PRAISE FOR *BLUEPRINTS*

"A story of growth . . . Delinsky effortlessly brings the components together—romance, career shifts, changes in parent-child relationships . . . A likable beach read with just a touch of gravitas."   —*Kirkus Reviews*

"Delinsky's moving story is filled with love, loss, betrayal, and passion. Readers will share the highs and lows experienced by the characters. This is a story for mothers and daughters everywhere."   —*RT Book Reviews*

"[A story] about the complicated dynamics of a family, the novelty of love no matter when in life you find it, and the importance of a good home makeover."   —*Pop Sugar*

Also by Barbara Delinsky

Sweet Salt Air

Love Songs

Warm Hearts

Blueprints

BARBARA DELINSKY

St. Martin's Paperbacks

BLUEPRINTS

For information address St. Martin's Press, 175 Fifth Avenue, New York, NY 10010.

Library of Congress Catalog Card Number: 2015012454

ISBN: 978-1-250-18235-7

Our books may be purchased in bulk for promotional, educational, or business use. Please contact your local bookseller or the Macmillan Corporate and Premium Sales Department at 1-800-221-7945, ext. 5442, or by e-mail at MacmillanSpecialMarkets@macmillan.com.

Printed in the United States of America

St. Martin's Press hardcover edition / June 2015
St. Martin's Griffin trade paperback edition / May 2016
St. Martin's Paperbacks edition / June 2018

St. Martin's Paperbacks are published by St. Martin's Press, 175 Fifth Avenue, New York, NY 10010.

10 9 8 7 6 5 4 3 2 .1

to finn,
for sweet blueprints
and love always

Prologue

The rain let up just in time. The final day of taping for the spring season of *Gut It!* was about to begin, and though the sun hadn't yet appeared, Caroline MacAfee's hopes were high. Well behind the stream of work vehicles pulling up on the road, the western sky was giving way to scattered patches of blue, as the June breeze pushed gunmetal clouds east, toward Boston and the sea.

How to describe what she felt as she stood at the head of an all-new cobblestone drive looking at the rebuilt facade of what had once been a weary old Cape? There was relief that the hard work was done, and surprise—always surprise—that everything had come together so well. There was also a sense of ownership. Caroline hadn't asked to be the mouthpiece of the show, but after nearly ten years as host, it was her baby as much as anyone's.

Gut It! was a local public television production, a home renovation series headlined by women—specifically, the women of MacAfee Homes. It touted neither high drama nor celebrity antics, just real work by real people with whom an audience of real women identified. The taping was done by a single cameraman, who was male but good, and directed by an executive producer, who was female and smart. If said producer was also prickly at times, the success of the show forgave it. Over the course of twenty projects, *Gut It!* had built a cult following that Caroline believed would only grow with this one.

Glancing skyward, she rubbed her hands together and grinned at the camera. "I wore yellow today to inspire the weather gods." She hitched her head at the approaching blue. "But how perfect is this? Welcome back to Longmeadow, Massachusetts, where we're putting the finishing touches on the latest *Gut It!* redo. As you can see"—she stepped aside for a worker shouldering a large roll of sod—"things are pretty busy right now." She skipped back again, this time with an excited "Hey," for a pair of furniture movers carrying a sofa toward the house. "Great fabric," she called after them and told the camera, "Our homeowners are planning to sleep here for the first time tonight, so we're hustling today. Lots to do."

Inviting viewers along with her chin, she started to walk. Talk came easily. She hadn't expected that, when she stumbled into this role, but she and the camera had become friends. "It's been six months since we began work on the small Cape that Rob and Diana LaValle put in our care. They needed more space, but since the house was originally built by Diana's grandparents and held the emotions of four generations, a teardown was out of the question. Our challenge was to preserve the heart of the house while we doubled its size, updated its features, and made its systems state-of-the-art efficient and green. Today is the day of reckoning. Let's see how we did."

Feeling a visceral delight, she guided the camera to her daughter, who was consulting with the general contractor as they watched the last of the exterior shutters being hung. That contractor, Dean Brannick, was the only male who appeared in every episode, but he had become such a fan favorite that no one minded. As he loped off, Caroline called, "Catch you in a bit, Dean," and slipped an arm around Jamie's waist. It was the kind of spontaneous gesture she had hesitated to show at first. Turned out, viewers loved it. Second to the female angle in appeal came the mother-daughter connection.

The resemblance between them was strong—same wide mouth, fern-green eyes, and auburn hair—but their differences were nearly as marked. Caroline let her hair wave, while Jamie blew hers straight; Caroline was five-seven to Jamie's five-three; Jamie wore the sophisticated neutrals of a young architect, but master carpenter Caroline, when not behind goggles and a chop saw, was known for color. Her yellow jeans were paired today with a matching tank under a slim-fitting turquoise sweater, all in contrast to Jamie's gray slacks and jacket.

"Talk to us, Jamie," Caroline invited. "As the architect of record for this project, you've been involved since Day One." She gestured toward the house. "Whaddaya think?"

"I'm *pleased*," Jamie replied as they walked on. "The best part of an architect's job is seeing a house go from modest to amazing, and this one did." Her pride showed; the camera hung on that. Cutaways of detail work would be inserted later, as would second or third takes, but for now it was all about feeling and flow. "The original structure had one and a half stories and a steeply pitched roof. By raising that roof, we were able to create three generous bedrooms and a loft on the second floor, with an expanded kitchen and a whole new great room underneath."

"Everything energy-efficient."

"Totally, from insulated floor joists to double-thick insulation and dual-pane windows."

"And that's just the inside." Caroline raised admiring eyes. "This exterior is something."

"I agree. The homeowners wanted to dress things up without losing the flavor of the original Cape," Jamie reminded viewers, "so we bumped out the front foyer and added fieldstone to the facade. And new gables over the second-floor windows? Wow." Her eyes touched the brackets under each gable. "Gotta love those corbels."

"Amen," smiled Caroline, who had carved them herself.

"Not *amen*," broke in the producer with a hand on the cameraman's shoulder to signal a cut. "This isn't about religion. Jamie, sweetheart, repeat that last line."

Jamie did. This time, Caroline managed a whole other kind of smile and said, "Absolutely," before moving on to the colors Dean had picked. The man was multifaceted. In addition to ordering supplies and hiring subs, he could handle any aspect of construction, including the egos of men who did grunt work in a world of women, and homeowners who had no clue about exterior paint. Here, cedar shingles picked up a deep gray from the stonework, while the trim was a startlingly pure white.

"Crisp and fresh," Jamie breathed. "And it all blends with the architectural shingles he chose for the roof."

"What we don't see from here, of course . . ."

". . . are the triple-junction solar cell panels. They're another aspect of the energy-efficient reconstruction of this house."

"All of which we'll get to later. For now, I'm just stunned at how elegant a Cape can look."

Jamie laughed her agreement. "This house used to be old. Now it has a reinvigorated sense of tradition. Take these cobblestones. Dean found them in a mill warehouse in New Hampshire. They date back to the turn of the twentieth century." She glanced at Caroline. "Remember the detached one-car garage that was here?"

"It was an eyesore."

"And inadequate. The LaValles have four kids who'll be driving soon, hence a new three-car attached garage at the back of the house. By leveling the old one, we not only removed a visual distraction but gained valuable land abutting the kitchen." A cutaway would show the new patio, replete with trelliswork and a raised fire pit.

After a discussion of the challenges posed by the topography of the lot, Caroline drew the camera's eye back to the front porch. "The stone columns add an arts-and-crafts element, which enhances the curb appeal tenfold. And just look at the front door. It's taller and wider than it was, and the sidelights make it grand. Jamie, you always envisioned an imposing entrance—"

"Wait," the producer cut in. "Caroline, you're talking too much. Let Jamie speak."

Caroline felt an inkling of annoyance. She wasn't doing any more than she ever did, but the point was too petty to argue. Thinking that she was ready to be free of Claire Howe for a few months, she said, "Okay. That's fine." She glanced at Jamie, who nodded.

"Let's start fresh with the front porch," Claire instructed, at which point Jamie re-created her mother's narration. Since there was no formal script, the words were slightly different, and Jamie's manner of speech reflected her age. She tripped once, but started again and went smoothly on.

They were heading inside when Caroline was distracted by the women in the shrubbery beds. Stopping Jamie with a hand on her arm, she called, *"Annie."* Annie Ahl was the show's landscape designer. Wearing mud-crusted boots, gloves, and a satisfied expression, she stepped out from between a pair of newly planted junipers. The pixie cut of her pure silver hair suited her diminutive size.

Caroline was looking beyond the junipers. "Do I recognize those?"

"Good eye," Annie said in the high voice that had nearly nixed her place in the show. Like the cameraman and his feel for light, though, her instinct for design was too good to pass up. She was the senior landscape architect at

MacAfee Homes, and Caroline's close friend. "We removed those azaleas last fall to protect them from the mess of construction. They wintered over in my nursery, and now here they are, back home. They actually bloomed two weeks ago. See the last of the flowers?" There would be a cutaway of those. For now, the camera stayed on the talent. "Naturally, we'll have to wait to see how they do here next spring, but I'm confident they'll make it. They're hardy."

"And they have company now." Caroline took in the new plantings.

"Uh-huh. One row—"

"Not *uh-huh*," Claire cut in. "I've asked you not to say that, Anne."

Annie said a particularly high-pitched, "I'm sorry. It's just natural."

"I like natural, but not *uh-huh*. And watch the voice. It's too high."

Caroline had never once read a complaint about that on their Facebook page, which she personally monitored. But Claire was the boss. In a voice that wouldn't reach the woman, she told Annie both of those things. Once Annie gathered herself, they resumed.

"When I first saw this house," she said perfectly, "the shrub beds were long and narrow, which was typical of beds at the time the house was built. I wanted greater depth to complement Jamie's new designs, so we widened and reshaped them. The taller shrubs in back are Andromeda, holly, and yew. I've planted juniper in and around the azaleas, and we're just now putting in perennials."

"Good job, guys," Caroline called to the two still planting, and let Annie go.

As she and Jamie climbed the stairs to enter the house, Caroline pointed out the solid walnut front door with its raised panels and bronze hardware. In the foyer, they saw Dean coming down the hall from the kitchen. "We're just tweaking the security system," he said. "Want to see the control room?"

The cameraman signaled a break. After cold drinks all around, they picked up in the basement with the security specialist, who was giving a rundown on the advanced features of a system that went far beyond security to include remote control of heating, cooling, and irrigation. Dean took the lead; he was easy on the eye and ear, and he understood electronics. When the plumbing and heating expert joined them to explain the environmental soundness of the new systems, Caroline backed off completely.

The sky continued to brighten, offering the dispersed natural light the cameraman loved. Dodging hustling crews, Caroline talked with the stone specialist, who was polishing marble in the first-floor lav, and the tile expert, who was finishing the kitchen backsplash. These scenes, largely included for DIY addicts who wanted to watch the process, would be saved or cut after the producer and her editors had a chance to log the videotape and decide how much time to spend on what.

When taping resumed in the afternoon, Caroline was in the kitchen with the homeowners, highlighting what was old, new, and repurposed, but the excitement quickly turned to the great room, where the show's interior designer, Taylor Huff, was supervising the placement of furniture. Sectional sofas complemented cushiony chairs, whose upholstery coordinated with window valences and chair cushions in the kitchen. Then came the media specialist, who was programming the remote for a huge flat-screen TV. *Gut It!* had worked with her before; she was at the forefront of technology and reliable to a fault when it came to installation. Unfortunately, she flustered easily. Even before Claire could intervene, Caroline stopped the taping to calm the woman, then reshaped questions to help her along.

One by one, the crews finished up, and neighbors and guests began to arrive. By early evening, as the lowering sun spilled through the dining room into the foyer, production assistants were arranging nearly forty family, friends, craftsmen, and crew for the group shot that had become a *Gut It!* tradition.

Caroline was front and center. Facing the camera a final time, she said with satisfaction, "There you have it, a recap of this season's *Gut It!* We took a sixty-year-old Cape that was too small for a growing family, too dated for a modern couple, and too wasteful in an energy-conscious town, and we turned it into a larger, younger, greener home. Now, we're here with homeowners Rob and Diana, at the foot of the stunning winding staircase that they always dreamed of having. I'm Caroline MacAfee, the host of *Gut It!* Thanks so much for being with us this season. We hope you'll join us next season for a whole new project." She looked around. "Everyone set?" Facing front, she slid one arm around her daughter and the other around Diana LaValle. "O-*kay*," she said, then, "Squish in, you guys," when the cameraman gestured as much. Seconds of compression passed. "All eyes on the camera." There was one click, then a second and third, then a communally held breath while the cameraman checked his playback. When he smiled, Caroline turned to her friends and raised a triumphant fist in the air. *"Yesss!"*

Chapter One

Jamie MacAfee would always be her parents' child. It didn't matter that she was twenty-nine and financially independent. When it came to her mother and father, she was still the little girl whose life had been shaped by their divorce and her need to please them both—which was why she was increasingly anxious as she drove across town for a quick breakfast with her dad.

The streets were early-morning quiet. School buses hadn't yet started to roll, lawn mowers remained stowed, and what other noises there might have been at seven were muted by a thick and ominous heat. June wasn't supposed to be this hot in New England. Humidity that had been oppressive the evening before remained trapped under the dense maples and oaks that lined her route, and the silk blouse she wore stuck to her skin. Her convertible top was down. Two streets into the drive, she jacked up the air and aimed the blowers at her neck, but her anxiety remained.

It ticked up a notch when she passed the corner of South Main and Grove, where the teardown being rebuilt by her major competitor as a Dutch Colonial was starting to look a little too good.

It ticked up further when she passed an Audi A5 that looked exactly like her fiancé's but, of course, was not.

Brad Greer had left her condo at six that morning after what should have been a sweet cup of coffee in bed turned into a set-to about picking a wedding date. They had been engaged for six months, and she hadn't done it yet. Her fault. Totally. Between taping *Gut It!* and working on a dozen projects in various stages of design, she hadn't had time to breathe. Brad was vulnerable when it came to love, though, and it tore at her when he got all down in the mouth, as he had earlier.

He hadn't called, hadn't texted. She would have driven to his place if there'd been time.

But there wasn't, which brought her to her father. He was the real source of her angst. He knew she had a special reason today to be with her mother, and for Jamie, there should have been no contest. Caroline wasn't just her mother; she was her best friend—and Jamie was all the family Caroline had. Roy, conversely, had moved on. Twice. Jamie hadn't cared for his second wife and wasn't sorry when the brief marriage ended, but his third and current wife, who was close to Jamie's own age, had become a friend. Moreover, Roy was absorbed enough with Jessica and their young son to leave Jamie to her own life.

Unless he needed her for something.

Which he apparently did now.

Still, she should have put him off.

But he had been dogged last night on the phone, evading every attempt she made to discuss whatever it was there and then. *This is about work,* he had finally said with unusual gravity. Work meant MacAfee Homes, where Jamie and every other local MacAfee was employed. She offered to be at the office by nine, but Roy had been adamant about seeing her before she saw her mother.

Those were his words. *Before you see your mother.*

That was what frightened her. The implication was that he wanted to talk about Caroline, but what could he say?

Caroline had been a master carpenter for MacAfee Homes since before marrying Roy, and their parting hadn't slowed her rising star. Roy's father, Theodore MacAfee, who headed the business, blamed his son for the divorce far more than he did Caroline. Theo adored Caroline. Whenever Roy tried to exclude her from plum assignments, Theo overruled him. Likewise when Caroline wanted birch burl or some such exotic wood and Roy claimed she was over budget.

Then again, Jamie realized, Roy's current emergency could be as simple as his wanting her to babysit two-year-old Tad while he and Jessica vacationed in Europe, which would certainly impact Jamie's work. Being a full-time mom was hard; she had watched Jess struggle, and Jess did not have a career outside the home. But Jamie did love her father, and she was totally smitten by her half brother, which meant she could never say no.

Jamie didn't think that warranted drop-everything-and-come insistence, but he wouldn't be denied. The best she'd been able to do was get him to meet at seven, so that she could still see Caroline before work.

And there he was, crossing the lot at Fiona's as she pulled in off the street. She waved through her open top and parked. Glancing in the rearview mirror, she ran quick fingers through her hair, but all she saw, to her dismay, were the freckles on her nose. So much for her expensive new concealer. The heat apparently melted makeup just as it swallowed up breathable air.

Resigned, she groped around for her shoes in the floor well and slipped them on, then slid out of the car as deftly as her short black skirt and those high heels allowed. The skirt showed off slim hips; the heels added inches she desperately needed. Pairing them with white silk, she was dressed to impress, though not solely for her dad. This was her typical take-me-seriously look for days that were filled with meetings. Most architects doing her level of work were older than she was, and while the family business gave her a leg up, it also gave her a name to uphold.

Freckles didn't help, but there was no erasing them now. The best she could do was to put her shoulders back and set off with a pretense of confidence—only to ricochet right back when the long strap of her shoulder bag caught in the door. *That* wasn't impressive, she mused, though it was nothing she hadn't done before. As physically co-ordinated as she was when focused, when distracted, she was pathetic.

Freeing the bag, she strode forward.

Fiona's was an upscale diner that offered the best break-fast in town, which meant that even this early in the day, it was humming. The parking lot was comfortably full; the air held the lure of hot corn muffins, chunky hash browns, and local maple syrup.

By the time she caught up to Roy, he was talking with two of Williston's finest, on their way home after a night on patrol. They had admiring smiles for Jamie as she hurried to keep up with Roy, who was entering the diner. He immediately began working booths filled with real estate agents, lawyers, plumbers, shopkeepers, husbands and wives—all local, all friends. Williston lay twenty miles west of Boston. Home to fifteen thousand residents, it was ruled by a Board of Selectmen, but if there had been a mayor, Roy would have been it. He was always smiling, always up for a meet-and-greet, always remembering names. Theo had done this for years until age crippled his mornings, at which point Roy smoothly stepped in. As the single largest employer in town, not to mention the raison d'être for many town shops, MacAfee Homes treasured lo-cal goodwill.

Roy made it happen. That he was strikingly handsome didn't hurt. With his keen brown eyes and perpetual tan, he looked younger than fifty-two. The gray that had spattered his hair a decade before had miraculously turned sandy, and, though Jamie didn't know for fact, she would bet that his forehead was medicinally smoothed. Not that she criticized him for it. He put in the effort to stay in shape—had likely gone running at dawn that morning, even in the heat. Now, dressed in a crisp blue shirt and fine gray slacks, he had a fresh-from-the-shower sheen.

For Roy, it was all about looking young—young body, young face, young wife. The irony, of course, was that with Jamie always trying to look older than twenty-nine, they were occasionally taken for brother and sister. Roy loved that, and while Jamie was proud of her father for his efforts and, yes, for his looks, she found the brother-sister comparisons awkward.

This day, she didn't get a formal greeting from him—no hug or kiss, no *hey, honey, thanks for coming*—just a possessive arm around her shoulder, drawing her into the small talk.

But small talk wasn't her strength. She could speak at length about architectural design, energy efficiency, or re-purposed barnboard, but she wasn't good at keeping track of whose mother was sick, whose son had gotten into college, or which tree service would take down the rotting pine in the center of town. Roy knew all that and more, in part because Jess picked up gossip at the local hair salon and shared it with him. Jamie would have forgotten it in two seconds flat. Not Roy. He remembered every last detail, pulling out whatever was appropriate in a way that endeared him to his audience.

Today, the talk was of the weather. *Beastly hot . . . not right . . . fierce storms coming.* Jamie smiled and nodded, but after a minute began to shift from one high heel to the other.

Her mother was waiting. Today was her birthday. And

she'd had surgery on her wrist less than twenty-four hours before. Jamie had texted her earlier but wanted to *be* there.

Finally, Roy guided her to a free booth. Fiona's wasn't so much a single railroad car as a square of four cars framing an open kitchen. The decor was a virtual history of the town, Fighting Falcon–blue wall after wall of framed high school senior class photos dating back to the mid-1900s, and laminated front pages of the *Williston News,* née the *Williston Crier,* memorializing the town during major events like the fire of '56, which wiped out half the town center, the blizzard of '78, which paralyzed town life for weeks, and the '04 Red Sox capturing their first World Series title in eighty-six years, which had been out-of-the-park *awesome* for a town in which two team members had lived. More old newspaper clippings covered the tabletops and were covered in turn by a thick sheet of glass, but the clutter ended there. Benches were upholstered in a soothing gray, place mats woven to match. Cloth napkins, knotted around silverware, filled a slim tin by the wall. Jamie automatically reached for two as they slid into the booth, passing one to Roy, who placed his cell beside it.

They were barely seated when the waitress brought the mud-strong coffee he liked and a pitcher of cream. Once both mugs were filled, Roy ordered his usual three-cheese omelet, Jamie her usual egg-white frittata.

What she really wanted was a side of the thick, sizzling bacon that smelled so good, but ordering it was out of the question, (A) because it was unhealthy and (B) because Roy would have felt the need to discuss that, and the last thing she wanted was to distract him.

Cupping her mug, she leaned in, anxious to hear what was on his mind. Before she could ask, he confided in a hushed voice, "See that guy behind me at the end of the row, the one with the red hair? He's a Barth."

Not urgent news, Dad, and nothing to do with Mom.

But Jamie glanced at the redhead in question. "Barths are blond," she said for lack of anything wiser.

"Not this one. He's buying the house on Appleton and plans to live in it. He just moved back from California with his wife and kids and is rejoining the business. The Barth Brothers teardown at the corner of South Main and Grove? It has location, magnitude, and visibility. They're making a statement with it. They want to make inroads here."

"Why here? Williston's our base. They have the North Shore. MetroWest is ours." MacAfee Homes had dominated the suburbs west of Boston since before she was born.

"They want the Weymouth acreage," he said, referring to the largest privately owned parcel in town.

"It's not even on the market," Jamie argued, though she knew that preemptive buys, negotiated directly with the seller, were common. "Is it?" she asked on an uneasy note.

"Not yet. But Mildred Weymouth has been dead nearly a year, and her kids can't agree on what to do with the place, much less afford the upkeep. The grounds have gone to shit, and property taxes are in default. Mildred's trustee says they have no choice but to sell." With a soft whistle and both hands on his mug, Roy sat back. "Thirty acres of prime wooded land? Pretty tempting."

Seriously, Jamie thought. Speculation had run wild since Mildred Weymouth's passing, and Jamie was deep in the mix. She envisioned a hybrid community of single-family homes and condos, all developed by MacAfee Homes. "We can outbid the Barths."

Roy checked his phone, put it down. "They'll drive up the price."

That was a problem, Jamie knew, but nothing MacAfee Homes couldn't handle. A single Barth moving to town didn't supplant the power of three generations of MacAfees who had lived here forever.

Roy proceeded to say as much in different combinations of words, and all the while, the little voice in Jamie's head was saying, *Come on, Dad. We could have discussed this at the office. Why here? Why now?*

Their breakfast arrived, but she barely looked. Teasing—not scolding, never scolding—she said, "This wasn't why you wanted to see me before I saw Mom."

Roy smacked the ketchup bottle over his omelet. "Hell, no. I only thought of it because that Barth was right there." Setting the ketchup aside, he softened. "I hear you saw Taddy the other night. Sorry I missed you. I was at the selectmen's meeting. How was he?"

Jamie gave a helpless smile. "Adorable. He calls me Mamie. I love that he's talking."

"Mostly he says *no*. Jessica's struggling with that."

"She seemed okay to me."

Roy frowned. "I'm talking tantrums. She has no idea what to do when he throws himself on the floor and kicks and screams."

"But all kids do that. Sometimes it's the only way they can express themselves. I saw one of his tantrums. It was actually pretty cute—I know, easy for me to say, since I leave when the going gets tough." But that couldn't be why her father had wanted to see her, either. "So, Dad. You got me here good and early."

"The early was your doing."

"And you know why." Caroline.

Ignoring the bait, Roy checked his phone, this time swiping once, then again. It wasn't for work, Jamie knew. He was checking Twitter and sports news. "There's a good point guard on the summer league team," he murmured, "but if the Celts don't trim their roster to get under the max . . ." With a grunt, he returned the phone to the table, then brightened. "How's Brad?"

Jamie sighed. There was nothing urgent about Brad—

well, there was, but her father didn't need to know that. "Brad's awesome," she said, as was expected.

"You know that I think of him like a son."

How could she not? He said it often enough.

"He's good for you, good for the business. Someday . . ."

He didn't have to finish. Someday, Brad would head MacAfee Homes. He had come to the company straight from law school, hired as an assistant to the in-house lawyer, who had become pregnant soon after and opted to be a stay-at-home mom. Though barely thirty, Brad had taken over. That was three years ago, and he had more than proven himself since. In his quiet, competent way, he had shown an understanding of the business that went beyond law. Since Jamie had no interest in these things, once they were married, Brad would be right behind Roy in the line of succession.

Theo liked that idea.

So did Roy, who, while he certainly wasn't ceding any real power to his future son-in-law yet, had already begun to share some of the more onerous tasks that he didn't care to do himself.

Grinning in a self-satisfied way, he tapped the plate with his fork. "I have to tell you, the stars are aligned. I thought Brad was the icing on the cake, but now there's more on top of that, and it is sweet indeed." Fork in midair, he came forward, brown eyes alive. "I met with Levitt and Howe yesterday to discuss the future of *Gut It!*" Brian Levitt was the general manager of the station that hosted the show, Claire Howe the show's executive producer.

Jamie was confused. As far as she knew, the future was decided. The fall project was in its final stages of production prior to taping, and the spring project had been picked, preliminary designs drawn, permits filed.

Roy's mouth curved into a smug smile. "You're the new host."

She drew back in alarm. "Mom's the host."

"They say we need a change. Things have been the same for a while. It's time for a facelift."

Scrambling for an explanation, she said, "A facelift would mean changing the format or the graphics or maybe taking on different projects. But I've been giving them cutting-edge designs. Don't they like them? Do they not want me to be the architect anymore?"

"They love your work, honey. They love *you*. That's the point." His fork urged her to eat her frittata.

Wishing it were bacon, she managed a small piece, but there was no comfort in it. She was thinking how much more satisfying the bacon would have been when he said, "They want you to continue doing what you're doing *and* be the show's host. It's really a no-brainer. You're beautiful and smart and talented. This would make your career, honey. You couldn't ask for better exposure."

"As an architect," Jamie said, setting her fork down with care. There was a whole other problem to changing the host. "What I do is intellectual. I'm more of a paper person than a people person."

"Who says? Not me. Not Claire. She gave you a leading role in several segments this season. Why do you think she did that?"

"Because the segments dealt with architectural design?"

"Because she was trying you out. You passed. You were great." Chiding, he added, "You told her you loved it."

Jamie might have, but specifics were a blur. "What else would I say? Claire's our EP, and she's tough. But talking about my own field is one thing. Talking about every other field in home construction is something else. And anyway, *Mom's* the host," she repeated, more loudly now, because this was the other half of the equation, and it was huge. "Our audience loves her. Ratings are good."

Roy ran a napkin over his mouth. "They could be better."

"Says *who*?" Jamie asked, frightened now, because, despite dozens of meetings with Levitt and Howe to prepare for the fall, no one had mentioned a ratings concern.

"Brian," Roy said. "He speaks for the network, and when he speaks, we listen. He got the show off the ground ten years ago, and he's been fighting for us ever since. If it weren't for him, *Gut It!* wouldn't be in half the markets it is. He's our guardian angel." His voice tightened. "He's the GM, and when the GM has his mind made up, crossing him is not wise. We need *Gut It! Gut It!* is good for MacAfee Homes."

The issue wasn't money, Jamie knew. The station funded the show through grants and syndication fees. It paid MacAfee Homes on a contract basis, and MacAfee Homes paid cast members from that sum. What remained in company coffers was less than the profit from a major construction project—less than the condo complex they had built in Foxborough last year, and certainly less than the potential for development of the Weymouth land.

No. *Gut It!* was about exposure.

"Do you understand what a marketing boon the show is for us?" Roy asked, clearly irritated that he had to explain. "Easily half the work we get is from people who either watch it or know someone who does. And then there are endorsements. Tools, 'as seen on.' Gloves, 'as seen on.' And the books documenting each season? The Barths have brochures; we have stunning coffee table books. They're a powerful marketing tool, but they're worth zip if the show is canceled."

"I know," she conceded. "We need the show. But Mom should stay on as host."

"It's done, Jamie." He lifted his phone, checked the face, put it down. "The station is not renewing her contract as host. She's out."

"Just like *that*?" Jamie asked, appalled by both sudden-ness and finality. She knew the station could do it. But out of the blue? With no warning? That was no way to oper-ate. Forget that Caroline was Jamie's mother; she was a human being who had basically shaped *Gut It!* with her bare hands. "Aren't our terms with the station meant to be negotiated? Can't we call our agent?" When Roy gave her an arch look, she winced. "Our *agent* thought this was a good idea?"

"He understands how things work."

"And how is that?" she asked quietly, but Roy got the point.

Blunt now, he held her gaze. "We're targeting a younger demographic."

Jamie wanted to weep. She had known this was his bot-tom line—of course it was—but hearing the words was something else.

"We want to win the couple buying a first home," he went on, "or the gold-mine techno-kids, or the Gen-Xers with a growing family."

"They think Mom is too old."

"I didn't say that."

But it's what you mean, said her little voice. *It's what you always mean.* Jamie loved her father, but she had no illusions. When his marriage to Caroline floundered, Roy had blamed his infidelities on her age and appearance, claiming that she had "let herself go," that he needed a more sexy wife. His second one was ten years his junior. His third was ten years younger than that.

"This isn't me, honey," he insisted. "It's Brian and Claire."

"But you can convince them they're wrong," Jamie pleaded. Her father was a consummate salesman. He could convince anyone of anything. "Mom is a master carpen-ter with incredible people skills. She's authoritative. She's experienced. She's reassuring."

"She's fifty-six."

"That's not old."

"For television it is. Age makes a difference."

"She looks *fabulous*."

"She looks fifty-six."

"And not only does she *look* great," Jamie rushed on, panicked on her mother's behalf, "but her work gets better and better. She's just hitting her stride."

Roy bounced an irritated glance at the window, then whined, "No one's asking her to retire. Brian and Claire want her to stay on the show. She just won't be its public face. TV needs young."

"Roy needs young," Jamie blurted out, because her little voice simply couldn't control the frustration, to which her father shot her a *watch it, honey* look. She might have taken it back, purely for the sake of keeping peace between them, if she hadn't had a sudden, awful thought. "Oh hell, Dad. Are you breaking this to me while someone else breaks it to Mom? Is someone at the house right now telling her—like, giving her the birthday present from hell—because today *is* her birthday, you know that?"

"Yes, I know it. And no, no one's there. I wanted to talk to you about how to break it to her."

"Well, *I* don't know," Jamie cried, feeling helpless. "How do you tell a woman she's too old for her dream job? Because that's what this is, Dad. Mom stayed with carpentry even when other opportunities opened up for women, because carpentry is what she loves. Then she got roped into hosting *Gut It!* She didn't want to do it at first, remember?" There had been an outside host the first season, but the chemistry was off, and Caroline had spontaneously filled in the gaps. "It was like she discovered strengths she didn't know she had."

"So will you."

"But Mom knows construction—I mean, *knows* it. She

can as easily help frame a house as carve a crown molding. I can't be on a roof the way she is. I hate heights."

"She or Dean will narrate those parts."

"But those parts," Jamie said with air quotes, "are ninety percent of the series. Framing, plumbing, heating, wiring—you name it, she can explain the entire process in lay terms. I can't do that. And handling the cast? Calming them when they're rattled? Mom has stature. We respect her *precisely* because of how long she's been doing this." When he said nothing, she whispered, "How can you ask me to kick her out?"

"This is about the survival of the show." He returned to his breakfast.

"What about Mom?" Jamie asked softly. When he simply continued to eat, she begged, "Fix this, Dad. Make them change their minds."

Midway through a triangle of toast, he said, "Honestly, Jamie. I want this for *you*."

"I don't want it." The words simmered over a backdrop of utensils, kitchen activity, and conversation. Jamie had never actively challenged Roy before. Even when she saw his face harden—even when she recognized the look as one he usually gave Caroline—she didn't soften her words. No, no, no, she didn't want to take sides, but if ever there was cause, it was now.

Eyes drilling hers, he sat back in the booth. "That wasn't the impression you gave Claire two weeks ago when she asked how you would handle the objections of the historical society to the new project." Jamie blinked, feeling used, but he wasn't done. "Or when she asked your opinion on those reluctant neighbors, and you assured her you could bring them into the fold. You knew where this was headed."

"Someday, maybe, but not *now*."

"Yes, now. It's about leadership. Tennis, architecture—

hell," he said glancing at her blouse, "the way you dress—
you're a natural competitor. It's what you do."

"Not against Mom." She didn't want to fight with Roy.
Did *not* want him displeased. She had never, not once, criticized him for criticizing Caroline. She had certainly
never said a word about the divorce. But punishing Caroline solely because of the date on her driver's license was
unfair, and using Jamie as the tool to do it only made it
worse. Lifting her mug, she took refuge behind it, sipping,
as she struggled.

She heard Roy's fork scrabbling into the last of his
omelet. She imagined he was regrouping and steeled herself.

Finally, sounding puzzled, he asked, "Don't you want
to be a star, even a little?"

"Of *course* I want to be a star," she cried. She had done
it in tennis—USTA junior champ for two years, ITF second seed in Paris—and had the trophies to prove it. When
it came to architecture, she had won local awards. To be
recognized for her work on a larger scale would be special.

The problem was Caroline. Jamie would rather die than
hurt her mother, and this would hurt.

She gave it a final shot. "And even aside from the Mom
issue, I don't have *time*. The host of the show does a ton of
behind-the-scenes work, but I'm already in over my head."
There were currently three licensed architects in MacAfee's
design department, but their head architect, Jamie's mentor,
was finally retiring after threatening it for years and had
bequeathed his major projects to Jamie. "We're talking ten
private homes, a library, two office buildings, two banks,
the *spring Gut It!* project, for goodness sake, and that's not
counting anything the Weymouth property may produce—
and then there's planning what *I'm* supposed to be saying
on air this fall about the design plans alone."

"You always do great on tape days."

"Because Mom leads. She sets the tone and asks the questions. Mom is *perfect* for this job. I am not."

Roy drained his coffee, set down the mug, and sat back. "If it's not you, it'll be someone else. Like I said, it's a done deal."

"For *fall*? Can't they wait another season or two?"

"Ratings don't wait. Consider that redheaded Barth over there. If he ratchets up the competition, we may need all the help we can get. Do you want MacAfee Homes to fall behind?" When she didn't answer, he said, "Claire's calling Caroline later to arrange a meeting."

Jamie sat back. "Please, not today."

"It has to be soon. Brian and Claire want this sewn up so that they can start putting together promo material. You know your mother best. What approach should Claire take?"

Jamie also knew her father. When his sentences came short and as fast as they did now, he was immoveable. Oh yes, the decision had been made, and it infuriated her.

She wasn't impulsive. She was a thinker, a studier, a strategizer. But her parents were her weakness, and what he proposed was untenable.

That was why, without thinking beyond the moment, she said something she would come to regret.

Chapter Two

I'll tell Mom. Claire can be abrasive, and this'll be hard enough on her without that."

Too late, Jamie saw his slow smile and realized that she had played into his hands. This was what he had wanted all along. It fit the image of a MacAfee family that was united and strong. To Roy, Caroline's age was dirty laundry that should stay in the bin, handled quietly and in private.

But two could play the game, Jamie decided in a moment's defiance. If she was the one telling Caroline, then she could do it in her own words and her own time. That gave her an element of control, which, given the anxiety she felt, helped her sit through Roy's prattle about how wonderful she was and what a great host she would make. The little voice in her head was answering each line with a sarcasm she hated, until finally the head of the local Lions Club appeared at their table. Thinking that the interruption hadn't come a moment too soon, she slid out of the booth, gestured the man into her seat, gave Roy a quick peck on the cheek, and left.

Back in her car in Fiona's lot, she was hit by the heat and a wave of second thoughts. She jacked up the AC as she turned onto the street, but those second thoughts weren't as easily fixed.

What have I done? Did I seriously agree *to host the show? How can I* ever *tell Mom?*

Brad would know how. Diplomacy was his thing. But he still hadn't texted or tried to call, and she couldn't very well call him without mentioning their own issues, which seemed small by comparison.

She left Fiona's upset. By the time she'd driven two blocks, though, she was angry. She didn't want to think that Roy had put the bug in Brian's ear, though it wouldn't have been out of character. Roy saw Caroline as his aging ex-wife. He was constantly making little digs about her hair or her face, and when Jamie told him Caroline was having surgery on her wrist, he sighed and said, "That's what happens . . ."

Like there weren't crow's-feet at the corners of *his* eyes?

Like *he* didn't wear orthotics in his running shoes to help a bum knee?

Like she hadn't caught him *napping* in the office after a late night out with Jess?

So Jamie was angry at Roy, who at the very least hadn't argued when mention was made of removing Caroline as host. And she was angry at Brian Levitt, who was behaving like a chauvinist. And she was *furious* at Claire Howe, who was a woman, for God's sake, and should understand a female audience better than Brian.

Another two blocks, though, and her heart was breaking for her mother. Caroline's self-esteem was higher than it had been at any time since the divorce. This would be a terrible blow.

How to deliver it?

One thing was for sure. Jamie wasn't breathing a word to Caroline today, not on her birthday, and likely not tomorrow, since she would be gone from dawn to dusk. And if she could convince Brian and Claire that this was a bad move, she might not have to tell Caroline at all.

She tried calling Brian, then Claire, but both calls went to voice mail. Vowing to try again later, she dashed into the bakery, then the grocery store for orders she had called in the day before. Back in her car, she sped through a world that was a myriad lush shades of green, with historic houses on every block and the scent of fresh-baked goods rising from the seat beside her. Habit had her waving at a MacAfee truck, then again when she passed a neighbor from her condo complex, and as she crossed through the little shopping area that marked the center of Williston, random townsfolk acknowledged her with a chin or a hand.

The closer she got to Caroline's, the better she felt. *Forever the child?* she wondered again. She hadn't lived at home since before college, and never at Caroline's current house, yet she was soothed simply turning onto her mother's street. It was one of the most untouched in Williston, which was why, in a preemptive strike that only a town insider could make, Caroline had snapped up the house before anyone else could make a bid. MacAfee Homes would have renovated; Barth Brothers would have torn down and rebuilt. And wouldn't that have been a crime? There was no place for new construction here, certainly not of the mega size the Barths would build on this kind of lot. A McMansion would change the entire character of a street where shade trees were old and luxuriant, lawns were thick with meandering roots, and drives were dirt or stone. The houses themselves were vibrantly painted Victorians, and while Caroline's was smaller than most, its Queen Anne style heightened its charm. Teal clapboard was below, mint shingle above, all of it framed by intricately

carved trim in pale blue with navy accents. Asymmetrically designed, it had a scrolled eave, a big bay window, a
handsome turret, and a modest play of steep-sloped roofs,
but it was the encircling veranda that Caroline claimed
had sparked love at first sight. Rounding out into an open
turret at the corner to allow for a wrought-iron table and
vintage chairs, it was a fresh-air parlor ringed with hanging petunias in a riot of pinks. In good weather, this was
where Caroline spent her free time.

Sure enough, there she was as Jamie drove up, lounging in a wicker love seat that swung from a thick chain.
Her bare feet were crossed on the front rail. A smile lit her
face.

With a popping of tires on gravel, Jamie turned into the
driveway. Her convertible was red, the same color as the
pickup parked at the garage, but while Caroline's truck was
the epitome of practical, with tools under its bed cover, dirt
on its tires, and the logo of MacAfee Homes on its dusty
flanks, Jamie's car was pure indulgence.

Gathering bags from the passenger's seat, she climbed
out. Those feet on the rail twitched in a little wave as she
started up the walk. Her mother's toenails were orange;
she had seen them the day before. Pedicures were one of
Caroline's weaknesses, and bright toenails were only the
start. She had been wearing jeans that were yellow, purple,
or green long before they became a fad. When she coordinated those jeans with shirts that were striped or plaid, she
was a standout. *Gut It!* addicts also loved the bright sweaters she wore in cool weather and the hot-red parka she
wore in snow. When the executive producer once suggested
that she try for sophistication with black, the Facebook uproar had been fierce. Viewers wanted boldness, and her
mother gave them that. There was nothing stodgy about
her. Too old? No way!

Jamie swallowed her dismay.

Caroline was pink and braless today, her soft tank and shorts a tribute to heat and a well-earned hiatus. Her hair was a messy knot of waves at her crown, her face bare of makeup and gorgeous in a totally natural way.

Less gorgeous was the thick bandage around her right hand and wrist, but the absence of last night's sling was a relief. More reassuring, though, was Caroline's face, which was back to its natural glow. Her recovery-room pallor yesterday had terrified Jamie.

Carrying the bags, she bypassed newly budding roses and climbed the front steps. "Is it better or worse now that you can feel the pain?"

"Better," Caroline said with warm fern eyes, "but anything would be. There's nothing more disconcerting than having a body part that feels like it belongs to someone else. You look beautiful."

Jamie bent to kiss her cheek. It smelled woodsy, like lily-of-the-valley body wash, which meant Caroline had managed to bathe, another good sign. "Happy Birthday," she sang and drew back. "How do you feel?"

"Lazy."

"Lazy is good on a day like this. Warm, huh?"

"I've worked in worse."

"Yeah, well, the doctor said not to do anything today," Jamie warned and looked around. The laptop was blessedly absent.

Not so Master, Caroline's cat. Shimmying its massive gray coat out from under the wicker chair beyond the swing, the Maine Coon gave Jamie's leg a rub. "Poor baby must be roasting," she murmured, before refocusing on her mother's wrist. "Does it hurt?"

"Compared to raging tendonitis? Nope."

"So yes, it hurts," she deduced, because Caroline wasn't

a complainer. She saw wrist problems as an occupational hazard that couldn't be helped. No one on the set had known she was in pain, and had that pain not grown progressively worse, she would never have agreed to surgery. Officially, now that taping was done, she was just "taking a few days off."

She looked thoroughly pleased with herself, which made Jamie suspicious.

"What are you taking?"

"Tylenol."

"You look too happy for just that."

Caroline laughed. "I'm relieved. I hate surgery. So now it's behind me, and here I am in my favorite place with my favorite person." The sultry quiet of the front porch was a far cry from recent days on the set. The only sounds here were the buzz of bees in the roses, the hum of a Weedwacker several houses down, and the gentle creak of Caroline's love seat as the chain moved to and fro. She eyed Jamie's armload. "Whatcha got?"

Wedging a drained iced-tea glass between her bags, Jamie managed to open the screen door. Master scooted into the house so close to her legs that she nearly bobbled the glass. "Food!" she called back as the door slapped shut.

The air inside smelled of age in a hallowed way, and though it was marginally cooler after the night, Jamie knew that wouldn't last. Her heels ticked along the dark hardwood of the hall as she passed a whitewashed grandfather clock and an L of stairs. The walls of both stairway and hall were navy, which should have closed in an already close space. But Caroline had known that between moldings, balusters, and newel posts, the white trim would bring the navy alive.

A window at the landing three steps up was open, with Master now frozen on the sill, stalking an invisible dove that cooed in the maple's depth. The living room on her

right was also navy, here over peach panels. It had originally been built in the old English style, with front and
back parlors, but the walls between the two had long since
come down, leaving only striking trim work to mark
what had been. Caroline had accessorized the room in
burgundy and placed a dining table at the far end. Large
and round, it was a magnificent walnut piece—she had
made it herself—and was the focal point of the room for
many who entered. For Jamie, though, the pièce de ré-
sistance was the swatch of Victorian lace that hung in a
frame on the wall. Taken from Caroline's mother's wedding
dress, it was a Rorschach test of sorts. Jamie had grown
up seeing her moods in the lace.

Rather than confirm turmoil there now, she simply
checked to be sure the two ceiling fans were whirring at
either end of the room and strode on.

The kitchen was a sage cubby at the back of the house.
High wainscoting covered its modest wall space and was
topped by a wide plate rail holding rescued antiques.
Though Caroline had added a line of ceiling cabinets, the
storage space was sparse.

Setting her bags on the lone counter, Jamie opened the
fridge and stashed what needed chilling. The rest went on
the stove simply for lack of space, not that any cooking
would be done here today. The room was already warm,
and the heat would only rise.

In anticipation, she turned on the ceiling fan. Then she
took a small plate from a glass-front cabinet. The china
was hand-painted, though sturdy enough to have survived
her childhood with only a single small chip. The plate she
held was blue-rimmed with an apple in the center; others
beneath it in the stack had different colored rims, different
fruits. And oh, the memories served up on these plates—
of apple wedges sprouting in eighths from a slicer (*Let's
count, baby, one, two, three*) of pound cake topped with

strawberries and whipped cream, of s'mores oozing marsh-mallow over chocolate over graham crackers.

Tucking nostalgia back inside, Jamie took a sticky bun from one of the bakery bags, a mini scone from the other, and napkins from the drawer. After refilling the iced-tea glass from the pitcher she had brewed the night before, she tucked a slim package with a red bow under her arm. Unsure, she set it back on the counter. Seconds later, she grabbed it again and headed back out to the porch.

She reacted more sharply this time to the slap of the screen door. "A pneumatic closer would eliminate that," she advised, placing the refilled glass on the swing's wide arm beside Caroline's phone and bandaged wrist.

"But I like the sound," Caroline said without apology. Taking the sticky bun from the dish Jamie held, she bit a pecan from the top. "The slap of a screen door adds something."

"Noise."

"Flavor. It's part of what I love about this place. MacAfee Homes builds a great house—we *renovate* a great house—but recycling and repurposing and replicating, say, period millwork can only go so far in adding character. Character has to mature. It takes years for that." The love seat shifted when she lowered her legs for Jamie to pass. "I have it here now."

Jamie sank down beside her. "Air-conditioning has nothing to do with character. That sun's heading for brutal today. You need central air."

Caroline slid an indulgent glance at the paddle fan whirring softly overhead. After taking a full bite of the bun, she offered one to Jamie.

Jamie shook her head. Having deprived herself of bacon, she had every intention of eating the scone. How else to deal with frustration? She *so* wanted to do something for her mother. Caroline just gave and gave. She was too independent to ask for much, and now, if she was going to lose something she loved, there had to be something Jamie could give in exchange.

"Okay. Forget air. What about the kitchen? We could punch out a wall and double the space."

"Why do I need more space?"

"Wouldn't you like more counters? Even a desk, think of *that*. Dedicated laptop space in your kitchen? If you don't want granite or quartz, we can use butcher block or maple or hand-painted ceramic tile, any one of which would work with this house. I'd add an eating island with barn board siding and bookshelves—"

"—for the cookbooks I don't own, because I rarely cook."

"Don't laugh at me, Mom. You have tons of other books. You read all the time."

Setting the bun aside, Caroline twined their forearms and gave Jamie's hand a squeeze. Her palm was callused, another occupational hazard, and though hand lotion partnered with scented soap at every sink, it could only do so much. Not that Jamie minded. Her mother's skin was unique. Had it been smooth, it wouldn't have been Caroline's. Hell, viewers loved her toughness, too.

"Which is why," Caroline was saying, "I fell in love with this house. It came with shelves in most every nook and cranny, and what wasn't there, I built myself. I love the claw-foot tub in my bathroom and the antique fixtures in the hall, and the farmhouse sink in the kitchen is an original."

"It's porcelain."

"What's wrong with porcelain?"

"You need copper."

Caroline's silence said, quite eloquently, that she did not need copper.

Resigned, Jamie rested her head on her mother's

shoulder. The ceiling beadboard was mint, a shade lighter
than the outer shingles. Her gaze slid to the railing, which
was the same pale blue as the rest of the trim, then the wood
floor, which was a shade darker. The wicker swing was
pure white only because its cushions were alive with flo-
rals that would mirror the riot of color in the flower beds
at summer's height.

Jamie had to admit that the overall effect held appeal.
Still, she would love to redo this place. "I want to design
something special for you," she tried to explain. "Rehab-
bing old houses is what we do, but you've done nothing
here."

"Not true. Look at my newel post and the crown molding in the bedroom and the detail work on the panels in
the parlor. And my garage."

"That doesn't count."

Jamie realized her mistake even before an indignant
"Excuse me?" came her way. Caroline adored her garage,
which she had doubled in size and outfitted with new electrical and air systems even before she'd moved in. This
was her prized workshop, where she made many of the
more intricate pieces that other carpenters had neither the
eye nor the hand to make. Oh yes, Caroline was a master
carpenter with the years of experience to prove it.

Feeling like a traitor in light of what she knew that Caroline did not and how wrong the whole thing was, Jamie
snuggled closer. She didn't care about sweaty skin. The heat
couldn't compete with this deeper need. "The garage is
for work. I meant living space."

"I painted," Caroline said in an indulgent way. "And
installed new systems for heat, plumbing, and electricity.
And added Wi-Fi. *And* got rid of the termites in the basement and removed the mold growing behind the bathroom
wall, and what about the metal underlayment I added to
my whole new roof?"

"I'm talking renovation, as in making it bigger."

"I don't need bigger. I live alone. Besides, this is my private space. I don't want a crew in here."

"You let Dean in."

"Dean's different. He's a friend."

"With whom you agree to disagree on a dozen little things."

"We have different tastes. That's all."

"Is he coming over later?" She tipped her head when her mother's phone chirped. "Speak of the devil."

"No, baby. Dean's ring is a gray owl. That's a whippoor-will, which means Annie." Jamie was a chickadee and her grandfather a trumpeter swan. Her father, bless his mis-guided soul, was a duck with an annoying honk. Not that Roy called Caroline much, but even Jamie would recog-nize that sound.

Misguided soul. *No more so than now,* she thought, but, really, what else was new? Sensitivity had never been Roy's strong suit where Caroline was concerned. Phone calls to the house, gossip around town, photos with his arm around pretty young things—he wasn't fazed. And Caroline's lows when the divorce was finalized? He was oblivious. Not Jamie. She was twelve when he moved out, and in the subsequent months, she had been the one who followed nighttime footsteps to where Caroline stood in the dark kitchen staring out at an inky world. Jamie was the one who saw her ignoring the phone and avoiding people and moving more food around the plate than ever reached her mouth.

Eventually, she had found strength. Jamie never knew from where; she suspected it had been a combination of work, Jamie's increasingly complex tennis schedule, and a dawning realization that the judge-of-all-things was now gone from the house. The change didn't come overnight, but once the emergence began, it was steady. Anyone watching her now could see how comfortable she was with her life.

Indeed, her soft voice held confidence. "Hey, A. Yeah, I'm good. Jamie's here, can I call you back? Promise. Thirty max." She ended the call, put the phone in her lap, and picked up where she had left off. "Dean's bringing lunch."

Jamie had been counting on that. She didn't know if she could get back until late afternoon, and though Annie would be only one of a stream of other visitors, Dean knew his way around Caroline's house. And he was good company. They might argue about what she should do with the house, but Caroline did let him speak his mind. Maybe when he saw her laid up, he would talk her into making the place more liveable.

That said, the Victorian had its strengths. Taking a long breath, Jamie sank into the cushions as the swing gently rocked. She might fault Caroline's refusal to renovate, but she had to admit that the house was serene. Serene went beyond quiet. Her condo was quiet, but it didn't have the feel of home that this did.

The screen door gave a quick creak and slap. Seconds later, the swing jostled, and Master was settling his big body onto a sliver of cushion. He ended up half on Jamie's thigh, which should have been too much in the heat but was not.

"Oh, baby," Caroline warned, "he'll shed on your skirt."

"I don't care." She ran her fingers through the thick coat, from his wide collar to his bushy tail, then did it again. The resulting purr was hypnotic. "I'd get my own cat if I wasn't gone so much of the time." She sighed as she stroked Master. "Aren't I lucky you're willing to take the cats I fall for?" While Roy scoured the *Williston News* for useful buzz, Jamie beelined it to the weekly shelter col-

umn. Kittens went fast. Older cats? Harder to place, but
they were the sweetest, most mellow creatures. Master was
one of three Jamie had given Caroline. The other two
stayed inside, largely on the upper floors where the sun was
strong and Master was scarce.

"I nearly got you a fourth for your birthday," she said
now.

"Good thing you didn't. I told you, three's my limit."

"She was abandoned," Jamie went on. "By the time
she was brought in, one of her eyes was so infected that
they had to remove it. They're guessing she's eight or
nine."

"Jamie . . ."

"Don't worry. She was adopted by the time I called."

Content with that, Jamie let the cat go. Just then, she
was content with most everything. The air was hot and so
much of her life murky, but as she sat here on the porch
swing, with her fingers in the oddly cool hair of the cat and
her mother's familiar scent spread by the ceiling fan, she
was revived enough to pull out the thin package with its
red ribbon. "I know you don't like me buying you gifts,
Mom, but since you won't take another cat, this'll have to
do. It's totally self-serving. Read the card."

Tucked under the ribbon, the card was handmade, as
Jamie's to her mother always were. Caroline kept every
one, occasionally pulling them out to show Jamie the progression. This year's was part computer-assisted, part cut-
and-paste construction paper, all geometrically shaped
navy and mint. And the note inside?

Caroline read it, set the card on her lap, and gave Jamie
a chiding look. "A weekend with you at Canyon Ranch. I
can't refuse that, which you knew." Slipping her good arm
around Jamie's neck, she gave her a hug. "Thank you,
honey. I will *love* it." Her eyes lit. "Let's go tomorrow."

Grasping the fingers at her shoulder, Jamie laughed. "We can't, because (A) your wrist has to heal, (B) I'm in Atlanta tomorrow, and (C) my calendar is crammed with meetings for the next ten days. The taping backed things up, speaking of which—" She hitched her chin toward the DVD case that lay on her mother's lap. Though its cover wasn't as handsome as what fans would eventually see, the red bow couldn't hide its identity.

"The uncut tape," Caroline said excitedly. "Perfect timing. I'll watch it later."

"No typing notes."

"I'll call Claire with a critique."

Oh no. Not good. "I'd hold on that, Mom. She wanted time off."

Without responding to that, Caroline angled herself and looked Jamie over. "I got used to seeing you in slacks while we taped. This is dress-up. Big meeting day?"

Grateful for the change of subject, Jamie gave her a rundown of appointments. She didn't mention having had breakfast with Roy and felt even more duplicitous for that. Wondering again whether Roy was behind the hosting change, she asked, "Is everything okay between you and Dad?"

"As okay as it ever is," Caroline mused lightly. "I rarely see him."

Jamie doubted her mother would have continued to work for MacAfee Homes if regular encounters with Roy were part of the job. They went their separate ways, his big-picture marketing to her detail carpentry. On the rare occasion that she went to the MacAfee Building, it was either to meet with the budget director or visit with Theo. She didn't seek out Roy.

"Which is good," Jamie said, considering.

"Which is good," Caroline confirmed.

"What'll you do when Theo retires and Dad takes the throne?"

"Work, same as always. Unless your father cuts my pay or tells me to use inferior material. I've been spoiled. Theo believes in top-notch everything, and he gives me free rein."

"He respects you." Jamie lifted her hair to cool her neck. "Besides, having a family business was always his dream. You may not be Dad's wife, but you're still my mom, which makes you family in Theo's eyes."

Truthfully, if Caroline had left the company after the divorce, Jamie might not have gone to MacAfee Homes straight from college. She and Caroline had always dreamed of working together, though, and her mother being on the family payroll was the clincher. The path to licensure was rigorous, and while Jamie's mentor at MacAfee had been patient and instructive, he was male. Her emotions weren't on his radar screen. But they were on her mother's. Caroline might glaze over when Jamie got going on a new piece of architectural software, but she was immediately, entirely present when Jamie needed encouragement.

And now this? Competitors for the same job? Jamie might have wanted that job in theory one day, but no way, *no way* could she take it today.

"You look troubled," Caroline said.

She gave a little headshake. "Sorry. I have a gazillion things on my mind and half of those on tap for today."

"But making wedding plans is not on the list. I thought that was Priority Number One once the taping was done."

"No," Jamie corrected, half-wondering if Brad had called Caroline to see how she was doing and mentioned his frustration, "wrist surgery was. You're key to my wedding plans. I can't go looking at venues with you laid up."

Caroline's phone cooed like the dove in the maple. "That's the hardware store. I gave them a tone because they call so much. They open early." She touched IGNORE.

"Maybe it's something important."

"Nothing's more important than this. Tell me what's going on with Brad."

Chapter Three

Caroline liked Brad. He was a sweet guy who was a good lawyer and had a solid future with MacAfee Homes, which meant that Jamie would be taken care of whether she chose to work or not. And he loved Jamie. Caroline didn't doubt that. Other things, yes. But not that.

Unfortunately, she couldn't discuss those other doubts. For one thing, they were vague, more a niggling in the back of her mind than anything concrete. For another, expressing them might hurt her relationship with her daughter. Besides, Caroline didn't need to love Brad. Maybe all they needed was an easy rapport.

Jamie started the swing with her heel. "It started innocently enough. He said kind of what you just did about my needing to pick a date. When he kept pushing, I lost it a little. I feel like he's harping on it."

"Maybe he feels like you're avoiding it."

"That's what he said, and he started looking all wounded and dejected, which upsets me every time, because I know where it's coming from. He was a lonely little boy whose parents were always there but never *there*. He never felt loved." She watched a robin fly in and perch on the corner rail.

"She has a nest in the Andromeda," Caroline explained

and, fully prepared to protect four helpless hatchlings, eyed Master. But the cat remained blissfully asleep under Jamie's touch. "Go on," she urged.

"He's such a nice person."

"So are you."

Jamie put her thumb to the underside of her ring. "I don't feel like it right now. I feel like a traitor." Her eyes shot to Caroline's.

Caroline wasn't about to judge her daughter. "Sweet people can approach things differently."

"Maybe." She focused on finger-combing Master's fur. "He says it's a matter of priorities and that if I love him, the wedding would be at the top of my list. But picking a venue isn't easy. Dad is adamant about it being a *big* wedding, which limits our options. I have to speak with people at each of the venues, but I just can't do it right now. That's driving Brad nuts."

"He's afraid you'll get away."

"I'm not *going* anywhere," she protested, still stroking the cat. "I keep telling him that. I text him all the time. I share my thoughts and show him my designs and ask his opinion, because I care what he thinks, and we talk about his work, too. I make his favorite dinner—well, pick it up at Whole Foods, but he's good with that." Her eyes rose. "Then he says, *You're too old to be afraid to commit*. Me, afraid to commit, like he has no idea where *I'm* coming from?"

Apparently not, Caroline mused. Jamie had learned commitment with a tennis racquet in her hand, playing at five, competing at eight. She had given her all to coaches, team sponsors, and opponents, and after discovering architecture in college had attacked that with the same fervor. Advanced courses, summer seminars, internships—she had front-loaded on all counts.

"Have I ever been afraid to commit, Mom?"

"No, baby."

"If I haven't had time to plan a wedding, it isn't because I'm afraid to commit but because I'm *busy,* and as for the too-old part, I'm only twenty-nine. I don't call that too old for much. How old is too old?"

Certainly not twenty-nine, Caroline knew. Women were getting married later and later, in part to establish careers, in part to be make sure they got the right guy. "Age isn't the issue," she replied, to which Jamie shot her a stricken look but said nothing. "You know commitment better than most." Her phone dinged. She glanced at the screen to read the text. "Taylor Huff . . . asking about my *wrist*?" She sliced Jamie a narrow look. "How did Taylor know about my wrist?"

"Uh, I may have let it slip. Inadvertently."

"Do I believe that last word?"

"People care, Mom. They *love* you."

Yes. Caroline knew that. And knew how lucky she was to be surrounded by people who cared. "Which brings us back to Brad," she said, returning the phone to her lap. "Your thumb keeps going to the backside of that ring, like you're either making sure it's there or it's irritating you. Are you worried Brad's right? Do you think there might be reasons why you haven't wanted to plan the wedding?"

"What, like subconscious ones?" Jamie separated her thumb from the ring. "Like what? Brad is perfect for me. He's smart. He works hard. He's our top lawyer at thirty-three, *thirty-three,* which means Theo has total faith in his talent. He's considerate and good-looking, and he adores me. Why wouldn't I be able to commit?"

"Maybe because your father and I committed and failed?"

The creak of the swing resumed at the bidding of Jamie's heel. "Your situation was different. You got married because (A) you were pregnant and (B) Granddad wouldn't hear of my being born out of wedlock. And you loved Dad back then."

It was a question without the question mark, but Caroline had known it would come. It always did. Her parents' relationship was Jamie's personal Achilles' heel.

"I loved him," Caroline assured her again.

"And you'd have loved him forever if he'd been a forever guy. *He* was the one who was antsy. But Brad isn't Dad."

"True."

Though Roy thought Brad hung the moon.

Which might be what bothered Caroline.

Which was certainly not a *rational* reason for Caroline's doubts.

Jamie pulled her cell from the waistband of her skirt. She flipped through messages, looking discouraged, then startled. She sat straighter, heels stopping the swing. "Oh, cripes, look at the time. I have to go. There's a problem that I have to work out before my eleven o'clock, and a couple of important phone calls."

"Think about it," Caroline said.

"About?"

"Commitment."

"Mom," Jamie said with audible frustration, "I do commitment better than anyone I know."

"Commitment to Brad," Caroline specified.

"I love Brad," Jamie vowed.

"Then there you go. That's it. You'll get through the rest." Caroline couldn't fight love.

But Jamie seemed upset at that, like she wanted more reassurance, like she wanted Caroline to tell her that Brad was the best thing to walk into her life. Lord knew, Roy said it enough. Well, Caroline couldn't gush over something she didn't feel. Besides, her focus was always on Jamie. If Jamie wanted to marry Brad, she was for it.

With a jingle of chains, Jamie shifted the cat so that she could shimmy herself out and push up from the swing. "Brad and I should elope."

"Your father would never forgive you."

"Would you?"

Caroline caught her hand and gave it a jiggle. "Absolutely, if it's what you want. I want you happy. Oh, baby," she said in alarm when Jamie teared up. "You'll get through this." She held out her arm and, when Jamie bent down, folded her in. "There's a reason why planning a wedding is so stressful. It separates the wheat from the chaff. Do you know how many couples don't make it?"

"No," Jamie whispered against her ear. "How many?"

"I have no clue, but there must be lots. It stands to reason, doesn't it?"

There was a soft snort. "You just made that up, then?"

"No. The Bible talks about separating the wheat from the chaff."

"I mean, the part about wedding stress."

"I'm sure I read it somewhere," Caroline said and gave Jamie a final hug before holding her at arm's length and thumbing away an unshed tear.

Jamie took a deep breath and smiled. "You're the best, Mom, know that?"

I'm only as good as you, Caroline thought. She hated that Jamie was upset, but loved that she was willing to share worries with her mother.

"It's weird seeing you doing nothing," Jamie remarked.

Caroline gave a facetious *ha.* "Enjoy it while it lasts. I'm not sure how much more idleness I can take. When I close my eyes, I'm in the garage working on that oak railing for the Millers' house."

"Don't even think it," her daughter warned and glanced at the books on the porch table. "You can read."

"Yes. I can read."

"Got something sexy and hot?" When Caroline shot her a look, she sang, "Your loss." But she was suddenly earnest. "Can I get you anything before I leave? Eggs? Cereal?"

"No thanks, baby. I'm good."

"Remember," she said as she edged toward the stairs, "I'm bringing dinner tonight. Lobster lazy-man style in honor of a one-handed birthday girl. Can I bring you more Tylenol?"

Caroline laughed. "It's only my wrist. I can walk." To prove the point, she stood and, taking Jamie's arm, escorted her down the steps, but they were barely at the bottom when they wobbled as a pair. "Maybe not."

"Oh please," Jamie muttered. "That's me." Reaching down, she freed her heel from the tiny crack between step and stone where it had caught, the front access being one more thing Jamie would have fixed had Caroline allowed it. "You're steady as a rock. Not that I wouldn't love to cancel everything else and stay here today."

"Don't you dare. You're behind already. Go. Really. I'm calling Annie back. She'll be here by ten. Then Theo's administrative assistant Allison's coming, then the LaValles, Rob and Diana, then Dean. I'm good."

Jamie started the car only when Caroline was back on the swing. Once on the street, she crawled forward to blow her mother a handful of kisses before giving the car gas. Seconds after the mint-on-teal Victorian was out of sight, though, she pulled over, picked up her phone, and tried Claire. When the call went to voice mail again, she tried Brian. Same thing.

This time, she redialed Claire and left a message. *Call when you can, and please, please, please, don't call Caroline yet. And don't mention the hosting issue to anyone else, please?*

Wondering how many other people already knew and, if the list went beyond three or four or five, whether it would be possible to put a lid on the secret at all, she headed for MacAfee Homes.

The MacAfee Building was several blocks from the center of town. A regal brick structure, it was designed to honor the Georgian Colonial style of the earliest homes built by the company. Its front door, which was oversized and paneled, had the requisite crown and columns, and its windows had multiple panes, but its six-story height had called for creativity. Though side gables and chimneys still rose at the top, its facade was a pastiche of those tall multipaned windows, with cornices, moldings, and pillared balconies strategically placed for visual appeal.

Jamie worked on the top floor, though not at the front of the building. That front, with its sunny southern exposure, housed executive offices that were spacious, one large desk per office and an assistant outside each door. At the other end, facing north, was the design team. Here, skylights allowed for available light, but none hit the computer screens so crucial to an architect's work. The floor space was open, broken by large L-shaped desks that were arranged in three-person pods to maximize the sharing of ideas and advice.

Jamie shared a pod with her about-to-retire mentor and an architect-intern. The latter was already at her desk, struggling with an egress issue as she moved tracing paper over one of Jamie's plans. Normally, Jamie would have leaned over her shoulder to see where she was headed and perhaps move the translucent paper around herself, but she didn't have time now for that. Waking up her computer, she checked for e-mail from Brian or Claire. Finding nothing, she set off to see Brad.

His office was on the floor below. The central area here

held desks for a receptionist and secretaries, as well as comfortable chairs for guests. Glassed-in offices ran along either side, housing Brad, his paralegal, a one-person billing department, the MacAfee in-house real estate agent, and a resident computer nerd. Dean and two other general contractors, who were in the field more often than not but loyal enough to MacAfee Homes to merit dedicated desks, shared a large office at the end of the hall, as well as a conference room nearby for meetings with subcontractors, suppliers, and clients.

"Hey, Miranda," Jamie said, nearly beside the receptionist before the woman's eyes flew up.

Startled, she pushed the book she was reading out of sight. "Jamie," she said, blushing. "Hi. I didn't hear the elevator."

"I took the stairs," Jamie explained, but kept on walking to minimize the woman's embarrassment at having been caught reading on the job, much less reading a book with as recognizable a cover as that one. Miranda was as good a receptionist as MacAfee Homes had. She was attractive, personable, and efficient. She was also happily married and had three children in various stages of daycare and school.

Jamie might have wondered why she was reading erotica, if her mind hadn't been on Brad. She knew his schedule and had hoped to find him alone, but his clients had arrived early and were seated in leather club chairs while Brad reviewed their agreement with MacAfee Homes.

Her steps slowed. He was leaning against the front of his desk, his wire-rims on his nose, and he was a calming sight. Tall and rangy, he had short, side-parted brown hair. His blazer, slacks, and loafers were sedate and well tailored; they were nowhere near as expensive as Roy's clothes, but Brad wasn't about money or show. He was about competence. As he turned from one page to the next, he had his clients' undivided attention.

Then he spotted her, and she felt a moment's doubt. This wasn't the time to talk through the argument they'd had, certainly not to discuss Caroline. But his face lit with pleasure seconds before he waved her in. Yes, pleasure. Hard feelings from earlier? Gone, at least for now. She was barely through the door when he held out an arm, inviting her over in a gesture that might have been inappropriate in another place of business, but MacAfee Homes was about family. *Family Builds.* The words were on every piece of stationery, every contract, every bit of marketing the company used. It was hokey, perhaps, but Theo MacAfee couldn't say it enough.

Brad had become family. When he took her hand and drew her close, she felt safe. Not that clients intimidated her; she was with them all the time. Brad was particularly good with them, though. Content to socialize in ways she was not, he was the glove that fit her MacAfee life.

It had taken her a while to see that. He had already been with the company for several years when she joined it fresh from RISD—the Rhode Island School of Design—and there were no instant sparks. Jamie wasn't looking for a lover, much less a husband. She was focused on work. They became friends joking about everyone who *wanted* them to be more, only in time discovering that they shared other things as well. Once they started to date, sly smiles were rife, and when they became engaged, the celebration was office-wide.

The sense of safety was mutual. Jamie was Brad's security, too. She felt it in the way he held her to his side as he returned to his clients and said, "You remember my fiancée, Jamie MacAfee. Jamie, the Abbotts, David and John."

The two rose to shake her hand and were still on their feet when Brad said, "Would you excuse us for a minute?" and led her out of the office. In the hall, he whispered, "How did it go?"

Her meeting with Roy. "Awful," she whispered back. "They want me to take over as host of the show."

Behind his glasses, his eyes came alive. "He told you?"

"You *knew*?"

"I don't negotiate the contracts, since I'm not an entertainment lawyer, but Roy told me they wanted the change. This is so good, Jamie. You'll make an amazing host."

Jamie was startled because (A) he had known and hadn't told her and because (B) he thought it was a good idea. "I can't be the host. Not if it means kicking Mom out." Brad should have *known* that. He should have argued with Roy when the issue first came up. "Oh God. Dad asked you to side with him."

"He didn't have to. I think it's a good decision."

"You think Mom's not doing the best job?"

"She's done a great job, but so will you."

Jamie let out a discouraged breath. "I can't do it, Brad. This is my mother. And I have a *wedding* to plan." She squeezed his hand. "I'm sorry about this morning. My mind's been on too many other things."

He shrugged and, in the next breath, asked, "How's Caroline's wrist?"

"Better today."

"Did you wish her Happy Birthday for me?"

"I was barely able to wish her Happy Birthday from me. Thanks to Dad, we didn't have much time together. Can you and I talk later?" If Roy could enlist Brad to convince Jamie, Jamie could enlist Brad to unconvince Roy. Brad could also advise her on handling Brian and Claire. "What's your schedule?"

"Lighter than yours. You tell me. What time is good?"

She had clients coming at eleven for a second-round consult on the design of their home, a budget discussion over lunch concerning renovation of a public library, and, when that was done, an on-site check of the construction of one of her banks. Between it all, she had to review her Revit schematic and send it to the plotter so that she would have two full sets to take with her to Atlanta tomorrow.

"Three?" She had a short break then. "Out back, maybe?" There was a large patio behind the office, created to showcase MacAfee landscape designers. Client meetings were sometimes held there, though more often it was where employees went for coffee or lunch. It would be hot today, but there was shade. More important, there was privacy.

"Three, out back," he whispered. He kissed her lightly, raised a brow and grinned with a touch of mischief that said she was his, and returned to his office.

Jamie should have been reassured by his kiss, his grin, his conviction that she would make a great host. As she headed for the stairwell, though, she was uneasy. She wanted him to side with her from the get-go. He knew what her life was like, and he knew what she felt for her mother. He should have considered all that.

Shouldn't he have?

Chapter Four

Caroline hadn't moved from the porch swing. Granted, it was her favorite spot, but she had never spent the whole morning here. She'd never spent the whole morning off her feet, period—or hadn't since she'd had the flu, what, four years ago? She was the healthiest person around, and she wasn't exactly sick now. Her wrist ached, but had it not been her right one, she would have been in the garage working. *Gut It!* might be done for the season, but other work went on. Most of it involved intricate carving, which was better done here. She had her best tools in the garage, plus ideal lighting and her own music. The guys she worked with liked hard rock. Her sound was more mellow.

Mellow was an apt description for what she felt now, she decided, eyes still closed through a stretch. She had fallen asleep sprawled on the swing after Annie had left, and though she felt sweaty, she didn't rush to sit up. The birds were quieter, either tired of socializing or silenced by the midday heat. Not so the MacAfee crew that was framing the new addition to a house two streets over. As muted as the hammering was, it was a tapping she knew well.

Then came a closer sound, a human one, and her eyes flew open.

Dean. He was leaning against the front rail, hands braced on either side, ankles crossed as long, bare legs settled in with a brush of hair on skin.

Eye candy, Jamie called him, no small compliment since he was close to Caroline's age, but her daughter was right. Everything about Dean worked: the dark hair that spiked over his forehead, the silver tips of his sideburns, the just-there scruff on his jaw, the muscled shoulders, the lean waist. Had he come from work, he'd have been wearing jeans and boots, but with the taping of *Gut It!* done, he was taking off for a week. He still wore black from the waist up, always black, but today in the form of a button-down rather than a T-shirt. His sleeves were rolled, his khaki shorts pressed, his eyes amused.

She tried to muster anger but was too logy. Besides, he was so much like a brother—why waste the energy? The best she could do was to chide, "That isn't very polite, Dean."

"What?" he asked innocently.

"Watching someone sleep without her knowing. How long have you been here?"

"Not long. How do you feel?"

"Great."

"Which is why you were sleeping just now."

"I was just sleeping off the last of the anesthesia. They called it a local block, but there was enough sedation in that IV to last a week." She eyed the mass of gauze and tape on her wrist, rolled it one way, then the other. It felt heavier in the rising heat. "This is just a gimmick to keep me from working. The incision is tiny." She eyed his knee. "Much neater than that." The scar there ran a jagged eight inches, the upshot of a hand saw misused by an apprentice carpenter several years before. It was usually hidden by jeans. "That still looks mean."

"It adds to my appeal, don't you think?"

"Absolutely," she mocked, though there was some truth to it. The scar fit the image of the rugged outdoorsman, and it wasn't alone. He had a white line over one eyebrow, a pinkie that didn't quite work, and numerous scars in other places habitually exposed to his work. Most people wouldn't notice; a man's skin wasn't smooth to begin with. But he and Caroline had a running competition. He showed her his; she showed him hers.

"I'm still ahead," he said.

"Only because you're reckless. I get credit for caution."

"Reckless has nothing to do with it. I learned the trade through trial and error. You learned it from a father who was not only a master at carpentry but totally protective of you."

She had been fortunate in that, and not only when it came to learning. Much as she loved both of her parents, she and her father had shared something special.

"Thinking of them?" Dean asked kindly.

Her parents, on her birthday? Of course. She had been a late-in-life child, "our little miracle," her mother always claimed. As though to prove themselves worthy of that, both had lived well into their eighties.

"They were proud of you. They loved watching the show."

"On some level," Caroline said with a sad smile, remembering the phone calls during the early *Gut It!* years. "Mom thought it was an ad, and Dad, well, Dad recognized me the first year or two, but after that he was too far gone. His mind just . . ." She flicked her hand toward nothingness and then, needing a regrounding, ran her eyes down Dean from head to foot. He was wearing flip-flops. Her eyes shot to the street. From where she lay, only the top of his truck rose over the porch rail. "No bike?" His passion was a Harley. He rarely skipped work without it.

"It's too hot."

Too hot. Definitely. Pushing up, she lowered her legs to the floor and stretched her back, then wiped sweat from her forehead with her good arm. She wasn't the only one sweating. Dean's tanned skin held a sheen. Naturally, it looked fine on him, which wasn't fair at all.

"I nearly brought you flowers. Good thing I didn't," he said with a glance at the porch table. "That is funereal."

Four arrangements had come, two from people who shouldn't have known about Caroline's hand. "My daughter has loose lips. But her intentions are good. Same with yours, though I told you not to cancel your trip." He was going fly-fishing in Montana, or so he claimed.

"I didn't cancel it. I just put it off a day."

"So who are you really going out there to see?" she teased as she always did, and as he always did, he smirked.

"No one you know."

"Meaning, a craggy old man who owns a fly-fishing business."

"Don't knock him. He's a find. He's fished the Big Hole River all his life and knows where the trout are best. He boats me in each morning and picks me up at the end of the day." His phone dinged. Taking it from his pocket, he studied the text. "Hick Weston underestimated the amount of piping he needs for the house on Smithfield. On. Its. Way," he said as he typed, then repocketed the phone. "Anyway, it's a solitary week."

Caroline actually believed him. He had been married for many of those Montana years and would never have cheated. In the three years since his divorce, those fishing trips had been pure escape from thinking about the woman who had rejected him, taken their then-eleven-year-old son back to her hometown, and reconnected a little too quickly with the childhood sweetheart to whom she was now married.

There had been anger, and when it came to his son,

there was an ongoing sense of loss, though Caroline was one of the few to know about either. She might not be wild over things like his preference for dogs over cats and black over color, but Dean was a good man. If fly-fishing gave him a buzz, she was all for it.

Sitting forward, she pushed herself up. By the time she was standing, he had reached for her arm. "Where are you going?"

"The bathroom," she said drolly, "and no, I do not need help."

Hands up, he backed off. "Ooo-kay. How about I plate our lunch?"

Spotting the telltale bag on the floor by the door, Caroline's eyes lit. "Is it what I hope it is?" That would be a marinated chicken breast on focaccia, with Boursin, sliced tomato, and Bibb lettuce. It was Fiona's lunchtime specialty. Caroline could eat it every day, which Dean well knew, since they went there often enough. Not that he ate chicken breast with Boursin. His choice would be roast beef or ham topped with aged cheddar, hard and sharp.

Now he said, "Would I bring anything else on your birthday?" and shooed her off. When she came out of the bathroom, he was leaving the kitchen juggling plates, napkins, and drinks. His mouth was filled with something from the bakery stash Jamie had brought.

"Ah. You found the minis."

"Um-hmm." He finished off the mouthful. "I'd ask where you want to eat, except the front porch is the coolest place right now. You need AC, sweetheart."

Ignoring the remark, she took one of the bottled waters he carried and washed down a pair of Tylenol before following him out. After she'd set the water on the arm of the swing, she left-handedly peeled wisps of damp hair from her neck and pushed them into the knot above. Then she sank into the swing and took the plate he offered.

The side chair he pulled up was white wicker matching the swing, but large enough so that he didn't look silly in it. He had actually been with her when she bought both pieces, and had tried it on for size then. Now he sat back and sprawled his legs.

Content that he was content, Caroline closed her eyes as she took a bite of her sandwich. The first hit of flavor to her taste buds was always the best. "This is amazing. *Gracias, amigo.*"

"*De nada.*" He passed her a napkin. "So who else came by?"

"Allison. She brought roses from Theo. Then Rob and Diana." The LaValles, whose Cape *Gut It!* had just transformed. "Recognize the azaleas? They're from the shrubs Annie replanted. And Jamie was here."

"Are she and Brad getting away now that the taping's done?"

"I doubt it. She's backed up with work. Besides, she needs to plan the wedding."

In the silence that followed, Caroline felt a throb in her wrist. It was a quick jab, here and gone, but she feared it reflected a pang in her thoughts.

"How're you feelin' about that?" Dean asked quietly, surprisingly. Of all the things they shared, she had not told him her qualms.

She gave a little smile, a little shrug, a little look that said it wasn't her place to tell her grown daughter what to do. Again she wondered what her own problem was with Brad. Jamie certainly could have done a lot worse.

"Want me to get the Harley? It'd take your mind off things."

"Thank you, no." The Harley terrified her. "My mind

is fine right where it is. Trust me, I am not obsessing about
Jamie and Brad." She only thought about it when issues
like wedding planning arose. The rest of the time she was
fine.

Dean's phone dinged again. This time it was the fore-
man on one of his jobs calling about a problem with de-
fective skylights, but it was nothing Dean hadn't dealt with
before. His voice remained low, the phone was soon stowed,
and stillness returned.

Then came the rumble of an approaching engine, and
a van pulled up with another delivery. Caroline moaned.
"Who all did she *tell*?" This arrangement was beautiful,
though—white callas, blue delphinium, and the deepest of
green herbs. She read the card. *"Heal well. You're still our
carpenter."* She frowned at Dean. "Well, duh. That's
weird. From our cameraman. See, this is why I didn't want
anyone to know. Tell one person, and the whole world
knows." He was suddenly looking a little too sheepish.
"Oh, Dean, who did you tell?"

"Just Mike." Michael O'Shay was one of MacAfee's
electrical contractors.

Her shoulders slumped.

"What's wrong with people knowing?" he asked.

"I don't know." She struggled for the right words. "It
makes me seem weak. Worn."

"No way. It shows you're tough. You do jobs most men
couldn't handle. That's a war wound, sweetheart."

"War wound," she echoed, doubtful.

He bit into his sandwich, chewed, swallowed. "You're
just sensitive because it's your birthday."

"No, I'm not. I'm fine with my birthday. I like my life."

"Well, Mike's a good guy. I asked him to be on call for
you while I'm gone, and since everyone knows how self-
sufficient you are, I had to give him a reason."

"You couldn't lie?" she asked meekly.

He didn't respond. No, Dean couldn't lie. It was alternately his best and worst feature. Whether she liked it or not, she always knew where he stood.

One consistently good thing, though. He was comfortable with silence and didn't fill it when he had nothing to say, which she appreciated just then. She was feeling lethargic, no doubt a by-product of heat and surgery. Halfway through her sandwich, she couldn't take another bite.

After finishing his, he stood and pointed at the half she had left. "Can I wrap it?"

When she nodded, he stacked their plates and took them back to the kitchen. A short time later, he returned and handed her a mini scone. He was eating a second, with a third in his hand, when another van pulled up. Scratching the stubble on his jaw, Dean shot her an *uh-oh* look before trotting down the steps and meeting the deliveryman on the walk. The arrangement was huge. Back on the porch, he lowered it so that Caroline could remove the card. *"Happy Birthday,"* she read aloud. *"You're the best."* She smiled. "That's sweet. It's from Brian and Claire."

Brows raised in question, he hitched the vase toward the table.

"Living room," she suggested. The screen door slapped behind him. When she heard his flip-flops returning, she called, "Want to play Scrabble?"

"Nah." He came through the door. "You always beat me. And I have to leave." The door slapped shut.

She had another idea. "Jamie brought over the uncut tape. Want to watch?"

He shook his head to that, too. "I'm on vacation." His eyes grew shrewd. "Uh-uh, Caro. Don't work today. I know you love Facebook, but MacAfee has a paid staffer to monitor that. Marketing isn't your job."

"Right," she admitted. "It's Roy's."

"And doing it under his nose is part of the pleasure."

She had to laugh. "I like you, Dean. You get it." She was thinking what a good friend he was when she felt a sudden pang. "Oh boy. I'm so out of it. How did it go in Portland?"

He had been there yesterday. Given the demands of lead time in construction, planning for the spring *Gut It!* had to be under way even before the fall season taped. They had decided to renovate and enlarge a coastal cottage in Cape Elizabeth, and while Jamie only had partial designs done, Dean had enough to start interviewing local subs. "I was able to get a few leads, but it's hard to find women. We could bring up our own, but it's a trickle-down thing. Get someone local and they have local connections, which is a help when weather puts us behind schedule and we have to scramble. Besides, local people add flavor."

"Flavor" meant local accents, and Caroline had to agree. Most of the subs they used talked Boston, but Maine was unique. "It'll be a fun project," she said. "Very different from the one we're doing this fall." That one involved a small historical home that had been bought by empty nesters wanting to downsize. Jamie had no sooner finished a redesign of the house than two of the couple's sons decided to return home to live, so the gut-and-rebuild of a carriage house entered the mix. The last-minute change had caused mild panic, not to mention doubling Dean's work, but it made the project far more interesting.

Mildly disgruntled, Dean folded his arms. "I'm still not sure why the Millers want their kids in a separate house."

"You're confusing how much you wish you could be near Renny with the fact that most adult parents need a little space from their kids." Renny was fourteen and increasingly involved in a life far removed from Dean's. In Maryland for the last three years, the boy had embraced a new family, new friends, new school. Dean knew football; the boy was into lacrosse. Their Lego days together were

gone. From what Dean could see, the boy's free-time pal
was now his iPad.

Caroline felt his frustration, but she also understood
this client. "The Millers are at a different place. And I
hear what they're saying. I love Jamie, but I don't want her
living with me, not after those last few years before she
finally moved out. Her stuff was everywhere. Books, keys,
hair ties, large purses, Sharpies, electronics, half-filled
bottles of water—you name it, all in plain sight. Her bedroom was always neat, which is rare for a child, but common space in my house? Fair game. It was like she had to
mark her territory each time she came home from school."

Dean's eyes remained dark. "Wouldn't it just have been
easier for the Millers to buy a bigger house?"

"Then where would that leave us? I *like* this project."
But she knew what he was thinking. "You wait. When
Renny is older, he'll visit. You'll see."

"Not the same."

She understood that. Dean had clung to a bad marriage
for the sake of his son. He went to Maryland often, but
he was a spectator in his son's life. So no, it wasn't the
same. And no amount of smooth talk from Caroline about
things changing with time could help.

Again she pushed at the pieces of hair on her neck. They
hadn't stayed put. Her left hand did a lousy job.

"I should brush your hair before I go," Dean muttered.
"It's a rat's nest up there."

"Thanks a lot," she drawled.

"Hey. I'm just kidding. You look beautiful."

The compliment was unexpected. She wasn't sure she
believed it, but along with surprise came an odd pleasure.

Seeming done with melancholy, Dean took a breath and
pushed off from the rail. "Too bad you don't like fishing.
You could come with me."

She was thinking that in another life she might when a bark came from the truck. She should have guessed Champ was in the cab from the way Dean had parked in the shade and lowered the windows. He knew not to bring the dog inside. A German shepherd, Champ had traumatized her cats enough times that they made themselves scarce at the first sniff of Dean. He did love that dog.

"Poor guy. Who's watching him while you're gone?"

"A neighbor. They have a shepherd, too. Champ'll be fine."

"Spoken wistfully."

"Well, he's my pal, like you." Leaning in, he put his soap-clean stubble to her cheek and his mouth to her ear. "There's a quart of yogurt in the freezer."

She drew in a fast breath. "Moose Tracks?"

"Um-hmm."

"My *favorite*."

She could feel his smile against her cheek. "I think I knew that." Straightening, he backed away and started down the steps. "Consider it a peace offering. I bought the country house."

Caroline was so taken off guard that she was a minute following. Then, "Oh no. No, no, no."

"Done," he said as his long legs ate up the walk.

She sat forward and called, "That place is in the middle of nowhere. It has water problems, zoning problems, *access* problems, *and*"—she raised her voice when he didn't stop—"it's so infested with carpenter ants that you'd be best burning the thing to the ground. You don't want that place, Dean! There's no way you can make it salable, and isn't that the *point*?"

But he was already in his truck, and once the engine turned over, her shouting was pointless. As he drove off, she grabbed her phone. It took her longer than usual to type, what with holding the phone steady against her bandaged right hand as she worked with her left. She had to delete numerous times until the letters made sense, and then it was simply *Big mistake*.

Thank you, Mom, he wrote back. *Be good while I'm gone.*

Chapter Five

When noon came without word from Claire Howe, Jamie left a second message, as well as one for Brian Levitt. The fact that neither picked up or called back said they were avoiding her, which made her insane. Her fear was that the more time passed, the more word of the hosting switch would spread at the studio, and the more Caroline would be hurt when she learned it herself. At its extreme, Jamie's fear had someone at the station leaking word to a columnist at *The Boston Globe* and the whole world reading a blurb in tomorrow's paper.

She made it through her lunch meeting intact, though when she arrived at the site of the bank construction, she immediately knew something was wrong. What had looked fine on paper lacked the element of welcome that the bank wanted for its branch, which meant Jamie had to rework the plans. It was no big deal and could be easily fixed, but she hated getting things wrong.

She needed Brad, *definitely* needed Brad. By the time she crossed the back patio to the bench where he sat, she was feeling the heat. The air was thick, and she was desperate enough for support to set aside the issue of his knowing about the host change before she did. But when he opened with "Hey, TV star," she was not happy.

"Okay," she warned, "now's the time when I need you to say you're just kidding with that, because you know I don't want to do this yet, and you also know Caroline is still the best one for the job."

His gray eyes held steady behind his glasses, his voice quiet and smooth. "What I know is that you'll be a great host. The more I think about it, the more excited I get."

It went downhill from there. She rebutted his arguments; he counter-rebutted hers. And when she finally asked, "What about Mom?" he said, "She had her turn, now it's yours."

His confidence in her was as sweet as his loyalty. But there was a larger picture here, a more personal one, a picture of Caroline heartbroken at being ousted on account of age, by her daughter, no less, and he was so not understanding of that that she was beside herself.

He wouldn't help her with Roy, or he would have done it at the get-go.

And Roy had already made his feelings clear, which meant that they would only argue, which she did not, did not, did not want to do.

Her grandfather was her last best hope.

Theo MacAfee was eighty-two but as sharp mentally as a man half his age. The problem was his body. Bad knees, bad hips, bad back, bad cough. Fine to say he had brought the last on himself, but as he told Jamie whenever his cough alarmed her, "We were young and stupid. What did we know?" By some miracle of fate, whatever was there hadn't evolved into lung cancer, though there had been a melanoma scare a few years back—and it was fine to say he had invited that, too. But he first learned the trade by working construction himself, and how could he have possibly built a business in that field without spending time in the sun? Add foolhardiness to the mix, and he had been known until recently to climb a ladder in a snit and show a framer the *proper* way to mount plywood sheathing to the outside wall of a house.

He was a perfectionist, which was probably how Jamie came by the trait. He could be short-tempered when things weren't done right, and he could be painfully blunt. Beneath his impatience, though, was a kind heart. He treated his family well.

Jamie was counting on that now.

"Got a minute?" she asked, poking her head into his office and feeling a catch inside at the sight of him. When she was a child, she had always thought him tall and imposing. She had gained perspective on that as she had grown herself, but hunched over now, he seemed frail. He didn't smile when he saw her, but those blue eyes lit.

Theo was an older, more leathery version of Roy. He had a head of white hair that was only beginning to thin, and though his blue eyes were rheumy, they remained riveting. In his later years, finally accepting that he couldn't be harassing electricians at a job site, he had taken to wearing a jacket and tie, and his manners had grown courtly to match. He started to rise now. Slowly.

Hoping to spare his arthritic spine, Jamie scooted around his desk and eased him back down with her hug, then leaned against the mahogany not far from his trouser leg.

His eyes were keen, his voice gravelly. "I'd congratulate you, little girl, but you look like you lost your best friend."

"It might come to that," Jamie said with a little huff. "So you know about the *Gut It!* switch?"

"Your father told me. He said you were on board."

"That is not true."

"He said you asked for the change."

"To replace Mom? Why would I do that? Mom loves

the job, and she's great at it. This isn't a good move, Granddad. You know it's not."

"No, I don't know it's not," he said as he calmly put his elbows on the arms of his chair and cupped his gnarled hands, one in the other. "It sounds logical. The producers want a younger face, and yours is a winner."

"What about age before beauty? Who always said that?"

"Your grandmother, rest her soul, but she didn't know the television business. Neither do I, which is why I defer to your father on this. Beauty before age seems to be the way of the world today."

Jamie was dismayed. "Is that why I'm working my tail off now, so that by the time I hit my stride, I can be laid off because I have wrinkles?" She searched her grandfather's face, finding wrinkles in abundance. "Is anyone saying *your* face is too old and asking you to step down?"

"No," he said with a dry quirk of his lips, "because I own the company, so I'm the one who decides, and I'm not ready to step down."

"What if Mom isn't either?"

"Has she said that?"

Jamie let out a frustrated breath. "No. She doesn't know about this yet. I'm hoping to get it changed before she has to. She'll be devastated. Think of what you'd feel if someone said you were too old to do what you do best."

"They'd probably be right."

"I'm serious, Granddad."

"So am I, but everything is relative. This is television, which apparently is a whole other ball game when it comes to age. Personally, I like seeing those little blondes reading the news in their cocktail dresses—not that I'd want your grandmother to know that," he said with a penitent heavenward glance. "But I do understand why the station wants you. Roy is proud."

"Roy is blind," Jamie countered, knowing that if she

was out of line, Theo would blame it on her youth. And wasn't that an irony? "He isn't thinking about Caroline at all. But you love her. You always stand up for her."

"And I would now if I felt that show was her future. She's much more than a carpenter, and—no offense to you—she's much more than a host. I see her doing other things."

"On the show?"

"In this company."

"Like what?" Jamie asked, because, as gratifying as Theo's confidence in Caroline was, this was the first she'd heard of her mother doing other things within the business.

Theo only waved a knobby hand. "Not important right now."

"Okay. So right now, why not let her do what she loves? All it would take is a phone call."

"Oh-ho, no you don't," Theo scolded with a spasmodic shake of his head. "A phone call to any one of three people who have their minds made up? I've learned to pick my battles, little girl. This is one I'm not fighting."

"But *why*?" she asked, not understanding how after so many years of protecting Caroline, he could desert her now. "Mom's been loyal to you." She took his hands between hers. "Speak to Dad. Speak to Brian or Claire. Please? You can make them change their minds."

But Theo refused to commit, and she wasn't about to wheedle. *I've learned to pick my battles, little girl. This is one I'm not fighting.*

More and more, she felt like a lone warrior, but at least Caroline was still in the dark. When Jamie arrived at the Victorian to make dinner, her mother seemed as blissfully unaware of any problem as she had been that morning, so at least Roy was keeping his word on that.

With the heat so oppressive, Jamie had opted for

lobster salad. No cooking was required, since she bought the lobster meat already boiled and out of the shell, and turning it into salad was so easy to do that she couldn't screw up. That was important, given how distracted she was. Theo was Theo; she could accept his position. But Brad? He was the one who gnawed at her as she cut the lobster into chunks. She didn't understand why he couldn't see her mother's side of things. Actually, she could. He wasn't close to his own parents. They lived in Minneapolis and didn't travel. Jamie had only met them once. They had been sweet enough to her in a polite, aren't-you-lovely way, but chatty they were not. Throughout Brad's upbringing, they had never shared thoughts, much less invited a discussion of problems. Caroline did both.

As Jamie took mayonnaise from the fridge and spooned it into a cup, she worried. Brad knew how important Caroline was to her, but hadn't made the connection that she should be important to him, too. He would in time. Only they didn't have time when it came to *Gut It!*

Cutting a lemon in half, she squeezed it over the mayo and stirred, then poured the mixture over the lobster chunks and folded it in. There was plenty for two, but not enough for three. She hadn't invited Brad. From the start, she had envisioned Caroline's birthday dinner to be strictly mother and daughter, as it had been for so long. She wondered now whether excluding him was only perpetuating the distance between him and Caroline, causing jealousy, resentment, even dislike.

Knowing she was getting carried away, she reached for the tomato she had bought. It was huge and locally grown, which meant that it was likely a sin to discard the insides. "No problem," said a woman who stood beside her at the tomato bin. "Save the insides for salsa or, even better, for homemade Bolognese." Like she had the time to make either? Ignoring the guilt she felt, she sliced her tomato in half, scooped the innards down the drain, and piled in the salad. Once the stuffed tomato lay on a bed of Boston Bibb lettuce, with a mound of marinated mushrooms, a fresh baguette on the side, and a glass of wine nearby, the plate was gorgeous.

Where to eat? There was the Caroline-made dining table in the parlor, but that would mean seeing her own tension in her grandmother's Victorian lace, and the porch table was covered with flowers. So they ate on a quilt in the backyard, where the sun had fallen enough to allow for shade and a small breeze stirred the air.

Thinking that her mother was the only person on earth with whom she wanted to communicate just then, she turned off her phone.

The downside of that, of course, was turning it back on. Her home screen had barely appeared when the dinging began. She told herself not to look. Dinner had been great, an escape from all things unpleasant. But just cruising away from Caroline's with the streetlamps flashing sequentially in and out of her car, she felt her serenity begin to slip away.

The phone didn't help. It lay like a coiled snake on the seat beside her. She ignored it as she passed through the center of town and continued to ignore it as she approached newer homes. In contrast to Caroline's neighborhood, parts of which were settled in the early 1800s, this side of town had been farmland into the mid-1900s. Tract by tract, houses began to appear then, first a gaggle of ranch-style homes, then small regiments of Colonials, and then split levels that were a hybrid of the two.

Her condo complex was an eight-year-old MacAfee Homes development that captured the spirit of New England in shingled faces and gabled roofs. Each condo was two stories high, with its own walled patio and built-in garage.

Pulling into hers, Jamie turned off the engine and, resigned, picked up the phone. Why not? Every one of the day's worries was back anyway, from Roy's bombshell reveal early that morning to Brad's one-sided cheerleading to Theo's refusal to stop the change.

She studied the screen. There were several work-related messages. She skipped over them to the personal ones. *How'd it go?* Brad had texted an hour earlier. *Did she like the cupcakes?*

The cupcakes were birthday ones that she and Caroline had thoroughly enjoyed but that should not have been his first concern. She would have confronted him on it if he'd been staying with her that night. Just then, she was glad he wasn't.

Her thumbs typed *Yup,* then SEND.

His answer came in seconds. *No mishaps?*

Still not the right topic, but a wry one. He knew her well. *Nope.*

What time's your flight?

6:58.

Sure I can't drive you to the airport?

No need. Client pays for parking.

Okay. Have a safe flight.

It was an innocuous exchange that left her feeling empty as she sat in her garage. *And you, Brad?* came the snide little voice that was usually reserved for Roy. *Did that little back-and-forth do anything for you?*

She knew she was being unfair. A text was a text. Only he could have called once he knew she was in. Or asked her to call him. Or sent a longer e-mail. He might have even insisted on driving her to the airport so that they could talk, though attempting serious discussion at 5:15 A.M. was dangerous, as they had proven this morning with regard to choosing a wedding date.

Wedding date. *Gah*. Another problem to try to solve.

But first, Roy. He had texted her, too. More than once. She could guess why.

Grabbing her purse, briefcase, and the heels she'd kicked off to drive, she left the car and went inside, where she dropped her things on a glass table in the short hallway that connected the garage to the main living space. Right there, determined to face the devil before she stepped farther into her home, she pulled up Roy's texts.

Theo just called, he had written shortly after she arrived at Caroline's. *Why did you involve him?* Then, an hour later, *Have you told your mother yet?* And an hour after that, *Did you tell her?*

It was ten now. Like Brad, Roy slept with the phone by his bed, but Jamie couldn't bear to go into the *Gut It!* dilemma with him now. She was emotionally drained and physically tired, and she still had to run through a checklist for tomorrow. And, oh yeah, she had to be up at 4:30 A.M.

But she knew Roy. He would keep at it until she wrote back.

Quickly, she typed, *Just got this. Am leaving for Atlanta early tomorrow, back late. Talk Saturday.*

She hit SEND, connected the phone to the charger on the table, and walked away with only her briefcase and shoes.

Entering the body of the condo, she felt instant relief. The foyer was open to a small dining room, beyond which were an eat-in kitchen and a great room, all of it done in a soft white with accents in soothing shades of sand. Setting her briefcase on the island, she sank low in a leather sofa, put her feet on the limestone coffee table, and listened.

All was quiet. She appreciated that for all of two minutes, at which point she began hearing echoes of the day.

Needing to escape them, she was off the sofa in a flash and barefooting it up the stairs. There were two bedrooms here, one for sleep and one for work. Both were decorated in the same minimalist way, everything low and sleek, done in varying shades of white with sprinkles of sand—the bathroom marble, the bedroom dresser, the wall-to-wall on the office floor to soften the effect of the starker white desk and chair. Color came from art on the walls, though there wasn't much. What she had was large and contemporary, bringing in the neutrality of brown, khaki, and blue. She couldn't say what she loved about each, other than that it had spoken to her on a visceral level. Each was soothing and, regardless of hue, pristine.

She took slow, deep breaths as she undressed and pulled on a silky T-shirt and shorts, and she breathed her way into the bathroom to wash her face. When her freckles appeared, she eyed her mirrored self in despair. *She's had her turn,* Brad had said of Caroline; *She's fifty-six,* said Roy. *But me?* Jamie thought. Twenty-nine going on twelve, to judge from that freckled face.

Closing her eyes, she braced her hands on the marble countertop and continued to breathe, ignoring the voices as she focused on the movement of her diaphragm, belly, breasts, and hips. She really needed an hour with her yoga instructor. She used to do classes several times a week, but weekends seemed the only time for them now.

Saturday was the day after tomorrow. She could make it till then.

Clinging to that thought, she brushed her hair and piled it on the top of her head, then went back downstairs and opened her briefcase. Before leaving the office, she had packed it with every folder that she might have even a vague chance of wanting. Now, needing it as streamlined as her home, she sorted through. She did not need bubble diagrams, since she had two sets of formal plans ready to travel. Nor did she need printouts of every e-mail to and from the client. She did need her notes from multiple meetings with the client on his vision and the needs of his company. These she would reread during the two-and-a-half-hour flight, so that they would be fresh in her mind during her presentation.

She skimmed those notes now, along with the quote package Dean had prepared. The bottom line was more than the client wanted, which meant that there would be hard discussions. Best-case scenario, they could reach a comfortable compromise. Worst-case scenario, she would be paid for time spent and discharged. Hoping it didn't come to the latter, she repacked the briefcase. She had barely placed it by the garage door when she saw the message light on her phone.

That would be Roy.

Unable to deal, she headed upstairs to pick clothes. Her closet was built in behind a hinge-less white door and organized to the extreme, with full-length spaces for dresses and pants, half-length ones for skirts and blouses. There were a dozen drawers, as many open shelves, and more shoe cubbies than she could ever fill herself. Brad would help with that if he moved in. That said, he had a condo. She had a condo. Pooling resources, they could afford a house. They talked of this often—dreamed of it.

But she loved her place. It was the first one she'd ever owned.

For tomorrow, she picked a chocolate brown suit in a summer-weight merino that refused to wrinkle, and a pale silk tank. Once she had set her alarm for 4:30 and drawn off the fitted duvet cover, she climbed into bed with the remote. She didn't usually watch the news on television, preferring to read it online, where she could skim or not. The instant she tuned in now, though, she was riveted. *Personally, I like seeing those little blondes reading the news in their cocktail dresses,* Theo had said, and to her amazement, he was right. The co-anchors were female, with long blond hair and impeccable makeup. They couldn't have been any older than Jamie, and they looked disturbingly alike in a Barbie way. The main things setting them apart were their dresses. One was red, the other purple; one had cap sleeves, the other no sleeves; one had a plunging neckline, and the other was ruched to show just a hint of cleavage.

What had happened to chic business suits? Or to trying to win the respect given a man by dressing like one? Or, at the very least, to rejecting the stereotype of the sexy little woman?

Did Jamie hear the story being reported? No. She was too busy frowning at the cleavage on display and thinking how inappropriate it was to be dressed to the hilt to read the 11:00 P.M. news. She couldn't imagine either of these women actually going out into the field to gather information. Clearly, that wasn't their job. They were entertainers.

Did she feel confidence in someone her age who did this? No. They moved their hands, looked at the camera in a comfortable enough way, looked disappointed or downcast or jovial at just the right times. Did she trust that they had insight into world affairs? *No.*

Maybe brains didn't matter when there was someone else to write the words. In fact, the lead story, to which they returned repeatedly during the broadcast, was the weather. The heat and humidity would be around for another day at least, with no storms to bring relief until Saturday. Since Jamie was flying morning and evening tomorrow, this was good news.

Mesmerized in the way of morbid curiosity, she kept watching. *Beauty before age,* Theo had said, and that might work here, but not on *Gut It!*

Or did it? What if Brian and Claire wanted her to host

solely because she was young and attractive? What if she were as noncredible, as *interchangeable,* as these women? If so, she hadn't accomplished anything in life, at least not where *Gut It!* was concerned. She was simply being rewarded for her age at the expense of her mother, who was being punished for hers.

It was all wrong. Caroline was a hands-on host who knew what she was talking about. Even when smiling, she had a gravitas that these two on the screen lacked.

The news ended, but Jamie was aggravated enough to be hearing voices again. Aware that she had to be up in five hours, she pulled up reruns of *American Idol* and let the music exhaust her.

Soon after dawn, she was on her way to the airport, and, yes, there were messages on her phone from Roy and Brad. Ignoring them, she read one from Caroline thanking her for the birthday celebration, and several from clients on project issues. Once she boarded the plane, though, she turned off her phone. Minutes later, the plane took off, and she was on her way to Atlanta, oblivious of the disaster about to unfold at home.

Chapter Six

Caroline was sitting in the middle of her unmade bed, in a mess of fuchsia sheets and scattered sections of the newspaper, when she called the MacAfee shop Friday morning. Fresh from the bath, she had placed herself directly under the ceiling fan, so that it would cool her as it dried her skin.

At the other end of the line, she heard the high-pitched screech of a table saw, then the voice of the shop's manager. "McGinn here."

"Hey, Brady, it's Caroline. Just checking in. Have my dowels arrived?" The dowels in question were small pins that would anchor the top to the legs of a trestle table she was building from white oak. The pins were a hybrid of wood and steel that was new enough to the market to make them a special-order item.

"Hold on. I'll look."

He was gone for several minutes, during which time the upstairs cats joined her on the bed—Biscuit, the youngest, to bat at the newspaper, AnneMarie, the mama's girl, to stretch out along Caroline's thigh. Caroline was stroking her orange back when Brady returned.

"I don't see them. They should've been in by now. Want me to track 'em down?"

"That'd be great. Thanks, Brady. What's doing there?"

"Same old. Norris and Watts are working on prefabs for the Connolly house. Turino's cutting decking."

"Not on-site?"

"He says it's too hot. Me, I'd be out there anyhow. It's pretty hot in here, too."

Caroline didn't doubt it. Her house seemed to be absorbing more humidity with each passing hour, and though she had every ceiling fan running on high, they could only do so much when the moisture became entrenched. Lethargy was the order of the day, not that she was about to do anything strenuous, like take a wood chisel to teak. Her wrist was still achy.

Phone calls were fine, though. She made a few more before extracting herself from the cats, pulling on a white tank and denim shorts, and trotting barefoot down the stairs. The place smelled—cloyingly—of roses. She might have tossed them, had they not been from Theo.

She poured herself an iced tea, pulled a stool up to the kitchen counter, and opened her laptop. It was a minute before her e-mail began loading. One day offline, and an amazing amount piled up. MacAfee had a digital assistant whose job was to monitor *Gut It!* Facebook posts, forward notes to whoever of the cast could best answer them, and post their replies. As host, Caroline got the most mail. For that reason, and because she liked doing it, she wrote and posted replies herself.

Today, there were questions on refinishing butcher block, building bunk beds into a gabled alcove, and replacing an out-of-code banister, but she had barely skimmed the list when Master began weaving through her legs. She managed to haul him onto her lap—no small feat with only one arm and significant cat girth—but once there, he butted her chin with his furry gray head by way of thank you, turned a circle in search of just the right spot, and settled in.

How to restore salvaged barn board. She started with that. Her right thumb was a problem, since the bandage holding it in the proper position for her wrist kept hitting the space bar at the wrong time. Other than the occasional twinge, though, the typing caused no pain.

Caroline loved this part of her job. There were times when that still surprised her. Born and bred a carpenter, she had never dreamed of doing anything but working with tools. But now this—writing letters, giving advice, sharing her knowledge with people who turned around and put it to good use? Life was good.

The doorbell rang. Easing Master to the floor, she left the kitchen. And there, at the far end of the hall on the other side of the screen, was Claire Howe.

Caroline's first thought was that Claire would *not* like what she was wearing. She rarely did. Not that the woman was a sharp dresser herself. Tall and lean, she seemed oblivious to her sloppy appearance, as in ill-fitting skirts and half-tucked blouses. And sneakers? Even Caroline knew that flats or low heels were better with a skirt.

Not that Claire needed clothes to exert command. Her deep voice did that all on its own, and if not her voice, her eyes. They rarely blinked. The intimidation factor didn't bother Caroline, but she spent her share of time on the set soothing others who suffered a bruising Claire stare.

But they weren't on the set now. This was Caroline's turf.

"Claire. Hi." She smiled as she opened the screen. "This is a surprise—and before you say anything, I watched the tape. It's amazing. Our best season yet, don't you think?"

Claire didn't reply. She was eying the bandaged hand. "That looks serious."

Caroline turned the wrist back and forth. "Not to worry. This is by design. My doctor has a perverse sense of humor. And thank you for the birthday flowers." She glanced toward the living room, where the arrangement from Brian and Claire positively burst from its vase. "Come." She gestured. "You have to see these."

"I can certainly smell them," Claire remarked as she followed Caroline into the living room. She glanced at the flowers, said a dismissive "Pretty," and returned to Caroline with cautious eyes. "You look calm. Does that mean you're okay with everything?"

"With what?"

"The change."

"What change?" When Claire's eyes darkened in annoyance, Caroline tried to think of something she might have forgotten. The woman certainly wasn't talking about menopause; she never got personal. Caroline could only think of one possibility. "You mean the underwriting change?" A new sponsor would be on board for the fall. But Claire's frown said it wasn't that. Uneasy, she said, "Spill it, Claire. It's not like you to hesitate."

"It's not like Roy to lie," Claire shot back.

Ooooh. Caroline wasn't touching *that* one. "Please," she invited, "what *is* it?"

With a low chuff, Claire looked away, then almost angrily back. "We're changing hosts."

Pause. "Excuse me?"

"We're making a change in who will host the show." The words, enunciated in pairs, were barely out when she declared an irritated "I was not supposed to be the messenger here. We discussed this at length. Roy said Jamie already told you."

Caroline was doubly confused. "I was with Jamie yesterday. Twice. She didn't mention any change."

"Well, I don't know why not. She was the one who offered to tell you. This has been in the works for a while. We've been prepping her behind the scenes. She'll be taking over as host."

Caroline was floored. "Ex*cuse* me?"

"Jamie is the new host. We want a new face."

Caroline recoiled. "What's wrong with mine?"

"Nothing, Caroline," Claire said in a pedantic way, clearly still annoyed, "except you've been hosting for a while. It's time for something fresh."

Caroline had an awful feeling. "Define fresh."

"Young. Our backers feel strongly about this, and focus groups tell us that Jamie is the one they like best."

"At least they have good taste," Caroline managed to say. Jamie would make a great host, but that wasn't the issue. The word "young" was echoing, echoing, echoing. She felt blindsided, gutted just as she had been when Roy had told her she was no longer "young" enough to be his wife. "Oh boy," she muttered. "This is Roy's doing." It was the only thing that made sense. He loved everything about *Gut It!*'s success except her role in it.

Claire was strident. "Roy does not make the decisions here. He may know about marketing for your family business, but television is not his world. No, Roy didn't initiate this, but he's been on board from the start."

From the start? Like months and months? And Jamie knowing, too? That thought had her reeling.

"Jamie is good, Caroline. She won't let you down."

"Her ability isn't the issue."

"It was Jamie's idea to make a contest out of choosing the fall house."

"She's definitely savvy about marketing gimmicks, but how does that correlate to hosting *Gut It!*?"

"She's of the generation we want. It was her idea to

bring Taylor Huff on as interior designer this spring. Taylor is thirty. Focus groups liked her, too."

"Who all were *in* these focus groups?" Caroline cried. "*College* kids?"

"Accept it, Caroline. It's a fact of life, and it isn't just television. Every entertainment platform puts a premium on youth."

"What about Oprah? She's not thirty. Neither is Katie Couric or Cokie Roberts or . . . or Diane Sawyer."

"You're no Diane Sawyer."

"And *Gut It!* is no *This Old House*," Caroline shot back, because one put-down deserved another. But there was little satisfaction in it. Something inside her was withering. "I'm just gone from the show, then?"

"Oh no," Claire said quickly. "*Lord* no. We want you to stay on as master carpenter. You'll still anchor certain segments, especially if the wedding takes place during the taping, and Jamie and Brad are in Paris."

"Paris."

"Am I speaking out of turn? I thought they were honeymooning there."

The woman certainly knew how to stab and twist. Caroline felt the pain but refused to show it. "They haven't decided," she replied, though suddenly wasn't certain.

"Well, whatever. When it comes to *Gut It!* we want you to do everything that you've been doing."

"Like smoothing things over when you offend people on set?"

Claire stared. "Do you have a point with that?"

"Absolutely," Caroline said, perhaps brashly, but what did she have to lose? "I do a lot more on set than hosting, and it's because I am who I am at the *age* I am that I'm able to do it."

"And we appreciate your efforts. But the person facing the camera is going to be Jamie."

With that bluntness, Caroline was blindsided all over again. How to process this, when it didn't make sense? She and Jamie shared everything. Besides, hadn't Jamie just said she didn't have time to plan a wedding? Add hosting responsibilities to that—unless she was *already* factoring in hosting responsibilities?

"There'll be a learning curve," Claire went on. "She understands that. But you have to agree that this will lead to big things for her career. Her name will be front and center. She'll be a celebrity in architectural circles."

"I'm not arguing with any of that. But why *now*?" Jamie was twenty-nine. Caroline had been midforties when she took the helm.

"Because our new sponsor feels strongly about it. Jamie was instrumental in securing this sponsor, by the way. She was in on all the meetings last winter. It's about demographics. We want to aim for the twenty-five- to forty-year-olds."

"Well, that's very PC," Caroline said in a burst of pique, "but they're not the ones spending the money."

"Increasingly, they are. Advertisers know this."

"They should tell *that* to those twenty-five- to forty-year-olds, who either have low-paying jobs or—if they were lucky enough to go to college—huge debt to repay. In the ten years our show's been running, what was the youngest age of a homeowner?" In response to silence, she said, "Correct. Forty. Which is at the very top of that demographic. The average age of homeowners has been fifty. Our fall homeowners are nearing *sixty*. Do advertisers want that to change, too? Should *Gut It!* start focusing on redoing the one-bedroom condo that the average thirty-year-old might be able to afford?"

Needing fresh air, Caroline left the living room and went out the door to the porch. Oh yes, the heat was brutal, but that wasn't why she was sweating. Claire was poison.

She wanted the woman out of her house. But even the porch was too close. She went halfway down the walk, where she put her hands on her hips and waited.

Behind her, the screen slapped. Hit by a new wave of bewilderment, she turned as Claire approached. "Was it something I did? Something I said? Something I *wore*?" Not that she was about to change her look. Viewers loved her color. She constantly got mail on that.

Claire said nothing.

"Just my age," Caroline concluded in defeat.

After another moment's silence, Claire waved away a fly. "So . . . are you okay with this now?"

They had come full circle, but Caroline was more confused than ever. "How could I be okay with it? I totally disagree with this decision."

"You don't want your daughter to move ahead?"

"Whoa," she cautioned with deadly calm, "I *always* want my daughter to move ahead. I've devoted my *life* to having my daughter move ahead. Do not *ever* think that I would do anything to hold my daughter back."

It was true. But Caroline knew that the issue here wasn't job advancement. It was caring. It was honesty, or the lack thereof, and the hurt it caused. It might even be betrayal, though she refused to go that far before she spoke with Jamie.

Claire was still backing her BMW out of the driveway when Caroline went inside and, heart pounding, tried Jamie's cell, but the call went straight to voice mail. Realizing that the plane might not have touched down in Atlanta, she waited another few minutes, then tried again. This time, after the beep, she said, "Call when you land," and clicked off.

Claire was gone.

Jamie was silent.

Caroline was too old.

Sinking down on the steps in the front hall, feeling deficient in ways she hadn't in years, she waited for Jamie to call back. Antsy, she wandered out to the front porch, frowning at nothing in particular until her eye fell on the flowers the *Gut It!* cameraman had sent. *Heal well,* his card read. *You're still our carpenter.* She had thought the wording strange at the time, but it took on new meaning now.

Who else knew? Claire and Brian, Roy and Jamie, the cameraman. Were e-mails making broader rounds even now? Was she the *last* to know? Had they purposely chosen to break the news when they knew she would be at home and out of commission?

Striding angrily down the steps and across the lawn, she paused at the junipers growing in the shade of a curbside oak. They needed pruning. But not now. Totally aside from the heat, her *wrist* wouldn't work.

Because she'd had to have surgery on it. Because she'd been using it for so long.

Discouraged, she went back to the steps, sat on the lowest one, and hugged her knees. A neighbor returning home slowed and waved. She waved back but was in no mood to talk. Instead, she went back inside and tried Jamie again, wondering if Jamie had forgotten to turn her phone on. She didn't usually. Whenever Caroline was with her, she turned on the phone the instant the wheels touched down. It was habit, even compulsion perhaps.

Unless she had deliberately not done it now because she didn't want to be reached. Unless she had actually, horrifyingly *planned* to be away so that Claire would have to break the news.

Trying not to panic, Caroline went through to the

kitchen and out the back door. Even as she headed for the garage, though, her mind remained in the kitchen. Jamie wanted to renovate it. She had been increasingly insistent. Out of guilt? That would make sense if she had known about this for a while or, worse, had lobbied for it. Would she seriously have done that?

Roy sure as hell would. Caroline had no doubt about that, as she slipped into the garage. He might not have come up with the idea, but he was probably on the phone with Claire right now, grinning that cocky grin of his as he reveled in Caroline's demotion.

Inhaling the familiar scent of sawdust, she ousted Roy from her mind. She didn't want him here. This place was hers.

Up until five years before, she had lived in the house they shared while married, and though it was a dozen years before that when he moved out and signed over the deed, that house had never felt entirely hers. This one did—both the main Victorian and this garage, which had the same facade as the original carriage house but was a totally different beast inside. Oh yes, it had a small office in the second-floor loft, but more important to Caroline was the belly below.

The equivalent of a generous two-car garage, it was outfitted with superb lighting and the latest in ventilation systems to remove sawdust from the air. That said, there was just enough of it gathered at the feet of the worktables to bring her comfort. Add to its smell the fainter ones of glue, wood stain, even a lingering electrical smell from her new belt saw, and she was in her element. Her tools were on shelves and wall hooks, or mounted on tables, with goggles and gloves lying nearby. Mingling among them, though, and just as precious to her were the relics from her father's workshop. Most were small hand tools. Running

her hand now over a palm sander that had been revolution-
ary in his day, she was taken back to her roots.

She was a carpenter. The scent of sawdust, like comfort
food, was an anesthetic. She was okay, she told herself. She
didn't need to host a TV show.

Momentarily soothed, she tried Jamie again, but when
she hit voice mail, the soothing leeched away. Jamie knew.
Jamie prepped. Jamie plotted.

But knowing Caroline would be hurt?

She thought about asking Roy and quickly vetoed the
idea. All he would do was gloat.

Theo, on the other hand, was her champion. He might
have insight into what was happening and why. But running to her ex-father-in-law at the first sign of trouble just
wasn't her way.

Unable to work because of her hand and too unsettled
to sit still, she left the garage and paced the yard as she
waited for Jamie's call. But the cell in her hand remained
silent, and the longer it did that, the more damning things
seemed. Jamie was taking her sweet time returning her
call, which was so not like Jamie that there had to be more
going on.

Plane trouble? Back inside, she checked the airline's
website. ARRIVED, it said.

She thought of calling Dean. But he was in the air somewhere in the middle of the country, and besides, his solution to life problems was either to ride on the Harley or
to hunt.

Annie would be as angry as Dean. But she was doing a
huge installation at a MacAfee project an hour away. And
Caroline didn't want to involve anyone else until she talked
with Jamie.

She wanted to convince herself that being upset was
petty and that she'd be fine as long as she was still part

of the show. She wanted to say she didn't care if Jamie hosted.

But the silence grew louder with each minute that passed, so that by the time Jamie finally called, Caroline was ready to believe the worst.

Chapter Seven

Jamie's heart lurched when she heard Caroline's message. It was too short and too tense, not like her mother at all. And though Jamie was in a car with her client and needed to maintain a semblance of professionalism, there was no way she wasn't calling right back.

Picking up, Caroline said her name, just her name.

"What's wrong?" Jamie asked in the lowest of voices.

"Claire was here."

Jamie pressed her fingers to her forehead, as much to shield her voice from the driver as to keep herself calm. "She wasn't supposed to do that."

"How long have you known?"

"One day."

"That's not what she said. She said you've known for a while."

"Not true."

"She said they've been grooming you for this."

"I had no idea."

"She said you were all in favor of it."

"She lied."

"But you did know about it both times you were here yesterday."

"Yes. But the time wasn't right to discuss it." Nor was

this, what with a client sitting three feet away. Voice even lower, she said, "I can't talk right now. Can I call later?"

She heard what sounded like a frustrated sound, then a click, and the line went dead.

Caroline's rational self understood why Jamie couldn't talk. The emotional one did not. Thinking that if Jamie was as innocent as she claimed, she would find a way to call back, she waited anxiously on the porch. She walked through the house. She spent time with the cats.

Again she considered calling Dean. He would get the aging part. Again she considered calling Annie. She would get the betrayal part.

I do not want this change, Jamie texted an hour later.

Caroline didn't reply. Texting was a cop-out.

But another came a short time later. *I did not ask for it. They just want it to look that way. I've been used.*

You're not the victim here, Caroline shot back. When she calmed a bit, she typed, *Who used you?*

Brian and Claire. Dad.

What did Roy do?

Supported the other two. He should have said NO.

Your father? Caroline wrote back with sarcasm aplenty.

Jamie didn't respond as they got into the lunch hour. Caroline's hopes rose when the phone rang, but it was Brad.

"Jamie is panicking," he said. "She's had two minutes in the ladies' room, no other time alone. She's worried about you. She's worried you're furious. How are you doing?"

"I've been better," Caroline said in what she thought was a commendably benign voice.

"She feels terrible about this."

"Which part—the switch or her role in it?" she asked and instantly regretted it. She didn't want to discuss this with Brad. Jamie should have called her during those two minutes in the ladies' room.

Apparently Brad didn't want to discuss it with her either. What he said was focused on the narrowest angle. "She doesn't want you angry at her. She's agonizing down there."

"Well, I'm agonizing up here, but that doesn't help either one of us, does it? Listen, I appreciate your calling, but Jamie and I really need to talk."

"Can I tell her you're okay?"

"No. That would be a lie. Hey, Brad, I have to run. Thanks for calling."

Stuck in a car with her client in thick traffic thanks to an accident, Jamie was late getting back to the airport, and then reached her departure gate only after a fiasco at security during which she spilled the contents of her bag. Frazzled and no small amount exhausted, she corralled runaway print tubes from under the conveyor belt while the security guards watched in amusement. Knowing the plane was boarding, she ran. It wasn't until her things were in the overhead bin—actually, in a bin farther back, since those over her own seat were full—and she had climbed awkwardly over the legs of a large man who chose not to stand, for some reason, that she was able to call Caroline. Her mother picked up right away, but Jamie spent so long trying to explain why she hadn't been able to call sooner that she sounded defensive even to herself.

"I'm landing at ten," she concluded as the flight attendant began the instructions for takeoff. "Can I drive right there?"

Caroline nixed that. When Jamie asked why, she said she needed time, and when Jamie insisted they had to talk, Caroline said, "Not tonight."

Jamie didn't mention Brad's call, though she knew he

had made it. He had texted that it went just fine, but she
didn't know what that meant, and she hadn't had time to
call him to find out.

So she didn't stop at Caroline's on her way home from
the airport. She did talk with Brad, but when she tried to
pin him down about his conversation with Caroline, she
didn't learn much. "She's feeling self-pity," he suggested.

"Seriously?" Jamie shot back, unimpressed with his
analysis and thinking that her mother had a right to feel
that and more. To his credit, Brad was contrite. He didn't
offer to drive over to comfort her, though, and for a second night in a row, she was glad. He had meetings with
clients Saturday morning, and she planned to sleep in.

In fact, she slept poorly and was glad for an excuse to stop
trying as soon as daylight appeared. Though clouds covered the sky, she was able to drive to Caroline's with the
top down, but took no pleasure from it this day. The stifling air reflected her mood, which undermined the comfort she normally felt approaching the Victorian. When she
thought of her mother, she ached.

The truck was parked at the garage, but Caroline wasn't
on the porch. When Jamie stuck her head in the front door
and called, Master's meow was the only response. As she
scrubbed the back of his neck, she heard a faint noise over
his purring.

Ducking back out, she followed that noise to the garage.
The shrill buzz of the table saw was as familiar to her as
a lullaby. The sheer normalcy of it raised her hopes.

Caroline couldn't hear her over the noise of the saw. Nor
would she catch movement, with her goggles distorting her
peripheral vision. She wore a T-shirt so faded that it looked
gray and very old, very worn jeans. With her hair in a high
knot and protective gloves on her hands, she was carving
a piece of wood at one of three worktables. If her wrist

hurt, she was ignoring it. The intensity of her forward stance suggested full concentration.

Jamie was wondering how to get her attention without making her jump when it struck her that Caroline knew she was there. Her jaw had grown tighter. Likewise her forearm. And rather than surging and ebbing as she shaped the wood, the whir of the saw was steady, determined, angry.

Not good.

"Mom," she called, then did it again. Finally, with a sigh, Caroline silenced the saw and straightened. After raising the goggles, she removed her gloves—gingerly when it came to the right one. The bandage on her wrist was gone, replaced by a Velcro support.

"That's an improvement," Jamie said in a tentative voice. "Is it okay?"

Caroline brushed at the wood, smoothed it with her hand, and bent to eye it from a different angle. "It's fine."

But her mother was not. What little Jamie could see of her face looked pale. Her failure to look at Jamie spoke volumes. "You're angry at me."

"I'm angry at the world," Caroline declared in a resigned burst as she straightened to her full height. Jamie might have appreciated her honesty if those so-like-her-own eyes hadn't met hers then. They were guarded to the point of being foreign. "*Should* I be angry with you?"

"For not telling you myself? Yes," Jamie readily confessed. "For Claire's decision? No. I had no part in that, Mom. Didn't ask for it. Don't want it."

"Have you told that to Claire?"

"No. She won't return my calls."

"Did you tell Roy?"

"Yes. He said they'd just hire an outside host and that I'd be jeopardizing the show."

"He's right." She didn't blink. "It's our family that's

associated with *Gut It!* One of us has to host it, and they don't want me to do it."

"But that's not *right*," Jamie cried. "They're discriminating against you because of your age. You have to fight."

"Oh, I plan to," Caroline informed her, "but will I win? Doubtful. Let's open our eyes here, Jamie. When I look at the rest of the entertainment field, this isn't unique."

"But you love your role on the show. You haven't been this happy since—"

"—the divorce." Caroline raised her chin and said, "So here's a question for you. I've gone out of my way all these years not to put you in the middle, but I need an honest answer. How hard is your father pushing for this?"

Jamie did feel sandwiched. She chose her words with care. "He says he wants it for me. He keeps telling me how good it would be for my career."

"Brad clearly agrees with your father. And they're right. This would be a great move for you. You'll make a fabulous host—and you're ready. It didn't occur to me, not once during the Longmeadow taping, but when I look back on it, you hosted more scenes than you ever have before."

"It didn't occur to me either, Mom," Jamie came back in a beseeching voice. "That's what I'm trying to say. It's only in hindsight that I can see what they were doing. I didn't plan it."

"Jamie!" Caroline shouted. "You were instrumental in choosing the next project and securing new sponsors. You brought in Taylor Huff, who is *your* contemporary. You even narrated segments on the hand-crafted built-ins that I made. How could you not see what was happening?"

"Did *you* see it?" Jamie asked. Her stomach was churning.

"No, because you're my daughter, so I wasn't threatened. Besides, I wasn't in on your meetings with Claire.

But you did tell me you were meeting with her. As I recall, it was practically every Tuesday morning."

That was damning, Jamie realized. "Honestly? I just thought she wanted my perspective on things. I thought she was picking my brain."

"You also took her shopping."

"For shoes, because she has zero taste."

"You went to a concert with her."

"Because you hate Nine Inch Nails, and she got complimentary tickets."

"You told her you and Brad were honeymooning in Paris. You didn't even tell me that."

Jamie was livid. "*She* mentioned Paris. *She* said it would be a good place to honeymoon. I agreed with her because there was no point in arguing, but if I haven't picked a date for my wedding yet, how can I plan my honeymoon? Claire is a bitch, Mom. She's making trouble." She had a bizarre thought. "Are you *jealous*?"

"Of Claire Howe?"

"Of her thinking she's my friend. She isn't because (A) I have no time for friends and (B) you're the only friend I need."

"I'm not jealous. I'm just looking at the evidence and thinking that there's no way you could have spent that amount of time with her without knowing on some level what she was planning. You're too bright to have missed all the signs. You had to have known, even subconsciously, but you said nothing to me. This is my *life*, Jamie. Shouldn't I have been involved in the conversation?"

"*Yes,* but it wasn't my call, Mom. I guess I'm *not* so bright, but I did not know what they were doing until Thursday morning. I said I'd be the one to tell you, because Claire is abrasive and Dad is a bulldozer"—her voice rose—"but was I seriously supposed to tell you when you were recovering from surgery? And on your *birthday*? Was I supposed to tell you on your birthday that you were being replaced because of your age? Give me credit for sensitivity, at least."

"But you do want this job."

"Not at your expense. If it didn't mean replacing you, of *course* I'd want it. It's a dream opportunity. Who *wouldn't* want it?"

"There you go."

"That doesn't mean—"

"Call it subconscious, but you were lobbying for it."

"No, Mom. I've been doing what Claire wanted me to do. I'm the dunce here. I just went along."

Caroline stared at her before whipping the goggles off her head and tossing them on the table on her way to the door. "Poor Jamie. She didn't plan any of this. Well, poor Jamie is the one who stands to gain here." She stormed toward the house.

"You sound like Grandma."

Caroline whipped around. "Who was paranoid at the end because she suffered from *dementia*. Hah! The truth comes out—I am an old fool."

"Mom," Jamie moaned as Caroline whipped back and strode on, "I can't do this. I *hate* confrontation."

At the back steps, Caroline whirled around again. "Life lesson here. Confrontation is what happens when you are less than honest and you get caught."

Jamie was losing it. Her relationship with her mother was more important to her than anything else in the world. "Okay," she said, trying desperately to stay calm, "I'll do anything to make this right. I don't care about *Gut It!* Let it be canceled. Is that what you want?"

"Excuse me? Are you putting the burden of that on *me*?"

Jamie threw her hands in the air. "I can't win. What do you want me to say? Okay." She was beyond reason. "I wanted this. I planned it. Is that what you want me to say? It's not true, but do the words make you feel better?"

Caroline trotted up the back steps. At the door, she shot a look back, but her gaze was so forbidding that Jamie couldn't take another step. All she could do was to watch her go inside and close the door.

Driving back home, Jamie was beside herself. For the first time in her life, something stood between her and her mother. It wasn't a person or even a wall, but more like that screen door slapping hard in her face. She could still see her old mom—same wavy hair, same green eyes, same strong arms—but now on the far side that she couldn't reach. Anger was so not part of her mother's usual behavior that Jamie didn't know how to begin to handle it.

"How'd it go?" Brad asked, sounding concerned. He had been trying her, but it wasn't until she was inside her clean, neat, sleek white condo that she found the where-withal to call back.

"She totally blames me."

"This is not your fault," he said innocently enough.

"No? I played into Claire's hands. I played into *Dad's* hands." She began wandering. "I should have seen it coming, but I didn't, and she's right, I'm the one who stands to gain from this. She used to trust me. Forget that now." Her feet stopped moving. "When you called her, Brad, what did you say?" Whatever it was hadn't helped, but she needed to know.

"I told her how worried you were."

"About her."

"Yes. That's what I got from you."

She felt a spike of frustration. She knew that Brad wasn't good with parents, but this was as much about his understanding Jamie as anything else. "Did you not tell her that I think this change is a mistake?"

"It isn't a mistake. It's a carefully crafted move to improve the show's ratings—"

"—which haven't declined. So it's a preemptive move."

"That's how successful ventures work. They have to stay one step ahead."

"This isn't a corporate venture. It's a family show. Does that not count for anything?"

"It's more than a family show." He barely paused. "By the way, did you hear the forecast? Bad storms are moving in."

Jamie couldn't have cared less about the weather. "*Gut It!* is about MacAfee Homes, and MacAfee Homes is about family. When it comes to the show, Caroline is the matriarch. She's the glue that holds it all together." With a quick breath, she begged, "I need you to hear me, Brad. I don't want this job. Maybe in the future, but not now. My mother earned it, she does it well, and viewers aren't complaining about the way she looks. If they're firing her because she's too old, that's grounds for a lawsuit." She paused, got no reply, finally asked, "Don't you think?"

"Actually, they're within their legal rights. Her contract runs from year to year. They're not kicking her off the show. They're just shifting the cast around. And I mentioned the weather because if we get torrential downpours, having dinner in Boston tonight may not be smart."

Their reservation was at a restaurant on the waterfront that had opened earlier that spring, but Jamie couldn't think about dinner just then. "Claire admitted it was about age."

"It might be, but this is entertainment. Actresses audition for roles all the time and fail to get them because they're too old. Do you see them suing? I looked into precedent, Jamie. Caroline can sue, but the case will be tossed out before it ever reaches a court, and she'll be out fifty grand for the attempt."

"MacAfee will cover it."

"We won't. I asked."

"Asked *who*?"

"Theo. Roy wanted to know. Neither one of them wants that kind of publicity. Listen, I know you're upset, but stand back for a minute. If she can't win this, wouldn't it be better to accept the inevitable?"

"You mean, go out with dignity?" Jamie mocked.

"Yes," he insisted with more enthusiasm in that single word than in any of the others preceding it, which annoyed her all the more.

"Okay, Brad. *You* stand back. Suppose I take this job. Suppose I hold it for a dozen years, and maybe the show has moved through a handful of mutations but is still going strong, and we're married with three kids—"

"Two kids."

"*Three* kids, and I'm over forty and maybe not so slim after the kids, and they decide they want someone twenty-five so they're easing me out, how would you feel then?" Silence. "How would you feel if they did that to *you*?"

"I'm in a different field."

Jamie simmered. "The correct answer would be 'I'm a man. That would never happen to me.' And you're right. But how unfair is that? Your dad is bald, so *you* could well be bald. Think MacAfee buyers will ask for a younger lawyer? No, they will not, because your age gives you authority. It suggests knowledge and experience. Well, the same is true of Caroline MacAfee."

"Jeez, Jamie," Brad burst out, sounding bewildered, "what do you want me to say?"

Jamie could think of a dozen things, but she refused to spoon-feed him. Either he felt the cause or he did not.

Right now, though, she wanted to get off the phone and go to yoga. There was a class at one, and after a disastrous time earlier with Caroline and now a disappointing discussion with Brad, she needed a break. Granted it was barely ten. One was a ways off, and the class wasn't far. But she had plenty to keep her busy, starting with the drawings for a residential project, for which she needed to visit a stoneworks company that MacAfee hadn't used before but that carried the fieldstone she desperately wanted to use on this house.

"Gotta go," she said.

"We have to keep talking. We don't agree yet."

"Brad, we're not going to agree on everything. I need to go to yoga."

"Watch the weather."

"Okay. I'll call you later."

Concentration was a problem. She couldn't sit still to work on the drawings, didn't see the fieldstone she wanted, and when she got to yoga, the instructor was so like Caroline in age and looks that Jamie had to keep her eyes shut. Without a visual example, she was distracted and kept reverting to shallow breathing.

Brad had been right about the weather. By the time her class was done, the morning's clouds had darkened to slate. Her mood was correspondingly grim. She needed Caroline.

As she drove home, she called. "Mom?" She paused. Nothing. "Are you okay?"

"I'm fine," Caroline said. She didn't sound it, but at least she had answered the phone.

"About this morning—"

"I don't want to talk about it, Jamie."

"We were both upset."

"Right, so I'm not going there. Let it rest."

"Nothing gets resolved if it rests." She realized she sounded like Brad.

There was a pause, then a quiet "When it's raw, it does, unless you want to do more damage?"

Invitation? Dare? Threat? Jamie felt like she might cry. "No," she conceded and swallowed, but an ominous lump remained in her throat. She had to clear it to ask, "What are you doing tonight?" It was a petty question, but it kept the connection going.

"Having dinner with Annie, Linda, and Dawn."

That was good. Jamie didn't want her alone. "Dawn?"

"From the nail shop. Like Linda. Their husbands are all going to Fenway."

"The game may be rained out." Jamie thought she heard distant thunder, until she saw a truck roll around the corner a block ahead. "Okay. Well, be careful."

"Yup." No *You be careful, too,* no *We'll work this out,* no *I love you, baby.* Just *Yup,* and the call ended.

Chapter Eight

Jamie was bereft, which was why she caught a little breath of hope when she turned onto her street. Parked in front of her condo was Jess's silver SUV with its yellow TODDLER ON BOARD cling-on decal in the back window. Seeing Tad was the one thing sure to distract her.

When the SUV started to pull away, she honked and waved. *Wait! I'm home! Wait!* The SUV stopped. After pulling into the garage, Jamie ran back outside with her eyes on the backseat.

"Hey, Taddy!" she called, waving at the shadow that would be the boy, then at the real one when the window smoothly lowered. His milk-chocolate hair was a mop of soft curls that were longer than Roy wanted but shorter than Jessica did. His eyes were an even warmer brown, his little cheeks red as ever.

"Mamie, Mamie!" he shrieked.

She reached for the door just as it clicked to unlock, and shot a thank-you smile at Jess. Only Jess wasn't the one unfolding from the driver's seat.

Seeing Roy, Jamie felt a stab of dismay. He was the last person she needed right now. Granted, he wasn't looking as together as usual. He wore running shorts and a baggy tank, and his hair was messed. But his eyes were sharp, anger focused on her.

Stomach churning, she opened the door and released Tad's harness. "Hi, monkey," she said and scooped him up for a hug. His arms went around her neck, his legs around her waist. She closed her eyes, savoring. Tad always made her feel loved. Had from infancy.

Having rounded the front of the car, Roy kept the open door between them as he gripped its top. His voice was low to protect the boy, but nothing protected Jamie. The words came at her with a simmering ire.

"I can't tell you how disappointed I am. You promised you'd tell your mother, and you did not. You went behind my back with Theo and tried to do it with Claire. *She* had to tell Caroline herself, which made it harder for both of them, so if you were trying to protect your mother, you failed. I didn't ask you to tell Caroline, you offered, and I told Claire that you'd do it, so now I look like a fool and, by extension, so does MacAfee Homes." He threw up his hands. "What were you waiting for? Did you think I was kidding? That if you waited long enough, this would all just go away?"

Wearing Tad like a shield, Jamie kept her cheek tucked against his hair as she swayed from side to side. When the little boy sang her name, she drew back. His brown eyes held excitement. He babbled something.

"Say it again, monkey," she urged.

He pointed back. Fallen over on the car seat that it must have been sharing with him was a furry brown moose. "Oh my," she said in awe. "Is he new?" Indeed. The tag was still attached to its side. "What's his name?" She studied Tad's raised brows and caught in a breath. "Oh. No name yet. Should we call him Moose?"

Tad lit up. "My Moose."

"Absolutely, your Moose," Jamie said.

"Did you *hear* me, Jamie?" Roy asked, seething. "I'm not sure what your mother said, but Claire was pretty offended, so there's harm done on many fronts. Do you fully understand the stakes here? The station will go on with this show—don't ever doubt that—but if we can't come together and make it work, they'll remove the MacAfee Homes label from it."

Jamie burrowed the moose against Tad's neck. The child giggled and contorted.

"Maybe they should," she said softly and shot her father a look. His hands were on his hips, knuckles white, and his blue eyes sharp. He had clearly been stewing about this.

Tightly, he said, "I want you to call Claire and apologize. Explain why you didn't tell your mother on Thursday like you promised me you'd do, and tell her that you talked with your mother today and everything's settled. Tell her that your mother agrees with the reasoning behind the switch and is totally behind your moving up. Tell her you'll be *honored* to host the show from here on." Coming around the door, he reached for Tad. "Come on, boy. We have to go to the store for Mommy, and I want to do it before the rain comes."

With the child no longer in her arms, Jamie backed away from the car. "Wait," Roy ordered. After belting Tad in, he stalked her. "You want to feel loyalty to your mother, fine, but now is not the time. This is about loyalty to MacAfee Homes."

She didn't want to argue, but he was on a mission. When she stepped back, he followed.

"It's about business," he nearly shouted. "It's about MacAfee prominence. Did you not get it when I pointed out that Barth at Fiona's? Our competitors don't like what we have with *Gut It!* and would do most anything to have it fail. If it does, that hurts all of us." She took another step back, but he followed, hands on his hips now, upper body leaning in. "It's not just you, Jamie. You have a responsibility to the rest of the cast, too. Some have families to support, what about them? And what about your own future? Has it not occurred to you to get your foot in the door as host before you and Brad have kids? Once you've built a following, no one will blink if you're pregnant, and I'm talking about Brian and Claire, because they're the ones who count." He lowered his head so that their eyes were level. "Is anyone home? Can you speak?"

"You're crowding me," she murmured and took another step back. This time, when he followed, she held up a hand.

"I need you to speak now, Jamie. Tell me what I want to hear."

Her insides were knotted up. On a wisp of breath, she tried to be conciliatory with a mild "I think we're both upset." Caroline had said it earlier, so the statement couldn't be without merit.

Roy straightened, drawing up to his full height. "This is about your mother. That's your bottom line, isn't it."

It would be yours, too, if you had an ounce of compassion, shouted the voice in her head. The one that emerged from her mouth was less reckless. "Some things in life are just as important as MacAfee Homes."

"Like Caroline MacAfee—and hah, she wasn't so quick to give up my name, not when she was getting mileage from it. So what's the problem here? She's had her day in the sun. Now she needs to step aside and let someone younger host the show. Ah, but that's it, isn't it? You think for me it's all about age. You've always thought that. Well, let me tell you, it takes two to tango. Your mother was as much at fault for the failure of our marriage as I was. She knew I needed someone with pizzazz, but she refused to even try."

Jamie waved both hands spasmodically.

"Don't want to get into that?" Roy goaded. "Not your

business? Well, you've made it your business with this . . . this show of misguided loyalty."

"Mom worked so hard to rebuild after the divorce."

"Ah, hell. She had lots of help. Theo worships her. But he's not stepping in on her behalf right now, is he? He knows when to let smarter people make the decisions. Your mother may be good at what she does"—he rolled his eyes—"but she's just a carpenter."

"If she's just a carpenter," shouted the angry voice in Jamie's head, "then you're just a salesman!" Only when his eyes widened did she realize she had actually spoken.

A sound came from the car. Tad.

Jamie was upset enough to ignore it. "I only say that because you did. If we're boiling it down to one word—"

"The difference being that your mother will always be just a carpenter, but I'm the next head of MacAfee Homes. Your calling me 'just a salesman' is not only insulting but ignorant."

Another sound came from the car.

Roy sent an aggrieved look there before it shot back to her. "Do you hear what I'm saying about all this? You won't listen to Brad, who is nearly as frustrated as I am, but I want you to listen to me. You're being selfish and shortsighted."

"You're being insensitive and cruel."

"Excuse me?"

She didn't apologize. He had insulted Caroline. He had insulted her. He had been pushing and pushing, spoiling for a fight. She was simply stating the truth.

Suddenly, he had a finger in her face. In a low, lethal voice, he said, "I named you my son's godmother because I thought you would be the most responsible person for the job. But if you can't behave like a grown-up—if you can't separate this fixation on your mother from what everyone else knows is for the best—I'll gladly change that."

"For what it's worth," Jamie burst back, hurt enough to be reckless, "as godmothers go, I'm a totally positive influence. I'll teach Tad sensitivity and compassion, which is more than you will."

"*Excuse* me?"

She stood her ground, staring at him in defiance. He seemed stunned, and understandably so. She could count on one hand the number of times she had stood up to him.

Tad began to cry full out. Swearing, Roy simmered for a last minute before he turned on his heel and strode off. Within seconds, the SUV peeled off from the curb, and Jamie began to shake.

She wasn't sorry, absolutely was not sorry. In a perfect world, she might have used a different tone, so that she sounded less bad-tempered and more adult. But this wasn't a perfect world, and she didn't regret the words themselves. They were the absolute, positive truth.

Still, she reran the argument constantly as she showered and dressed. She muttered some lines when her eye shadow was too dark, barked out others in the closet when a hanger wouldn't release the blouse she wanted. When Brad came to pick her up, though, she didn't mention Roy's visit. She was having enough trouble processing it herself. Granted, Roy had goaded her. But now *both* of her parents were upset with her.

Then there was the line that stuck in her throat for a different reason. *You won't listen to Brad, who is nearly as frustrated as I am.* The implication was that Roy and Brad were talking and in total agreement about her stubbornness. She knew to beware. Roy was perfectly capable of twisting Brad's words, or worse, hearing in Brad's reply only what he wanted to hear. It was possible that Brad had in fact argued on her behalf.

But she doubted it.

Add to that the weather, and she felt totally off. The rain began even before Brad picked her up and continued through dinner without bringing a change in temperature, which meant that the very warm air was now also very wet. Her hair curled; her freckles bled through her makeup; her jeans stuck to her thighs despite all manner of shifting in her seat. Their dinner companions were Brad's law school friends, and she tried to be part of the conversation but didn't always succeed. Law talk wasn't exactly small talk, and it could be technical.

Returning from Boston, they drove through steady, heavy rain. By the time they got home, thunder had rolled in and was growing louder by the clap. When lightning joined it with a ferocity that confirmed Brad's prediction, it was reason enough to snuggle beside him on the sofa watching reruns of *Homeland*. They had to raise the volume. The rain that sheeted against the patio doors drowned out everything but what became near-continual thunder. Mix in a driving wind, with sudden, sharp gusts, and there were times when the condo shook.

Then came a deafening clap, a brilliant flash, and the power went out. Without lights or TV, they went to bed and made love. It seemed the only thing to do that didn't involve thinking too much.

Brad was happy. Feeling loved, he fell asleep soon after. Jamie wanted to follow, but her body wouldn't settle. She was on edge. Storm? Her parents? Sex?

She lay against him for a time, listening to the rain on the skylight as the flashes of light weakened and the thunder moved off. Eventually, she put on a robe and went downstairs, but bits of conversation followed—her mother's distrust, her father's anger. Groping for a match, she lit the while pillar candle that sat in a clear glass lamp on the kitchen island. The candle flickered. Hoping to be lulled by the dance of the flame, she watched it, but long minutes after, she was as troubled as ever.

Wondering how far the power outage stretched, she opened her front door and leaned out. The rain had slowed to a drizzle, which fell off rooftops and trees to dapple an otherwise eerie silence. The surrounding houses were as dark as hers. She assumed that the problem had already been reported, and was wondering whether she should call herself simply to find out when the power would return, when a pair of headlights turned onto the street.

She didn't think a neighbor would be driving so late in such bad weather, and this vehicle being a car, rather than a truck, ruled out the power company. Startled, she watched the headlights pull up at her house.

Her first thought was that someone casing the area had seen her open door and that she needed to close it, wake Brad, and call the cops. Before she could, though, both car doors opened, casting enough light into the lingering drizzle to bounce back on itself.

It *was* the cops.

At her house.

At one in the morning.

The strangeness of it made her uneasy, no less as their flashlights made a path to her door. The men wore rain gear. When they were close enough, she recognized the younger as one of the officers who had been leaving Fiona's when she arrived there Thursday morning. The man in front of him, older, more portly, and plodding forward under the weight of the world, was the chief of police. Paul Logan was a local boy who had left town, learned the ropes of law enforcement elsewhere, and returned. He and Roy were high school buddies, close then and now.

"Paul?" she said uneasily.

He hitched his chin. His voice was rough. "Can we go inside?"

Heart pounding, she held the door open. "What's wrong?" A dozen thoughts went through her mind as she opened the door wider, but the scariest part was Paul. After he shook the rain off his cap, she got a good look at his eyes. They were filled with sorrow.

"There's been an accident."

She barely breathed. "Who?"

"Your father and his wife."

She was suspended in time. "Bad?"

He nodded, then looked past her as Brad approached, wearing jeans and an unbuttoned shirt. "What's up?" He was looking at Paul.

"Dad had an accident," Jamie whispered, terrified. "He and Jess." She forced her voice into sound. "*How* bad?" When Paul swallowed, she urged, "*Tell* me."

"Lightning hit a tree. It fell on their car." He paused briefly before saying, "Your father didn't make it. They're rushing Jess to the hospital, but it doesn't look good."

"Didn't make it," Jamie repeated, needing something more definitive.

"When?" Brad asked. "Where?"

"We're guessing it was when the last cell hit, but we won't be sure until forensics looks at the car. It was over on River Run."

Not heavily traveled, Jamie thought with rising panic. Dark as pitch unless the moon was full, which it wasn't even behind all those storm clouds.

"What do you mean, didn't make it?" she asked.

Paul's tired eyes said it all. "I'm sorry."

She might have swayed, but Brad was at her shoulder. *"Dead?"* she asked with barely a sound. It didn't make sense. There had to be a mistake.

But Paul was Roy's friend—*and* the police chief. Wouldn't Paul know?

Omigod omigod omigod. She looked past him to the other officer, but his frightened expression said he hadn't had to make a visit like this before, which was telling.

Her eyes filled with tears. Unable to grasp *dead,* she focused on details. "A tree fell. Did it crush them, push them into another car, make them go off the road, maybe flip over? Part of River Run has a really steep drop-off."

Brad cupped her shoulder with a hand that said, *Not important now, Jamie,* but the police chief understood her. Gently, he said, "The car was on the road under a large tree. A forensic team from the state is on its way there now. We won't know whether the cause of death was blunt force trauma from the tree or from the sudden stop until an autopsy is done."

"Do you think it was instant?"

"For Roy, yes."

"Was Jess conscious?"

"No, but breathing. I don't know who of her family to call, and there's the matter of whoever's staying with Tad. Someone has to call Randi." Miranda MacAfee was Roy's only sibling. She lived in California, well removed from MacAfee Homes. "First, we have to tell Theo. Would you like me to do that?"

Feeling a soul-deep dread, Jamie looked up at Brad. His eyes were wide behind his glasses, but he did get this. "You should be with Tad," he said. "Should I go to Theo's?"

"No. Um, no. No." She cleared her throat. "Mom will. She'll know how to do it." Caroline was the *only* one who could tell Theo. Jamie had no doubt of that, but she was struggling with who else to call and what to say, trying to order her thoughts in a nightmare for which she was ill prepared. "Maybe you can go to the . . . scene."

* * *

Jamie didn't cry. There was too much to be done. After hurriedly throwing water on her face, she stuck her hair in a ponytail and pulled on jeans and a shirt. She grabbed for her phone with such a shaky hand that she nearly dropped it before getting a grip.

Brad had already put up the convertible top. He gave her a hug before she climbed in. "Are you sure I can't come with you?"

She nodded. "I'm okay."

As she headed out, though, she wondered. Jess might survive, but *dead* was final. Just as she hadn't been able to grasp her phone, she couldn't grasp that Roy was gone. Part of her wanted to go to the scene first. Until she saw her father's car, she wouldn't believe this was real. He drove a BMW. People didn't die in BMWs.

But Paul Logan had seen the car, and his pain was clear.

Hands tight on the wheel, Jamie drove over roads that were slick and littered with branches and leaves. At least the sporadic house light said there was power on Caroline's side of town.

Only as she turned onto her mother's street did she remember their rift. Rift or not, though, Caroline would be there for Theo. That was who she was.

The front walk was as littered as the street, the front steps soggy. Even the porch showed wear and tear from gusting winds. Ignoring the wrought-iron chair overturned near the table, Jamie reached for the doorbell and was about to press it, then pulled out her phone instead and dialed. Caroline slept with her phone on the nightstand—*in case you need me,* she always said.

I need you, Mom, she thought. *I need you now.*

She heard the phone ring inside once, twice, and pictured Caroline groping for it and squinting at the caller ID as it rang a third time. Just shy of voice mail, there was a groggy "Not now, Jamie. It can wait till morning."

"Dad's dead," Jamie said in a breathy rush. "I'm downstairs at your door. Someone has to tell Theo."

There was a long pause. Jamie was wondering whether she should ring the doorbell after all when she heard a hurried footfall descending inside.

The porch light came on and Caroline opened the door. *"What?"* she asked in quiet alarm as she pushed the screen open.

"Paul Logan just came to my house," Jamie said and rushed out the details she knew.

Her mother looked stunned. After a frozen moment, she gave a tiny headshake and wrapped her arms around Jamie. "I am so sorry," she whispered, "*so* sorry." Her hold was strong and precious. It wasn't long enough to stop the trembling deep inside, but Jamie was grateful nonetheless.

Too soon, Caroline drew back. Eyes clouded in disbelief, she asked questions, like where Roy and Jess had been and whether air bags had deployed, but they were filler, simply buying time for news that was unreal to sink in. Finally, plowing both hands—the right with its Velcro wrap—into her tousled hair, she held her elbows up and cupped her head. "Theo will be devastated. I'll go there."

"That would be huge," Jamie breathed. "Brad went to the scene. I have to call Jess's mother. She lives near Leominster and can be here in an hour, assuming she wants to come." Jess had no siblings, just a mother and stepfather with their own children, their own interests, their own lives. There were issues, Jamie knew, not the least being resentment of Roy and the easy life he offered Jess.

"Of course she'll come."

"They weren't on good terms." Nor were Jamie and Caroline, yet here they were. She raised tearful, fear-filled eyes. "What do I tell Tad's sitter? She's probably, like, fifteen. She'll freak out."

Seeming bewildered for a minute herself, Caroline finally inhaled. "Just say that Roy and Jess are detained—uh, that they're having car problems and that you're filling in."

"Dad usually drives her home."

"One of her parents will have to come. You should call them yourself."

Definitely. She could do that. Trust Caroline to know what to do. She was always level-headed. "Mom, about before—"

Gentle fingers touched her mouth. "Shhhh. We'll talk later. Right now, you need to deal with Tad."

"But how? What do I do? What do I say?"

"He'll be asleep a while longer, so you have time. If Jess wakes up, she can tell you what she wants you to say."

"What if she doesn't wake up?" Jamie asked. "What if she's in a coma for days . . . or . . . or in a permanent vegetative state?"

"Don't go there yet."

But how could Jamie not? *I named you my son's godmother.* They were the most innocent of the angry, vindictive words she and Roy had exchanged—their last words to each other on this earth—less than twelve hours before he died. Now they took on even deeper meaning. Two years ago, shortly after Tad's birth, Roy and Jess had asked, and Jamie had agreed, that she also be the boy's guardian should anything happen to them.

She hadn't thought twice about it. Nothing would happen to Roy and Jess.

Now something had.

Most people lost parents. It was the generational order of things. But so soon? So *suddenly*? She couldn't begin to grasp that Roy was gone. For Tad's sake alone, she could only pray Jess would survive.

Chapter Nine

Theo MacAfee lived in a Tudor-style home at the east end of town. It had been one of the company's first showcase properties in Williston, and Theo's wife loved it too much to sell. Caroline had always thought it dark, though as she approached it this night, the darkness was internal. Roy was gone. Crushed. Silenced forever.

It was surreal. Oh, she knew he was human, knew it better than anyone, perhaps. But he had always been so cocksure of himself. Sudden death did not seem possible.

Other than a residual dripping from trees, the rain had stopped by the time she pulled under the portico and climbed up the broad stone steps. Her heart was heavy as she rang the bell. She waited, wishing she were anywhere else but knowing she had to be here. She was more vigilant when she pressed the button a second time, listening for the bell, hearing it, knowing it worked. *Patience, Caroline.* Theo had day help, but nights he was alone. He would be startled from sleep and slow to descend.

But descend he finally did, put on a light, and opened the door with a groggy caution. His eyes widened a fraction when he saw Caroline. Seeming to know that only something desperately wrong would bring her to his door in the middle of the night, he stood aside.

She slipped in, closed the door, spoke quickly and softly. For a split second, she saw panic in those blue eyes. He looked at the floor and swallowed once. Then, either because he was overwhelmed with too many emotions or simply unwilling to think, his face went blank. Caroline was midsentence, saying that Jamie was going to be with Tad, when he turned, went to the phone on the hall table, and punched in a number with a large-knuckled hand.

"MacAfee here," he barked. "Get me the chief." The police dispatcher must have been waiting for his call, because he was immediately patched through. Frozen in place with his shoulders bent, he said a gruff word here or there but mostly listened. The conversation was brief. When he hung up, he murmured, "Paul's coming." Holding up a shaky *stay* finger to Caroline, he went back upstairs to dress.

She would have waited even without the command. She couldn't leave him alone at a time like this. Sinking into a Louis XIV chair that was nestled into the newel curve, she looked around at old-world furnishings, original art, creative ceramics that Patricia MacAfee had collected. What she kept seeing, though, was the look on Theo's face in the instant she'd told him the news. Panic was one word for it, but it also held shreds of horror and loss. It was here and gone in a second, but she knew that look. Her father had worn a similar one at the beginning of the end— knowing what was happening, not knowing how to deal. The look was wrong in both men, the kind of expression that a person who had led a full and commanding life should never wear.

Feeling lost herself, Caroline thought about calling Dean. But without more information?

She shifted in the chair. With nothing to do but think, she had a growing sense of the enormity of what had occurred. Theo had lost his son, Jamie and Tad their father, Jess her husband. The town had lost a leader. MacAfee Homes had lost its heir.

At the sound of a motor, she jumped up. She reached the door just as a cruiser pulled in behind her truck. Paul approached wearing a devastated look.

"How's Jessica?" Caroline asked.

"On life support. They're not optimistic."

She pressed a hand to her mouth. Life support was more definitive than unconscious, not good at all. Jamie would need to know. Now that Paul was here, Caroline could drive to Roy's to help her there.

Just then, though, Theo came down the stairs. Seeming older and more frail, he was gripping the banister, taking one step at a time. He cleared his throat as he met Paul's eyes.

"I'll leave you," Caroline said gently, but the words were barely out when Theo grasped her arm.

"No." He shot her a look that reprised a world of fear, then said a lower "Stay. I'll ride with you."

Could she deny him? He had been her father-in-law once, and in the years since, he had been in her corner more times than she could count. He was such a solitary figure now—such a *tragic* figure—that, much as she wanted to be with Jamie, she couldn't leave Theo just yet.

Jamie had stopped trying to differentiate windshield spatter from tears. More than once, when she could barely see, she thought about pulling over. But she needed to be at Roy's. She had to let the babysitter leave and then call Jess's mother. She wasn't looking forward to that, but it was probably an easier task than the one Caroline faced.

Tougher, for Jamie, would be seeing Tad.

Her headlights cut a bleeding swath through wooded streets. As many times as she had visited here, she had never done it at this hour or with this burden. Her throat was an aching knot by the time she reached the house.

It was one of the newer French manor homes built by Roy on a triple-size lot. It was bigger than anything he and Jess would ever need, and far too pretentious for Jamie's liking. Separated from neighbors and surrounded by woods, its lights were a beacon in the dark.

As fate had it, the babysitter's mother was already there. Apparently, Jess had promised that they would be home by midnight, and when that had been missed by an hour with neither texts nor phone calls answered, the girl was worried enough to call home.

Holding it together by a thread, Jamie explained that there had been a problem and that she was filling in. It wasn't a lie. They would know the truth soon enough. Williston had a handful of citizens who monitored the police frequency for sport. For all she knew, word had already begun to spread.

Apologizing profusely, she overpaid the girl, saw them out, and headed for Tad's room. Despite the many times Roy had talked of buying a toddler bed, it hadn't appeared yet. Tad was in his crib, sound asleep on his side with an arm around his favorite stuffed dog, the new moose fallen over behind him, and a zoo of other animals scattered about. She barely breathed as she listened for his soft, steady sounds. The child was blissfully unaware of the unfolding tragedy.

Child? *Try "baby,"* Jamie thought. He was a *baby* who would now never know his father. How could that *be*?

Overwhelmed with anger and unable to help herself, she started to cry. She quickly left the room so that she wouldn't wake Tad, and ran down to the kitchen.

Struggling to stem her tears, just needing to get this

done, she searched for Jess's mother's number. Naturally, it would be on Jess's iPhone, but that would be in the car, a brutal mental image there. Plan B had her opening Jess's laptop to pull up Contacts. But . . . password? Jamie had no idea. Plan C—and there it was, *Maureen Olson,* at the very bottom of the list of emergency numbers in the kitchen drawer. Jamie suspected it was wishful thinking on Jess's part that the woman would actually be there for her in a pinch.

Nonetheless, Jamie felt deep sympathy waking Maureen in the middle of the night with news like this. The woman was stunned. When she couldn't get a word out, her husband came on to ask specifics of the accident.

Jamie wished she knew more. She wished she didn't have to now call her aunt. She wished her father, whose last words to her—and hers to him—had been ones of anger, would drive up any minute and walk through the door. She wished her mother were here.

In lieu of that, she texted Brad. *Where are you?*

At the scene. You don't want to come.

Bad?

Yes. Happened earlier than we thought. Took a long time to find and extricate.

She pictured a large clawed machine being brought in to lift the tree that had fallen and remove the roof of the car. And the scene beneath?

Squeezing her eyes shut, she was trying to blot out the image when Brad texted again. *Your mother just got here with Theo.*

How is he?

Stoic. Did you call Jess's mother?

Yes. She's going to the hospital. Any news from there?

Life support.

Jamie let the phone fall to her side. Jess gone, too?

No. No. If miracles happened, she could still wake up. But whole and functioning?

By the time dawn arrived, Jamie had wandered through the first floor of the house over and over again, library to living room to dining room to great room, hating the place more with each round. She felt like she was in a mausoleum. Aside from a small den filled with sturdy leather and toys, the decor was an ultratraditional mix of velvet and silk, with elaborate mahogany millwork and brocades of blue and gold. The walls were jam-packed with paintings, the tables with bowls, vases, and lamps. Had these things been family heirlooms, the effect might have been different, but the family heirlooms were at Theo's. Roy had simply bought what the designer advised, that designer being Roy's favorite, a longtime MacAfee employee whose style was too busy for Jamie's. She felt suffocated here; with so much stuff packed in, she couldn't breathe. And it wasn't just the current horror that made it so. She had never been able to handle staying here for more than a day or two; when she was watching Tad for longer, she brought him to her condo.

This house was a showpiece, no doubt about that, but the thought of raising a child here gave her the chills. Not that Tad had free run of the place. His things were consolidated in kitchen, bedroom, and den. He could also play in a finished basement, a paved driveway, and a huge backyard. He wasn't deprived by a long shot.

Not materially at least. But to lose parents who would be only the merest threads of memory? *Stuff* was worth squat compared to that.

The circles she walked didn't include the upstairs. She couldn't bear to see the room that Roy had shared with Jess. Rather, her base was the kitchen counter, where her cell phone lay beside the baby monitor, both of which lay beside the Keurig, which she had repeatedly used more for warmth than caffeine. She was chilled to the bone, perhaps because Roy kept the AC low, perhaps because she was in a state of shock. She hadn't slept, doubted she could have even if she tried. Her thoughts were a muddle of disbelief and fear, her mind a demon of gruesome images, and her insides wouldn't stop shaking.

Brad and Caroline were with Theo, and while she wished one or the other were with her, she understood Theo's need. She exchanged texts with them, but there was little of comfort to be had there. Nor did repeated calls to the hospital help. None offered good news.

When she heard Tad crying at six, she panicked. Praying he might fall back to sleep, she didn't move. Barely a minute passed before he called again, this time with more force. *"Mommmeee."*

Swallowing a cry of anguish, Jamie headed for the stairs. She knew the early morning drill—change diaper, warm sippy cup of milk, fix breakfast. She had stayed with Tad enough to know that when she opened his door he would be standing against the bars of his crib—and there he was. His milk-chocolate hair stuck up in random curls; his brown eyes were clear, his cheeks pink. His thumb was in his mouth but popped out when he saw her. In his innocence, he wasn't confused at all but cried her name in delight.

It was so sweet, so *sad,* that she thought she would die. He had no idea how his life had changed. It was all she could do not to bawl.

"Hi, monkey," she whispered so that he wouldn't hear the shake in her voice. He held out his arms as she neared the crib. Gathering him close, she left his arms around her neck while she unzipped his sleep sack. Then she scooped him into a tight hug, rocking him from side to side as she struggled not to cry.

Focus, Jamie. That's a big fat diaper against your arm.

Regaining a bit of control, she eased off the hug. "Did you have a good sleep?"

"I wan Moose," he said and reached back toward the crib. She put the pet in his arms and tried to lay him on the dressing table, but he squirmed until she set him on his feet on the floor. This was a change since she had stayed with him last. But okay. Doable.

That said, changing his diaper while he was standing up was a challenge. If he wasn't dancing off toward his Playskool garage, he was reaching for a dump truck or twisting to pick up the driver when it fell out of the cab. Thinking that he definitely needed to be potty trained— *would Jess be here to do it?*—Jamie struggled with the clean diaper. She had never been as adept at this as Jess, simply hadn't done it as much, and Tad wasn't helping her out. It took three tries before the tapes were tight enough, and then she pulled on a pair of jeans to hold the diaper in place.

Sitting on the floor, he played with the truck and a bulldozer, gathering other drivers, handing one to Jamie and telling her what to do. He was actually quite clear with his instructions. "Put man dere . . . No, dis one . . . Brrrrm, brrrrrrm . . . Dump, Mamie." Having her here was a game.

She was thinking how grateful she was that he didn't know better when without warning he ran out the door toward the stairs. Heart pounding, she caught him just as he might have tumbled, though once she was beside him, she saw that he was already holding the banister. He climbed down facing front, knew to take one step at a time and move his hands accordingly. Physical coordination had never been a problem for him.

Or for his dad, Jamie realized, *who would never see him ride a bike, serve a tennis ball, score a basket.*

Aching inside, she gave him his milk, which he drank as he wandered around the kitchen. Then she fixed him a bowl of cereal, put it on the island counter, and reached for him. He had long since rejected a high chair, but now refused even the booster seat. "Dis one, Mamie," he insisted, patting a stool, and when she set him there, he patted the stool beside it. "Mamie eat."

Jamie wasn't up for food, but after a few minutes, she went to the fridge for yogurt and fruit and, to encourage Tad, swallowed a few blueberries herself. When she put some in his cereal bowl, he howled in protest. *"No blues!"* She snatched them back out and crossed the kitchen to get another plate. By the time she returned, he had tipped the cereal bowl and was drawing pictures in the milk that pooled on the granite counter, and when she reached for a paper towel, half a dozen sheets left the roll.

She might have been upset if there hadn't been so much else on her mind—like what to do with Tad when breakfast was done. They could play inside, outside, or at one of the playgrounds in town. But how could she play? How could she smile and laugh and run with the sun rising on the saddest possible day?

Focus, she told herself again. But how to do that with God-only-knew-what-else going on? Tad was lucky. He was a child. He could be blissfully ignorant. Or not.

"Where Mommy?" Big brown eyes held hers.

Uh. Uh. Omigod. What to say?

"She had to go out" seemed the best stopgap, and yes, the child was blissfully ignorant of the absurdity of Jess going out at this hour. "You're stuck with Mamie today," she said and let him help mop up the milk. He had fun with that. She let him drag it out.

She barely made it to seven before texting her mother.

It was a few minutes before an answer came, and the exchange that followed was choppy. Caroline was driving Theo home. There was no word on Jess. Funeral plans would wait until they knew more. Theo wanted her to start calling MacAfee people.

You can do this, Jamie, read her final text, and while Jamie needed more, she understood. It sounded like Caroline had her hands full with Theo, perhaps even more so than Jamie with Tad. Theo knew what was happening.

Brad's appearance at Roy's shortly thereafter was small comfort. His hair was mussed, his face pale, his eyes shadowed. When she asked for details of the accident, he just shook his head, then did it again when she asked how Jess was, and when she tried to verbalize what had been hovering in the back of her mind, haunting her, his bleak look cut her off before she said a word.

Had the remoteness of the scene affected the outcome? Would Roy be alive if help had arrived sooner? Would they ever know?

Thinking that the answer was no to all three, but that Brad was grappling with gruesome images and could probably use breakfast, she left him in the den to play with Tad, but within seconds of her leaving the room, the boy followed, and she didn't mind. His presence filled a void and kept her mind from dwelling on Roy. Brad might have been the one physically viewing the scene of the crash, but her imagination pinned her right there as well.

She returned to the den for pieces of the wooden train, then set it back up in the kitchen while Brad planted himself on a stool with his forearms on the granite and his eyes distant. When she rubbed his shoulder, he gave her a weak smile.

She could have used words of solace in return. But what did one say in a situation like this?

* * *

What one said, she discovered when, within the hour, the phone started to ring, was *Thank you, I appreciate your thoughts, Yes, we're shocked.* What one said, she realized when more calls came and the questions narrowed, was *I'm sorry, I don't know, Maybe, No plans yet.* And when the calls grew solicitous, she could only express gratitude. *I'll remember that, I haven't thought that far, Thank you for offering.*

The last had to do with watching Tad, even for the funeral, but she couldn't go there yet. She couldn't think beyond the next hour.

There was a certain cruelty to the sun shining after the havoc wreaked by the storm the night before, but Jamie needed to get out. Brad had barely eaten and remained in a visible pall. Was it easy for *her* to carry on? No, but someone had to do it for Tad. She told herself that the child was too young to grasp what had happened, but even apart from the occasional cry for his mother, if the way he was clinging to Jamie meant anything, he sensed something was up.

Before they could make it to the backyard, though, Maureen Olson arrived in a deluge of tears. Tests had shown an absence of activity in Jess's brain. The local team had even consulted with neurologists at two other hospitals, but "brain dead" stood. Machines were all that kept her alive.

Jamie was crushed. When her eyes filled with tears, it wasn't so much for Maureen as for Tad. He would never see his mother again. She would never be coming home. Jamie had always prayed that he wouldn't have to be a child of divorce, but this? Unimaginably worse.

Maureen spoke in a rush, explaining that she had begged the doctors to tell her there was even the smallest sign of life, had begged them to try something, *anything,* but they insisted that nothing would change what the tests showed . . . that she thought it better to let her daughter die with dignity . . . that she couldn't possibly take Tad back to Leominster with her, that her other children were grown, her husband couldn't take the noise, and she couldn't handle a toddler.

As if Jamie would have even considered letting him go?

Misinterpreting her horrified expression, Maureen blathered on about money, time, arthritis, even a planned cruise, until Jamie stopped it with a hand on her arm.

"Tad is mine," she said. Her heart beat wildly as the fact of that set in for the very first time. Needing an anchor, she looked back at Brad. "When he was first born, they named me his legal guardian, but I never, *ever* thought . . ." With Brad looking as stunned as she felt, she faced Maureen again. "We'll bury Jess with Roy."

The woman simply nodded, gave Tad an awkward hug, and excused herself to return to the hospital.

Tad is mine Tad is mine Tad is mine. The words echoed along with the deeper meaning that they implied. With Brad remaining silent, Jamie shifted her frustration to Maureen, wondering how in the world the woman could so easily walk away from the only thing she had left of Jess.

Feeling rejected on Tad's behalf, she gathered him up and held his face to her shoulder. His warm little body settling into hers was an unexpected comfort. *He's all I have left of my father,* Jamie thought, but an even more terrifying thought came fast on that.

I'm all he has.

Without a word to Brad, she went out the back door.

Chapter Ten

When Brad joined Jamie a short time later, Tad was gliding forward and back in his bucket swing. The movement was repetitive, predictable, mindless, all of which she needed. When the bucket came back at her, she gave it a push, then raised anguished eyes to Brad.

He looked drained. A living nightmare and zero sleep could do that to a person. But she was living the same nightmare, and she needed comfort. She needed reassurance that things would be okay, that they could handle this, that he would be a father to Tad.

Instead, he stood at her side without a word.

To get him talking, Jamie asked, "Will she have them turn off the machines?"

"I'd guess."

"I don't envy her that."

The swing returned. She sent it forward again. And again. And again.

Brad remained silent.

Having been leaning over the front of the bucket, Tad straightened and looked back as the bucket approached her. *"Out, Mamie!"*

Catching the swing, she lowered it to a stop and lifted him, but the bucket twisted when his sneaker caught in the leg hole. "Brad . . ." She breathed a plea for help—he was standing right there—but by the time he figured out what to do, she had freed the sneaker herself.

The child took off for the sandbox, where he picked up a plastic rake and began combing the sand. Though Jamie's eyes were on him, her thoughts were on Jess. "I really liked Jess. She had a good heart."

"Not her mother."

"No. Jess became a third wheel the minute Maureen remarried. It got worse when the half sibs were born. I guess it's in character that she's washing her hands of Tad, but it still boggles my mind."

"She was being honest. She's not prepared to take in a child."

"Neither am I, but do I have a choice?"

Brad didn't reply.

"Neither do you," she said quietly. "This is my lot now."

"I didn't know you were his guardian."

"I never thought to tell you. I never thought it would happen."

"You're not set up for it."

"I can be."

"How will you work?"

"I haven't thought that far."

"You'll have to soon."

"Dad hasn't been dead a *day*," she protested and might have said more if a sudden scream from Tad hadn't brought her head around. One look at him sprawled on his face, apparently having tripped climbing out of the sandbox, and she bolted forward in a fit of worry and guilt. Had she been standing right there, paying closer attention, she would have caught him before he fell.

By the time she reached him, he was on all fours and crying bitterly. Snatching him up, she saw dirt on his knees but no blood. Heart pounding, she clutched him to her. "It's okay, baby, shhhh, you're okay, I gotcha."

"I wan Mommy."

Jamie identified with that, oh boy, did she ever. There was something about letting it all go and sobbing for a mother to make everything better. She was bereft about Roy, distanced from Caroline, uneasy over Brad, and Tad was crying his little heart out. She felt his pain, felt as lost and alone as he did.

Holding him back, she wiped big tears from his cheeks with her thumbs, kissed his forehead, and hugged him again. "You're such a good boy, Mamie's right here, I am not letting go."

And she didn't. Ignoring the phone, she held him while he ate a snack. When family friends arrived and began congregating in the kitchen and living room to murmur together in horror and shock, she escaped with Tad to the den, where she held him on her lap and read board book after board book. When he began to squirm, she took him outside again, this time to the toy-filled garage. The child wanted for nothing except a mother and father.

And how cruel is that? Jamie wondered in silent anguish.

Well-wishers joined them, speaking kind words that inevitably led to questions she couldn't answer. She did her best to be polite, but after a while, her mind clotted. Leaving them texting others in town, she pushed Tad down the sidewalk on his tricycle while he walked his feet along. She went farther than she should have and ended up walking back with him on her hip and the tricycle trailing off her hand. By the time she reached the house, Brad was gone, headed to Theo's to help make calls.

People left. More arrived. Some were personal friends of Roy and Jess, some friends of the business. They were devastated and didn't know how to help, but the best Jamie could do was promise to let them know when she figured it out herself.

By midday, the people who came carried food. Sandwiches and casseroles, cookies and cakes, a watermelon filled with cut fruit—all so generous, she knew. But the gift she appreciated most was the arrival of Desideria Carmel, who cleaned for Roy and Jess and was stricken. Desperate to help, she took over the kitchen.

When it came to helping with Tad, though, Jamie smiled a thanks-but-no-thanks. She needed to do this herself. Sifting through foil-covered dishes, she took bits of chicken and pasta and sat him on her lap. He didn't eat much. There were too many people around, too many voices droning on through the house. She had a little more luck with fruit, and total luck with a cookie, but even before the last of that was gone, he was rubbing his eyes with his fists.

He was exhausted. So was she. She carried him upstairs, changed him, and put him in his crib. He was asleep within minutes, and within minutes of that, slumped in a nearby rocker, so was she.

When the doorbell rang, she bolted awake. That brief sleep had been so deep that it was a minute before she got her bearings, at which point reality returned in a biting rush. Stomach knotting, she scrambled up to check Tad. Mercifully, he slept on. Likewise, mercifully, everything downstairs was under control. With more people than ever milling about, the dining room table was beautifully set and offered a spread of food and drinks. There were no paper goods here, but rather the fine china and crystal for which Jessica had registered before the wedding. The elegance of it all would have pleased Roy.

He would not have been pleased with Jamie's T-shirt and jeans—it seemed a lifetime ago that she had pulled them on—but there was nothing to be done. She refused to run home for nicer clothes lest Tad wake while she was gone, and a good decision that was. Nicer clothes wouldn't have worked. By the time he woke up, she had so OD'd on well-meaning friends that she knew if she didn't escape she would go mad.

The town playground was a five-minute drive from the house. Jamie had driven Jess's SUV often enough that the eeriness of doing it now wasn't so bad. But then, she had no alternative. Her convertible didn't have a backseat, and the playground was a must.

Always before, though, she had taken Tad here during the week. This being Sunday, the place was packed with families, so arriving alone with Tad was a stark reminder of their loss. She actually stood at the fence for a minute, wondering if she could bear it. If a break from people was what she needed, she could always drive around for an hour.

But Tad was standing between her legs, his little fingers clutching the links and impatiently rattling the gate. Telling herself that his needs came first, she lifted the latch. He ran off toward a broad climbing dome, and though she was quickly there, he knew this piece of equipment. Scrambling up, he sprawled from one foothold to another, reckless and unafraid.

Jamie was moving around the dome in anticipation of where he might fall off when she was spotted. Even wearing sunglasses, she was a familiar face, if not as a former classmate then as a MacAfee.

"Jamie! Oh my God! You poor thing," cried one parent. And another, "Jess was my playground buddy. We always sat here together." And a third, this a dad who sold flooring to MacAfee designers, "We heard the sirens, but had no idea it was Roy."

Nodding, Jamie continued to shadow Tad around the dome. When he slid off and raced to a nearby rope ladder, others migrated there as well. She kept her eye on Tad, saying only as much as was necessary to avoid rudeness, but all the while she was growing frantic, wondering how word had spread so fast and why these people couldn't see that she needed to pretend, for a few minutes at least, that this hadn't happened. She helped Tad climb to the top of the ladder, then lifted him off, knowing that he was going to have to learn how to climb down as well, but not today.

Today she needed a quiet corner. There was only one—the old sandbox, which was huge and contained many more pails and shovels than children. Only one little boy was there; she guessed him to be three or four. The man she assumed to be his father sat alone on a bench on the far side. He wore sunglasses and a ball cap and was reading a book.

Thinking that something about him was keeping the other parents away and that maybe, just maybe, the repellent would work for her, too, she sat down at the end of his bench. She had no idea if he saw her. He didn't say anything. Which was good.

Her eyes hung on Tad, who stood utterly still by the rim of the box as he watched the other child shovel sand into a pail, pack it down, and turn it over. The sand was damp; after last night's rain, it would be a while drying out. Climbing in, Tad went to within three feet of the child and continued to watch.

"Will you have custody of him?" came the low voice of a woman kneeling at Jamie's elbow.

Jamie hadn't seen her coming. She cleared her throat. "Uh, yes. I will."

A minute passed. Then the woman said, "Jessica adored Tad. She was good with other kids, too. She told me she wanted another one and that she was trying to get pregnant, but I guess it hadn't happened yet."

Jamie swallowed. She tried to let the words go over her head, but they only created another source of loss.

"If I can help, you know, maybe host a play date for Tad, will you let me know?" She rattled off her name; Jamie didn't catch it. She was thinking that she couldn't process play dates just yet when she saw Tad pick up a shovel and dig into the sand. Without a word to the woman, she left the bench and entered the sandbox. Pulling over a pail, she set to helping Tad fill it with sand. When it was full, she tipped it to make a mound beside the three that the other child now had. None was perfect. All were crumbling somewhere or other, but that didn't matter. Looking around, she spotted a plastic piece in a castle shape, but while the other child helped her fill it, Tad sat on his haunches and watched.

They worked in silence. Jamie thought about asking for the boy's name. Or his age. But doing something, anything, without having to think was a respite. So she let it go.

When she returned to the bench, the woman was gone. Jamie dug out her cell and called Caroline. She didn't care if her mother was busy. She needed to hear her voice.

"Mom," she breathed, bending over herself in dire relief. "Mom." Barely a sound.

"Oh, baby. You sound awful."

She took a steadying breath. "Is Jess gone?"

There was a pause, then a sad "Yes. Theo just got the call."

Jamie wrapped her free arm over her head. "Oh God," she whispered.

"I know," Caroline whispered. "The enormity . . ." Her voice trailed off, then, "I'm guessing the funeral will be Wednesday."

"Together?"

"Yes."

"How's Granddad?"

"Terrible. The house is swarming with people."

"Roy's, too. It's overwhelming."

"Here. Brad wants to talk."

"Wait—" Jamie wasn't ready to let her go, but Brad must have grabbed the phone.

"Hey."

"Hey."

"Can you meet us at the funeral home?"

"Right now? I, uh, no." She cleared her throat. "I'm with Tad." She peered around her arm. Tad was holding his own.

"Can't someone watch him? Someone at the house?"

"I can't leave him right now."

"What about the housekeeper?"

Yes, Desideria would watch Tad, but Jamie needed to be with him. "I'll have to let Mom and Theo handle it. Gotta run, Brad. Talk later."

Ending the call, she pocketed the phone and, hugging her stomach, huddled into herself. Tad continued to play, not so much with as alongside the other child. From time to time, he sat back on his heels, but even then, he wasn't looking for Jamie.

She half-wished he was. She half-wished she was so instrumental to his existence that he couldn't bear to have her out of his sight for more than a minute. That would justify her not going to the funeral home. But the truth? With Jess declared dead and Tad her own child forever more, she was having trouble breathing. Dealing with the reality of a funeral—burial clothes, hymns, obituaries—would have been way too much. She couldn't even think about picking out a dress to wear herself.

When her eyes filled with tears, she pressed a hand under her nose to squelch out-and-out crying.

"I'm sorry for your loss, Jamie," came a new female voice. "What a fluke accident. If only that tree had come

down in the hurricane we had two years ago—" The voice
suddenly stopped.

Startled by the abruptness, Jamie looked up, then followed the woman's gaze to the man at the other end of the
bench. His hand was raised off his book just enough to say,
Enough. Leave her alone.

Amazingly, the woman pressed her fingers to her
mouth, nodded, and, seeming duly chastised, left.

The angst of the past few days notwithstanding, Caroline
would have driven over to see Jamie if there hadn't been
so much to do here. Each time she went looking for Theo
to say she was leaving, the front door opened, and more
people arrived. She knew them all, if not through work
then through Williston, and if not through the town
then through her marriage to Roy. With Theo looking as
fragile as the antique French armchair on which he sat—
"Patricia's favorite," he said each time she suggested he
might be more comfortable elsewhere—she couldn't desert him. She guided friends his way. She reassured him
that the picture of Roy in the newspaper obit would be a
good one. At his urging, she dug through files in the library
to read the write-up of Patricia's funeral and see which
hymns were played.

She also brought him water and tried to get him to eat.
"You need strength," she told him in a private moment,
squatting beside his chair with her back to the room. "Roy
would not want you to starve. Here's tuna salad. You like
tuna." When he waved the plate away, she set it on the lamp
table. "You're exhausted. Why not go up and rest for a few
minutes? We'll all understand."

Seeming not to hear, he said in a rough murmur, "It
wasn't supposed to happen this way. This wasn't in the
plan. You think about the life you want, and you follow
the rules and try to do the right things."

Caroline squeezed his hand. "You're a good person, Theo."

"And still he died." Sad eyes met hers. "Roy had his faults. But he was my son."

"He had many strengths. You raised a good man. He loved his family."

Indeed, she had never once doubted his love for Jamie. Wondering if Jamie knew that, she thought again about going to Roy's, but as she stood, Theo's eyes went to the door. "There's the president of the bank. Talk to him, Caroline. Answer his questions. I can't go through that again."

So Caroline talked with the president of the bank. When Brad showed up, she drew him in to take her place. This time, when she went to tell Theo she was leaving, he came up with another person she needed to call, so she went into the library to use the phone.

While there, she left another message for Dean. It was the third one. He would want to know what had happened, and though she knew that cell reception was iffy on the river, she also knew that he would connect to a hot spot at least once a day for emergency's sake.

As the afternoon passed, exhaustion crept up, but her own strain was nothing compared to what she heard when Jamie finally called. Given that, she was annoyed when Brad suggested Jamie join them at the funeral home. She wasn't needed there. Nor was he, actually, and though he offered to drive, Theo insisted Caroline do it. He claimed she knew as much about Roy as anyone, and he was likely right. As distant as they had grown personally, she knew about the work that he did, could list projects that he had single-handedly made happen and charities that he championed.

Jessica was more of an enigma. Her mother had little to offer beyond basic biographical facts, given tearfully and tersely. Caroline texted Jamie a few questions, like whether Jessica was an avid athlete and what flowers she liked. The feminist part of Caroline regretted that Roy's life so overshadowed his wife's. But there was no help for it now.

As she talked about Roy at the funeral home, something else hit her. She had been so focused on everyone else's loss that she hadn't considered her own. Reminiscing with Theo and the funeral home director, she realized that a person who had been a part of her life for more than thirty years was suddenly gone. Love him or not, his death left a void.

She was feeling that emptiness when they returned to Theo's, which made Dean's call perfectly timed. They talked as she stood at the kitchen window, overlooking the lush beauty of Theo's backyard patio.

"Just like that, Dean. In a heartbeat, he's gone. I haven't loved him for years, but we shared a lot once. I've never lost a friend before. I've been lucky, I guess."

"You and me both," Dean remarked. He had asked question after question at the start of the call. Now he was subdued. "The guy was my age." He fell silent. Still, Caroline took comfort from knowing that he was there. Finally, quietly, he said, "I'm just . . . stunned."

"Yeah." She sighed. "Me, too."

"How's Jamie?"

"Hanging on, I guess. She's young. She's busy. Theo's the shaky one. He has me driving him places. I'm not sure he'd get to where he's going alone."

"Is he confused?"

"Distracted."

"Well, you're doing a good thing, sweetheart. I'm coming back. I'll help."

"Oh no, Dean. Don't come back early. That's not why I called. I just felt you'd want to know." She had also needed to hear the voice of a friend.

"I should be there out of respect."

Well, there was that. But had Roy earned it? Dean didn't yet know about the *Gut It!* fiasco. When he learned about that, he would be livid.

So Caroline said, "There are too many people here already, Dean. Wait. Stay there. Stay fresh. That way you'll be even more of a help when you get back."

Chapter Eleven

That night, once Brad had returned and she was sure Tad was asleep, Jamie clipped the baby monitor to Brad's belt and dashed back to her condo for toiletries and clothes. By the time she returned, guests were gone, food was stowed, and the monitor was on the kitchen counter.

Brad was slouched on a stool nearby. Wrapping her arms around his neck, she tried to focus on the familiarity of his warmth, but the old comfort wasn't there. Oh, the house was quiet and under control, but nothing else was. Not really. Death didn't stop at the end of the day; it was the one guest that refused to leave for the night.

Jamie's life had changed forever. She wasn't sure Brad was on board.

"Nightmare," she whispered and felt him nod against her cheek. "Want to stay?" Sex was the last thing she wanted, but maybe in bed she would feel his warmth? She kind of needed that. Yes, he was feeling the shock of sudden death and perhaps even instant parenthood, but it was *her* father who had died, *her* friend who had died, *her* half brother who was orphaned. Okay. Brad needed time to adjust. She didn't have that luxury, and if he didn't see that, if he couldn't rise to the occasion and be supportive, what hope did they have?

But he shook his head. "I need my own space for a few. I have to go the office early tomorrow, then to Theo's. Can you handle things here?"

Jamie thought she could. But Monday was a repeat of Sunday, the only difference being that she *started* it worn down by the house, the guests, the mood. When it became clear that even with the onset of the workweek, even with mourners at Theo's and at the funeral home, Roy's was still the go-to place, she knew she had to move. Tad was growing confused, his little brow increasingly furrowed, his baby voice crying for his mommy more often, his eyes filled with something just shy of fear. The constant flow of people in his home who weren't his parents had to be upsetting.

Or so Jamie guessed. She couldn't ask. How could a two-year-old understand the questions, much less articulate answers? She was on such shaky ground here. She needed a book on parenting. She needed *ten* books on parenting. Actually, she needed her mother, but Caroline was tethered to Theo.

The longer she stayed at Roy's, though, the more oppressive it grew. His assistant helped pick burial clothes and ran them to the funeral home, which was a huge help to Jamie but brought little lasting relief. As soon as the woman returned to help Desideria at the house, Jamie packed several duffels of clothing, baby supplies, and toys and took Tad to her place. Short-term, that was always a novelty for him, and at least it was quiet. They played on the patio, went to the market for milk, mac 'n' cheese, and mangos, and returned for lunch. This was familiar, she decided, thinking of other times she'd had him here, and refusing to think beyond.

Once he was down for a nap, though, she had no choice. She couldn't hide behind him forever. She was a MacAfee.

Totally aside from the issue of responsibility, she wanted to see Theo, who was suffering. She also wanted to see Caroline, if only for a few minutes. They were at the funeral home, which was the last place she wanted to be. But Roy had attacked her during their last awful talk. *If you can't behave like a grown-up . . .*

She could. She *would*.

She had a sitter. The receptionist in her department, a longtime family loyalist, had a grandchild Tad's age and a sincere need to help Jamie. When she showed up at the condo with the makings for chocolate chip cookies, Jamie quickly showered, dressed, and left. She wished she had her convertible. It would have made her feel more herself. But how absurd a thought was that? Her convertible was at Roy's and not much good to her now, which raised a lifestyle issue she couldn't begin to deal with yet.

Heart heavy with dread, she approached the funeral home all too soon and parked the SUV beside Theo's Cadillac sedan. Once through the front door, she was surrounded by townsfolk, but her eye kept going to the pair of coffins at the end of the room. They were closed. The reason why was chilling. She went to the one with her father's picture on top, touched the polished wood with one hand and her mouth with the other, and began to cry.

Firm arms came around her shoulders, bringing a familiar scent that was so woodsy and light and perfectly Caroline that it brought more tears. Jamie had no idea how long she stood there sobbing quietly—two minutes, five, ten—only that there was nowhere else she could fall apart but in her mother's arms. When a tissue materialized, she pressed it to her nose, blotted her eyes, and released a shuddering sigh.

Turning Jamie's face up, Caroline kissed her forehead and gave her a sad smile. "Better?"

"Yes," Jamie whispered. "I'm not very good at this."

"Nor am I. Or Theo." Her gaze crossed the room and returned. "He's anxious to see you. Are you ready yet?"

Jamie took a breath and nodded, at which point Caroline guided her to her grandfather, who held out his arms. Jamie hugged him and clung. He was such a part of her heritage, and with an even bigger part of that now gone, she couldn't let go. His body wasn't as solid as Caroline's; she felt a tremor in the arms that held her. When she finally drew back and focused on his wrinkled face, those teary blue eyes were hollow, and Caroline was gone.

Though Jamie stayed for a time, Caroline always seemed to be engaged with others. *By choice?* Jamie wondered, and quickly dismissed that thought. Whatever problems they had with *Gut It!* paled in the face of untimely death. It was enough, Jamie told herself, that Caroline had held her for those few minutes. There was hope here, at least.

She returned to Roy's more for the sake of politeness than necessity. No one seemed to need her, and Brad was a far better host than she could be. He was content to stay until the last of the guests left Monday night, go home to his own apartment to sleep, and return Tuesday morning. Though appropriately subdued, he filled Roy's social shoes with ease.

Jamie was alternately pleased and annoyed. On one hand, in stepping up so comfortably, he made a statement about continuity at MacAfee Homes. On the other hand, his dismissal of Tad was increasingly disturbing. He didn't ask how the child was, didn't offer to help with him, didn't praise her, as so many others did when she said Tad was hers, other than to say that she had been wise to leave him at the condo before coming to the house.

The little voice in her head went to work.

Did he not understand that her father had specifically

wanted her to raise the child in the event of something like this happening?

Did he not understand that there were priorities in life, and that, yes, she knew she would have to make changes?

Did he not understand that she *wanted* to do this?

No, no, and no—which meant, bottom line, a storm was brewing.

Tuesday morning found Caroline visiting a succession of major MacAfee construction sites. Given a choice, she'd have been in her own workshop. Her wrist was fine, with little more than a bandage covering the stitches, and she needed the therapy of drilling, shaping, and sanding, needed the smell of sawdust and her father's old tools. But having been with Theo every waking hour since Sunday morning, she welcomed a break—from Theo, from tragedy, from distress.

That said, when he asked her to site-hop, she couldn't say no. The gesture was a good one. Yes, every MacAfee higher-up had been personally called, and most had come to visit, but there were scores of hands-on workers who would be wondering what effect Roy's death would have on MacAfee Homes. Her personal appearance made a statement that the business would survive.

Unfortunately, delivering the message meant a juggling of sorrow and optimism on her part, and it was exhausting.

Emotionally drained, after talking with a group of carpenters who were doing finish work in an office, she walked out into the sun and saw a Harley parked by her truck.

Dean.

Her heart lifted.

She needed a friend, and Dean was that.

Smiling as much as several days of darkness allowed,

she approached him and, shading her eyes with a hand, looked up. "I said you shouldn't come."

Sunglasses hid his eyes but not his smirk. "Since when do I listen to you?"

Never. But she was too pleased to see him to fight. Wearing a black shirt and midnight jeans, he was certainly dressed right. "Well, thank you for coming," she said, exhaling tension. "It's been wild here."

"Wild?"

"Tearful. Tragic. *Bleak*." And here was Dean, the antithesis of these things. His nose and cheeks were sunburned, which was saying something about skin that had started with a good base tan. "Looks like you did get some fishing in. I'm sorry it was only two days."

"Not your fault. You didn't make that tree fall on Roy's car."

"At least if I had, I could say that what I'm doing now is penance." That sounded bitchy, she realized, and explained, "Don't get me wrong. I choose to help Theo. He's like a father to me, and the poor guy is beside himself. No one ever thinks his child will go before he does. But it's awkward. Roy was my ex twice removed, and Jess was more Jamie's contemporary than mine."

"How's Jamie doing with all this?"

Caroline felt Jamie's agony acutely. "She's struggling. She has custody of Tad."

Dean gave a little start. "Seriously? Did she know she would beforehand?"

"Yes."

"Can she handle it?"

"She'll have to."

He considered that. "Talk about life turning on a dime."

"Mmm. Lots of complications hitting at once." Not the least being the *Gut It!* change, which would be an even greater challenge for Jamie if she was dealing with new motherhood at the same time. But of course, Dean didn't know about the show. She wasn't quite sure how to broach it.

"Keep frowning like that," he remarked, "and you'll need Botox."

She tried to think up a smart reply, only her mind went off in a different direction. Botox meant wrinkles, wrinkles meant old, old meant death, and death was as final as those closed coffins at the funeral home, an image that did nothing good for her frame of mind. She had been feeling shaky since Jamie had shown up at her door Sunday morning—had actually been feeling shaky since Claire had shown up Friday—and while's Dean's comment was just Dean being clever, something about his presence snapped whatever element had been holding her together. To her horror, her eyes filled with tears.

He jerked back. "What's this?"

It would have been so easy to swipe at her eyes with the heel of her hand and blame the past few days for emotions too close to the surface, but the words wouldn't come for that either.

"Hey," he said more gently, then, "I need lunch. Want some?"

She nodded.

"Follow me."

Fiona's was back in Williston, and Caroline wouldn't have wanted to go there anyway. Seeming to know that she needed anonymity even before she pushed huge sunglasses onto the bridge of her nose, Dean led her to a sandwich place not far from the site. He waited until they were seated, with the wood wings of the booth back shielding them from other diners. Then he waited again, until after they ordered, before he said, "I was kidding about the Botox."

"I know." They might bicker, but he wasn't malicious. "It just touched a raw nerve." Sitting back in the booth with her head against the wood, she considered his mottled green eyes, dark hair, and burnished skin. He was the image of honed energy and health. By comparison, she felt positively ancient. "It's like you've been gone a year."

Those eyes grew puzzled. "Why am I sensing something else going on?"

Perhaps because he knew her better than most and could read her too well, she realized, and gave a self-deprecating shrug. "It doesn't matter. It's silly to even be talking about in the same breath as two deaths."

"Spill it, Caro. Nothing you care about is silly to me."

"You're sweet."

"I'm serious."

Knowing that he was, she nearly teared up again. Before that could happen, she said, "As of fall, I'm out as the host of *Gut It!* Jamie's the new host." He flinched, but didn't speak. Clinging to the steadiness of his gaze, she told him about her meeting with Claire. She was still watching him closely when she finished. "You don't seem surprised."

"That they want younger?" A sound of disgust came from the back of his throat. "I read, I see, I hear. It's happening everywhere. I'm not happy that it happened here. To you." His eyes rose to the server who brought their sandwiches, roast beef for him, shrimp salad for her. Once they were alone again, he picked up half of his sandwich and considered it, then considered her in the same puzzled way. "Are you sure Jamie was involved in the decision?"

"No. All I know is that she knew before I did and had ample opportunity to tell me but did not, and that makes me uncomfortable."

"Uncomfortable?"

"Like she was hiding it because she agrees with the de-

cision but knew that I would not." Having removed the
bread from her sandwich, she waved a fork. "Roy's death
has kind of taken over right now. Jamie's going through
so much. I know she needs me, but at odd times, I feel a
twisting inside." She mimed the motion with her fork.

"Anger?"

"Hurt."

"You need to talk with her." He opened the bag of chips
on his plate and crunched one. When it was gone, he said,
"You used to tell me to do that with my ex."

"And you used to say it wasn't easy." Caroline sighed.
"You were right." She had always heard him out, then rebutted his arguments with a certain insistence. Now that the
tables were turned, it struck her that she hadn't fully grasped
the emotions involved. "I'm doing what I can to help her.
My heart wants to do more, but my mind fights it."

"Your mind is going through a lot."

Where to begin on that? She felt betrayed, sad, and worried, and those emotions had to do solely with Jamie. Add
the age issue, which had dredged up feelings she thought
were long buried, and Roy's death and Theo's fragility, and
she was hopelessly mired.

They ate in silence until Dean ran a napkin over his
mouth. "Will she opt out of hosting the show because of
Tad?"

"Maybe. I don't know. This is new ground for Jamie."

"What about Brad?"

"New ground for him, too. He wants her to do the show.
She says she won't because of me, but if she says no and
they threaten to cancel—"

"You could sue."

"How can I do that? It would only hurt Jamie." She set
down her fork, studied her lunch and then Dean. "I love
my job, but I love my daughter, too." Retrieving the fork,
she ate another piece of shrimp.

"What's wrong with your bread?" he asked.

"Nothing. I just don't need two pieces."

"Since when?"

"Since I'm sitting around like a sack of potatoes that hasn't worked in almost a week."

"Like you're getting fat? You've lost weight, Caroline. How's the hand?"

Lost weight meant looking haggard, a dismaying thought there. "Fine," she snapped.

"Spare me the fight, and save it for Claire. You must be furious at her."

"Absolutely. And at Roy, like that'll get me far." She scooped a forkful of shrimp salad off the plate and into her mouth. Talking around the food, as if that would gentle the words, she said, "And then I come back to Jamie again. She may not have known what Claire was up to, but there's been a whole lot of girlfriend time between the two of them. Shouldn't she have seen where Claire was headed?"

"Not if she didn't want to see. Is the decision irrevocable? No changing their minds?"

"Claire said not, but that was before Roy died." She had probably said the words "Roy died" dozens of times in the last two days, and still they shocked her. It wasn't that she loved Roy. There were times she wondered if she ever had. But he was still the father of her daughter, and his death was out of the blue. It was going to take some getting used to. "The problem is that they need to know soon. We can put them off out of respect for Roy, but they won't wait forever."

Nor could Caroline. There was a slew of prep that she always did in the months leading up to taping, and promo for the station was the least of it. She had to get to know the homeowners, so that they were comfortable with each other. She had to get to know abutting neighbors, who would be physically close to the work. She had to get to know the town well enough to give viewers a feel for the location, and had to work through house plans with Dean and the other specialists.

If she wasn't hosting the show, these things wouldn't be her responsibility. They would be Jamie's. Like Jamie had time for all that?

"Aren't you eating those chips?" Dean asked, but when she pushed the bag across, he didn't rush to open it. "You like chips."

She shrugged. "I'm not real hungry."

"Well, *there's* a convenient excuse for every anorexic woman. Not real hungry."

"I have never been anorexic."

"Not yet, but I know what you're doing. Roy did a job on you about the age thing. So now Claire Howe is saying the TV show needs younger, and you're thinking you're too old, too wrinkled, too fat—"

"*Please,*" Caroline cut in, "this isn't the time."

He settled back and finished eating.

She might have done the same, if *too old, too wrinkled, too fat* hadn't continued to echo. "But I'm right to feel some of that," she insisted. "You can joke as much as you want, but I do have more wrinkles than I did ten years ago. I may not be heavier, but my shape has changed, and my voice isn't as rich. I know these things." Every woman of an age did. Changes like these came with menopause, which she had gone through several years before, though she wasn't saying that to Dean. In her few instances of big-time public sweat, she had been able to blame hot weather. Fortunately, her hot flashes had eased up. "But I didn't expect I'd be axed because of them. I thought it was my personality that viewers liked."

"They like all of it."

"Apparently not."

"Claire's full of shit."

"Maybe, but she and Brian get to decide, and their decision is to go with Jamie. So where does that leave me? I like hosting the show. I feel so . . ." She searched for the word. "So *whole* when I'm there." Once started, the thoughts spilled. "I didn't plan it, didn't even realize it was happening, but suddenly when someone tells me I'm off the job, I realize how much store I put in it. It's become my identity. If that's gone, where am I?" She closed her eyes and pressed her fingertips to the tight spot between them. "I'm sorry. I shouldn't be carrying on. Roy and Jessica are dead, which makes my problems petty, y'know?"

"Don't apologize," he grumbled. "What, are you supposed to be a robot and not feel things? You didn't ask for this." Grabbing the check, he dug his wallet from his jeans. "Let's get outta here."

Leaving him at the cash register, Caroline went outside. When he joined her, she said, "Don't be angry at me."

"I'm not. I'm angry at them." He put his hands on his hips and glared at the street. "This is a stupid decision. The only thing it has to do with is sex."

"What does sex have to do with the show?"

"Sex has to do with everything. It's right fucking there all the time."

Caroline was appalled. "Well, isn't *that* a macho remark. Women don't think that way." Shoving her sunglasses on, she set off past sidewalk tables that held the overflow of lunch.

"Not Claire?" Dean goaded, keeping pace.

"No. She just resents my place on the set. She hates it that the crew looks to me before they listen to her. If sex appeal is the bottom line here, it's coming either from advertisers or the media. They're the ones who stoke this." When they passed a table where a woman was reading, she muttered out of the corner of her mouth, "And there you go, a perfect example of the ultimate hype. Can you imagine picking up something with the title *Legs*? If I see one more person reading that book, I'll scream. Since when is eroticism considered literature?" she asked and answered, "Since the media latched on to those books. I mean, talk about a whole load of hot air." Tossing Dean a quelling look, she huffed, "Sex is *so* overrated."

He eyed her strangely. Then, turning on his heel, he headed back to the table where the woman was reading and ducked his head to see the cover of her book.

Caroline could not believe him. Mortified, she cut diagonally across the sidewalk to her truck and was grabbing the door handle when he joined her. She fully expected another macho remark. When it didn't come, she homed in on his face. He wasn't exactly amused, wasn't exactly startled, though there were elements of each. In the aftermath, his eyes held a dare.

"What?" she asked, impatient.

"I could prove you wrong. About sex."

She pulled the door open and drawled, "Sure you could."

"I could."

With a foot on the running board, she looked back. "How?" It wasn't a question so much as a drawled *yeah, right,* but he held her gaze and slowly lowered his eyes to her mouth.

Not what she'd expected.

Head jerking back in alarm, she pointed a finger at herself. He nodded.

"Oh no." She waved a hand and backed away. "No no no. I did not see that nod." Angry that he would think to raise something so wrong at such a wrong time, she climbed into the truck and tugged at the door.

He stood in the way. "You asked."

"Not. Appropriate. We're planning a funeral here, Dean."

"I'm not saying it has to be now. It's just part of the other discussion."

"How can you even *raise* it now?"

"Maybe because I'm a man. And because I'd rather think about life than death. And because I do think you're sexy."

"We work together. We're friends, not lovers." She tugged at the door. "Move, Dean." When he didn't budge, she gave him a testy look. "Don't you think that if there was an attraction between us we'd have felt it long ago?" Lord knew, they had spent enough time together, and not only for work. There had been hours at dinners, on front steps, or in pickups talking about Dean's failing marriage, his fear for his son, Caroline's concerns about Jamie, her frustration with Roy. Dean had walked her through her parents' death. But this?

He looked hurt. "You don't find me attractive?"

"You're *very* attractive, but that doesn't mean we should sleep together—and anyway, this is *so* not the time to talk about sex. Roy is dead, Jamie's distraught, and Theo's as needy as I've ever seen him, meaning I have one hour before I have to be back there, and since the funeral is tomorrow and I don't own anything black, I need to shop."

What Caroline bought that afternoon and wore to the funeral Wednesday was a black flared skirt and peplum jacket with an ivory tank. She couldn't recall the last time she had worn a skirt, and since this one barely hit her knees, she wore sheer black stockings with pumps. The heels weren't terribly high. Still, she thought the outfit was stylish and young, which hadn't been the point at all, but the alternatives? Matronly, every one.

"You look amazing," Dean whispered as soon as they were seated at the church. Theo, Jamie and Brad, and others of the immediate families were in front of them, and the pews behind were filling quickly.

Keeping her eyes on Jamie's tense shoulders, she whispered, "I suppose amazing is better than sexy."

"If I'd said that, what would you have done?"

"Moved to a different pew."

"Right." He waited a few seconds before murmuring under his breath. "Trust me, though. That outfit's a slam dunk. It's good for Brian and Claire to see."

Caroline felt a twinge of unease. "Are they both here?" She had figured Brian might be, since he was the one who had worked closely with Roy, but she wasn't in any frame of mind to see Claire.

Dean nodded.

She let out a long, low breath, but it barely reached her anxiety. Leaning forward, she gave Jamie's shoulder a soft little rub. Large eyes in an unnaturally pale face looked back, which only unsettled her more. "Are you okay?"

The girl shook her head, but the minister rose then, the crowd hushed, and Jamie faced forward before Caroline could say more. Not that there was much to say. Her heart ached for her daughter—and not just because Jamie had to deliver a eulogy or even because she had lost her father. Caroline knew what Jamie faced long-term perhaps more than Jamie did herself, and that knowledge tore at her.

Motherhood was a lifetime commitment. It didn't end with a church service or ease up after a month or a year. Tad might be with Jamie's receptionist again today, but the woman would be back at work tomorrow, along with so many others who had offered to help but would now be resuming their lives. Jamie would be on her own.

Then again, maybe not. Caroline was likely jaded on this score. Roy had been there for the good times, but show him a dirty diaper, a sneaker reeking of dog poop, or vomit, and he was gone. Jamie had Brad, who would hopefully be a more hands-on father. He was definitely kinder than Roy, more devoted to Jamie than Roy had ever been to Caroline, certainly less ego driven. But good with change? Unfortunately, change was the name of the game right now when it came to Jamie's life.

The funeral began. Hymns, readings, even the minister's words were as uplifting as they could be; still, the weight of tragedy was oppressive, all the more so when Jamie rose to speak. At no point did she blow Roy up into something he had not been, but there was good to be acknowledged—Caroline could admit that—and Jamie spoke from the heart. From time to time, her eyes touched Caroline's for reassurance, but the reassurance was as much Caroline's. Being Jamie's mainstay had been far more a part of her identity than hosting a TV show, which was precisely why she was so bothered by the rift between them.

She was losing Jamie—and not only to Brad, though his arm was the one that circled her when she returned to her seat, while Caroline's fingers remained locked in her lap.

A large hand suddenly covered them, gave a gentle squeeze, and was gone.

Caroline didn't react. To look at Dean would have been to give the gesture undue meaning. He had sensed her loss and was trying to help, as simple as that. And he did make her feel less alone. With the warmth of his touch fading, though, it struck her that she hadn't been actually physically held by a man in anything but a perfunctory way in a long, long time. She shared hugs and linked arms often with Jamie and female friends. But with men? No. With men it was all about being professional. For Caroline, who had to work with them daily, it was about being asexual.

She might have dwelt on the necessity of that if the church service hadn't drawn to a close and the trip to the cemetery begun. She drove alone and, dreading what was to come, climbed the knoll to the graveside. This was the part that always bothered her most, the finality of lowering a body into the ground and then leaving it to the cold and dark, and turning away. And what had the minister said, that the focus of death had to be on living? Caroline wasn't able to do that as she stood in the crowd with Annie Ahl and her husband. She didn't see Dean again until she started down the hill, at which point she was too disheartened to do more than glance his way. She had to do more, though, when she reached the road and Brian and Claire approached.

There were the obligatory cheek brushes and words of sympathy. Then Brian said, "Caroline, about what Claire told you . . ." He paused.

Not the best time to discuss this, Caroline wanted to say. But she needed to hear what he had to say. "Go on."

"I don't want hard feelings."

She considered that . . . considered everything she wanted to say in response . . . considered the time and place . . . and held her tongue.

Not so Dean. She hadn't seen him approach, but there he was, a solid presence by her shoulder. "You could rescind the change."

Brian spared him a glance. "It wasn't a random decision. The reasons behind it are very real. We've already started spreading the word."

"You could say you changed your mind. This is a dumb move, Brian. Caroline is the show."

"Are you saying Jamie can't do the job?" Claire asked, putting him on the spot with Caroline right there.

He smiled. "Nope. Not saying that at all. She can easily do the job. What I'm saying is that viewers will be expecting Caroline. When they don't get her, they may be upset."

"We'll ease Jamie in gradually. Caroline will still be there."

"What if I'm not?" Caroline asked. She hadn't planned to, but with Dean's warmth at her shoulder and his antagonism toward Claire on display, she felt bold.

"Are you saying that if you're not the host, you're gone?"

"I don't know."

"We could always cancel the show."

"Do that," Dean warned, "and we'll take it to another station. We're the show, Claire. The players are all MacAfee people. If we leave, they do."

"Well, aren't you full of yourself," she remarked.

Caroline was thinking that he had a right, that he looked authoritative as hell with his dark blazer and tie, shadowed jaw, and combed-back hair, when Brian said nervously, "This is not productive." He addressed Caroline. "Feelings are raw right now. Once you get past Roy's death, we'll meet and hash this out. Agreed?"

"Absolutely," Caroline affirmed, but she wasn't thinking of any meeting when Dean walked her to her truck a short time later. She was thinking of Dean's hand at her back, guiding her with just the lightest touch. She was thinking that he hadn't ever done that before, that she should speed up her pace to shrug off his hand, that it didn't mean anything.

But it had been really nice to have him on her side against Brian and Claire.

Not that that meant anything either. These were extenuating circumstances.

Still. Given the hollowness she felt about so much of her life, a little protectiveness was nice.

Chapter Twelve

The funeral should have been the end of it, but Jamie's phone didn't stop ringing with Willistonians wanting to remember Roy. She couldn't cut them off; she wanted to remember him, too. But between talking with them, keeping Tad clean, fed, and busy, and trying to squeeze in little bits of work, she was exhausted—which was likely why she didn't see the potential for trouble before it hit Friday morning. She was making breakfast at the kitchen island, alternately dicing pears, stirring oatmeal, and watching Tad play. He was on the floor with Legos, and while the blocks were large enough for him to be able to snap together, his great joy just then—hands clapping, squeals of "Look, Mamie, Taddy do it"—was loading them in a box and dumping them out, again and again. After a particularly enthusiastic dumping, several blocks tumbled behind the sofa. She saw him run there and felt a silent alarm even before her beautiful tulip floor lamp began to totter. Dropping the paring knife, she whipped around the island and lunged to catch it, but it crashed to the wood floor, missing the area rug that might have protected it and shattering all four glass shades.

Tad's eyes shot to hers. They were huge. She was feeling a stab of desperation thinking of her lamp, her home, her neat life that was wrecked, when the little boy's eyes filled with tears.

"Don't move," she warned him and, advancing only enough to grab him, stepped gingerly away from the shards. She didn't breathe until he was safely on a stool at the island, but his eyes remained large enough to destroy her. Roy would have yelled at him; he had certainly yelled enough at her when she'd been a child. Roy didn't like accidents.

How ironic was it that his life had ended in one?

But thanks to that Tad was hers now, and Roy had challenged her to be *the most responsible person* in his life. She had to deal.

Framing the child's warm little head with her hands, she lowered her face to his. "It's okay, monkey. It's only a thing." So Caroline had always said. She hugged him close, humming to Pandora's rendition of "Old MacDonald" streaming from her iPad.

"I want Mommy," he whimpered against her middle. He was saying it more and more, clearly not satisfied with the nonanswers she gave. She would have to offer more one day, but what to say?

She was spared it now when he asked for the moose. Retrieving it from the sofa, she included it in a group hug.

Most. Responsible. Person.

With a steadying breath, she ignored the fact that her pristine white condo was in shambles and said, "Accidents happen, Taddy. You didn't mean to do it. But those little pieces of glass need to be picked up or these bare little feet"—she squeezed one—"will be cut." She was looking around, wondering where to start, when Brad came in from the garage.

"Oh look, sweetie. Here's Brad," to whom she called, "Careful," though unnecessarily. The dismay on his face said he had seen the damage.

"You loved that lamp," he said.

She didn't need the reminder. The lamp sprouted from a wrought-iron base into four stems of different heights, each topped with a tulip-shaped globe. For all the small items she had put away in the name of childproofing, she hadn't thought to remove this—likely because, yes, she had loved it.

It's only a thing. Same with her favorite glass vase, broken yesterday. It wasn't that Tad was destructive. He was two years old, active and curious, both good in the overall scheme—but that thought raised others. Was he developing normally? Was there a line between active and ADHD? Did he have learning disabilities or food allergies? How would he be socialized?

As an aunt, she hadn't had to worry about these things. As a parent, she did. Today was her sixth day in that role. Having no experience with other two-year-olds, she knew nothing. She had ordered a slew of books and had read site after site about what two-year-olds typically did, but no two articles were exactly the same, and none were as good as getting advice from her mother. But Caroline was busy with Theo and MacAfee Homes. And they hadn't resolved the host change, which hung like a sword over her head.

So she went with her new favorite mantra. "It can be replaced." Then, "Give me a hand here, Brad. Broom and dust pan first?" Holding Tad on her hip, she took the oatmeal off the stove and put the knife out of reach before setting him up at the lacquered dining table with a coloring book and crayons. His strokes were wild, and he held the crayon wrong, but she wasn't about to correct him. Instinct said that his self-esteem was more important than perfect form.

Or was this the kind of thing she had to correct before his muscles formed memory? She didn't know the answer to that either. Caroline would. She would ask.

Worried about when they would talk and whether, totally aside from their current rift, she could seriously ask Caroline's advice on caring for Roy MacAfee's child, she busied herself vacuuming while Brad swept. The exertion was good, though when she knelt to run her hand over the floor and peer at it from a different angle to make sure every last shard was gone, she found a tiny piece of that earlier vase. *Not* good. She was a novice at parenthood to begin with, and mistakes didn't make her more confident. Always before, when she set out to do something big, she had a game plan. She had lessons, courses, mentors, coaches, and practiced until she got it right. This, here, now, was walking a high wire without a net.

She *desperately* needed Caroline.

"You look frazzled," Brad said.

She closed her eyes and massaged tension from her forehead, but, hell, she *felt* frazzled. It didn't help that Brad was rested, freshly showered, and neatly dressed for work while she wore yesterday's tee and shorts, a slapdash ponytail, zero makeup, and an expression that had to be strained. Beside him, she must look like something the cat had dragged in.

"I'm not sleeping well," she told Brad, which, of course, he couldn't know, since he hadn't slept over since the accident.

"I thought Tad slept through the night."

"He does. The problem is me. I wake up stressing and can't fall back to sleep."

"Maybe you need to be at Roy's house."

The suggestion alone made her stomach clench. "What difference would that make?"

"There's more room. You could spread out."

Half a dozen family friends had said similar things at Roy's after the funeral. *This house is gorgeous . . . You're lucky to have it . . . Easy enough to sell the condo . . . The yard here is perfect for Tad.* But totally aside from her own distaste for Roy's, being there meant that Tad would be waiting for his parents to come home. He would be expecting things to return to normal, without understanding that normal had changed. Her gut told her he was better off at her condo for now, and as for the tightness of the layout here, she didn't want to be more than a single wall away from him at night.

She doubted Brad would understand. He was clearly disheartened as he looked beyond the broken lamp, and oh yes, she knew what he saw. All sense of urban chic was gone, replaced by scattered toys, one empty sippy cup, clean diapers and wipes, one *half-filled* sippy cup, a mound of clothes newly removed from the dryer, and, on the floor, the pajamas she had just taken off Tad—all now with Raffi singing "Baby Beluga" in the background.

Her sanctuary was decimated. There were times when she looked around and couldn't breathe, other times when she couldn't see through panicky tears. It wasn't like she didn't clean and neaten, but as soon as she did, there was another stained shirt, another dirty sippy cup, another disgusting diaper. And toys? She was *constantly* picking up toys. But here they were again, so why bother?

"Are you sure you want to do this?" Brad asked very, very quietly.

Her eyes flew to his. "What do you mean?" But she knew, oh yeah, she knew, and was shaking her head before he could utter the name *Maureen.* "No. Absolutely not."

"She's his grandmother," he said in the same low voice. "She's an experienced mother—"

"—whose kids are grown and whose husband doesn't want Tad and who didn't even have a good relationship with Jessica. She can't take him, Brad. I wouldn't let her. She doesn't love Tad like I do," Jamie whispered with force, horrified as much by Brad's insensitivity as by the idea of giving up her half brother.

But Brad wasn't done. He didn't raise his voice, never raised his voice. She almost wished he would, if only so that she could yell back. The need was building in her.

"You don't owe this to your father," he said.

"Excuse me? I absolutely do! I owe it to him, and to Tad, and to *me*. I *want* him, Brad." Staring at him in fury, she tugged the elastic off her hair and finger-combed the long strands into a fresh ponytail. "And anyway," she said, still glaring, "Desideria's coming Monday to clean."

Looking unsettled—she had never before spoken this harshly, but was tired of coddling him—he pushed up his glasses. "Okay." He was buying time. She could see him trying to think. And he had two choices, he realized. He could be positive, as in *We'll make this work. What do I need to do to help?* Or he could be negative.

Her heart fell with his opening "*but*."

"But it's only a stopgap, Jamie. You can't stay here long-run. It's way too small, and you can't do with only Desideria. You need a nanny. It helps that MacAfee is closed this week, so you haven't had to work—"

"Oh, I've worked," she cut in, annoyed that he would suggest she was slipping. "Our clients need jobs done. That's what I do when I wake up in the middle of the night."

"Where?" he asked—a valid question, since her office was now Tad's bedroom.

She eye-pointed to the table where Tad was happily coloring—and gasped. "Oh *no*." She rushed over. "No, no, monkey, keep it on the paper." She showed him how, then scrubbed at one of several crayon marks that marred the white lacquer, but a bare fingertip wasn't much of an eraser. A cleaning spray would work—or hurt?

Taylor. Taylor had chosen the table. Taylor would know.

Brad stood nearby with his hands in his pockets, shoulders slumped. "You need a dedicated office, especially if you'll be working more at home. You can have that at Roy's."

"Not happening," Jamie insisted.

"Why not?"

"(A) That house is too big, (B) it gives me a headache, and (C) it's my father, not me."

"Redecorate, and make it you."

"Why spend the money? We're planning to build our own house anyway. I'll sell Roy's house, and we'll build something that's plenty big enough for us and kids." Not that she had drawn up any plans. She had kicked ideas around, both in her head and with Brad, but time hadn't allowed for more. And that was before Roy's death.

Brad looked troubled. He might want a house, but he didn't want Tad. He was so not ready for this. She was about to scream that he needed to be a *responsible person,* too, when the phone rang. She was upset enough to answer without checking the screen first.

"Jamie, it's Claire."

She grimaced. Claire had been calling daily, and though the messages she left never asked for callbacks, their regularity pointed to a motive beyond saying hello.

"Hey, Claire."

"How *are* you?"

Jamie looked around the wreck of her condo and said, "Hanging in there." She watched Brad lean over Tad and point at the lines of a clown's hat to show the child where to color. "Things are a little weird, if you know what I mean."

Fisting a green crayon, Tad scribbled over the clown's feet.

"I do. I wouldn't be bothering you if I wasn't getting pressure on my end. We need a final decision here.

Publicity wants to put together preliminary pieces before
the Fourth. Are you ready to commit?"

"Oh, wow. I'm sorry, Claire. I haven't been able to really think about it," which was a bald-faced lie. Jamie had
thought about it for *hours*. She knew that if Claire could
get a commitment from her, Caroline would back down—
and Jamie's relationship with her mother would be per-
manently screwed.

Claire was using her again.

She might have said something to that effect if Brad
hadn't been trying to reposition the crayon in Tad's hand.
She was rounding the island when Claire said, "It's been
a hard week for you. When you're ready to talk, will you
give me a call?"

Jamie was about to remove Brad's arm when Brad
did it himself in response to a cool stare from Tad. "Sure,"
she told Claire. "Thanks for understanding." She ended
the call.

"I don't think he likes me," Brad murmured.

Well, duh, said the little voice in her head. *You don't
like him. He feels that.*

With a defeated breath, she slipped an arm through
his. "He doesn't know you. You have to play with him."
Brightening on an idea, she said, "Stay home with us today, Brad? A few hours, and Tad will *love* you. You said it
yourself. The office is officially closed."

His gray eyes ruled it out even before she finished.
"There's still a skeleton crew, and a family member should
be there. But I miss you. We haven't been alone together
at all. How about dinner out tonight, just us two? Can you
get a sitter?"

Trying to weigh his needs against Tad's, she said a sad
"How can I? Right now, he needs me with him. It hasn't
even been a week."

Sweet children's voices sang, *If you're happy and you know it wear a smile . . .*

She pegged a stare at the iPad. *Seriously*?

Brad shared her dismay, likely for a different reason. "What station is that?"

"Toddler Pandora."

. . . tee hee . . .

He wasn't amused. She saw disappointment, concern, maybe even annoyance—and she tried to understand. He didn't know where he stood now that she had Tad. He was feeling left out, feeling *unloved*. He needed reassurance.

But so do I!

Which basically put her between a rock and a hard place.

"Okay," she said as much to herself as to him, "maybe this weekend? If a sitter comes after he's asleep, he won't know I'm gone."

"What happens with work next week?" Brad asked.

She hadn't thought that far—actually, she had and had pushed the thought aside. That probably wasn't the smartest thing. Once the weekend was done, she would be down to the wire. "How do I find a nanny? How do I know who's good?"

Brad shot her a bewildered look. Then he glanced at his watch. "I have to run."

She might have begged him to stay if she felt it would help. But really? His being there was only one more messy thing.

"Say good-bye," she mouthed, hitching a glance toward Tad.

Brad ruffled the boy's hair. "Have a good day, sport."

Jamie walked him to the door, where he gave her a kiss that was sweet, gentle, and totally devoid of passion. For the first time, that bothered her—angered her, even.

She needed something stronger, something that said he was on board with this change to her life, something with *promise*.

"About what you told Brian and Claire at the funeral," Caroline began, leaning forward to see past Champ, who rose from the backseat like a sentinel. They were in Dean's truck on the way to a new project for which he wanted her to build custom cabinetry. She had plenty of work of her own, but it was a small house—and the truth was, a new project was always a distraction, and she needed one of those. She ached when she thought of Jamie, ached when she thought of *Gut It!* She also ached when she thought of Theo, who seemed to be aging by the day, which she would do one day, too, and then what?

Dean seemed to know her frame of mind. Since the funeral, he had rarely let a few hours pass without checking on her. He hadn't said anything about sex. She wondered if he regretted mentioning it in the first place. That would probably be best, she told herself, though the part of her that was feeling old and unwanted was sorry. Whether she wanted sex or not, being pursued was a good thing.

"The possibility of taking *Gut It!* to another station?" she reminded him. "I've been thinking about it. It's not a bad idea."

"I've been thinking about it, too," he said in a voice that rumbled over a cracked road. Nudging Champ back, he shot her a look. "It sucks." No rumble there, just a deep voice disagreeing in a familiar way.

"Why?"

"Because the risk is too great. We're already with the strongest local station. No other one will do the show as well or be able to match the syndication schedule. Switching stations would have been easier if Roy was here to work a deal—"

"We don't need Roy."

"I can understand your being angry at Claire—"

"Anger doesn't begin to describe it, and I'm angry at Brian, too. It's fine to say Claire is into the power of it, but Brian is old enough to know better."

"He's listening to market research. He's answerable to moneymen up above."

"How can you defend him?" Caroline asked as he pulled up in front of a barely framed house.

After shoving the stick into park, he reached for her hand. It was a surprisingly gentle gesture, matched by his eyes and his tone. "I'm not defending him. I'm trying to understand. But there's another reason why we need to back off. If you start shopping around, Jamie will take it personally. You haven't talked with her about this. I keep telling you to."

"I can't."

"So you're suffering." He gave her hand a jiggle. "I'll bet she is, too. There are so many crossed signals here that every day makes it worse. You need to talk with her, sweetheart. And you need to see the boy. They're a team now, those two."

Caroline wanted to argue. Only, he was right. Without Jamie, she was missing a limb. And his calling her sweetheart? He had done that in the past, but it sounded different to her now. Given the upheaval in her life, she needed the endearment, *and* the hand-holding. He seemed to know that, too. Even if he had changed his mind about the sex. Which was probably for the best, since they did have to work together. Which brought her back to *Gut It!*

"What if I talk with Jamie and she agrees?" Caroline suggested, mellow as she linked her fingers with his. "We need a bargaining chip. She knows how that works."

"Assuming she doesn't want to host."

It was a big assumption. Caroline wanted to believe

Jamie, *desperately* wanted to believe her. Being the star of the show, though, was a huge lure, and Jamie had said that, yes, she wanted it, but only some day. So there was room for compromise here. Caroline could more easily accept a gradual transition than the abrupt change the station wanted. Every bit of common sense in her—every bit of maternal instinct—told her Jamie would agree.

Unless she didn't know Jamie at all. Which had occurred to her more than once lately.

Seeming to sense Caroline's fear in this, too, Dean said, "Tell you what. You talk with Jamie. If she's on board, I'll make some calls."

Chapter Thirteen

The morning flew, as mornings always did when Jamie had nonstop meetings. She met with a checkout clerk at Whole Foods, one at the Container Store, and one at Toys "R" Us—the last, an emergency stop when Whole Foods didn't have the Huggies Tad wore.

Big mistake, that last stop. He threw a full-out tantrum when she tried to remove him from a Cozy Coupe that was definitely too big for her condo but ended up in the SUV nonetheless.

Next time, she would buy Huggies at CVS.

No. Next time, she would buy Huggies online.

Actually, next time she would get *lots* of things online. Taking Tad in and out of the car seat, walking him in and out of stores, and stopping to take things from his hands and replace them on shelves took twice as long as running errands alone.

Armed with a new respect for Jess and every other stay-at-home mom, she returned home to unload the car, switch towels from washer to dryer, and make lunch, all the while ignoring the marks the Cozy Coupe left on her polished hardwood floor as Tad propelled it round and round.

His nap brought a brief reprieve. She could have fallen

asleep in a nanosecond herself, but time without Tad was too precious to waste. So she organized. By the time she was done, she had a bin for diapers, a bin for stuffed animals, a bin for Legos, and a bin for trains, which was all well and good until Tad woke up from a longer-than-usual nap cranky.

He didn't want his diaper changed, didn't want a snack, didn't want a story. He didn't want the Cozy Coupe or any of the toys now neatly housed in the den. He squirmed out of her arms when she tried to gather him in and lay back on the floor, crying for his mother.

The novelty of being with Jamie was clearly gone.

But what to say? Tad didn't know what death meant. Even if he were old enough to grasp the concept of finality, how could she tell him that he would never, ever see his parents again?

Frantic, she simply sat beside him with her stomach in knots and finger-combed his chocolate curls until he quieted and asked for milk, and all the while she felt like a fraud. She was an architect, not a mother. She was clueless when it came to baby moods, not sure at all whether she liked the pressure of being *the most responsible person* in her orphaned half-brother's life.

Needing a shoulder to cry on—and desperate enough to risk being rejected—she put Tad back in the car and this time headed for Caroline's. The mere act of driving the route held normalcy, and once she turned onto the tree-lined street, the familiarity was a balm.

Her eyes flew ahead in search of the dusty red truck, but the driveway was empty. Her heart fell. She needed to see her mother—physically *see* her—needed even just a hint of Caroline's lily-of-the-valley scent, whether they talked substantively or not. That scent, as light and delicate as the tiny white bells that appeared so briefly each spring, was ageless. Caroline's mother had worn it before

Caroline, and though Jamie was always looking for something new to give her, it was never perfume. That fresh, subtle sweetness was resilient.

But it wasn't to be right now, and Roy had thrown down the gauntlet. *If you can't behave like a grown-up . . .*

Clearing the lump from her throat, she said with surprising enthusiasm, "See the trees, Taddy? They're called maple trees. They're very old. See how big they are?" He didn't answer, but the rearview mirror showed him looking out the window. "What color are they?"

"Blue."

"Blue . . . or . . . maybe green?"

"Gween!"

"Good boy! Annnnnd"—she turned into the driveway—"here we are at Mom's house."

She backed out and parked in front. Taking Tad from his seat, she carried him halfway up the walk before catching herself, setting him down, and taking his hand. She was holding him too much, wanting to shield him from loss, but the loss was a done deal, and he was starting to rebel. *No, no, Mamie, Taddy do it.* He wanted to move.

As soon as the screen door squeaked back and she opened the wood one, he ran inside. "Kitty, kitty, he-ah kitty." Amazing that he remembered, since she had only brought him here a time or two before. The two upstairs cats would be warned off by his high-pitched shout, but Master sensed a playmate and came close. While Tad crouched low, Jamie showed him how to stroke the cat from neck to tail, how to throw a scrunched-up paper ball for the cat to retrieve, how to drag a piece of string along the floor for Master to follow, and all the while Jamie struggled to capture the tiny wisps of woodsy scent her mother had left behind.

When the cat wandered off, Tad chased him. That was good for five minutes. Ten passed on the front porch with crackers and cheese, another five scrambling over the low arms of a copper beech in the backyard, and through it all, Jamie listened for Caroline's truck. Finally, she texted, *I'm at your place with Tad. Master was a hit. Where are you?*

Office, Caroline wrote back. *Theo is trying to decide who'll cover for Roy.*

It involved more than covering, Jamie realized with a stab of grief. Roy's death left a huge hole in the company. Brad wasn't a marketer. No one in the family was, which meant they would have to hire from the outside. Theo wouldn't be happy about that.

Not quite sure what Caroline's role with Theo was, she typed, *I need to see you. Want Tad to see you. He's my son now.*

The statement was blunt, provocative enough to warrant an instant reply. When none came, she felt starkly alone. Feeling suddenly unwelcome in Caroline's house, she bundled Tad back into the car. She was nearing the center of town when her phone finally vibrated. When she stopped at a light, she read, *I need to see you, too.*

Tucking hope into a snug corner of her mind, she headed for the playground to kill a few more minutes before having to think about another meal. This being a weekday, it was quieter than last time, with no big families and fewer cars parked by the gate. Two moms and what looked to be a nanny sat together watching little girls dressed in bright shorts, shirts, and bows. Well beyond them, off in a corner of the grassy playing field, was the dad she had seen last time. At least, she assumed he was the boy's dad. He wore the same sunglasses and similar nylon T-shirt and long shorts, but no hat today, and his hair and the child's were identically dark, straight, and neatly cut.

When Tad headed for them, Jamie followed. She

stopped behind him at a baseline etched in the grass and watched the game on the diamond unfold. Standing at the ready ten feet or so from home plate, the dad rolled in a soccer-sized rubber ball. The boy's first kick grazed its top, sending it feebly to the side. Loping forward, the dad retrieved it, loped backward—a pretty cool move, Jamie thought—and rolled it in again. This time, the boy's kick was solid.

"Way to *go,* Buddy," the dad called and, shagging the ball, narrated, "He's rounding first." The dad trotted toward second base, made an exaggerated attempt to tag the child, and missed. "Bad move, *pitcher,*" he sang, "and the runner is heading for third . . ."

The boy wore a wide grin and, between mischievous glances at his dad, was running for all he was worth. Laughing, Jamie bent over Tad. "Are you watching, monkey?" she asked and drew him back a step.

The child barreled past, heading for home as his father made a show of trying to chase him down and coming up short. *"Score!"* the man shouted, arms raised. "That's six for the Bud-man, two for Dad." Snatching the boy up, he held him high and shouted, *"The winner!"* He slid him back to the ground and turned to Jamie and Tad. "He's getting too good for me." Tossing the ball behind him for his son to chase, he ambled over. He was loose-limbed and tall, well over six feet.

"How old is he?" Jamie asked as they stood side by side watching the boy.

"Three and change."

"I was guessing four. That tells you how bad I am at all this."

"Not bad," he said. "Just new."

So he did know who she was. She felt she should know him, too. There was a vague familiarity to him. "Thanks for helping me out last Saturday. With the moms."

"No sweat. They can be overbearing. I hide in a book whenever I can."

Tad had inched over the baseline and stopped. The other child was sitting on the ball, watching him approach.

Jamie leaned in from behind. "You can play, sweetie. Go on." She raised questioning brows to the dad, who nodded.

"Roll him the ball, Buddy," he called. The boy stood and gave it a try, but the infield grass quickly slowed it.

"Is Buddy his real name?"

"Nah. It's Baker, but no one calls him that."

"Is his mom around?"

"Nope." One word. No discussion.

The ball lay idle halfway between the boys. They continued to stare at each other.

"Show him how," the dad called to Buddy, who didn't budge.

"Tad's two," Jamie offered lest the dad think him older and wonder at his failure to engage. He was tall for his age. Roy had loved telling people that. "Twenty-eight months, actually."

"Does he understand what's happened?"

His parents' sudden death. "No. We're both in denial. I'm still pretending to be the aunt who's babysitting."

"That's as good a bridge as any to a brave new world."

She had to smile. The man did get it. "I'm Jamie, by the way."

"Charlie," he said and trotted out. "Okay, guys. We need an ice-breaker here." Squatting between the two, he pointed. "Buddy, Tad. Tad, Buddy."

The boys remained silent and staring.

"Super," said the dad—Charlie—as he snagged the ball with one large hand. He looked from face to face. "We're playing tag. You ever played, Tad? No? That's okay, there's always a first time." He rose, then folded at the waist, knees bent, elbows on his thighs, shifting slightly from hip to hip, the quarterback huddling with his squad. Jamie assumed he was explaining the rules, though his voice was too low for her to hear until he said, "Ready, set, *run!*"

She was thinking that Tad couldn't possibly know what to do—when he started running after Buddy. With Charlie chasing first one, then the other, there were high-pitched shrieks, lots of legs wheeling and bodies tumbling, and, bless him, though Charlie reached out numerous times with the ball in that one large hand, he just couldn't manage to tag one of the boys.

Finally, with loud panting sounds, he pulled up. "Time out. You guys are too good." Dropping the ball, he trotted over to stand beside Jamie again. Not in the least winded, he put his hands on his hips.

"You're good with kids," she said.

He shrugged and cupped his mouth. "Circle the bases, Buddy."

Jogging in an exaggerated way, Buddy headed for first, rounded it, made for second. Tad followed more slowly.

"Do you come here often?" Jamie asked.

"Couple of times a week. We have a yard, but this one's better for hell hour."

"Hell hour?"

"Five to six."

How could she not have guessed? She had resorted to Elmo videos the last day or two, although the playground was infinitely better. "Do you live here in town?"

Charlie nodded. "In my folks' house. I got it when they retired. They divide their time between Florida and Vermont."

Longtime Willistonians, then? She might have asked the name—might have recognized it—might have even gone to the same school as Charlie at some point—if she hadn't been so needy for other info. "Are you a full-time dad?"

He snickered. "It sure as hell feels that way, but no, I have an outside job. Buddy's in daycare till four."

"Where?"

"First Unity." The church. "There are some other good ones, too." He watched the boys. Buddy had rounded third, lengthening the distance between him and Tad, but Tad didn't stop. "I'm sure you got a rundown from friends."

"I don't have friends," she stated. "Give me the rundown."

When he turned to face her, dark lenses didn't hide his skepticism. "How can a MacAfee not have friends?"

"I've always been too busy. What are my daycare options?"

Flipping his glasses to the top of his head, he rubbed the bridge of his nose and looked at her. "After First Unity, there's one at the Community Center. There's a pre-K at Underwood"—one of the elementary schools in town—"but he'd be too young for that." He saw her staring and replaced his glasses.

Too late. Jamie knew who he was now. Added to height and physical dexterity, those blue eyes gave him away. "Chip?" she asked in puzzled surprise.

"Charlie."

"Chip Kobik."

"Charlie," he corrected again. "Chip is long gone."

She might have asked more if, just then, the ball hadn't hit him square in the back.

"Whoaaaa," he drawled in a higher voice as he turned and, with slow challenge, said, "What. Was. *That.*"

His son apparently knew teasing when he heard it because, with a high giggle, he turned and raced off with his father in pursuit. The ball forgotten, they played tag using hands. The big guy quickly tagged his son, caught him up by the waist, and jogged over to deposit him beside Tad. When he said, *"Go,"* Buddy took off again. This time, Charlie scooped Tad up and raced off with him pinned to his hip.

Frightened, Jamie put a hand to her mouth—and not because Chip Kobik was holding her child. Tad didn't know the game. He didn't know the *man*. And he was only *two*.

When Charlie turned, though, the child's face was filled with delight, and once Tad tagged Buddy, he squirmed to be put down. Both boys stood close in the huddle, with Charlie bent over between them. He was shifting his weight from hip to hip again—a cool move that was no mystery now. Chip Kobik, physically coordinated to the nth degree, had dropped out of college to play professional hockey. He had been incredibly talented.

Jamie didn't know what he said, but when he was done, he turned both boys in the direction of second base and sent them off.

Her throat tightened, eyes filled. Tad was joining right in, seeming older than twenty-eight months at that moment and content in a way he hadn't been since his parents died. His happiness was infectious. She basked in it, even for a short time.

Charlie returned to her side. He watched the boys go all the way to the outfield with Buddy leading, Taddy lagging but not stopping. "The point of this is to wear them out. Buddy'll be asleep by seven thirty." He shot her a look. "You okay?"

She was actually feeling emotional, but the practical distracted her. "Is seven thirty his bedtime?"

"Mostly, but I don't like to be rigid."

"He must be in a big-boy bed."

Acknowledgment came as a grunt. "Double-edged sword there."

"How?"

"His face in mine at six in the morning."

"How long? I mean, when did you switch him from a crib?"

"When he was two and a half."

"Is that the usual age?"

He stretched his neck, one side to the other. "Depends on when the child is ready." He cupped his mouth and yelled to the boys, who stood with their backs to the chain-link fence at the very end of the field, "Come on back!"

"How do I know if Tad's ready?" Jamie asked.

He cut her a half-smile. "Are you?"

"I have no idea, but I have to decide ASAP. The Pack 'n Play isn't big enough. Either I bring his crib over from the house, or I buy a bed."

"Buy a bed."

"With all the other changes in his life right now?"

"What's one more." No question. Because it made total sense. Like keeping Tad at her place to allow the past to fade and the future begin.

"What about potty training?"

"Use M&M's. Bribery works wonders."

"Should I be training him now?"

"Is he compulsively neat?"

"Omigod, no." She pictured her condo. "He could care less."

"Then wait a little. Buddy was slow. It's harder for boys anyway—y'know, two things to learn to do."

Jamie might have been embarrassed discussing male body function with Chip Kobic, except that she found herself breathing, truly breathing, *deeply* breathing for the first time in forever. She had gotten more solid information in the last fifteen minutes than in all of the last five days. Amazed, she looked up at him. "Who'da thought Checker Chip would have answers like this?"

"Who'da thought Just-So-Jamie would deign to ask?" he shot back.

Well, she deserved that. Chip Kobik had been two years ahead of her in school. They had never been friends, had never spoken to each other, but nicknames transcended social circles when it came to standouts. En route to the pros, Chip had played hockey on local and state squads and was widely considered an ace at checking, hence Checker Chip. King of the jock crowd, he had an ego to match. Jamie had no ego, at least not at school. Nor, actually, did she have a crowd. Just-So-Jamie, fastidious to a T, had been too focused on tennis to care.

Seeming to regret the sharpness, he said more gently, "It's Charlie. And I have a list of babysitters at home. What's your e-mail address?" Taking a phone from his pocket, he keyed it in. "They probably aren't a permanent solution, but they'll help for now."

"I'll take any help I can get." She was without pride. "I am up the proverbial creek without a you know what."

"Speaking of which," he called over his shoulder as he guided his son toward the gate, "there's Toddler Swim at the town pool Tuesdays and Thursdays. He'd probably like that. And story hour at the library. The days vary, but there are always other kids. It's good for socializing."

Checker Chip a parenting resource? Who *knew*. Jamie was amused enough, curious enough, *needy* enough for a frivolous break to explore the surprise. After putting cheese tortellini on for dinner, she settled Tad in the crook of her left elbow with her iPad streaming a Handy Manny video, opened her laptop on her right, and Googled Charlie Kobik.

He taught PE at Emory Elementary.

Not what she would have expected, though seeing him on the playground with the boys, it made sense. Still, it was a turnaround from the wild behavior reported in earlier articles. He had gone to Harvard to play hockey, then dropped out and signed with the Montreal Canadiens, the Buffalo Sabres, and the Pittsburgh Penguins in quick succession until his three-year contract expired and the NHL summarily let him go. After an undocumented period spent, she assumed, getting his act together, he had enrolled at UMass, earned a degree in education, and been appointed to the Williston School Department. Summers, he ran a hockey camp at an indoor ice rink. According to the *Williston News,* it was hugely successful.

There was nothing about a wife and son, but given how he sat by himself at the park hiding under shades and a hat, she figured he was making a statement. What he did on his own time was his own business.

And yet, there came his e-mail, as promised, containing the names of half a dozen babysitters. *You are a godsend,* she typed back. *Thank you SO much.*

With the phone at her ear while she drained the tortellini, she secured a babysitter for Saturday night, then called Brad in triumph.

"Great," he said but sounded tired.

"Will you stay over?"

"Of course."

"Want to come tonight?"

"Nah. I'll be here working a while."

"You could come later. Or how about tomorrow morning? I'm taking Tad bed shopping. Want to meet us at the store?"

"Isn't he too young for a bed?"

"Not according to the reading I've done." No point mentioning Chip. "We can get a bed that's low and has bars, and the floor is carpeted, so it's not like he would hurt himself if he fell out. Come with us, Brad? It'd be really neat if he associated you with his new big-boy bed."

But Brad had other plans. "I just got into a foursome." Golf. "I need the break. It's been a nightmare week."

Jamie stifled the miffed little voice in her head that wanted to point out that it had been a nightmare week for her, too, and that he was part of a family now. Only he wasn't part of the family that was her and Tad. He didn't seem to want to be.

They had to talk.

Chapter Fourteen

When a sharp knock on the door woke Caroline from a deep sleep early Saturday, her first thought was Jamie. No surprise there. Thoughts of Jamie had kept her awake into the wee hours more times than she could count, and last night was bad.

But no. Not Jamie at the door now. Jamie wouldn't knock. She had a key.

Nor would Jamie drive over in Dean's truck, which was what Caroline saw when, bleary-eyed, she scrambled over cats to squint out at the street.

Dean, who had said *I could prove you wrong about sex,* whose hand on hers during the funeral had brought comfort, whose palm at her back following the confrontation with Claire suggested he was more than just a colleague, and whose sensitivity and gentleness yesterday in his truck brought tears to her eyes now—all of which was bizarre.

Unnerved, she climbed back into bed, but only until he knocked louder. Then, resentful of being woken after the night that had been, she threw back the sheet and trounced barefoot down the stairs. She was wearing an ancient MacAfee T-shirt, once red but now faded from a gazillion washes. It was big enough to cover her sleep shorts and any body parts that were also faded from a gazillion washes, and if that didn't turn him off more, the mess of her hair would.

Jaw tight, she pulled open the door.

His eyes widened. Recovering quickly, he grinned. "Hey, Sunshine."

"Sunshine?" She cleared her throat. "Not. Quite."

The amusement in his eyes didn't waver. "Got up on the wrong side, did we?"

"*We* didn't."

"Through no fault of mine," he said with such innocence that once upon a time she would have laughed.

Now, confused and feeling unfit to deal, she simply pleaded, "Why are you here so early? It's the weekend. You sleep late." She narrowed a glance back at the grandfather clock. "What time is it even?"

"Eight," he said, "and I brought breakfast makings." He pushed past her—close, tall body brushing, *deliberate*, and not entirely unpleasant—as he strode into the house and down the hall.

She considered making a statement by going back to bed. There were two reasons she didn't. First, she would never fall asleep with him in her kitchen, and second—*worse*—he might follow.

That said, she was not changing her clothes. She didn't care that he was newly showered, hair still damp, T-shirt and jeans fresh. This was her house, her Saturday morning, *her* routine. "And don't ask if I called Jamie," she shouted after him, "because since you last asked, nothing has changed." Padding down the hall, she found him unloading bags in her itty-bitty little space.

"Bacon, eggs, cheese," he listed. "And bread."

"I have all those things."

"Bacon? Really?"

"No. Not bacon. Bacon's bad for you."

"Not for me. And I doubt you have this bread, which is

thick-sliced organic whole grain, fresh-baked this morning in town." He arched a questioning brow.

"No," she admitted. A quart of fresh-squeezed orange juice stood in a signature glass bottle from the same bakery. Taking out two glasses, she filled them. Dean was frowning at the lower cabinets by then, clearly not knowing what was where. She nudged him aside. "I'll cook."

"That wasn't my plan."

"Maybe not, but my kitchen is too small for both of us, and I know what's where. And if you're going to tell me it's too warm in here, you can go wait on the porch." She removed a skillet from a low cabinet, put it on the stove, and lit the gas. While it heated, she separated bacon slices and laid them in one by one. The sizzle accompanied the *whooshhh* of the Keurig.

"Want some?" he asked. The fridge opened; he added cream to his coffee.

"Tea, please. K-Cups are—"

"Got 'em." He removed one, studied the label, removed a second and did the same.

"Either is fine. Surprise me." While he brewed it, she cracked four eggs in a bowl, whipped them with a fork, flipped the bacon slices. Messy curls slid forward as she worked, blocking her vision so that she was startled to find him close when she turned to the fridge.

Whipping her hair out of the way, she stepped back and cleared her throat, but he didn't move. Instead, he set her tea down near the skillet and asked, "How's your hand?"

Thinking a diversion was good, she showed him her bright red scar. "The stitches came out yesterday. It's fine." Proving it, she used that hand to push him aside. "Please. Take the orange juice and these"—she plunked napkins and forks on the counter—"to the porch." After giving the skillet a shuffle, she stood waiting, watching as the bacon shriveled and curled.

She felt his warmth at her ear seconds before she heard, "Mmmm. There is nothing like that smell." Though he meant bacon, she was thinking coffee, which was on his breath as he nuzzled her hair. "And this. Is it shampoo or you?"

She swallowed. "Shampoo."

His voice moved off a bit. "It smells like you."

"Because I always use it." She had torn off a handful of paper towels and was in the process of forking up the bacon to drain when she felt a hand slide up her spine. Fork in hand, she whirled around. "What are you *doing*?"

He took a step back, actually seeming guilty. "Just wondering what's on under this."

She refused to look away. "Nothing, Dean. Nothing. I just woke up."

"You're gorgeous."

She wanted to yell, scream, kick him out. Only he seemed to mean it, and—*traitorous, vain self*—a little part of her ate up the words.

Embarrassed, wishing she had put on clothes or washed her face or at the very least used mouthwash, she turned back to the stove. After draining bacon grease from the skillet, she poured in the beaten eggs and shook on a layer of shredded cheddar.

"More," he urged from her temple.

She added more, and when his warmth stayed behind her in as clear a message as could be, she set down the bag of cheese and, sighing in resignation, sagged back against him for a single weary minute.

Actually, it wasn't a single minute. It was probably a quarter of that, and it wasn't weary so much as bewildered. There was warmth and strength here, and a commanding height. There was a sense of being enveloped that felt better than it should. There was familiarity, and trust, and something else that she hadn't felt in many long years. *Why now why now why now?*

Confused, she came forward, taking her own weight again. "Oh, Dean," she murmured, stirring the eggs as they cooked.

Not moving far, he turned to lean against the sink, where he could see her face. "What does that mean?"

"It means this is strange." She focused on the eggs. "I don't understand what you're doing or what I'm feeling. Why is this happening all of a sudden?"

His hazel eyes darkened. His voice was quiet. "There's nothing sudden about it on my end. I've always been attracted to you."

That startled her. "Even when you were married?"

He looked uncomfortable, finally shrugged. "I wouldn't have acted on it then. And after my divorce, our relationship was comfortable. I needed your friendship more than I needed sex."

She studied him, her fifty-six-year-old self wondering if he was reading *More*. But he was serious. "And what's changed?"

He considered, seeming puzzled, then just gave another shrug.

Caroline was just as puzzled. "I'm not soft or sexy or feminine."

"Is that what Roy said?"

"He didn't have to. I'm not blind. I look in the mirror every morning. I see myself through the eyes of dozens of men every week. Besides, I'm older than you."

"Which *is* what Roy said."

She scrubbed the air. "Forget Roy. Roy is dead."

Dean stood straight, eyes suddenly clear and intense. "That's it, Caro. Dead at fifty-two. And what is the lesson from that? I'm fifty-*three*. Will I be gone next year or the year after that? Maybe fall off a roof or crash the Harley?

I don't know, I really don't, but suddenly I'm thinking of the things I'd regret in those last few minutes before death. You'd be one."

She didn't know whether to laugh or cry. "So I'm on your bucket list."

"Actually"—he didn't blink—"you *are* my bucket list."

Caroline swallowed, trying to digest *that*. "I'm a carpenter, Dean. I do man's work. I have calluses and scars. And I'll be *sixty* in four years."

"You're sexy."

"*Sixty* in four years."

"You're fixated on age because of Roy and Claire—"

"Just stating facts."

"Like they matter once you're past, what, forty? Come on, Caro. That's just dumb. I don't care how old you are. I think you're hot."

Hot. Well, there was a potent word.

Caroline searched his face. When she saw nothing but earnestness, she felt a tightness inside. Roy could sling the bull, sling it often and long. Not Dean. Dean was all down-to-earth, tell-it-like-it-is practicality. He wasn't driven by ego. His expression right now—*vulnerable*—attested to that, giving new meaning to *I could prove you wrong.*

What she had initially thought was pure swagger was not. This wasn't a dare. It wasn't a game for him. And *that* was the sweetest, most frightening realization of all.

"You look terrified," he said.

"I am. I don't know if I can do this. I don't know if I want to."

He shifted again, this time caging her with both elbows as he took the skillet from the stove. Then his hands closed on her forearms. Dark against her skin, his fingers were long and scarred, with a pinkie that didn't fully straighten but took nothing from the strength of the others. His voice was low and surprisingly intimate. "You think I'm not nervous? You think I don't worry I'm not good enough? You think I don't know the risk? Think again. But Roy was younger than me, and he died. That's a reality check. Put things off and they may never happen. Ever. At some point in life, you have to go for what you want."

"Fine for you to say," she mused. "Apparently, you knew you wanted this. I've been in the dark."

"You're not in the dark now. You either feel it or you don't."

"Those are words, Dean, just words. So is this a philosophical challenge?"

He paused. "Why do you ask that?"

"Because."

"Because why?"

"I can just tell."

"How?"

"Because," she blurted, "you're standing against me, and we're talking about it, and if it was really a *sexual* thing, I should feel, well, feel you, but I don't—" She stopped short when he brought his lower body against hers, proving her well and truly wrong.

Dean had barely headed off in his truck when Caroline speed-dialed Annie Ahl. "Where are you?"

"Sitting in weeds at the Blaine site." The home in question, a current MacAfee job, was more an external facelift than an internal redo, which meant that Annie, Jamie, and Dean were more familiar with it than Caroline was, but she certainly knew the address.

"I'll be there in ten minutes." She dressed in two, fed the cats in two, and drove in six, which was truly too fast, but there was an urgency here. Dean's erection had stolen her breath. She should have been angry or embarrassed, should have been *turned off,* for Pete's sake, not intrigued. That erection had been impressive. Add to it earnestness and vulnerability, both of which she had seen in Dean during their discussion, and she was about to OD on confusion.

Annie was her closest friend. Having met on a job fifteen years before, they had bonded over girl things, like mani-pedi afternoons, breast biopsies, brown spots, and menopause. Caroline hadn't told Annie about *Gut It!* yet. She hoped she wouldn't have to. Annie was even closer to sixty than she was; if the hosting switch held, she would fear for her own job.

Besides, *Gut It!* definitely took a backseat to an impressive erection.

Pulling up behind Annie's van, she spotted the silver-haired pixie in the garden, trotted over, and sat. "We need to talk."

"About what?"

"Sex."

"My favorite topic," Annie sang in her high voice as she pulled up a clump of weeds.

"Is it overrated?" Caroline asked. When Annie shot her a *where did this come from* frown, she said, "You've been married to Byron for thirty years. Your sons are in college, and you're not having more kids. Is sex still important?"

Annie was oddly wary. "Why do you ask?"

"Is it?"

"Yes."

"Do you think about it a lot?"

"Yes."

"As much as you used to?"

Annie started to blink and stopped, seeming not to breathe. "More."

That surprised Caroline. Puzzled, she asked, "Because of those books?" Annie made no bones about having read them multiple times.

"No." Annie tugged up another handful of weeds. "Because I'm not ready to have it end."

"Why not?"

"Because it's fun. It's exciting. It's a way to feel alive. And young. And *feminine*."

Dean had certainly made Caroline feel feminine. He had also made her feel protected—a totally bizarre thought, since she could take care of herself.

Seeming halfway between cross and sad, Annie sat back on her heels. "I don't want to dry up. Use it or lose it."

"Then things are better with Byron?" Caroline asked. Annie had once confided that her husband was losing interest in sex. When it hadn't come up again, she had assumed an improvement. But her friend wasn't answering now. "Annie?" Silence. "Oh, whoa. What is going on?"

Barely above a whisper, Annie's words came in a rush. "Don't worry, it's not like that, I haven't done anything wrong. It's just, I *think* about it." She leaned closer. "There's this guy—"

Caroline cut her off. "Byron is wonderful!"

"Yes, he is, wonderfully the same, getting older and not caring, but I do. There's this guy—" She stopped abruptly. Eyes flying past Caroline, she broke into a smile. "Hey, Jordan. I thought you were paying bills while Mandy was at the hair shop."

"Your being out here is too tempting."

The man who had come from behind the house wasn't particularly tall, muscular, or young, wasn't notable in any way other than the intensity of his focus on Annie.

Taking a brief break, he extended Caroline a hand. "I recognize you from the show. Jordan Blaine, homeowner." They shook, but his hand was barely free when he walked on. Coming up behind Annie, he steepled his fingers on the top of her head and said to Caroline, "Is this woman amazing or what? On a Saturday, no less."

Annie tipped her head back to see him. "It makes sense to clean now, so that I'll know what to dig up next week before our crew starts tossing off old siding."

"I'm happy to dump all of these plants and start fresh. I told you that."

"But some of them are worth saving. If there's no place for them in front, there is in back."

He glanced at Caroline. "How rare is a landscaper who comes up with a high-end design and still wants to save me money?" His fingers slipped to Annie's shoulder. "I'll be inside. Ring the bell when you're done." With a little squeeze, he was gone.

Annie followed his departure before shifting wide eyes to Caroline. Wide, *expectant* eyes.

"Him?" Caroline whispered in surprise. She didn't find Jordan Blaine sexy in the least.

"He touches me, y'know? Byron doesn't do that any-more. I could be a piece of furniture that he happens to screw once a month," which was pretty much what Annie had told her before.

Caroline's heart sank. The touching she had just wit-nessed seemed more friendly than sexual, like Annie was building it into more, but even that was a shame. Byron was a gentle soul who was faithful and adoring. It didn't seem fair that he should be cheated on because of sex alone. "If it's still bad, you need to talk with him."

"I *did.*"

"Do it again. And again. You owe him that, Annie."

"I know," she wailed.

"Not to mention," Caroline remarked, "that there was a big fat wedding band on the hand that stroked your hair just now."

"I *know,* but, *God,* the attraction's strong. His eyes, his hands, his body—when we're alone, he's there."

Okay. Caroline's presence might have kept a lid on the fire.

"He doesn't even have to touch me and I feel alive," Annie went on achingly. Grabbing Caroline, she pulled her up and, linking their arms, put distance between themselves and the house. "Maybe all I need is the tease. There isn't any of that in my marriage. No tease, no mystery, no adventure, no spice. How can old marrieds not get bored?"

"You're asking the wrong person. My marriage never made it to the old-marrieds stage. We lasted twelve years. Roy was bored after one."

"Were you?"

"Not bored."

"Satisfied?"

Caroline looked at her fingernails. Given her line of work, she had no business painting them. Feet, yes, but hands? She had only done it because she had known the surgery would keep those hands idle. Now the orange polish was starting to chip. Roy had thought her hands masculine; hence the concept of hand care had taken root. Had years of moisturizing made a difference? Or sexy lingerie or designer perfume? Had sex with Roy been satisfying?

Tucking her hands in her armpits, she leaned against Annie's van. "Our sex was good the first few times. Then I got pregnant, and it went downhill. By the time Jamie was born, Roy had tuned out." She met her friend's gaze. "We still had sex, but he climaxed and was done. My pleasure wasn't part of the package."

Annie hung on her forearm. "I'm sorry. That makes my complaints seem petty."

"No complaints are petty. Everything is relative. You've had something with Byron that I never had with Roy. Yours may be on autopilot now, but Byron's still a good man."

"I know, I know, I know. But right there, that's the trouble. I *know* Byron inside and out. We're the same people, bringing the same cards to the table over and over again. I try to suggest new things to do, but he's no change agent. I tell him change is good and healthy and how we stay young." She wagged a finger between them. "How often do you and I change nail color?"

"Nail color." Caroline failed to make the connection.

"Okay. Bad example. Try hairstyle. I cut mine short, then let it grow long and cut it again. I drive Claire nuts, but I'm sorry, I like novelty when it comes to hair and nails and food. Shouldn't I like novelty in bed, too?"

Caroline thought of Dean. She didn't know how he made love, what positions he liked, whether he was silent or vocal. Anything he did with her would likely be a novelty after Roy, who had been a die-hard missionary guy and didn't welcome her input. For all she knew, Dean was the same. Worse, he could be addicted to another position that she liked even less.

"Variety is *good*," Annie said into the silence, and Caroline couldn't argue with that.

"But we're older. Our bodies respond differently."

"Different doesn't mean worse."

"I hate my thighs. They're lumpy."

"Most people call that muscled, but there's a solution for that. It's called darkness."

But Caroline was thinking about things that lighting couldn't hide. With anyone else, she might have been more hesitant to be blunt, but Annie was Annie. "What about dryness?"

"CVS sells lubricants."

"Do you use them?"

"With Byron I do. I don't think it would be an issue . . ." Her eyes touched the house and returned.

"How do you know?"

Annie stared at her pointedly.

Ahhh. Wetness just thinking about it.

"I mean," the pixie burst out, "you and I are at an incredible stage in life when we don't have to worry about getting pregnant or even being discreet since we don't have kids around. Why can't sex just be pleasurable and fun, and if my husband doesn't want that, should I be punished? Why can't I once, just once before I go senile, have a hot, passionate, incredibly romantic love affair? I've been so good all my life." She paused. "So have you. I didn't know you when you first got divorced. Did you think about having affairs back then?"

"Yes. I tried with two different guys. It was disappointing with both."

"Was it more than one night with each?"

"Yes. I really did try." One was a client whose house they had finished, the other an independent furniture maker. She had chosen them carefully to avoid fallout at work. Dean, now, Dean was a whole other can of worms.

"You were on the rebound," Annie offered, bringing her back.

"No, the sex just wasn't great, and I've been okay with that," Caroline insisted. "I like my life. It's rewarding and full." Until now, if the *Gut It!* change held. Being on the show as the host emeritus would make her feel older than God. Not that having sex with Dean would change that.

"But I see guys watching you. Aren't you ever tempted?"

She thought about that—and about why she had been totally unprepared for Dean's move. "Sex just . . . hasn't been on my radar screen."

"You've repressed it."

She considered that and conceded, "Maybe."

"Because Roy sucked at it."

She smiled sadly. "Either Roy or me."

"Roy," Annie said. "Every woman *feels*. It just takes the

right man to make things combust. So Roy wasn't right, and clearly neither of the other guys was. But aren't you curious?"

"Curious enough to risk awkwardness, embarrassment, and pain?" Which raised the issue of why she was even *beginning* to consider sleeping with Dean. She wondered if Roy's death was a wake-up call for her, too, a red alert that she had to go for what she wanted while she still could. Granted, she hadn't thought she wanted sex. But she was getting older. If her recent birthday hadn't told her that, being put out to pasture by *Gut It!* would have, which brought her back to the issue of sex for a woman her age.

You either feel it or you don't, Dean had said, and a week ago she would have denied feeling a thing. But she was here talking to her best friend because she had felt something. Dean's erection—God, it was weird thinking of him that way—his erection had made her buzz in a way that made his argument real. He had put his money where his mouth was, which raised an interesting thought. His mouth. They hadn't ever even kissed. It was all well and good to be eye candy, but if his kiss turned her off, they had a problem that no advice from Annie would solve.

Still, that erection had given her a quick blast of heat.

"How long has it been?" Annie asked.

Caroline had done the math more than once since Dean had changed their relationship with his challenge. "Seventeen years since the divorce, ten since I last had sex, or tried."

"I knew you ten years ago. You never told me—"

"Because we weren't that close then, and it was bad. Oh boy," she breathed. "I am *so* out of my league here."

Annie's sidelong stare lasted long enough to make her squirm before a breathlessly high voice said an amazed "You're considering it! That's why you wanted to talk. Oooh, this is good, Caro. Who *is* he?"

Caroline moved a hand *no*. She couldn't tell Annie. Annie knew Dean. It would be unfair to implicate him in something that might absolutely never come to pass.

Mercifully, her friend let the identity piece go and chided softly, "You're thinking of doing it, and you're scared. Do not be, Caro. If the guy is right, it'll work, and if he isn't, it's no loss." Caroline was thinking that it wasn't so simple, that a working relationship was at risk, not to mention a friendship, when Annie said, "I'd give my right arm to be as free as you are. Sex is an integral part of womanhood. When I think of never feeling that . . . that *rush* again, I feel incredibly sad. It would be a loss."

"Loss of?"

"Pleasure. Possibility. Power." Annie raised hope-filled eyes to hers. "That's what I get from those books that you refuse to read. It's like they remind me that my body is capable of doing more, like I have to let go of preconceptions, like I can open my mind to growth in this, too." Her voice fell to a whisper. "I have not done anything with Jordan, I swear I haven't, but when he touches my shoulder or my hand, I feel powerful, like I'm the one making it happen. Don't you want to feel that?"

Actually, no. Power wasn't part of Caroline's equation. Hers was less lofty. She knew what it was to feel passion for work and for her daughter, but stripped-naked, bare-ass passion with a man? Exposure to the extreme? Being *that* close with another person, that *trusting*? That might be something she did want to feel.

But with Dean? It could either be the best thing that ever happened or the worst.

Chapter Fifteen

Dinner with Brad Saturday night was a disaster. Jamie had hoped that eighteen holes of golf would loosen him up, and that since the other three in the foursome had kids, he would warm to the idea of being a father himself. But beyond color on his cheeks, his features were their usual calm selves. She had always found that reassuring. Now it angered her. If ever they needed to actually share thoughts, this was the time, but he remained distant. He nodded when she told him about organizing the condo and did it again when she said she had possible nanny contacts. His eyes glazed over when she described her dilemma at the furniture store that morning, and when she asked his opinion, toddler bed versus twin bed, he held up his hands and said a gentle "You'd know better than me" with an infuriatingly sweet smile. By the time he had given versions of the same answer with regard to staying with Jessica's pediatrician, feeding Tad the sugary breakfast cereal he wanted, and, finally, formalizing his adoption in court, she'd had it.

"I'm not asking for a definitive answer, Brad, just an opinion. What do you *think*?" She had lost interest in both the steak on her plate and the garlic mashed potatoes topped with onion rings that she would have normally devoured. She was too filled with annoyance to eat.

"I don't know," he said helplessly. "I have no experience in this."

Sorry, bud, said her irate mind-voice, *helplessness does not work here.* "You *do.* You spent a law-school summer interning for a lawyer who specialized in child custody cases."

"That was after my first year, and I hated it so much that I did a one-eighty the next summer and never looked back. I'm a real estate lawyer, Jamie."

"But you know how this state works. I want to know whether I should ask Theo to pull strings and speed things up."

"Why do you need speed? It's not like there's anyone else who wants custody."

Jamie recoiled. "Like Tad's a booby prize?"

He gave a tiny frown and silently reached for his wine.

"You think he is," she charged. She kept her voice low; it wasn't in her to yell. She couldn't control the tiny tremor in it, though. Her heart was breaking. She shouldn't have to work so hard to remember why she loved Brad. But after spending the week tiptoeing around him, soothing his ego, and giving him time to adjust, this issue remained huge. "You and I swore we would talk things out, so let's talk. You don't want Tad."

Yes, I do, he would have insisted in an ideal world, because Tad was an adorable, smart, healthy little boy whose now-dead parents had named Jamie his legal guardian. Just as important, how could Brad not want what Jamie so badly did?

Instead, he was silent as he considered his answer. It was only after a pensive swallow of wine that he set down the glass and said, "It's not Tad. It's fatherhood. I was hoping we'd have time to ourselves before that."

"Well, so was I. Do you know how often I think about the fact that if my father had been on that road five seconds sooner or later he'd be alive now? No," she answered, still quiet despite the ache inside, "no, you don't know, because I'm afraid to tell you, because it's so obvious that everything about Tad annoys you."

"Not everything—"

"You hate his noise, his food, his music, his mess. You hate his existence in the condo, but on little more than a week's notice, I don't have a better option—and do *not* suggest Roy's house. You know my feeling on that. You also know that my mother and I are barely talking, and that she might have been a resource for me if it hadn't been for the *Gut It!* mess—and that's *another* thing you and I disagree on. This is not the time to make a host change, Brad. My mother is too good at it, and I suddenly have a whole other job."

"The show is important to MacAfee Homes."

"And MacAfee Homes has always been my first priority, but it isn't now. Tad is." She knew Brad well enough to recognize the flash of hurt in his eyes, and she nearly caved. He needed love. But so did she. And so did *Tad.* So she whispered, "Don't, Brad. Please don't. Selfishness doesn't work right now."

"Selfishness?" he asked, sounding offended, but at least that was something. "It's not selfishness. It's concern for *you*. You've worked your tail off building a career. To just throw it away—"

"There's nothing throwaway about what I'm doing."

"You're an architect."

"And I can't be a mother, too?"

"You can, but it means compromise. You've never been one to do that."

"Brad." Frustration beyond belief. "Things *change*. What would you have me do? Where would you have me put Tad?"

He didn't answer.

"Where?" she repeated, desperate for an answer. If she and Brad couldn't find a middle ground, there was no hope. "Remember I told you how my father came over just hours before he died? He accused me of being selfish and short-sighted, and he wasn't talking about this"—she wagged a finger between them—"clearly he couldn't have been, but his words haunt me. He told me to act like a grown-up." Her eyes filled with tears, not very grown up at all, but when it came to self-control, she was depleted. "I'm trying to do that, Brad. I'm looking at a situation that was not my doing, and I'm trying to figure it out. Buying a bed for Tad may seem like a stupid little thing to you, but if it's the very first major purchase I make as a mother, it isn't stupid at all. This is my life, Brad. This is who I am from here on out. You're either on board or you're not."

He didn't take a stand on that, and Jamie didn't push it. Clinging to a last lingering hope, she told herself that he needed time to consider what she'd said. But the rest of dinner was awkward, and, though he came home with her, she wasn't sure why. She half-wished they were fiery people who fought and made love, fought and made love. But sex didn't happen that night either. Not that she wanted it. Still, he might have tried, at least.

And then they were barely asleep when Tad woke up crying. Naturally, the monitor amplified his sobs, which brought a groan from Brad, who murmured a groggy "Shut that off," which, Jamie later realized, said it all. At the moment, though, she was simply worried about Tad.

Taking him from his crib, she bundled them both up on the living room sofa, where they slept until she heard Brad let himself out at dawn.

Much as her heart ached, she didn't get up. Tad hadn't woken, and she decided he needed the sleep more than she wanted to run after Brad. Every minute of peace and quiet with Tad was a treasure.

So she lay on the sofa with him, appreciating the whisper of the AC, the cycling of the fridge, and the gentle sough of baby breath, as she alternately studied his rosy-cheeked face, fingered the ring on her left hand, and wondered how she could simultaneously feel so in love and so hollow. It wasn't until Tad opened his eyes and snuggled closer that she realized the "in love" part had to do with the child.

What Jamie wanted to do that Sunday morning was to race to Caroline's. She didn't because, for starters, Caroline hadn't called, which meant she was still angry. Then there was the fact of Tad being Roy's son, and Roy had been awful to Caroline for years. Finally, though, Jamie had to behave like a grown-up, and a grown-up didn't run home at the first sign of trouble.

Besides, she was a mommy herself now, and if she planned to be an architect at the same time, she needed to work. Her MacAfee inbox was starting to clog, and it wasn't that her clients were insensitive. Inevitably, they expressed condolences. But they quickly got to the point, which was wanting to know whether she had made progress on their house, office, or bank.

In nearly every case, she had not.

So she spent much of Sunday morning meeting with sitters on Chip's list. All three were warm and affectionate with Tad, but only one was interested in a nanny slot.

One was all she needed. Jamie hired her.

Wanting to thank Chip, she picked up her phone and realized she didn't have his number. So she e-mailed. *Good news. June Flores will be here tomorrow at seven. She's lovely. I can't thank you enough.*

Feeling victorious and more hungry than she had in days, she took Tad for lunch at McDonald's, where she proceeded to eat every last crumb of a Quarter Pounder and fries, plus more than a few crumbs of the Happy Meal she had torn into small pieces for Tad. Then, feeling too stuffed, she drove by Roy's for the jogging stroller. She didn't go into the house, simply backed up to the garage and piled in the stroller and as many other outdoor toys as the back of the SUV would hold. She had a patio, she reasoned, and Brad was already disenchanted with baby gear, so would a little more hurt? *No.*

She wasn't quite as bold when it came to Tad, though. Praying that he wouldn't notice where they were, she left him in his car seat, playing with his Happy Meal bendy dog. She was barely back in the car when he asked for his mother.

Her insides twisted. Buckling her seat belt, she said an apologetic, "Oh, sweetie, Mommy's not here."

"Daddy?"

She put the car in gear. "He's not here either." Her voice was higher now, filled with tentativeness, because how did one discuss such a cruel truth with a child? She had wondered it before, but the question plagued her. Blogs offered a dozen different answers. Which to use? Caroline would know, but she was temporarily off-limits. Next best bet would be a pediatrician or even a grief therapist. Now that she had a nanny, she could consult one, but what was she supposed to tell Tad at this very moment?

"Woof?" came his little voice, sounding curious but not tragic, and she was saved.

"Woof? Oh my *goodness.*" She couched her relief in exaggerated excitement as she started down the road. "That little dog on the wall?" It was a painting in Tad's bedroom. He used to wave at it when he walked by, but it hadn't occurred to Jamie to take it along. "Good *thought,* Taddy. We'll have to get him another day, because right now we are going for a nice, healthy run and then," with drama, "to a *puppet show.*" The show was held every Sunday on a green several towns over. Jess had never taken him, which was partly the point. It would be a new memory with minimal connection to things Jamie couldn't discuss, like death.

I'm glad June signed on, Chip e-mailed that evening. *She's motherly and mobile. Give her a car seat and she'll take Tad to kids' programs in the area. Are you nervous about leaving him?*

Oh yeah, he did get it. *VERY,* she wrote back in caps. *It's easy to leave him with a sitter for a few hours when he's sleeping, but leaving him for the whole day, mostly awake, is something else. But I don't have a choice. I have to work. BTW, what pediatrician do you use?*

Jake Babineau. He's with Williston Medical Associates, in the center of town. He went into private practice after a stint at Children's, so his qualifications are good. I like his way with Buddy. And he's good with me, too. He's alarmist enough to take my alarms seriously, but not so alarmist that he makes me alarmed. Does that make sense?

Absolutely, she typed with a smile of relief. *And I appreciate the vote of confidence, since he's the one Jessica used. Tad saw him right after he turned two, so he's not due again for a while, but I need some advice. He's asking for his parents more, and I don't know what to say. Does Buddy ask for his mother?* Jamie still didn't know the details of that. Several of the local articles, like the one announcing Chip's teaching appointment, mentioned his son, but only in passing.

He didn't used to. When he was little he didn't know that having a single parent was any different from having two. He's started asking now because some of his day-care friends talk about their moms. I tell him his mom loved him but can't be here. He seems satisfied with that for now. Each time he asks, I get nervous and think this is it, I need a better answer, but his mind moves on to something else pretty quick. Babineau says when he's ready to handle more, he'll ask more. He tells me not to push the issue.

Hadn't Tad's mind moved on to something else back at the house? Normal, then. She felt less guilty for having happily evaded the truth.

Does Buddy ever see her? Jamie wrote.

They had been e-mailing back and forth so steadily that she guessed he had to be sitting with his laptop the way she was—okay, maybe not curled up in a corner of the sofa . . . maybe, actually, in bed wearing nothing. *That* was a frivolous thought. The relief at being able to talk so freely with him was making her giddy.

He was slower to reply this time. Fearing she had overstepped and thinking that she could not afford to alienate a friend who was an amazing resource, she was about to apologize when his answer arrived.

No. She basically gave birth and handed the baby to me. She didn't want any part of either one of us. It's pretty sad when you think of Buddy, but once I embraced (haha) the terror of being a father, I was fine with it. She and I were together one night. Neither of us wanted more. We came from different places and were heading different places. She told me she was protected, so I thought it was over and that I'd never see her again. Turns out she didn't believe in birth control any more than abortion.

Would you have wanted her to abort? Jamie wrote back and instantly wished she hadn't. She feared she had overstepped here, too.

But this was what friends did, wasn't it? Okay, she had no close girlfriends to judge by, and Chip was male, but did that matter? If he didn't like the question, he could just not answer.

He did, albeit taking a little longer again. *I want to say no. But at the time, I wasn't sure I could take care of myself, much less a child. I had just finished college— slightly late, but I finally did finish—and I didn't know if I'd be any good as a phys ed teacher. I had to do a practicum to get my degree, but the school arranged that. I didn't know if I'd get a job on my own. Some of my past was, well, out of control. I think the only reason Williston gave me a chance was because I grew up here.*

Jamie figured that might have been part of it, but his e-mails were intelligent, his manner at the playground smooth. He had been something of a local hero before losing focus in the pros. He had charisma; she felt it herself.

That said, he was clearly haunted by his past. *Do you worry she'll show up someday?*

If she does, I'll just have to deal. At some point, Buddy may want to know her, and I'll have to let him. You're lucky that way. You may have inherited Tad with no prep time, but at least he'll grow up with a mom and a dad. I hear your fiancé is a nice guy.

Without conscious thought, she let her fingers fly. *Poor guy is pretty upset with me right now. I haven't had time to plan the wedding or draw plans for a house for us, which is especially critical now that I have Tad, who has taken over my office, meaning that I have no place to work, which is especially crucial since I won't be able to work the kind of long hours at the office that I used to or even be able to travel—I've barely thought about that. Sorry. Just broke out in a cold sweat. Must be a panic attack.* She sent it off before she could think twice.

His reply came quickly. *Want to talk? What's your number?*

She sent it. Her phone rang seconds later. Caller ID didn't identify him, but the timing would have been too coincidental for it to be anyone else. So she picked right up and said an embarrassed "Hey. I'm sorry. I didn't mean to lose it like that."

His voice was kind. "Think I didn't lose it at the beginning? Think I still don't?"

"Yeah, I think that. You seem totally on top of things."

"At the playground, sure. Sports are what I do."

"Do you miss hockey?"

"I teach it summers."

"I mean playing professionally."

"No. That became lethal for me. Do you still play tennis?"

"I call my old pro once in a while, but then I get out on the court with him and it isn't fun like it was. I'm totally out of shape."

"I can't believe that."

"I'm so bad now there's no way I'd ever win a match."

"But you're not playing matches."

"Tell that to my competitive self. It thinks I need to win and gets really, really upset when I serve into the net or hit one out. 'Course, I won't have time to do even that now that I have Tad. Tell me the parental panic gets better."

"It gets better."

"Are you just saying that because it's what I want to hear?"

"No. It does get better."

"I hope so." She took a deep, steadying breath and glanced in surprise at the clock. They had been going back and forth for an hour, and though only the last had been voice to voice, it had calmed her. "I should let you go. But thank you. I'm totally grateful for June's name."

"Any other questions, just text."

She gave a self-deprecating laugh. "You may come to regret that."

"Only if you tell the other moms. I try to keep this number to myself."

It was a warning. She held up a hand he couldn't see. "It's safe with me. No friends here, remember? But actually I do have another question. Toddler bed or twin?"

"Twin. Tad's tall. He'll outgrow a toddler bed in a year, and then you're stuck buying another. I suppose you can afford that."

"Maybe in terms of money, but not time. Twin it is. Thanks, Chip."

"Charlie," he corrected.

"I really like Chip."

"I don't."

"Okay. Charlie." She had to give him this, since he'd given her so much. "Thank you. Have a good Monday."

As the new week approached, Caroline was frustrated on three counts.

The first involved Jamie, who hadn't returned with Tad. No, Caroline hadn't called to invite them, but, having agonized over pros and cons until she was a tangle of nerves, she believed that Jamie had to be the one to reach out. Since she was the one laying the groundwork for a core family of her own, she needed to show Caroline her place in it. The idea that showing involved not calling or coming over sent Caroline into a tailspin.

The second involved Theo, who called often enough that Caroline was becoming unsure of her role. He seemed to want her in on discussions that went well beyond holding his hand. He was asking her opinion, as if she were in management, and, bottom line there, she didn't know what she was doing.

The third involved Dean, *Gut It!*, and work that perhaps, just perhaps, she shouldn't be doing. Over the years, she had made a practice of spending time with the homeowners well in advance of a taping, her belief being that for an unscripted show to flow, the major players had to be fully comfortable with each other. She had set a date with the Millers weeks before and might have canceled if Dean hadn't offered to go with her. They agreed not to mention a host change. But if the change went forward and Caroline's on-screen time was reduced, Dean would be able to fill in. Well beyond that rationalization, though, his presence was a comfort. Seeming to understand that she was feeling fragile, he kept his hands to himself when they were with the Millers and limited himself to a brief touch now and again when they were not. For the Caroline who was starting to look at his hands as sensual tools, starting to realize that he smelled like a river banked with pines, starting to wonder, still and again, whether he had lost interest, and if not when he would make his move, it was frustrating as hell.

So by the time Monday morning arrived, she was looking forward to doing her own work in her own garage with her own tools.

But the day started badly. When she went to the MacAfee shop to pick up the dowels that had finally arrived, she found herself disconcertingly aware of the men. Five were there. She had worked with each at one time or another. They were physical guys in a physical trade, which meant that on a virility scale of one to ten, all were seven or above.

Irrelevant, she told herself, but that didn't stop her from noticing things she didn't usually notice, like shoulders and chests. She even darted covert glances at a fly or two while she reviewed a stack of invoices relating to her work.

It was unsettling. Maddening, actually. She wasn't about to jump any of them, but after spending a lifetime of blending in with the guys, what she saw now made her feel very different from them.

Angry that Dean had awakened her to this, she grabbed her dowels, strode back to the truck, and was heading home to the sanctity of her garage, where she could work with no one to ogle, when Theo called.

"Can you come to the office?" he asked. He didn't sound imperious—Roy's death had scraped away that rough outer layer—but he remained firm.

Caroline released a disappointed breath. "Now?"

"Please. We have a Barth problem."

Oh dear. "Another one?" The first was the all-too-visible Dutch Colonial on the corner of South Main and Grove.

"Actually, a second and third."

"Where?"

"One is a small frame near the town line. They can do what they want with that one, but the other is the Italianate in the center of town."

A large house with a belvedere tower and arched windows, the Italianate was in as prominent a spot as the Dutch Colonial. "The Ellwells' house? Why did we not know it was on the market?"

"That's what we have to discuss," came the rasping reply, and she agreed. Totally aside from whether she should be in on those discussions, her competitive edge went on alert.

Pulling into the first driveway she came to, she turned around and headed back into town. She arrived at Theo's office to find Brad and Dean already there. Dean shot her a quick look to say that he was as puzzled by his presence as she was.

"Where's Jamie?" Theo asked Brad.

"She's not in yet. She had a new nanny coming. I'm sure she wanted to get Tad settled before she left. Her assistant knows to send her up as soon as she arrives."

Theo grunted. He looked from face to face. "I don't know what happened. We should have known about those other two houses."

"Roy would have picked up on them," Caroline said

gently. "That's why we need to hire someone to fill his spot."

"No. This goes beyond marketing. It's about being part of Williston." He glowered at Dean. "That's why you're here."

"I was wondering," Dean rolled it right back. "I'm not family."

"But you know Williston as well as anyone here," Theo argued gruffly. "Have you not heard the rumors about Barth projects—framers defecting, plasterers stolen?"

"From us? Nope. Our guys are loyal. I'd guess the Barths are smart enough to use their own people. They start poaching our guys and they'll be in trouble."

"You can make that happen?"

"Oh yeah. Anyone who defects can kiss good-bye any hope of ever working with us again. Besides, the lumber-yard knows me. One word, and Barths'll find their stuff on backorder. I'm guessing they'll use their own resources there, too, but I can spread the word. Once our guys know to look, they'll report back anything fishy."

Theo grinned. "And that, my man, is why you're here. You're the central clearinghouse when it comes to local subs."

Caroline chuckled, thinking the term was apt.

Dean tossed a chin her way and asked Theo, "What's she?"

"She's family."

"So is Dana," Caroline said, referring to MacAfee's in-house Realtor, "but she isn't here."

"She doesn't deserve to be," Theo groused. "She does fine when clients come to us, but she knows nothing about reaching out, and she doesn't know Williston. She doesn't live here. She doesn't even *like* the town. Send her over to Fiona's to schmooze and she sits alone in a booth eying her salad like it's crawling with bugs. She does more harm than good."

Caroline might have disagreed out of family loyalty; Dana MacAfee Langham was the daughter of Theo's long-dead brother. But Theo was right. Dana was off-putting. "Have the Barths affiliated with a Realtor here?"

"Don't know."

"We'd better find out," Caroline reasoned. "It's all well and good for Dean to sabotage the Barths while they're trying to build, but it'd be better if they had nothing to build in the first place. There are a couple of terrific Realtors in town who have an ear to the ground."

"If that's so, why didn't we know about the Italianate?"

"Because those Realtors aren't beholden to us. One of the best is a friend of mine." From the nail shop, but Theo didn't need to know that. "Would you consider putting a nonfamily Realtor on the payroll?"

Before he could answer, Jamie rushed in. Closing the door behind her, she slipped into the only free seat. "Sorry," she told Theo. "I just got the message. What's up?"

Jamie tried to focus while Brad filled her in, and again when Theo argued the pros and cons of *Family Builds,* but her pulse was racing from the dash to work and refused to settle down. The morning had been a nightmare from the get-go. Tad threw a tantrum when she put him in his SpongeBob T-shirt instead of the Handy Manny one he had worn the day before. "Hannymanny want Hanny-manny," he kept crying, but Handy Manny was in the hamper with chocolate pudding streaks on the front. She pulled off SpongeBob, pulled on Bob the Builder, pulled off Bob the Builder, pulled on Diego. "Not dis not dis," he yelled until he saw Jake and the Never Land Pirates, but then he wanted her to read him the board book while she was trying to shower and dress. "June will read any book you want," she promised him through the mirror as she tried to cover her freckles, a hopeless task what with sweat from nerves. Tad either picked up on her nerves or wanted his mommy and not a nanny, because he took one look at the woman who walked in the door and, in a burst of tears, clung fiercely to Jamie, which meant that when she finally pried him off, she had to change her skirt—because she had tripped carrying his cereal bowl to the sink and forgotten to clean up the puddle, which Tad must have played in while she showered.

He was still crying when she left. She felt like the meanest mother in the world.

And now this meeting. Again she told herself to focus, but her specialty was design, not management, and, being so far behind in her own work, she didn't know why she was there. Brad must have seen that she was upset, but he didn't so much as squeeze her hand.

Caroline saw. Caroline knew. Jamie sensed both, but she was still startled when Caroline suggested that they needed to hire not only an experienced marketer and a Williston-based Realtor but another architect.

"Why?" she asked, feeling a chill as she faced her mother across a terrifying chasm.

"Because one-third of your team is retiring, which means you'll be the senior architect in your pod, and you could use the help."

"I'm fine," Jamie insisted and told herself it was true. But by the time she finally got back to her desk, she was alone with a lineup of folders that had her approaching panic.

When a hand touched her shoulder, she jumped.

"Are you really fine?" Caroline asked quietly, hunkering down beside her chair to keep their conversation private. As empty as Jamie's pod was just then, the two other pods were filled.

"I will be once I get some work done. Believe it or not, Mom, my clients want me, not someone else."

"You were offended."

Jamie hadn't called it, but yes, she was offended. Trust Caroline to home in on that. She had always been attuned to Jamie's feelings. Add a negative overlay, though, and you had Caroline seeing a Jamie who couldn't do her design work, or plan a wedding, or be a good mother without losing it over a dirty T-shirt, and therefore couldn't *possibly* take over as the host of *Gut It!*

Feeling a wave of anger, she was trying to think how to respond without provoking an all-out confrontation when Caroline said, "You've been telling me for a while that once Malcolm retires, you'd need to hire someone else. Why not now?"

"Because Malcolm hasn't retired yet."

"He's not even working half time, and most of what he does do is from his retirement place in Vermont. He's rarely in the office. He'd probably be relieved to have an excuse to clean out his desk."

That desk was perfectly neat, proof that the man wasn't around. Jamie's intern's desk was messier, though the woman was currently at a site rechecking specs.

"Yes, I know your clients want you," Caroline said. "I don't blame them. But why can't you be the name designer and the brain power behind a project while a new hire does the follow-up work?"

"Because," Jamie said as she swiveled to face her mother, "that isn't how it works. A good architect won't want to play second fiddle to me. (A) she'll want to work with her own designs so that she can build her own name, (B) if she's fully licensed, she's probably older than me, and (C), given (A) and (B), if she isn't a MacAfee, she'll feel threatened."

Caroline made a dismissive sound and stood. "The family thing has to change. We need a real estate agent, we need a marketer, we may well need a CEO if something happens to Theo, so what's one more architect? Okay, if you don't want to bring in a new person, what about shifting work around? We have two other design teams already on staff. Let them help."

Jamie told herself that her mother cared. But if she did—if she had a *clue* what Jamie was facing with Brad, with Tad, with her own insecurities—she wouldn't be harping on this.

"You think I can't do my job," she said.

"Which job are you talking about?" Caroline asked. "Seems to me you're working three right now." Her eyes softened along with her voice. "You don't have to do this all on your own, Jamie. When you were a singles star, it was just you out there on the court facing an opponent, and it had to be that way. But this doesn't. No one expects you to do everything yourself. There is nothing wrong with delegating."

Jamie barely heard. She was stuck back on *three right now*. Those three jobs would be as an architect, a mother, and what else? A wife-to-be? Maybe. More likely, though, a player in *Gut It!* Caroline hadn't specifically mentioned the last, but it was right there, under the skin like a burr. The message for Jamie, of course, was that if she couldn't handle the other aspects of her life, she shouldn't take on the show.

"I've got it, Mom. I'm on it. Trust me."

When Caroline folded her arms, Jamie glanced at her desk. She could have sworn the pile of folders had swelled since last she looked. She badly needed to work, which meant her mother had to go. But a hint of lily-of-the-valley hung in the air. Jamie didn't want to find comfort in it, but did.

In the next instant, the comfort dissolved. "Has Claire called?" Caroline asked. Her tone was too neutral.

"Not today. I think she got the point."

"Which was?"

"That I want her to back off."

"She won't. You know that."

Choking up with so much else on her plate, Jamie whispered, "I can't talk about this."

Caroline eased back. "But you did get a nanny."

"Yes." A breath of relief for both June and the return to safer ground. "Thank goodness."

"Do you like her?"

"She seems great."

"Does Tad like her?"

"He didn't this morning. He was screaming when I left, but he stopped. I checked while I was driving here. She was taking him to story hour at the library."

"That's nice," Caroline remarked, seeming sincere. "How's he doing otherwise?"

"Who knows? He can't verbalize much. He wakes up crying in the middle of the night, needing to be held. He misses his parents." Jamie glanced at a clock on the desk. "I keep wanting to call the nanny."

"She has your number, doesn't she?"

"God, yes. Cell number, office number." *Your* number, she might have added, because it was right there on the list.

"Then you're good."

"Good" lasted until Jamie got home from work and found June Flores in tears. Something was terribly wrong.

Chapter Sixteen

W hat *happened*?" Jamie asked. She was trying to imagine what it might be, but the only thing that registered was Tad crouched on the floor putting Little People on a yellow school bus. He was clean and content.

But June was already gathering her things together. Bad news had come from El Salvador, she explained in an accented voice that was broken by tears. Her mother had died. She had to go home.

Jamie sucked in a breath, feeling the shock of Roy's death again. "Sudden?" she asked.

It was. Barely seventy and in perfect health, the woman had suffered an aneurism and died instantly. "I'm so sorry," Jamie repeated with each new bit of information, but it wasn't until she asked when June expected to return that the extent of the situation hit. As fate had it, June's father was the one who was chronically in poor health. With her mother gone and two brothers living on the other side of the country, June would have to be his caretaker in San Salvador. Having raised her own children in the United States, she would return to visit but not to work.

Jamie understood. She wouldn't have expected any different from a kind and caring woman. Digging out money, she paid June for a single day and smiled when the woman told her how sweet Tad was. Within minutes, though, June was gone and panic set in.

What to do what to do what to do?

Stay calm, Jamie told herself, but she was back at square one, with no names on a nanny list and only slightly more than zip accomplished that day at work. Maybe her mother was right. Maybe she did need help.

Grabbing her phone, she called Chip. "It's Jamie," she said the instant he picked up, "and this is probably a terrible time. Are you at the playground?"

"We're on our way home. I can talk. You don't sound so good."

Hearing his voice made her feel better. With only a handful of words, he sounded like he cared, like he *wanted* to talk. It was invitation enough.

"June's mother died today, so she's moving back to El Salvador. She was terrific, Chip. I called a couple of times because Tad was sobbing this morning when I left, but she was totally on top of things. I know it was only one day, but she was a lifeline, and now she's gone, and none of the others want weekdays." She paused. "You still there?"

"Still here," he said. "Keep going."

She tried to rein in her voice. She was a grown-up. "This is so wrong of me. Her mother died. I should be more understanding than anyone. I do feel bad for her. I have no right to feel abandoned."

"You have every right. You need child care."

Soothed, she spoke more rationally. "My gut tells me I should stay home for a while to bond with Tad. I also need to look for a new place, because my condo is *so* not going to work long-run. Only I'm falling so far behind at work that it could start reflecting on the company"—not to mention proving to Caroline that she *couldn't* handle things—"so I need a sitter for tomorrow. But if that person won't nanny,

I'll have to find someone else, and isn't it worse to be passing Tad around? I'm thinking daycare, but honestly I can't bear the thought of spending tomorrow scoping them out, and I don't even know what to look for. You like First Unity, right?"

"I do."

"Then I'll call First Unity, but is there an application process? How long before he can start, and is it a problem if he isn't toilet trained—no, of course not, if they take babies," she thought aloud, "but will they even have room for him?" Meekly she added, "What do I do?"

"What you do," he replied, "is meet me at First Unity in ten minutes. Know where it is?"

"Yes, but it's too late in the day, isn't it?"

"It's a daycare center. They're open till six. That gives us twenty minutes."

"But it's such a bad time for you."

"Did I say that?" No. He hadn't. "Are you game?"

"I'm game," Jamie said before he could change his mind. "Ten minutes. See you there." She hung up, grabbed Tad, and raced out to the car.

There were only four children left at the daycare center, so Jamie didn't see the place in full operational mode. But three of those children were cleaning up a finger-painting project under the guidance of one patient teacher, the other teacher was cuddling a one-year-old who looked tired, and Chip was amazing. He introduced Jamie as a friend, and though there would normally be an interview with the center's director before accepting a child, he made it happen without. Granted, he exaggerated the critical nature of Jamie's work, and when he insisted that Tad wouldn't be a problem, it was like he knew the boy really, really well, which he did not. He also made sure, albeit in a subtle way, that the women knew what a coup it would be to have a MacAfee child enrolled.

"That was easy," he told Jamie when they walked to the car shortly after six. His was a Honda Pilot, parked behind her SUV.

Looking up at him to respond, she felt a spasm of shyness. He was tall and broad-shouldered, his sunglasses hung on the neck of his shirt in a way that showed a sprinkle of dark hair, and those blue eyes held hers. They were powerful, direct, *interested*—which, of course, she was seeing because she needed to feel the connection, which was probably not appropriate, but what was a single minute of make-believe?

Gathering her composure, she smiled. "*So* easy. Thank you. You went above and beyond. I'm sorry you had to bring Buddy back here again after you'd already picked him up. Did he not mind?" That Buddy was with Tad in the play yard, rather than hanging on Chip, said something.

Chip's lips twitched. "Oh, he minded. He counts on having his nights with me. I told him that if he came without a fight, I'd take him to Town House of Pizza for dinner."

"That's bribery."

"It works every time." He cupped his mouth. "Buddy!" He waved him in. "Bring Tad."

Jamie watched as Buddy reached for Tad's hand. He seemed to be a totally obedient child, certainly not like the Tad she had seen that morning. "When you say he 'minded' coming back here, how did he let you know?"

"Verbally. And physically. He started kicking the seat in front of him, *bam-babam-babam-babam*."

She might have laughed at the way he said it, nodding sharply with each *babam,* if she hadn't been heading somewhere with her question.

"Is he often physical?"

"Oh yeah. I'd say it's a boy thing, but I've seen girls get pushy and shovey on the playground when they don't get their way. The thing is, girls have an option. They can mouth off. Boys don't have that gene, so they kick." He tipped his head, ducked it, and asked a cautious "What did he do?"

The way he guessed her point—the way he asked—was adorable. She really liked Chip. Not caring in that instant whether it was appropriate or not, she related the T-shirt drama. "I was rushing to get ready for work and praying that June would actually show up, so I'm sure he felt my nerves, but when he continued to scream, I just yanked off one T-shirt after another. I mean, there was no finesse. How do you *deal* in a situation like that?"

He had long since straightened, and while he should have been studying her as if she were a pathetic mommy wannabe, there was no censure. His eyes were warm. They were appreciative. He liked her, too—and that meant a lot to her. From the corner of her mind came a whispered *tsk tsk,* but she was needy enough to ignore it.

"Sometimes not very well," he replied.

"What do you mean?"

"I lose it, just pick him up and put him in his room."

"Time out."

"Not that it's a solution if you're on the clock and have to get to work. Then I go with the two-choice rule. Two shirts, which do you want. Two sneaks, which do you want."

"What do you do if he refuses the choices?"

"Use force. I just put one of the damn shirts on him, usually the one I know he likes least, which is the pissed side of me coming out." Self-conscious, he scratched the back of his head. "So I get my satisfaction, and he learns that a little choice is better than none." He dropped his hand. "Kids this age want control, but they don't know how to make decisions. I can't tell you how many parents I hear offering choices their kids can't possibly make."

"Like?"

With a quick little jerk of his eyes, he lowered his voice. "That mom picking up the little girl over there just asked a wide-open 'What do you want for dinner?' That kid is probably eighteen months old. How in the hell does she know the choices, much less know which one she wants? Two choices. That's more than enough. You have to teach them a little at a time."

Jamie was charmed. "Did you learn that in college?"

"I wish," he said with a self-conscious snort. "No, I learned it by making every mistake first. I'm good at making mistakes."

If it was a reference to an earlier life, she didn't think it fit. "You're very good at parenting."

"Brilliant in hindsight. I've already been through what you're going through now, so I've mastered that stage. Now I'm muddling through the next one. Parenting is a work in progress. It never ends." He smiled crookedly. "I think I did get that from one of my ed courses. It's more profound than I am." He put a hand on Buddy's head. "Ready for Town House?"

"Yeah," the boy said enthusiastically.

"Join us?" Chip asked Jamie, but in that instant, leaning down to lift Tad, she dropped the daycare papers. She might have blamed it on being flustered at the prospect of dinner with Checker Chip, if she hadn't had such a history of fumbles.

Embarrassed, she knelt to gather them up. Chip was right down there with her.

"Sorry," she muttered. "Multitasking is always a challenge. I'm not the most coordinated being."

"I find that hard to believe," he said and passed her the

papers as they stood. "I watched a tape of your last big match on YouTube."

She was ridiculously pleased. "You did?" Chagrin followed. "I lost."

"Daddy." A whine.

"In a sec, Bud," he told his son, then said to her, "You're very pretty to watch."

She was beyond ridiculously pleased. The way he was looking at her made her breath hitch. She had to swallow before she could say, "Was. But thank you."

"Mamie," Tad piped up, echoing Buddy's whine.

She took his hand. "I was eighteen then and totally focused. Real life is not that way."

"No." He eyed her, questioning. "What do you say? Town House?"

She wanted to go, *really* wanted to go, which confused her. She liked Chip a lot. Did that mean he was a good friend, like a girlfriend, only male? She worked with men all the time and considered many of them friends. This was different. She found Chip exciting—yes, because he had answers, and because he understood what she was going through, and because having a friend was a novelty for her, but also because he had strong hands, broad shoulders, and hips that could move in a purely male way. When he looked at her with those riveting blues, like he was doing now, she felt something deep inside.

Okay. So it was just a pizza place. But if they were seen together, word would spread, and though groups of parents and kids ate there all the time without sexual overtones, she wasn't feeling totally innocent in that regard. And it wasn't just her. She might not be as experienced with men as Chip had to be with women, but she knew enough to know when a man was interested, and he was. She would have been shocked by that alone even aside from the fact that she was engaged to Brad.

"It's not a big thing," he finally said.

"It *is*," she insisted and let her eyes say more, "but I should probably go home." It was safer that way. She couldn't focus when she was with him, but she needed to think about being engaged to one man and attracted to another. "I can't thank you enough, Chip."

"Charlie."

She blinked, laughed. "Sorry. I have this fixation on Chip—oh God." She felt her cheeks heat. "That so did not come out right. Chip is habit, okay?"

"Change it," he said, but she caught the edge of a smile on his cheek as he strode off with his son.

Jamie's confidence lasted until Tad was in bed and she was in the kitchen filling out daycare papers, at which point she took an objective look at what she was doing. In the panic of June's leaving and the nonexistence of replacements, she had rushed to the daycare option. Now she wondered whether she had been rash, whether Tad would get the same kind of care outside the home, whether the social experience of daycare would compensate for the lack of one-on-one attention a nanny could give.

She might have called to ask Caroline's opinion. But Caroline thought she should hire another architect and step back from the everyday grind, and Jamie wasn't ready to do that. It would take her out of the competition.

She might have called to ask Brad's opinion. But he had made it clear that he wouldn't have one. Besides, she wanted to put some distance between them. When she focused on him, she was angry. Their relationship had gone off the rails, and if he didn't see that—if he didn't care enough to come to her to discuss it—if he couldn't finally step up—if he was so *spineless* that he couldn't act, they were done.

That left Chip. But there was no need to call. She knew

where he stood on the daycare issue, and she trusted his judgment. He taught kids. He would know what was best. Besides, she couldn't keep running to him every time something went wrong. She had to behave like a grown-up.

Her resolve lasted into Tuesday, when she dropped Tad at the center. It remained when one of the teachers called to say that he had begun crying inconsolably when asked to nap without Moose, prompting a truncated client meeting so that she could run home, get the stuffed animal, and drop it off. When she picked him up at the end of the day and smelled a nasty diaper, she reasoned that he might have done it seconds before climbing into the car rather than hours before, and when, the next morning, he didn't want to leave the house, much less leave the car when they reached the center, she told herself it was the strangeness of it all.

When she went for pickup late that afternoon and read the note that accompanied him, though, she lost it.

Head lice.

Two days into daycare, and Tad had been exposed to *head lice.* All parents were being advised to take precautionary measures, and while the note outlined what those would be, Jamie was too horrified to take them in. Stomach churning, she picked up the phone and punched in a number she now knew by heart.

"Guess who," she said the instant she heard Chip's voice. "I swore I wasn't going to keep calling you, but the idea of lice is freaking me out." She heard crying in the background. "Are you treating Buddy?"

"Against his wishes." His voice angled away. "The sooner we do this, the sooner we go back out." He sounded frustrated. Perversely, that made her feel better. Returning to Jamie, he said, "This isn't the first time a note's come home, so I have shampoo enough for ten. I'm at 403 Beech.

Feel free to come." As the crying grew, he angled away again. "Hold still and it *won't* get in your eyes." Then he was back. "Gotta go." He clicked off.

Beech was a rangy street that wove through meadows on the west edge of town. There was none of the dense green-ery of Caroline's neighborhood or the sleekness of Jamie's condo, just a modest mix of houses, the spread of a tall tree on each acre, and lots of grass. Other than an occasional truck, the driveways held family cars.

Chip's home was a bungalow in the Craftsman style, shingled in weathered gray with black trim. A single wide dormer broke through the front roof above a generous overhanging eave. Beneath it was a white-slatted front porch braced by columns anchored in stone. The windows were multipaned above, single-paned below. The front door was wood and wide open.

Carrying Tad for the sake of expediency, Jamie climbed the steps and rapped on the jamb. "Hello?" she called and, shading her eyes, peered through the screen.

Buddy came running, wearing only shorts and a head-ful of damp, spiky hair. When he struggled with the door handle, she helped him out, then had to smile.

"Hey, Buddy. Your hair looks fabulous." But he was al-ready running in the direction from which he had come, clearly having been sent to do a particular job.

"Back here," Chip called from what turned out to be the kitchen. She heard the clang of pots and the slap of a cabinet door. When she rounded the corner, he was just straightening. A dish towel draped his shoulder; overly ca-sual hands hooked his hips.

"Were you seriously cleaning up?" she teased.

With a self-deprecating snort, he lobbed the dish towel onto the counter. "The place can be a sty. I don't put any-thing away that I may use again within a week." He reached for Tad and told Jamie, "There are different kinds of shampoo. I find the wet stuff easier to use. You massage it into the scalp for three minutes and rinse it off. No hair wash for twenty-four hours after that. You good?"

"I'm good."

"Okay. Here goes Treatment Number Two." He had efficiently removed Tad's T-shirt and laid him on the counter with his head over the sink before the boy could complain.

Jamie held his ankle to let him know she was there. "I could have picked up the shampoo at CVS myself, but the offer of moral support was too good to pass up." Still, she felt guilty. "Can I do that washing?"

"Do you seriously want to?"

"Uh, no."

He laughed. "Relax, then. I'm good. Close the eyes, Taddy."

When Tad scrunched up his face, Jamie braced for a scream. But he was simply . . . closing his eyes. He didn't even start crying when Chip started to scrub, not that he cried when Jamie washed his hair, but this wasn't your normal rubber-ducky-in-the-bathtub scene. Granted, his little body was stiff, but he clearly recognized authority.

Show. Authority.

It was a lesson for Jamie, but for another time. For now, she was very happy to cede authority to Chip. "I couldn't get myself to check his scalp," she confessed, grossed out even now by the thought. "Did you find anything on Buddy?"

"No, but a little shampoo doesn't hurt." He was cradling Tad's head with one large hand while he scrubbed with the other. "Be grateful these guys have short hair. Long hair sucks."

"Long hair *sucks,*" came an echo from his other side.

Chip drew in an exaggerated breath. "I did not use that word the right way, Buddy. What do we suck?"

"A juice box."

"But what goes in the juice box?"

"A *straw*."

"Correct. What else do we suck?" When no answer came, he gave a hint. "What does Nana bring?"

"*Lollies.*"

"Bingo."

"Do you see your parents often?" Jamie asked as she watched him work. If he was at all freaked out at possibly touching nits, he didn't show it. His fingers moved with efficiency and grace.

"They have a place in Vermont for summers, so we're back and forth. Winters, Buddy and I fly south when we can."

Jamie thought of Caroline, who lived five minutes away, and suddenly it seemed ludicrous that they weren't seeing each other all the time, like at least every few days. Caroline would keep lollipops in the house for Tad. She would take him to the garage and help him make something from scraps of wood. She would be a good grandmother, once she accepted the role, *if* she accepted the role. She might have easily done it if a grandchild had come the normal way, but now, especially after the *Gut It!* fiasco?

Yes, now, Jamie thought with sudden anger. Brad wanted children to come at a more convenient time. *That is not how it works, Brad. Get with the program, for God's sake!*

"You there?" Chip asked quietly.

She blinked, smiled. "Sorry. I was just feeling a wave of envy." When he shot her a curious look, she explained, "For what you have with your parents." She wanted to tell him what was going on with Caroline, but he already knew that she was a basket case of a mother and didn't particularly want him to think she was also a dysfunctional daughter. So she asked, "What's it like traveling with a child?"

He studied her a minute longer, as if he knew she was holding back and wanted to know why. Then he simply shrugged. "Better now that I can slap on headphones and a video. When he was little, I used to chat it up with flight attendants—you know, single dad, not good at this, desperate for help, hint hint."

Jamie tried not to laugh. "Did it work?"

"Every time," he said. "When they had breaks, they'd walk him up and down the aisles. The ones my age thought it might translate into a relationship, and the moms and grandmoms just couldn't resist a cute child and a helpless dad."

A *gorgeous* dad, Jamie amended. Between that dark hair and shadowed jaw, and a T-shirt that stretched over an impressive back and pulled up enough to show just a sliver of bare skin when he reached for the sprayer, he was totally sexy.

"You're shameless," she decided.

"When necessary," he admitted. His eyes met hers in a way that gave her a jolt. She could keep telling herself that she was imagining things, that Checker Chip was way too cool to be interested in her, but she had felt it before, and the look in his eyes now revived it. For a minute she couldn't look away.

Finally, he hitched his chin toward a clean towel lying on the counter. Refocusing, she passed it over. "Are you also washing the bedding and stuff?" The instructions from the center were extensive, and as disgusting as the thought of lice remained, it was safer than dwelling on an attraction she didn't know how to handle.

"I probably should, but Buddy wasn't itching, so I'm not too worried." He sat Tad up and began drying his hair. "Almost done, bud," he said, then, in answer to Jamie, "I'll wash what he brings to the center and do pillowcases, but that's it. You can go nuts with some of this stuff. I have to obey certain rules at school, but here I follow only one."

"Which is?"

"Common sense. And moderation."

"That's two."

"They're actually the same. Think about it." He reached for a small metal tool and held it up, like evidence at a trial. "Lice comb. For removing nits that are stuck on the hair shaft. Their shafts look pretty clean—" He paused for a split second, smirked into a wry little headshake, and went on. "It's probably overkill with our guys, but since they both have short hair, it's easy enough to do." He arched her a questioning brow.

She waved a hand. "Do it. Please." But he was right about common sense and moderation. For a minute she was silent, watching him start with the comb at Tad's nape. The child's body seemed frozen, only his eyes moving sideways toward Buddy, who stood in the middle of the kitchen holding a very wrinkled booklet and looking at Jamie.

"Whatcha got?" she asked and, crouching down, took the booklet. It was worn but intact. She didn't have to look far to see that it held instructions. "Whoa. Do you have wood blocks? *Real* wood blocks? I mean, authentic, *old-fashioned* wood blocks?"

"They're my daddy's," Buddy confirmed. "He said you could make me a building."

"Buddy—" Chip scolded, but Jamie spoke over his protest.

"So cool! I would *love* to make you a building. I'm a good builder." She ignored a snicker from Chip, but couldn't quite ignore Tad whimpering her name. "I'm right here, sweetie."

"Why does he call you that?" Buddy asked.

"Mamie? Because it's close to Jamie, which is my name." She considered. "Halfway between Mommy and Jamie, maybe?" But the whimper was a warning. "Can we do blocks when your dad finishes Tad's hair?"

"How many minutes?" The boy held up three fingers. "This many?"

"That's a good guess. You know your time. Like your dad knows his rules."

"Speaking of which," Chip said when she returned to the sink, "I'll contradict myself. What is *not* common sense is that if your child gets lice it has nothing to do with hygiene. Lice prefer clean heads."

She chuffed. "Not reassuring, but good to know." Leaning back against the counter, she looked around. "I like your house."

He shot her a skeptical glance. "It isn't your usual style. I've seen the homes you build. This one's old."

"So's my mom's house, but I love going there." She actually missed it—tight spaces, vintage fixtures, and all. Her condo was starting to look different to her. Sleek and clean was just fine until you couldn't keep it sleek and clean, at which point it just didn't feel right. "When was this built?"

"Thirty-eight years ago. My parents built it when my oldest sister was born. It was a stretch. Dad didn't earn a hell of a lot—"

"Bad word!" shouted Buddy.

"You are right," Chip said quickly. "Daddy forgot. Thank you, Bud." Under his breath, he murmured, "My mouth is a problem."

Jamie didn't think it was. His lips were lean, strong, masculine.

"He managed the hardware store in town and went out on a limb for this, but it served us well. They raised three kids here. They'd have made a bundle on it if they'd sold it on the open market instead of giving it to me."

"But they must have done okay if they have two homes now." When he was quiet, looking oddly guilty, a light went off. "Ah. You bought them those."

"It was the least I could do. Rink time at six in the morning, then a full day of work? My mom was a nurse. She did the night shift three days a week so she could be home while Dad was at the store. They'd be juggling my practices while one was coming and the other going." He set down the comb. "Done." He put Tad on the floor. "Want to take Tad to the backyard, Buddy?"

"Mamie promised me blocks."

"She may not—"

"Absolutely," Jamie cut him off "Where's the best place?"

"Are you sure?"

She smiled. She was unable to think of anything she wanted more. She wasn't ready to return to the real world. "Where should we do it?"

"The blocks are in a rolling bin in the living room. You could go out to the front porch."

"Inside, Daddy."

"Okay. Dining room table. We'll eat here in the kitchen. Is chicken-broccoli-ziti okay for you?"

Jamie had Tad's hand and was reaching for Buddy's when she realized Chip was talking to her. "Oh Lord, you don't need—"

"I want. Will Tad eat that?"

She was about to protest. After everything else he had done for her, dinner went above and beyond. But here, in this escapist moment, dinner was something she wanted to do even more than build with ageless wood blocks. "He'll eat it. So will I. Thank you."

* * *

"This is great," Jamie said an hour later. Having left a fac-simile of First Unity Church standing tall and proud on the dining room table, she was now sitting in the kitchen with Chip, two boys on their knees on chairs as they ate with a mix of fingers and forks, and a near-empty casserole dish. "It's the single feature I most love about Craftsman-style homes. A breakfast nook has to be the warmest family element ever."

"Unless said family is bickering, which my sisters and I often did. This nook is small."

"Cozy."

"Small. The whole kitchen is small."

She took measure of the room. "It doesn't feel that way, because the cabinetry is on the perimeter, and besides, architecture is about proportion. This kitchen is perfect for the house. I like your Shaker cabinets. And the dark floor. And these," she said, smiling as she touched Tad's milk glass. He had needed help, but the problem was only partly drinking from an open glass. The rest was his want-ing, at the same time, to look at the Bugs Bunny etched on the front. Buddy had Donald Duck on his, but he had made Chip take ones with Tom, Jerry, and Tweety from the cabinet. Lining them up and comparing them had oc-cupied the boys between bites.

"Welch's jelly jars are vintage," Jamie marveled. "Did you get these on eBay?"

"Nope. PB&Js were staples in our house."

"You mean your parents saved the jars all these years?"

"They did. I want to say it was pure sentimentalism, but they were practical people. These are the right size, and they're sturdy."

"Can I be done, Daddy?"

With a glance at the boy's mostly clean plate, Chip slid

from the booth to let him out. "Good job with dinner, Bud."

Tad didn't ask, just squirmed against Jamie, clearly wanting to follow. Though she would have sat a while longer, she followed Chip's lead.

"Show Tad your room, Buddy. Go Ninja on the stairs."

"Ninja?" Jamie asked, about to follow the boys. Stairs made her nervous.

"Hands and knees. Show him how, Buddy."

When Jamie would have still gone to help, Chip caught her arm. He held up a finger and listened. There were thumps, then lighter thumps, then lighter thumps still, then ample running footsteps overhead to prove both children had made it safely.

Gratified, Jamie began gathering up dishes.

"Don't worry about those," Chip said.

She made a sputtering sound. "I'm feeling incompetent about too many things, but I can load a dishwasher." She went at it while he cleared the table. "This dishwasher looks brand-new."

"The old one died last month, but it was time." He piled glasses and utensils beside the sink. "The hot water tank is up next, and in another year, a new heating system. I want to green up the place. Appliances today are energy efficient."

After standing the last of the plates on the bottom rack, she pulled out the top. "But expensive."

"I have the money. I just have to decide whether to stay here or move."

The glasses were easily loaded. As she reached for the forks, Jamie-of-the-sleek-white-condo surprised herself by asking, "Why would you move?"

"I grew up in this house. I worry I'll grow old here. I moved back when Buddy was born, because Williston is a great place to raise kids, and my parents wanted to leave. My sisters were both living away, so the house was here. But change is good. I keep an eye on the local market. When I hear of a place up for sale, I look."

Jamie envied him this house. Even all these years later, she felt tension when she thought of her childhood home. Then, unbidden, came the image of her grandmother's Victorian lace. She had always felt connected to it, all the more so after Caroline sold the big house and settled into her own. That lace was a relic of Jamie's past. She wished she had more.

"You'd leave these memories?" she asked Chip now.

"To make room for new ones, yeah. To start fresh. There are times when I feel like I'm hiding."

"From?"

He frowned, seeming unsure for the first time. The eyes he raised held vulnerability. "Myself. My future. Taking a chance. Being able to handle a challenge without going off the deep end."

"You can handle it."

"You didn't know me before."

"I see you now." She also saw herself in that instant, felt priorities shifting. Forget being an architect. Forget starring in reality TV. "Raising a child alone has to be the greatest change in the world, and you haven't gone off the deep end. You can handle a new house."

His lips twitched. "Says the woman who could sell me one."

"Who could *design* you one."

"Well," he sighed, "it's still hypothetical. I haven't seen anything great yet. The good news is that I did well when I went pro, so when I do, I can act. My dad insisted I bank half of what I earned. The money's grown."

Squirting soap on a scrubber, Jamie worked on the casserole dish. "I could tell you about land that's just been snatched up by our competitors, but I do not want you dealing with the Barths. Whether you move to a new place or renovate this one, MacAfee Homes is a better choice."

"I take it the Barths are your rivals?"

"Lately, yes. It's a game to see which of us can sniff out houses first and preempt a sale."

"Who's winning?"

She stopped scrubbing to look up. He was leaning against the counter on the other side of the dishwasher, all dark hair, blue eyes, and amused mouth.

"It's not funny," she said. "They've scored lately. That's not good for us."

"You'll come back."

"I hope so. Williston is a transitional town. It has a huge inventory of old houses ripe for renovation or teardown. There are cycles. Every five years, a different neighborhood starts to change hands. Yours is probably on the cusp. If you wanted to stay," she coaxed as she rinsed the casserole dish, "I could draw you some nice plans."

His mouth quirked. "I'll bet you could."

"I'm good." She held out the dish.

He took it and began to dry. "I know you are."

"I'm serious."

"So am I."

"You're humoring me, Chip."

"It's Charlie. And I'm not." He paused. Looking away, he opened his mouth, flexed his jaw, closed his mouth. Then, setting down the dry dish, he looked at her again, and in that instant, with humor gone, everything changed. "I have a problem," he said in a low voice. Intense blue eyes held hers, slowly falling to her mouth, then her breasts, before rising again. Everywhere they touched, she felt singed.

She didn't move, *couldn't* move.

Catching her left hand, he fingered her engagement

ring. "I don't date much, Jamie. I haven't wanted to since Buddy was born, but I'm thinking about you a lot. I need you to tell me to stop."

She couldn't speak. She could barely breathe, her hand burned so, and the burning inside was even worse.

"Tell me to stop, Jamie."

"I can't," she whispered, because she had never, ever felt what she did now, and she couldn't think with him near.

It wasn't until she was back in the car on the way home with Tad that she realized there wasn't much to think about. That was when terror set in.

Chapter Seventeen

Six had come and gone when Caroline finally finished her meetings and went down the hall to see Dean. He sat with a mess of open folders at one of three desks in the general contractors' office. Wearing thin-framed glasses, he was poring over what she knew were either subcontractor bills or supply invoices. Using a pencil to keep track, he darted her a glance over the glasses, then returned and made several notes.

Caroline liked seeing him this way. It was a different side of him. Perversely, she liked the glasses. They made him look his age.

Sinking into one of two chairs facing the desk, she put her elbows on its arms and exhaled.

He tossed the glasses aside. "You look exhausted."

"I am. How can four hours in an office do what eight at a worksite cannot?"

"Was it tough with the Realtors?"

She shot him a dry look. "Is Dana ever any other way? She had a chip on her shoulder from the get-go because of the time. She didn't want to get stuck in rush hour traffic, even though she lives in Boston and does a reverse commute. We couldn't meet earlier, because Linda had a closing, but our only other option was waiting until next week, which I didn't want to do."

Linda Marshall, Caroline's friend from the nail shop, lived in Williston. With four children who were not only attending local schools but were involved in every sport, she was in a prime position to know what was happening in town before it happened, and she had agreed to work with MacAfee Homes in that regard. Caroline had sold Theo on the idea of hiring her, but with the stipulation that she sell the idea to Dana; hence today's meeting.

"Dana isn't happy," she told Dean now. "No matter how vehement Linda was about not wanting to touch the buyer side, Dana just didn't want to hear. She likes things the way they are and doesn't see any need for change."

"Did she come around?"

"Grudgingly. Not that I care if she up and leaves the company. My gut says Linda is worth it. She just gave me tips on two houses we may be able to buy." She slid a piece of paper his way. Coming forward, he put on his glasses to study it.

"Interesting," he said, then, "Good. I'll check them out in the morning."

Dean was vital to a preemptive buy. With a quick look, he could tell how much a property was worth and what MacAfee Homes would have to spend in order to turn it around and sell it for more. His instinct rarely disappointed—which was why Caroline refused to begin to discuss the country house he had bought. That one was doomed.

Removing the glasses, he sat back again.

"I *like* those specs," she taunted, knowing he hated them enough to wear them only when his eyes were tired, but she was tired, too, and the country house was a bad move.

"You would," he said, undaunted. "Has she picked up chatter on the Weymouth place?"

"Only vague speculation."

"That's the land we want."

"Oh yeah." Caroline closed her eyes. "I dream of developing it for *Gut It!* We could have three seasons right there—a continuing saga. We've never done that. It'd be great from a marketing angle." Opening her eyes, she saw reality in Dean's sympathetic expression. "Not that I'll be around for that, and if I am, they shouldn't listen to me anyway. I'm no marketer, which is why my interviewing marketing candidates for Theo was pointless." Just prior to the Realtors' meeting, she had spent time with three potential replacements for Roy.

"Not pointless," Dean argued. "You have years of experience working with marketing."

"With Roy. By comparison, none of the people I met today felt right—and trust me, I wanted to think one of them, at least, would be better than him." Weary and confused, she sighed. "I'm no executive."

"Theo is grooming you to take over."

"You think?" She did, too. It only added to her stress. "I shouldn't be here, Dean. This isn't my job to do. Yes, I can do it. Yes, I can handle people. But I'm *so* much better with wood." Wood was easy to nail down, and being nailed down was what her life lacked right now. Without Jamie to love, *Gut It!* to anticipate, even Roy to resent, she was feeling adrift—all that even before factoring in what she was or was not with Dean. "Lately I've been a little of this and a little of that, but not a lot of any one thing. So who *am* I?"

At first, he said nothing. She knew he was thinking of Jamie—could see it in the planes of his face. To hear him tell it, all it would take was a phone call on one of their parts. But it wasn't that easy. She had said it a dozen times and wouldn't say it again.

Seeming to sense the extent of her frustration, he began

pushing papers into folders and folders into a pile. "Go home, Caro," he said as he stood and scooped everything into the ratty canvas messenger bag he had been using for as long as she'd known him. "I'll pick you up there in an hour." He put the strap on his shoulder. "Wear jeans."

And oh, she knew what that meant. "No, thanks. I don't want to ride on the bike."

"Too old?" he taunted, standing right before her now.

She looked up. "Too smart."

"What if I promise to go slow?"

"On a big, burly new Harley?" She snorted her disbelief.

"What if I promise to grill us some fish?"

That stopped her. "What kind?"

"Whatever kind I can get at the market."

"I want trout," she said.

"Would that make things better?"

She was about to say that nothing would when he took her face with his free hand, lowered his head, and kissed her. She was so taken off guard that she couldn't push him away, and then so curious that she didn't want to. His mouth was firm but fluid, controlling the kiss—and then gone. He raised his head and, while intense eyes held hers, dropped his hand.

"How about that? Did it help or hurt?" he asked quietly.

"I don't know. It was too short."

A slow smile spread across his face. "Good to know." Throwing an arm over her shoulder, he walked her to the door.

Caroline showered, put on dark green jeans with a sleeveless blouse in a matching green and orange plaid, and took care to tack her hair up in a way that might survive a helmet, because she was sure that despite her objections Dean would be on the bike—and she wouldn't refuse it.

She needed an escape, maybe even needed danger or risk. He must have known that, which possibly explained why he had kissed her at that moment, in that way. The kiss was actually better than expected, not because she didn't find Dean physically appealing, but because she had always found kisses either too tame, as in closed-mouth and dull, or a slobbering mess. Dean's kiss had fallen somewhere in the middle—aggressive enough without *invading*. She hadn't felt violated. And as for being too short, that was perhaps why it had been good—as in, quitting while he was ahead.

Now what? He had taken his time making his first move. She wondered if he had anything planned for tonight. She assumed he would be taking her back to his place, a doddering A-frame several towns over that he was rebuilding and would sell for a profit when it was done. In the meanwhile, he had a grill on the back lawn and plenty of grass.

Last time, he'd done a mixed grill, steak for him, chicken for her. She liked the idea of trout. But the physical stuff? Not so sure about that. She had shaved for the sake of a sleeveless blouse, not Dean, and if she slathered on more body cream than usual, it was to counter motorcycle wind. She had also worn a bra, which on a warm night she might have foregone, but the blouse definitely looked better with lift.

Waiting on the front steps, she was restless. Master soothed her by rubbing one ear and then the other back and forth against her leg. She loved this cat, loved *all* her cats. They didn't care if her breasts sagged, her neck wasn't smooth, or her hand had an age spot.

Master's purr grew louder.

No, not Master. Dean's Harley.

Lifting the cat, she put him in the house, checked to make sure her phone was in a pocket, and locked up. She was midway down the front walk when the big machine arrived with its helmeted driver on board. His jacket was black, his belt wide, his jeans faded, his boots old. He silenced the bike, kicked down the stand, and climbed off. Setting his helmet on the handlebar, he came at her with a spare one, along with a jacket from the saddlebag.

She felt an alarming excitement, so much so that she might have turned and run if he hadn't already reached her. "The jacket's lightweight," he said, "but you need leather on your arms." He rolled the helmet on her front to back, pulled the strap tight, and, with a large hand spread, jiggled it to make sure it was snug. With the face shield still raised, he brought his eyes level with hers. "You okay in there?"

She was terrified, and not of the bike, not even of how tough and male Dean looked with his dark hair mussed from the helmet and his hazel eyes direct. What terrified her was the buzz in her own body. Again she thought about turning and running, but it was really too late for that now.

"This smells new," she said of the helmet.

"It is. I got red to go with your hair." She might have said red could easily clash with auburn, if he hadn't already been holding the jacket open like a gentleman, then zipping it before she could do it herself. The jacket was snug, bringing his fingers straight up her torso, but they didn't stray, just did their job and left.

Taunting, yes—but sweet, too. He made her feel like he was taking care of her, and, given that the weight of the world was on her shoulders, being taken care of was nice. He lowered her face shield, then turned and, after putting on his own helmet, straddled the bike. When he extended a hand, she took it and swung her leg over the back.

Too old? She'd be *damned* if she was that. She knew the moves, knew to put her Chucks on the foot pegs and her hands on his hips, knew to lean into corners with him and use her thighs to hold her in place. True to his word, he didn't speed—at least not until they passed through the center of Williston and hit open road, and even then she wasn't bothered. His body protected her from the force of the wind, and the Harley was surprisingly smooth. Imagining that the weight on her shoulders was lighter for the sheer unreality of the moment, she let him do his thing—until she realized that they were headed in the wrong direction.

She tapped him on the shoulder. He slowed fractionally and tipped his head.

"Where are we going?" she yelled.

"My house," came the muffled reply, followed by a resurgence of speed, and all at once she knew *exactly* where they were going, because there was only one house that Dean owned in the boonies.

Sure enough, he turned off the main road onto a side road, then again onto a rutted drive, and here the Harley wasn't so smooth. By the time it stopped, he had gone up a steep incline, and she was holding the back of his belt for dear life.

Riding on a rush of adrenaline and relief, she climbed off and removed the helmet. Her hair spilled free, its band God knew where, but she was too gripped by the house to care. It had the bones of a Victorian, but where her own spoke of age and charm, this one reeked of the dead. She had thought it spooky when he had first brought her here, and nothing she saw now changed her mind. This late in the day, with the sun low in the west, the house was all shadowed angles and peeling paint.

Dean traded her helmet for a bottle of wine. Taking two grocery bags from the Harley's trunk, he showed her up the side steps. He had gutted the kitchen, which was some improvement from the graveyard of broken-down appliances that had taken up space here before. In their place against the wall was a cluster of tools. A large worktable sat in the middle of the room. He set the bottle and bags there, then clicked on a single bare blub.

Wondering how he was going to pull off grilled trout, she folded her arms. Yes, she felt smug, because the how of it was not her worry. She was a guest. Since she was against this purchase, nothing here was her fault. She had zero responsibility.

Seeming off-balanced by her docility, Dean said in a tentative voice, "The grill's outside. And a table and lanterns."

She nodded.

He added quickly, "Just so you know, I had a geologic analysis done to pinpoint where to dig the new well to avoid rust, and the zoning board is granting an exemption from conservation land use. Rollers are coming next week to level the road." He frowned, tapped his forehead.

"Carpenter ants," she cued.

He straightened a finger. "Right. There were two nests. We destroyed them and treated everything nearby. I've already replaced the infected wood."

"Well, then," she said lightly, "you're all set."

He remained visibly wary. "You're still mad I bought it."

She had to laugh. "I'm actually not." She had seen enough gutted kitchens to be able to picture this one rebuilt, though she wasn't telling him that. Nor was she telling him that he was adorable when he was nervous, or that she felt removed from the world here. "I'm just tired and hungry and wondering if you're seriously going to be able to produce an edible meal."

That quickly, he grinned. "Just watch."

He was true to his word here, too. While she alternately explored a lean-to that held firewood and old farm tools, wandered to the edge of the woods to listen to the *yiiiip-*

yip-yip of a coyote, and returned to sit backward at the picnic table and watch Dean work, he decanted wine, made a salad, and warmed French bread on the upper shelf of a grill while the trout cooked below.

She offered to help, but he refused, even when it came to serving the food. And she was tired enough, greedy enough for care, caught up enough in a time and place that was far from reality, to let him do whatever his little heart desired.

That included cleaning up afterward, although, given the lack of a kitchen sink, the sum of the task was stuffing paper goods and plastic wineglasses in a trash bag. The air had cooled by then, and it was dark, the crescent moon a hazy smile that left the job of lighting to the lanterns' pale glow. When she heard the coyotes again, she limited her wandering to an outcropping of rocks that she had earlier skirted. Easily climbing them now, she sat facing the woods and listened. The coyotes called again, though from a distance. From an even greater distance came the drone of an airplane. Looking up, she spotted its lights against a wavering backdrop of stars. A rustle came from the woods and, farther off, the trickle of a brook that, if Dean's home inspector was correct, had overflowed its banks and flooded the house during more than one spring storm.

Thinking to shout a reminder to Dean that he would need a good drainage system *and* sump pumps, she turned to face the house. The lanterns softened its edges, but with a turret still higher than she was, it loomed dark against a darker sky. She chafed her arms, as much against the cooling air as the gloom. Spooky was putting it mildly, and that was before a large figure blotted out the lanterns and approached.

Climbing the rock, Dean settled behind her with his legs flanking hers and his hands on his thighs, arms brushing hers. She tried to transfer fear of ghosts to fear of a hungry male. But she couldn't fear Dean. Not with the way he was taking care of her, now shielding her from coyotes that were probably no threat, but who knew? Certainly not with the way he smelled of wood smoke or the warmth he brought. With so much of her life in flux, Dean was solid and physical and *there*. The real world was not.

"So, what do you think?" he asked quietly.

Like the moment, her reply was hushed. "Of the house? I think it's a big job, but it's yours, and if you want to do it, you should. I also think that what I think doesn't matter, since you've already committed to it. And," she added, layering her hands on his with a squeeze, then leaving them there because her fingers were cold and his were not, "I'm guessing you approached Jamie before you ever put money down."

He chuckled. "I did. She roughed out some sketches for me to work from." He turned his hands to surround hers. "Cold?"

"Good now. She didn't tell me."

"I told her not to. I didn't want you riled up. I figured I'd wait until I addressed some of your issues."

She angled sideways to look at him. "It shouldn't matter what I think."

He pushed her hair back with his chin. "It does."

"Why?"

"Because I trust your judgment."

"That's very sweet."

"It's very true."

His thumbs had been moving on her hands, sharing warmth as his eyes did now. Such a small movement, but oddly intimate, and Caroline didn't fight it. With the rest of her life treading water on the other side of town, she was here, with trout in her stomach, wine in her blood, and a growing curiosity.

She had barely faced forward when he circled her waist and pulled her close. Her breath caught.

"So?" he asked.

"So?" she managed. He was definitely aroused, and while the ramifications of that were clear, her curiosity kept growing.

"Do I have your approval?"

"For what?" She couldn't think straight. His forearms were inches—*inches*—from the underside of her breasts.

"Buying this place?"

"You have it," she whispered and forced herself to breathe into sound. "Grudgingly. I still wouldn't want to be alone here in the dark."

"No." He put his mouth to her ear. "I heard voices at three this morning."

She squeezed his thighs in punishment. "You're making that up."

"I am not."

"Why were you here at three in the morning?"

"I've been sleeping here."

Bracing her hands, she looked back in surprise. "On *what*?"

"A bed."

"*Where*?"

"Uh, the bedroom?" he suggested, amused.

She hadn't gone upstairs this day. Last time had been bad enough. Now, though, the idea of a bed in an otherworldly room lent itself to certain imagery.

He smiled. "Makes you think, doesn't it." Taking her head, he faced it forward and drew her back again. This time, his hands went to her shoulders, massaging in circles.

"What were the voices?" she asked, feeling those fingers dip under the edge of her blouse.

"I assume they were ghosts." With another round, then another, his fingers went deeper.

"And that doesn't make you nervous?"

His mouth touched her ear. "When was the last time you heard of a ghost doing anything violent?"

Caroline had no answer for that, and when his fingers grazed the top of her breasts and she arched to meet them, she had no answers at all—not for why this was happening now and with Dean, or for why her body craved things that two weeks ago she wouldn't have dreamed of, certainly not for who had just moaned like that.

Closing her eyes, she focused on sensation. A distant corner of her mind knew what he was doing. It was called foreplay, and it was exquisitely arousing. The anticipation of having Dean's hands—*Dean's* hands—on her breasts was stoking a startling heat.

"Tell me what you like," he said in a hoarse voice.

"I can't," she wailed with barely a breath.

"I want it to be right."

"What you're doing is right."

"What about this?" When he went all the way to her nipple, she cried out. He snatched his hand away. Laughing, she caught it and, feeling like a wild thing, pressed it to her while she scrambled not-so-gracefully around to straddle his lap.

"Now do it," she breathed against his mouth, and while she looped her arms around his neck, he explored her breasts, her belly, even the notch between her legs. And she touched him, *touched* that erection, which was all the more impressive in her hands. The fact that she wasn't embarrassed was as stunning as everything else. She didn't know this creature she had suddenly become, which was as liberating a fact as the distance from home, the wine, the dark, and Dean's obvious need.

But the creature was real. The fire inside her was real.

No nineteen-year-old virgin, she knew exactly what she wanted, and with that realization, something snapped. Suddenly, she had no patience. She needed more, needed it all.

"I want you in a bed," Dean gasped and in seconds managed to get them down from the rock. Holding her fast to his side, he crossed the grass in rapid strides and half-ran into the house and up the stairs. Ghosts? Caroline couldn't *begin* to think of ghosts with the way he was touching her, removing clothes, laying her on the bed and following her down. He took care to make sure she was ready, but she didn't need his fingers there to tell her. She felt the wetness. And she wasn't embarrassed. This was what being a woman was about. Besides, she needed him too much to be embarrassed. The creature she was—the one *he* had created—was hungry for everything she had pretty much forgotten.

Later, she would remember, time and again, that single first moment when he was fully inside. For now, it was about climbing hotter and higher until he brought her to orgasm, then let himself follow.

For a time, there in the dark of a bedroom that she would later learn had rotted walls, moldy rafters, and no furniture other than a king mattress on its frame, the only sounds were of shortened breath and stunned laughs.

"Who knew?" Dean finally asked against her hair. His voice was hoarse. "A wild woman. Where's she been all this time?"

Burrowing close, an arm across his chest, Caroline smiled. "Minding her own business. Well, at least, some woman was. I have no idea where this one came from. Actually, I do. You taunted her into existence."

"Taunted?"

"A look here, a touch there. It took you long enough to get to the main event."

"And whose fault was that? You didn't say a freaking *word*," he protested. "Did you invite me over and open the door wearing something skimpy and black? Did you promise not to sue for sexual harassment? Did you say you *wanted* this?"

"I said your kiss was too short."

"Yes. You did."

"Did you plan on this happening tonight?"

"No. I only wanted to get you away. You've been down."

"*Some* woman was down. This one's feeling pretty good."

"So," he asked cautiously, "what do you think?"

"About?"

He pinched her hip. "This. Do you still think sex is overrated?"

Tipping her head back, she met his gaze. "You're good. I have to say that."

"Good is not great."

"Tonight you were great."

"Well, *that's* a qualified endorsement."

"Once is once. Things are always great the first time."

"I'm up for a second."

"Now? You aren't." The wild woman slid a hand down his belly and, at the same time that she wondered how she could be touching *Dean* this way, discovered that he was. Up for a second. "Oh my."

"Is that a yes?"

"No. My thighs are screaming. I'd give anything for a bath."

"No bath here. No hot water here."

"I have both at my house. Take me home."

"Only if I can stay the night."

Caroline couldn't say no. By the time they were back in her Victorian, by the time he had showered and she had kicked him out of the bathroom so that she could soak alone, by the time lotion was soothing whisker burns on her breasts and the cats were ousted from the bed so that she could slip in with him—naked, because he was, and because it was still dark, and because a part of the wild woman had survived the return trip on the Harley and was still feeling bold—she wanted to sleep skin to skin. He was a quiet sleeper, breathing just shy of a snore, and he liked contact, maneuvering so that a part of him always touched her. Though she was used to sleeping alone and liked her space, much of which was now taken by his larger-than-hers body, the connection was novel enough to be pleasant.

With the summer solstice around the corner, though, dawn woke her early. She was instantly aware of Dean—could hear and smell him even before she opened her eyes—but was still startled to see his dark head on her pillow, his large body tangled in her fuchsia sheets. She might have lingered watching him, had she not needed a semblance of normalcy.

Ignoring the protest of hips, thighs, and private spots that had been stretched to the max, she slipped quietly from the sheets and wrapped herself in the towel she had dropped by the bed the night before. She tiptoed to the dresser for a tank top and shorts and, taking care to coddle a few notoriously creaky treads, went downstairs to dress. Once she had fed the cats, checked the *Gut It!* website, and taken a shawl from the kitchen hook, she carried her tea to the porch.

The air was cool, the sun bright, the tea fragrant. Sipping it slowly, she let memories of the night drift back. None were bad. Some startled her—namely, her own hunger and forwardness. But she didn't regret what she had done. Dean had satisfied her—actually, had done way more than that. She felt good. She felt feminine. Even despite that little bit of stiffness, she felt energized.

She thought about calling Annie. *So* much to tell.

But no. She wasn't ready to tell Annie what she had done, and as for what she felt, she was barely beginning to break it down. She had been someone else last night. Where that fit into the *Who Am I?* debate, she didn't know. And yet, in spite of that, in this early Thursday morning moment, she felt strong. She might have even felt *complete*, if things had been right between Jamie and her.

If she talked with anyone, it had to be Jamie.

Suddenly, doing just that seemed urgent.

Chapter Eighteen

Jamie might have woken Thursday morning with her stomach in knots if she had actually slept, but what she had done the evening before wouldn't let her. After leaving Chip's, she had driven slowly home. Determined to contain the terror she felt by acting in a deliberate and responsible way, she took her time getting Tad ready for bed, methodically read and reread him his good-night story, stroked his hair until he was deeply asleep, and all the while, she took slow breaths aimed at calming her nerves.

Leaving his room, though, she felt no different from how she had felt leaving Chip's. A truth had emerged that couldn't be ignored. Nor would it wait.

In the kitchen, she picked up her phone and called Brad. "Can you come over?" she asked softly.

"Now? I'm still at the office. There's a ton more to do here."

Much as she respected the work Brad did, time was passing. Her conscience couldn't have him choosing the office when doing the right thing meant acting now. "This is important, Brad. I'd come to you if I had a sitter, but I don't."

Her words were blunt, her tone no-nonsense. After a

moment's silence, he sighed. "I'll be there as soon as I can."

Forty-two minutes later, he pulled up at the condo. The time wasn't quite long enough to say he was making a statement, though it was plenty long enough for her to suffer. There were no second thoughts. She had to do this. But with each passing minute, her sense of dread rose. The last thing she had ever wanted was to hurt Brad. Now, she didn't see how she could avoid it.

In hindsight, she would think about the lack of a kiss when he arrived and wonder if he sensed what was coming. He wasn't angry to have been drawn from work so much as wary. He slipped his hands in his pockets, seeming determined to be cool.

She thought of gesturing him in, having him sit, maybe pouring him a glass of the Pinot he liked. But that seemed inappropriate. This wasn't a social visit. He seemed to sense that when she took up a position just inside the door. There was neither a glance beyond to see the state of her condo nor a glance toward the stairs to indicate an awareness of Tad. He stood with his glasses in place, his shirt collar open, and his eyes on her as he waited for her to speak.

For a final moment, she held her breath, knowing that once she did this, there was no going back. In that moment, she felt a last tug of conflicting emotions—loyalty and hurt, compassion and resentment, even love and dislike. Had he broken the tension with warmth of any kind, she might have reconsidered. But his aloofness validated her decision.

Carefully, she removed her diamond ring and held it out. "This isn't working. I think we both know that."

He stared at the ring, then at her face. His own was as composed as when he was with clients, but she had to believe he was feeling something inside.

"I do love you," she hurried on in an effort to soothe, "but we want different things now. You need a woman who wants those things, too."

He frowned, but remained silent, and right now that was fine. Jamie knew what to say. She had enumerated all the arguments in those forty-two minutes he had taken to arrive.

"I suppose it's good to find out before we're married," she said. "I mean, maybe there are other things we see differently, things we've just disregarded because in so many ways we're right for each other. But this is a big snag, Brad. I'd say it hit like lightning, except that would be crude, given how Dad and Jess died." She considered. "Only it did."

He didn't smile, didn't nod, didn't speak. So she said, "Remember the Logans? Theirs was one of the first jobs I did for MacAfee Homes. They spent a fortune on a tear-down and wanted a rebuild that was as big as the footprint would allow. I had just given them completed designs when he had a heart attack, and suddenly they needed a lifestyle change and wanted something more modest. Those original plans weren't good anymore. They had to be totally redrawn. That's kind of how I feel about us. The situation has changed. I'm not the same person I was when we got engaged."

"I am," he said, as if the problem were all her fault.

"Yes." She would take the blame if it made him feel better. "You are. But you don't like the person I am now."

"I didn't say that, Jamie, but there's the issue of honesty." His gray eyes were cutting. "You could have told me you were Tad's guardian."

"When? Tell me. I mean, I didn't deliberately keep it from you. I honestly never thought to announce it, because I never *dreamed* anything would come of it. You and I were barely dating when Tad was born, so was I going to warn you before we got more involved, like it was a disease? When Dad and Jess asked me, I was honored. I figured I'd eventually have kids of my own, and what was one more? I assumed that any man I wanted to marry wouldn't have a problem with it. I just didn't think about it again."

"It's the timing."

"I had no control over that."

"You could have told me right after the accident," he charged.

"You mean, like when the police were here?"

"The first I learned of it was when you were telling Maureen."

"Should I have been thinking about it before that? Should I have assumed Dad and Jess were *both* dead?" In a frustrated breath, she said, "Good God, Brad. Even if I'd told you six months ago, would you seriously have rejected me as wife material, just like that? *Please.* You would have thought the chances of Tad coming to me were as remote as I did." Her voice rose on a wave of anger. "Tad is an amazing little boy who is smart and cute and friendly and warm. He would make an incredible big brother for our kids." Brad's stony look gave her pause. "Ahhh. But he isn't yours. Is that it? Well, what if I hadn't been able to conceive? What if I had some problem—what if *you* had some problem? Are you saying that we wouldn't adopt a child? That you would not take in a child needing a good home and love him like your own if he doesn't have your blood? You never told me that."

"You never asked."

"Like you never asked if I was Tad's guardian?" she goaded. Yes, she wanted a fight. She wanted *some* show of passion from Brad. Calm and soothing were just fine until life demanded more.

She didn't get more from him, though, not at first. It occurred to her that his passivity was a form of punishment. He certainly wasn't making things easier for her. And that infuriated her all the more.

"Say something, Brad."

"What do you want me to say?" he finally charged. "I'm human. All I wanted was to have a *little* control over my life."

Confused, she shook her head. "Control? Have you been forced into something at MacAfee Homes that you don't want? Has being engaged to the granddaughter of the president of the company deprived you of freedom? Is the idea of one day heading a company so bad that—" She cut herself off. "Gah. This is going nowhere. There's no point in fighting." She held out a rigid hand. "Take the ring, Brad. We aren't a good match."

That quickly it was done. He took the ring, closed his hand, and without another word walked out the door.

Angry at Brad, shocked at herself, sad and relieved and worried—she just stood there in the front hall for a time. Eventually, she went upstairs, but she spent the night alternately hot and cold in a tangle of sheets, her mind too agitated to rest. Oh, she had done the right thing. She knew that in her heart. But for the right reasons? The ones having to do with Tad certainly were. But those to do with Chip? The idea that, even only in part, she had broken up with one man to be with another was so uncharacteristic that she felt like a stranger to herself.

By the time the sun filtered through the shutters and Tad shouted for her, she was dressed and waiting. For a long moment, she simply held him, a silent little monkey with his arms and legs wrapped around her. He had done the same thing the last two mornings, as though he knew something primal had changed in his life, didn't understand what, but needed grounding from Jamie. Much as she loved that, she needed grounding, too.

Setting him down, she grabbed the phone to text Caroline. Before she could, Caroline texted her.

It's time we talk.

Yes. Now. Her thumbs shook as she typed. *Can we come over?*

Of course. I'll make pancakes. Does Tad need milk?

Just water. Give us half an hour. She felt such relief, she could fly there.

I'll be waiting.

Eminently satisfied, Caroline pocketed the phone and stayed on the porch a bit longer enjoying her tea. When she returned to the kitchen, she sifted through a small index box for the dog-eared card her mother had passed down from *her* mother, who had printed the family pancake recipe in ancient blue ink. The recipe wasn't unique. Caroline figured an online search would turn up dozens like it. But knowing that her grandmother had created this card, that her mother had used it when Caroline was young, that Caroline had used it when Jamie was young and would use it now for Jamie's child—*Jamie's child*—made it worth the sentimental moments she spent thumbing through other cards in the box.

It wasn't until she had mixing bowl, skillet, and eggs on the counter that she remembered Dean, which meant that she was either totally brazen, entirely comfortable with him, or in full denial.

She raced up the stairs. "Dean! *Dean!*" He was sprawled facedown on her bed, dead to the world. Knowing that he was naked under the sheet—knowing exactly what his nakedness felt like against her and struck by the newness of it—she felt warmth suffuse her body into a blush. She shook one bare shoulder. "You have to get up, Dean. Now, right now. Jamie's on her way." When he opened an eye, seeming confused, she leaned in and said, "You have to *leave.*"

He finally focused and frowned. "Why?" His voice was morning rusty.

"She's coming for *breakfast.*"

"Can't I come, too?"

"No, you cannot. She's bringing Tad. *Please.* She and I have enough to talk about without this." She tugged at his arm. "You have to go now. There's no *way* the Harley would be in my driveway so early if you hadn't spent the night."

"Sure there is," he said with a lazy stretch. "Work starts early. I coulda come over."

"If you were going to work, you'd have come in the truck."

"You and I know that. She doesn't."

"Please don't argue with me right now," Caroline pleaded. "I don't want her finding you here."

"Are you ashamed of me?"

She barked out a laugh. "*That's* a joke. I'd parade you around, if it wouldn't be like rubbing her nose in my fun when she's been going through such a tough time." When she started to rise, he caught her hand.

"You had fun?"

"You know I did," she chided and, tugging free, made for the door. "But I can't have you here right now, please trust me on this. Weren't you the one who wanted me to talk with Jamie?"

"What's for breakfast?"

"Nothing for you, pancakes for Tad and her. My pancakes are beyond belief. I'll give you a rain check if you leave now." She gestured emphatically. "Up. *Please?*"

Having run out of words, she hurried down the stairs. She heard the thud of bare feet overhead as she cracked eggs, heard the shower as she whisked in flour, baking power, sugar, and salt. She melted butter in the skillet and cooked a first batch, then cooked a second with one eye on the clock—five minutes, four minutes, three minutes until Jamie was due.

"Dean!" she yelled seconds before she heard his boots. At the foot of the stairs, she raised her mouth for the quick kiss he sought. How natural it seemed, but she didn't have time to dwell on that, either.

"You owe me," he grumbled.

"I know." She pushed him to the door. "Go." She would have squirreled him out the back if there had been any other escape route for the Harley but the street. Holding her breath while he helmeted up, climbed on, and backed out—cringing as the raucous sound pierced the still of the morning—she breathed again only when the bike turned the curve at the end of the street and was gone. With a little prayer that he wouldn't pass Jamie, she hurried back to the kitchen.

Jamie was preoccupied. Along with a muddle of questions, doubts, and fear came excitement. She loved that Caroline wanted her there enough to make Great-Granny's panacea pancakes, that she wanted Tad to have them, too, and that, on some starter level at least, she had forgiven Jamie.

Right there, she had three things to be grateful for. But what she was suddenly thinking about as she backed out of the garage was the shiny red convertible in the spare bay, disappearing inch by inch as the garage door lowered. She loved that car. She hadn't planned to buy it, had actually gone shopping for a sleek two-door sedan, but one look at the convertible and something had clicked. It was flashier than any car she had ever owned, not the safest vehicle but spirited. What did that say about her—that she had a hidden wild streak, a repressed need to break out, a craving for risk?

Did she seriously *know* this person?

Roy would not have. He would have *freaked* over what his daughter was doing—and the risk she was taking with *his son*? Selfish. Shortsighted. The words echoed from their very-last-ever-on-earth talk.

But she couldn't turn back. Could. Not. Which was why she was racing across town at six thirty in the morning, while the rest of Williston was waking slowly, sipping coffee, lingering in the shower. Other than work vehicles and a lone motorcycle, her SUV had the road to itself, which meant she would get there faster. Indeed, the familiarity of turning onto Caroline's street was a lifeline. Once she parked in front of the mint-over-teal Victorian, she put Tad on her hip and hurried up the walk. The squeak of the screen was actually reassuring. And the smell of time when she stepped inside? Heaven.

"Mom?"

Caroline ran barefoot from the kitchen, stopped short, and put a hand to her heart. "Mother and child," she breathed and slowly approached. Her hair was a wavy mess, and her face blushed in a way that made her look forty, but her eyes, moist now, held adoration. Wrapping a firm arm around Jamie, she said by her ear, "We will not mention the show. It has no place in this house with us right now, okay?"

Jamie hadn't even thought about the show, and certainly couldn't think of it with Caroline's soft, woodsy scent soothing her nerves and giving her strength. "Mom," she began, drawing back, but Caroline was studying Tad.

"Oh my. A real little boy. Hey," she said softly and touched his hair. Jamie felt the warmth of the touch, but Tad just stared without blinking. "I think I know you. Aren't you Theodore MacAfee the Second?"

Those very big eyes were somber as he shook his head. "Who, then?"

"Taddy," came the baby voice.

"The Taddy who likes cats?" Caroline asked, to which he started looking around the floor, "or the Taddy who likes pancakes?"

"Pancakes, please," Jamie inserted. "I promised him we'd eat here. Mom—" She broke off when Master me-owed. Setting Tad on the floor, she waited only until he had run after the cat before turning back to her mother and holding out her left hand.

Caroline frowned. "You're shaking." She had steadied the hand with her own before she finally focused on that bare ring finger. Wide eyes flew to Jamie's.

In that instant, with this first oh-so-important disclo-sure, it was real. Jamie could barely breathe. "I returned it. Brad and I split."

"What *happened*?" Caroline whispered, but quickly caught herself. Cupping Jamie's face, she said, "First things first. I don't have a booster seat for Tad."

"He'll kneel on a chair. He looks like Dad. Do you hate him for that?"

Tad was on his haunches on the other side of the room, waiting for Master to come out from under the spindle legs of a lamp stand.

"I should," Caroline confessed, "but how to hate a child? He may have Roy's coloring, but he'll take on your expressions, and soon enough he'll look like himself. Be-sides," she gave a gritty smirk, "it's not like your father gets the last laugh. If he thought I was a withered-up old hag—"

"He didn't."

"Yes, he did. Isn't that what booting me off *Gut It!* was about?"

"You said we weren't talking about that," Jamie begged, knowing that despite this nascent reconciliation, *Gut It!* remained a huge issue. Not talking about it wouldn't make it go away, but she didn't want the intrusion of it now.

Caroline seemed to agree. She spoke more calmly. "Your father's opinion of me went way back to our marriage, so this, today, here, now, is satisfying for me. How happy do you think he is looking down from heaven to see his son at my house, chasing my cat and about to eat *my* grandmother's pancakes, cooked by me in *my* kitchen and served on a table *I* made?"

The part of Jamie that resented Roy for what he had made Caroline suffer shared her mother's satisfaction. She might have said that, if Caroline hadn't gone from bold to unsure in a breath. "I'm not equipped yet, baby. Does Tad need a bottle for his water?"

"No. He's done with bottles. Just a little water in a cup will do, since I forgot the sippy." In her rush to get out of the house, she had also left Moose, which meant she would have to go back for him before dropping Tad off, which meant she would be late for her first appointment, which she couldn't reschedule because she had back-to-backs all day, which meant she would have to postpone to another day, which wasn't good.

But she didn't care. Just didn't care. Right now, this was where she needed to be.

Her mother looked amazing—colorful, energetic, somehow soft, even when she was fired up about Roy. Not that Jamie minded the last. The anti-Roy sentiment was an ally. He would *so* disapprove of what she was doing.

Caroline took her hand and touched her ring finger much as Chip had done. The effect was totally different but no less potent. "When?"

"Last night."

"Who initiated it?"

"Me," she said, and that easily, the story unfolded. "I asked him over. He started to say he was working, but I cut him off and told him he *had* to come. I've tried to be understanding, Mom. I knew he felt wounded and left out, but finally, *finally,* we had to talk."

"About Tad?" Caroline whispered.

Jamie kept her voice low so that the child wouldn't hear. "Well, he was the catalyst. Brad can't deal with a child— doesn't *want* to deal with a child—doesn't want to deal with someone *else's* child. But Tad's mine now. This is nonnegotiable." Thinking back to the scene last night in her front hall, she was angry all over again. "Brad wants a neat little life that goes according to plan. Well, so did *I,* only that's not what I got."

Caroline touched her cheek. "I'm sorry. I know you like plans."

"But there's more, more that I didn't tell Brad," Jamie said, thinking of Chip, only Tad had returned and was looking expectantly at Caroline.

"Pancakes?" she asked him with an inviting nod, then said to Jamie, "Hold that thought," and returned to the kitchen.

Scooping the child up, Jamie followed. Once there, she set him down and opened a low cabinet. She shifted pots around until she found the one she wanted, grabbed a wooded spoon from a clay jar that held similar ancients, and showed Tad the art of drumming. "Mamie loved doing this when she was your age. See these dents? I made those." She demonstrated, handed him the spoon, and straightened. His banging was effective cover for more serious talk. "Am I a selfish person, Mom?"

Caroline was rinsing strawberries and raspberries in a colander. "For what?"

"Dumping Brad. This is a critical time for the company. Think of the meetings we've had this week. The Barths are creeping in, and we're short-handed without Dad. Brad would have grown beyond legal and moved up in time, but if he and I aren't married, there's no way he'll be CEO. Theo wouldn't want nonfamily in that position."

"Theo may not have a choice. We're running low on MacAfees." Caroline turned off the faucet and shook the colander. "Will Brad stay on now? More important, do you want him to?"

Jamie didn't know how she felt. This was all raw, and then there was the issue of Chip and what would come of that, and if something did, how comfortable Brad would feel having to see it all the time, which came back to the MacAfee Homes dilemma and whether Jamie had acted without considering the larger picture. "Do you think Brad has what it takes to be CEO?"

Caroline tipped the fruit into a bowl. "I don't know. I haven't worked with him enough."

"Then as husband material—did you like him for me? And don't say that if I was happy, that was enough. I need your honest opinion. You liked it when I got engaged, but were you thrilled?" She shook her own head in reply. "Why not?"

Easing her aside, Caroline took a jug of maple syrup from the fridge. Then she sorted through K-Cups, picking a coffee for Jamie and a tea for herself. Placing a mug on the Keurig, she made the coffee.

"Mom?" Jamie prompted. The evasion should have been answer enough, but she needed the words.

Caroline shot her a guilty glance. "Theo and Roy wanted him for you. He was preapproved, so to speak. Bitchy of me to think this, I know, but there were times when I worried that was part of his appeal."

Jamie hadn't thought of that—at least, not consciously. Considering it now, she admitted, "It probably helped. But I also did like him myself."

"Love him?"

"Yes. Just not"—she paused, struggling for the right word—"not *wildly*."

"He isn't dynamic or exciting or passionate," Caroline said in a burst, then gave a short laugh. "*That's* funny. I could never put my finger on it before. He's such a nice guy."

"But not dynamic or exciting or passionate." Chip was passionate. Jamie had seen heat in his eyes and heard need in his voice. "Am I those things, Mom? I mean, I broke my engagement at an unwise time, which is not the way I usually do things. Is what I did totally crazy?"

"Not if it's what you feel."

"You aren't shocked?"

Caroline gathered up food. "Honestly, I'm just so glad you're here that nothing much would shock me."

"What about sex?"

Her mother went still. "What about it?"

"How important is it in a relationship, really?"

Caroline blushed. "Uh, uh—hold *that* thought." Then she fled, which was the only word Jamie could use to describe the way she ducked into the parlor with breakfast. And the look of panic on her face? She had never been shy talking about sex with Jamie before.

Tad was still happily beating his pot—no attention deficit problem *there*—when Caroline returned for utensils and the fruit plates Jamie loved. Seeing the latter, Jamie teared up.

"Oh, baby."

"I'm okay. Just emotional."

"About Brad?"

"Actually," she realized and took a breath, "no. When it comes to him, I feel free. This"—she made a broad gesture to include kitchen, plates, her mother, and Tad—"this makes me emotional." Her voice broke. "It's a dream."

Caroline hugged her again, even tighter this time. Then,

plying her with plates and utensils, she saw to Tad herself—
kneeling beside him, talking softly, carrying him to the
dining room and settling him on a chair. She put a pancake on his plate and cut it up. "Syrup?" she asked Jamie.

"Oh yeah. He loves sweets." She dribbled syrup on her
own pancake, took a bite, and closed her eyes in pleasure.
The issue of Chip, sex, and her future remained, but right
now she was more aware of her past. Pancakes were her
past. So were Caroline's fruit plates and the framed Victorian lace, which looked down at her now from the nearby
wall as a patchwork of smiles. Swallowing a second bite,
she set down her fork. "I am so not good without you,
Mom. You have no idea. I've had decision after decision
to make, and it's probably been good that I've had to rely
on myself, but you have answers that might have saved me
hours—*days*—of emotional trauma. Like daycare. Dad
liked having Tad at home with Jess, but I can't be home,
and the nanny I hired didn't work out, and now that he's
in daycare, I like him there. It's totally different from what
he had before, and he's with other children."

"Which is precisely why I put you in daycare way back,"
Caroline said. "You were an only child. You needed so-
cialization."

"Did Dad like my being in daycare?"

"No. He didn't approve then and wouldn't now, but it's
no longer his decision. I know that sounds harsh, baby, but
it's true. Tad is yours. So are the decisions."

And the cleanup when things were a mess. "He's getting syrup on your table," she said as she started to rise.
Caroline's hand stayed her.

"It'll wash off."

"My condo is a wreck."

"Your condo is a thing."

With a happy sigh and a grin, Jamie scrubbed her fingers through Tad's curls. "See, Taddy? Haven't I said *that*

a gazillion times?" She sipped her coffee, thinking that half of those gazillion times had been aloud to Brad and had gone right over his head, but that was only one of many problems they'd had. "It was so weird."

"What was?"

"Last night. I'd been terrified of hurting Brad, but he was fine. Now I'm wondering whether I felt the pain and vulnerability more than he ever did. Did I imagine his sensitivity because I wanted him to be that kind of person?"

"Maybe. Maybe it was pride. Maybe he didn't want to show weakness, or, God forbid, beg for another chance."

Jamie had a different thought then and sucked in a breath. "Maybe he was relieved. Maybe he's drawn to someone else."

"Would that bother you?"

"Of course it would. We were engaged." In the next breath, she thought of Chip and was guilt-ridden. "Actually, it would make me feel better," she admitted. "I like to think our engagement wasn't working for him either. I know he's relieved about—" *Tad,* she finished with a glance. "Maybe he didn't want to be CEO either. Until the accident, that was hypothetical. Now it isn't. Maybe he's glad to be off the hook."

It was only speculation, though, and had little to do with who or what *she* was. Chip was never far from her mind. She didn't understand it. In high school, they had been at opposite ends of the social spectrum. He had a reputation for being fast. She was sure he'd slept around. Not her. But she couldn't think about much else now.

"So," she tried again, needing to get to it. "About sex."

Caroline set down the cup. "Sex? Hmm. Oh dear, let me get something for Tad's hands and face. He seems to be done." With a scrape of her chair, she rose and left the room.

Jamie leaned toward Tad. "Was that yummy?"

"Yummmmy."

"I loved pancakes when I was your age, and Nana Caro makes the best. *Mom?*" she called, so happy to be a daughter again.

"Yes?"

But Jamie suddenly spotted the fruit bowl. "Oh no," she said in mock horror, "we forgot raspberries." She spooned up a bunch. "Strawberries, too?"

"Noooo." He picked up a raspberry. There were six. Jamie was wondering how long he would take to eat them, and what else might hold his attention while she talked with her mother, when Caroline returned with a damp dishcloth, a pad of paper, and a pencil. The cloth cleaned up syrup; the paper and pencil bought time.

"I need crayons here," Caroline remarked. "Lead is lethal."

"It's okay. Pencils are made of graphite. But we're watching him. He won't put it in his mouth. What should he call you? I don't see you as a Grandma."

Caroline seemed startled. "Uh, no. Me, neither."

"Caro would be cute, only I want him to call you something no one else does. When I was talking with him a second ago, I said Nana Caro."

"Nana Caro. I like that. It feels . . . fresh."

Jamie sensed she had been about to say "young" but hadn't wanted to touch on age again, and Jamie was with her on that. *Gut It!* lay in wait, just beneath the surface but totally secondary to why she had come. "So, can we talk about sex?"

"Shhhh." Caroline hitched her chin toward the boy.

"Mom," Jamie begged, albeit in a hushed voice, "he doesn't know what sex is. I am not getting graphic, but I need to talk about this, and I have no one else."

"It could be," Caroline said, sounding baffled, "that I'm not the best one to ask."

Because she hadn't had sex in a while? But Jamie's questions were hypothetical. "What if I said it was boring with Brad? What if I said I didn't look at him and start to tremble?" Caroline's eyes went wide. "What?"

"Nothing." But she was blushing. "I'm good."

"Are you *embarrassed*?"

"No." She tipped up her chin. "I am not embarrassed. If Brad doesn't make you tremble, I'd say it's another piece to the puzzle of why you and Brad weren't good together."

"But how important a piece is it? A relationship can't exist on sex alone. Am I crazy to throw away a guy who may be good in every other way?"

"But he wasn't," Caroline pointed out with a nod at Tad.

"He might have eventually come around on that." Jamie grunted. "Or so I kept telling myself, stupid me. But I need to know about the other."

"Sex."

"Am I wrong to want more?"

Caroline considered. "No."

"How important is chemistry? Am I a sexual creature first? Second? Third? What proportion of a relationship should be dominated by sex?"

Her mother laughed. "Oh, baby. It isn't about proportions. Sex means more to some people than to others, and its importance in a relationship isn't static. It changes with life. And with time."

"I understand that, but shouldn't it at least start off pretty great? If it doesn't, what hope is there? I want it to be great, Mom. I want to look at a guy and melt."

Caroline was suddenly far away, dreamy almost, and, for the first time, Jamie realized she must have had lovers other than Roy. Her mother was sexy in an organic way, and her work constantly exposed her to men. As many times as she had sworn that she and Roy were in love when

Jamie was conceived, Jamie doubted the sex had been great. Roy was too into Roy. History had borne that out.

Cautiously, Caroline asked, "Was it never that way with Brad?"

"I thought it would be, because he really is sweet, and he wanted to please me. But sex with him was typical of our relationship—sedate and comfortable and planned. Even when he came—" She winced and waved a hand. "Forget I said that." Instead, she tried to articulate what she had felt in those moments with Chip. "Maybe I don't want it to be intellectual. Maybe I want it to be impulsive and hot. What does that say about me?"

Caroline was slow to answer, then oddly puzzled. "It might say that you're reacting to your father's early death."

"I don't think it's that."

"Have you always wanted more than Brad offered?"

"I wasn't aware that there *was* more." Jamie hesitated. How much to say? It could all amount to nothing. Right now, though, it was vividly real, and, even aside from re-building trust, she wanted Caroline's approval. "I met someone."

"Someone?"

"Chip Kobik."

Caroline's face was blank at first. Then her brows rose in surprise. "The hockey player?"

"Not anymore. Well, he runs a summer hockey camp for kids, but mostly he teaches PE at Emory, and he's a single dad. We met on the playground last week."

"Last *week*."

"I know. It's wild." A normal person didn't meet some-one one week and let it change her life the next. Unless she believed in love at first sight. Which was *really* push-ing it. "I mean, he is so not my type—or he wasn't, but he's different now. He's alone and I'm alone—I mean, I really am, Mom, because I haven't had Brad and I haven't had you—and I don't mean that as criticism, because I understand why you think I had a hand in what Claire did, but with Dad gone, if I'm choosing between hosting the show and being a mom, there's no choice, and if Claire—"

Caroline's fingers covered her mouth; suggestive eyes went to Tad. He had stopped scribbling. Large brown eyes were staring at Jamie in mild alarm.

"Well," Jamie drawled for his sake when Caroline's hand fell away, "*that* was a trip. Mamie got totally off-subject. What are you drawing, monkey?" She left her seat to study a havoc of lines. "That's so pretty!"

"At least he holds the pencil right," Caroline said appreciatively. "You were slow when it came to fine motor skills."

"Which is why I took up tennis." She scanned the coffee tables. "Do you have any old magazines you don't mind losing?"

"Would a catalog work?"

"Perfect. He decimated my *Architectural Records*." Moments later, with Tad on the floor engrossed in a tool catalogue ("Wow, Taddy, I'll bet Handy Manny uses this!") and Jamie hip to hip with Caroline on the love seat, she was calmer. "What are we going to do about *Gut It!?*"

"The show's on hiatus."

"Claire will be after me to do advance work."

"I'm already on it, so it'll be done for you if you host."

"She won't give up. She'll play dirty."

"We'll play dirty back." Caroline linked their hands. "But we said we wouldn't talk about *Gut It!* Tell me more about Chip."

Jamie didn't need forcing. "He's been amazingly helpful, and I don't just mean giving me lists of resources. He actually, physically, went with me to the daycare center to get Tad enrolled. His son is a year older than Tad, and he's a great dad. He's fun to be with and easy to talk to, and when he looks at me"—she drew in a shuddering breath—"it's *there,* Mom, everything I never had with Brad."

"When all did this *happen*?"

"Yesterday, and I know what you're thinking," she added quickly, "and you're right. I barely know the guy. But it's electric."

"Does he feel it, too?"

Piercing blue eyes. A tight jaw. *Tell me to stop, Jamie.*

"Oh, yeah. So maybe I like him because he's good with Tad or because he has answers I need or because he's a bad boy, or was, which makes him a little dangerous, and I've never *remotely* done dangerous. But can you fake chemistry? Isn't it either there or not?"

Caroline was so long thinking about this that Jamie wondered again about other men in her mother's life. She was about to ask when a second hand closed around hers and squeezed. "No, you can't fake it. But it may be dormant, like there without your realizing. If you're focused on other things and aren't looking—"

"I *wasn't* looking. I swear, I wasn't. I've never seen myself as that kind of person."

"Me either."

"My life has radically changed in two weeks' time. I don't know who I am anymore. How do I define myself? What do I *do*?"

"I haven't a clue."

"You have to."

A gentle laugh. "Why is that?"

"Because I need advice."

Caroline's laughter was higher this time. "What if I said that the last two weeks have been cataclysmic for me, too, and that my self-image has been turned upside down, so I don't know who I am either?"

Even without direct accusation, Jamie knew she was

responsible for much of her mother's angst. "I'm not hosting the show, Mom. That's my final answer. Maybe I would have wanted it once, but no more. It's too contentious. And I seriously, *seriously* do not have the time." That said, she checked the clock on her phone. "I have to go."

"Will you come again soon?"

"How about, oh, um, eight-point-five hours from now?" Jamie said with a snicker. In the next breath, she was self-conscious. "No. Maybe not."

"You want to see Chip."

"He calls himself Charlie. That's pretty much the only thing I have trouble with when it comes to him. And yes. I want to see him." Which was why she had so badly needed Caroline. "Am I awful for that?"

"If you're awful, I'm awful."

"Then you don't hate me for going from Brad to Chip so fast?"

"How can I judge you?"

"I need your *approval,* Mom."

"Well then, oooo-kay." She considered for another minute before taking a breath and letting loose an explosion of words. "Passion can take us by surprise, as in hitting suddenly, but maybe that isn't a bad thing. I'm thinking we can't overintellectualize life. Sex may be more important than some of us even *know,* because situations change, and life is a learning experience. Maybe your father's death is driving us, but if it's telling us that life is short, it's right. If we discover something better than we had, does it matter how we got there?"

"Is that an endorsement?"

"Um, yes, I guess it is. But be careful, baby," she added on a note of caution, "I don't want you hurt. And it isn't just you anymore. Now it's Tad, too."

Chapter Nineteen

Brad must have asked the receptionist to buzz him the instant Jamie arrived, because he was at her desk minutes later, leaning over her to talk with the same outward calm he would have shown any other day at work. He looked tired, as if he had barely slept. Heart heavy, she waited for him to say that they were acting too quickly, that he didn't want to break up, that he couldn't envision a future without her in his life. In fact, his glasses were straight, his eyes their usual light gray, his voice low and close. But his words were something else.

"I've thought this through," he said, intimate and low. "I want to hold off on making a formal announcement. Have you told anyone?"

Not regret, then. Just stark, cold practicality.

It was for the best, Jamie knew. Still, she was stung by how wrong she had been about Brad. "Only my mother."

"I doubt she was upset. Did you tell Theo?"

"Not yet. What do you mean, 'I doubt she was upset'?"

"It doesn't matter. It's over. But please don't tell anyone else. There's no need yet."

Jamie certainly hadn't planned on sending an e-announcement. Still, when they had first become engaged, word had spread on its own. "I'm not wearing my ring," she murmured. "People will notice."

"You can say you forgot to put it on."

"What about tomorrow? Or next week?"

"By then, I'll know what I'm doing."

That gave her pause. "What do you mean?"

Behind his glasses, his eyes were unblinking. "I've always had offers from other companies."

She was startled, then annoyed. "You never told me," she had to say, because he had made such a big deal the night before about her not telling him about Tad.

"I didn't tell you," he said, "because they were irrelevant at the time, but they aren't anymore. One's with a firm in Minnesota. I like the partners."

"You were entertaining job offers from out of state?" She could understand that he would be recruited by local companies he met through MacAfee Homes, but something out of state would suggest he had been actively soliciting jobs.

He didn't deny it. "I've often thought I'd like to go home."

"You never told me that." She had broken up with Brad as soon as she recognized her feelings for Chip. To learn that he had been looking elsewhere while they were engaged, knowing she was tied to MacAfee Homes, knowing that her work, family, and hometown were here, knowing that Theo and Roy were counting on his taking over one day—she was *stunned*. "You said you didn't want to be in the same city as your parents. You said you didn't *like* Minneapolis."

"And I believed it, but when I thought about it last night, I realized I had to make myself dislike Minneapolis so I could like Boston. The truth is, I'm a midwesterner. Minneapolis looks pretty good to me right now."

He was wounded and lashing out. That was the only

explanation Jamie could find. She had been engaged to marry the man. She had always thought him down to earth and totally transparent.

Only it sounded like he'd had this at the back of his mind for a while, like Plan B had been there all along on the chance that Plan A was nixed.

For a split second, she was hurt. In that second, she felt a whole new swell of anger, betrayal, dismay, not the least of it being how easily he had moved on.

But the second passed, and reality returned. She had moved on, too. Her heart wasn't here. And as she studied this detached Brad—she actually moved her desk chair farther from him—she felt better and better. She had believed him vulnerable for so long that the idea of his being strong and filled with purpose was a huge relief.

"Oh. Okay. I'm glad," she said and meant it. She had loved him, perhaps not the right way for marriage, but feelings didn't just vanish.

"So you won't tell anyone yet?"

There she balked. Feelings were one thing, principle something else. Brad might be moving on from MacAfee Homes, but she wasn't. She had her own credibility to protect. "I can't promise it. The best I can do, if someone asks, is to say we're on hold until things sort themselves out from Roy's death."

He studied her with what might have been pique before producing a sad smile. "You're tough."

"Apparently," she replied, sad as well, "so are you."

She should have known it, of course—should have known that there was a fine line between even-tempered and cool. What kind of man professed to want a family but couldn't open his heart to a two-year-old orphan who was his future wife's half brother and, PS, the son of a man who had given him so much and was now dead?

She should have known that a relationship so slow to

develop might, in fact, be more convenient than heartfelt.
And that two people coming from such different places
might just be *too* different.

Whatever, he seemed so comfortable now with his in-
dependence that she stopped worrying about him, especially when greater worries came a short time later in a
phone call from Claire. "Does the name Barth ring a
bell? . . . What do you know about the company? . . . Do
you personally know anyone there?" Apparently, one of
the Barths had contacted her about doing a season of
Gut It!

Jamie was horrified. "A *season*?"

"Not this fall or spring, but maybe in a year. I checked
them out. They're well regarded."

"But *Gut It!* has always been a MacAfee show. Are
you thinking of switching to an entirely new cast? Because of the *hosting* issue?" She found it unthinkable,
both change and cause.

"No. This goes beyond that. Alternating crews may be
another way of keeping things fresh. There would be continuity, since the Barths are in Williston, too."

"They're not here. Not like we are. Besides, part of the
appeal of *Gut It!* is that we're women. They aren't."

"Well, that's a hook that could work to our benefit. It
could be a competition between the sexes. Viewers could
even vote on their favorite crews. What do you think?"

"I think it's *awful*," Jamie cried, but Claire was un-
ruffled.

"It's certainly something to consider if you don't want
to host. Okay. I just wanted to mention it. Call me when
you're up to it, so that we can lock things in."

Moments after ending the call, Jamie was on the phone
with Caroline. "It's a threat, baby," she soothed, sounding
sensible and calm. "She's trying to intimidate us."

"With Dad not two weeks dead?"

"Claire wants what she wants when she wants it. That's part of what makes her good on the set."

"Well, I'm not hosting. Period."

"You'd be a good host."

"Not now."

"What if the choice is between your hosting or our losing the show?"

"Hosting is *your* job."

"Yes," Caroline said firmly, "and I do not like someone saying I'm too old to do it. But we're not the bank, and if the bank is calling the shots, we may be stuck."

The bank? Jamie kept coming back to a single person. "It's about power for Claire."

"Maybe," Caroline agreed. "Maybe she's getting pressure from someone above. It could be political, like she botched some other project and fears for her job if she can't swing this change."

Jamie was amazed that her mother could be so casual, given how she had been screwed. "But aren't you *angry*?"

"Only when I let myself really think about why I'm losing something I love. I'm trying not to do that, Jamie. I'm trying to focus on other things I love, one of which is spending time with my daughter. And with her little boy. *And* in Toys "R" Us just now."

"You didn't."

"I did. Dean and I were doing research in Warrenville." That was the site of the fall show. "Claire would die if she knew, but whichever one of us hosts will need to know more about the town. Remember how tough it was the first few seasons when people had no clue what we were? Now they fall over themselves wanting to help, even with Dean looking slightly disreputable."

Hearing an odd fondness, Jamie said, "You used to hate that."

There was a pause, then an indulgent sigh. "So I did.

But that look can be a turn-on. People who watch *Gut It!* know Dean and love him, but trust me, baby, they wouldn't open their hearts to any of the Barths that way. Claire's done us a favor by tipping us off about them. I'll let Linda know. She's connected. She'll do her best to shut them out." The more Jamie listened, the more she relaxed. "So, anyway, when we passed Toys "R" Us on the way home, I made Dean stop."

Jamie tried to picture it, but the truth was, she hadn't dreamed this far. Having Caroline buy toys for her child was as new a concept as Jamie's having a child at all. "Were you bad?"

"Awful. Dean was worse. I was picking up practical things, like sippy cups and toddler utensils and crayons and a plastic pool. He got toys. He said he knows little boys better than me. He's probably right." She paused. "Have you seen Brad?"

Warmed that Caroline was so accepting of Tad, Jamie was light-hearted. "Yes. No problem there. He's moved on."

"That easily?"

"I know. Seriously scary."

"Seriously upsetting."

"No. I'm relieved."

"Because of Chip?"

"Because the relationship was wrong. The scary part is my not seeing that. Brad doesn't want me telling anyone yet, not even Theo, but he'll be leaving the company. Will that be a problem?" Caroline did seem to be the one to ask, the one in the know, the one closest to Theo.

"*Definitely* leaving?"

"Oh yeah. Amazing, isn't it? He says he wants to go back to Minneapolis, which is the last thing I would've thought, which goes to show how much I did not know this guy. Theo won't be happy with me."

"I can handle Theo," Caroline assured her. "That's one advantage of being bumped up into the C-suite." She paused before asking in a gentler voice, "Does Chip know your engagement's off?"

"Not yet. He's at school till three."

"Jamie . . ." A warning.

"Caution. I know."

Caution haunted Jamie as the afternoon passed. Between meeting on-site with one homeowner and talking on the phone with two others, it occurred to her that she might have misread things and imagined something more than momentary lust on Chip's part. When that discouraged her, she pulled up her dream file, which contained whimsical plans for the Weymouth property. She added an arbor to the community amenities, had the computer insert wisteria, a few grapes, even a wedding reception. The last was telling. She hadn't been able to plan her own wedding. Caroline was right. Subconscious reasoning must have been at work.

And now? Caution meant leaving nothing to the subconscious, which meant understanding that Chip might have decided she wasn't his type at all, and that other than meeting at the playground, he didn't want to be involved with a single mom, which was likely the responsible thing, the *grown-up* thing.

Still, her excitement grew as the afternoon passed. It helped that Tad's day had been better—no crying jags and a nice long nap, his teacher reported. He had finger-painted Jamie a beautiful piece of art and chattered about it during the drive home. The chattering actually surprised her. Two days in daycare seemed to have jump-started his speech. Much of what he said was unintelligible, but his enthusiasm was catching. In that spirit, Jamie could always give an excited *Really?* or *That's so good, Taddy,* or *I love it!*

And she chattered right back at him—she'd read a study during lunch about how toddlers benefited from hearing complete sentences with good grammar.

Of course, her own talking might have been from nerves.

Was from nerves.

Back at the condo, she changed from skirt, blouse, and heels to T-shirt, shorts and flip-flops. Once Tad had snacked and pooped, and the clock reached five, she packed him back in the car and drove to the playground.

They were there. At the swings, Chip pushing Buddy at the same time that he coached, "Pump! That's it, Bud, use the legs." Tad ran toward them as if he knew the drill, his head down, arms and legs going for speed. Jamie followed more sedately, reliving every fear that what she had assumed to be mutual was not.

One look at the vivid blue eyes that watched her approach, though, and she knew she hadn't been wrong. Suddenly shy, she simply smiled and said, "Hey."

"Hey," he said with an answering smile. He gave his son a push, then caught up Tad, lowered him into the bucket, and got him swinging. He easily handled both buckets, with his wide arm span. "I wasn't sure you'd come."

"It's hell hour." The term held new meaning now; the temptation to be with Chip was greater than ever. *Caution,* she reminded herself and swallowed. "How was your day?"

"Challenging." He gave another two pushes, darting looks at her between. "Less than a week until summer break, and the kids are ready. They were antsy as hell." He looked her over. "I wasn't much better than they were today. Kept thinking about you." His gaze stuck on her hand. "Where's your ring?"

No one at work had asked that. Not one single person. They simply assumed she was with Brad, ring or no.

"Gone." He looked at her quizzically. "I broke my engagement."

"For me?" he asked with endearing excitement.

"For me. He and I had other issues, but once I realized I was drawn to you, I couldn't let it go on."

He smirked. "'Drawn' to is putting it mildly. At least on my side." He kept double-handing the swings.

"Mine, too."

He shot her a wary look. "I may be a lousy bet."

"And I'm not? I haven't ever done anything remotely like this."

"You're a MacAfee, I'm a Kobik. You're Phi Beta Kappa, I'm a party animal—"

"Am?"

"Was, but still, you're a TV star, I'm a gym teacher. You can do better than me."

"How do *you* know?" she asked with enough indignation to shut him up.

She stood close beside him, acutely aware of his long body flexing and reflexing as he pushed, and for several minutes, there was only the *whoosh* of the swings, the laughter of two little girls playing princess on the adjacent jungle gym, and the occasional "*Higher!*" from Buddy. When the latter became demands for the sandbox, they made the switch.

Then they sat side by side on a nearby bench, leaning forward, each with elbows on knees and fingers laced. Their thighs—his muscled and hair-spattered, hers lean and clear—were inches apart, yet the heat was enough to make her tremble.

When he muttered, "I need to touch you," she went up in flames.

She couldn't find breath enough to speak, she was shaking so inside. The best she could do was to lean that little distance closer until skin met skin.

Moaning, he shot her a sizzling look, then hollered at the boys, "Anyone in that sandbox hungry?"

"Me!" shouted Buddy and scrambled out of the sand. Tad imitated both the shout and the scrambling exit.

"Is pizza pickup on the way home okay?" Chip asked Jamie.

"Perfect." Anything would be. She was so not thinking about food, but there were the boys to consider, and Chip was much better than she was that way.

She followed the Honda to the pizza shop, then to his house. Once inside, she helped set out plates, napkins, and glasses—tonight Fred and Barney for the boys, no choices there. Other than catching the pocket of her shorts on a drawer pull, which she couldn't have done a second time if she'd tried, she breezed around his kitchen. Working together, they quickly joined the boys in the breakfast nook.

Did Jamie know what she ate? No. Nor did she know what she said, though she kept up her part, dovetailing with Chip through a running conversation designed to include the boys. All the while, if she wasn't looking at Chip's hands, she was looking at his mouth, or his once-broken nose, or the shadow on his jaw. Everything about him was forcefully male, including, once dinner was done, the commanding voice that got the boys into the living room to watch Diego rescue dinosaurs.

"You guys stay here while Jamie and I clean up," he said with commendable nonchalance and, returning to the kitchen, promptly backed Jamie up to the sink. Framing her face with both hands, he tipped it up and held it steady, and a good thing that was. His kiss was hungry, slanting one way, then the other, using tongue, teeth, and lips in the undisciplined way of the starving—until Jamie was wild with need.

"Okay?" he whispered against her mouth. She had

barely begun to nod when his hands were under her tee, and while he pushed up her bra and thumbed her nipples, he kissed her again. This time it was all tongue, provocative and deep.

Jamie had been fisting his shirt, then rubbing her palms over his chest, but she needed more. The thrust of his hips drove her. Frantic, she breached the waist of his sports shorts and found him with both hands. He was so magnificently erect that she gasped.

"Nnnnnn," he groaned into her mouth. Then he bodily lifted her, guiding her legs around his waist, so that he was right where she needed him to be, or almost. Having clothes in the way didn't work.

Breathing hard, he put his forehead to hers. "Buddy has a bunk bed. Can Tad sleep on the bottom?"

"He'll have to," Jamie said with a low laugh, because there was no way she was returning to her condo without having Chip inside her first, and there was no way that could happen until the boys were down for the night.

"Okay." He seemed in pain. "Okay." He sounded determined. "I'm a lousy dad for having pizza too often and for not knowing what in the hell we were saying to them at dinner and for sticking them in front of the TV while we do this, but right now I'm going to redeem myself by cleaning up here and then running their bath."

With measured movements, he set her on the counter. Determined to be similarly disciplined, she slid forward and promptly overshot the edge. She would have tumbled if he hadn't caught her, but he was kind enough not to say that. Without a word, he crushed the empty pizza box and put it aside, then began to load the dishwasher as she ferried things from table to sink.

"Do you think it's okay for Tad to be sleeping somewhere different again?" she whispered as they corralled the boys upstairs for a bath.

He began filling the tub. "I don't know, but I can't think of another option."

She couldn't either, and Lord knew she had tried to find one. She tried once more as she retrieved Moose and the diaper bag from downstairs, but she didn't have a sitter who would come instantly and stay late on a Thursday night, and she certainly couldn't ask Caroline. Caroline would talk about caution, but Jamie's body wouldn't listen.

"Let's see how he does," Chip said when she returned. "We'll only be two doors down."

Two doors down. In his bedroom. In his bed. Naked.

Hit with another flare of heat in her belly, she rocked lightly back and forth as she knelt by the tub, and though there was some foreplay—*way* wrong word—with a dozen rubber dinosaurs, they quickly got down to soaping the boys. She did Tad. Chip did Buddy. There was conversation in which Jamie did participate, though she didn't retain any more of what was said than Chip claimed to have taken in at supper. She did read the boys a story. It seemed only right to do that. She sat on the lower bunk with Tad tucked against her from the start, and though Buddy kept an initial distance, by the time Peter Pan backed Captain Hook off the plank and into the water, where the tick-tocking croc awaited, he was sitting nearly as close as Tad.

Chip sat cross-legged on the floor, a distraction there. But he got to his feet—bare, lean, masculine feet—as soon as the story was done, nixed Buddy's request for a second, and hoisted him up over the safety rail and into the top bunk. There were kisses, instructions, promises, and good nights. Moments later, Jamie and Chip stood with their backs to the wall just outside the room.

Chip whispered, "He'll come down the ladder at least once for another animal." He took her hand. She could barely think over the thunder of her pulse and the pooling of heat in her body, certainly couldn't make out the low murmuring in the bedroom, but Chip did. "Giving Tad something," he whispered. "Likely a teddy."

Jamie wanted to say what a sweet child Buddy was, but Chip had swung around to press her into the wall and capture her mouth. Clearly still listening, he kissed her quietly, lips sliding along her neck and down to her chest. He paused when a sound came from the boys. Jamie felt his ragged breath and tried to tame the thud of her heart, but forget that. His mouth was warm on her skin and so close to her breasts that her insides sizzled.

She dragged him up by the hair. "I *need*," she whispered in desperation, and still he waited another one, two, three minutes, rubbing against her in the most subtle undulation as those blue eyes seared hers. When no further sound came, he lifted her as he had done in the kitchen and carried her into his bedroom with her legs wrapped around his waist.

Freeing one hand to close the door, he lowered her to the bed and followed her down, and, that quickly, restraint vanished. His hands were everywhere, fighting with hers to remove clothes, touch what was bared, and see each part between kisses. It was frenzied, but not without care. As awed as she was by his size and by the rough texture of his skin, there was an answering wonder in his hands as they moved over her body.

His gentleness undid her. She was so ready for him that her body was weeping with need, but when he rose above her and thrust deep, she cried out. The fullness was beyond anything she had ever known, a sense of completion that brought even greater hunger. In a tangle of arms and legs, they rolled over, then over again, seeming to share the same need to feel more, deeper, *harder,* and when they came, it was in quick succession, overlapping, endless.

He landed on top, but when he made to roll off, she held him still. "Don't."

"I'm too heavy."

"You feel good." She loved his solidity, loved the musky scent of his skin and the way the late-day sun glanced off one broad shoulder. As her breathing leveled, though, a germ of responsibility returned and, conscience-stricken, she sought his eyes—blue eyes that looked down at her with satisfaction, admiration, and such incredible warmth that she forgot what she was going to say.

"Taddy," he prompted gently.

"He's not used to a bed," she said in a rush before she lost it again. They had padded the floor with cushions, but still he was used to having sides and would be afraid if he fell. "Will we hear if he cries?"

Holding her gaze, he stretched one long arm toward the nightstand. There was a click, then the whispery static of a monitor. When that long arm returned, it began to explore—and, oh, she'd been wrong about not wanting him to move. When he slid lower, his mouth did things to her she hadn't dreamed it could. And how his hands held her? And his words of arousal and praise? The pleasure was unfathomable. When she came, she sobbed with the intensity of it. She might have been embarrassed if his throaty cry hadn't quickly followed. He had waited for her, she realized. Both times, he had needed her to climax first.

It was a while before her body calmed, and even then, with his arms locking her to his side, she couldn't move far, not that she wanted to. There was too much to see. In the dying sun, he was positively golden—strong facial planes, wide shoulders tapering over a firm chest to a lean waist. He was athletic, but nowhere near as bulky as he must have been once. She trailed a hand through the whorls of dark hair that spread wide before arrowing down his torso to his groin.

He caught her hand and, carrying it to his mouth, opened her fingers and slowly kissed her palm. The gesture was unbelievably sweet, particularly when he flattened her hand over his heart and said in a voice that was husky and real, "You are my dream."

Her heart caught. "I'd say you're mine, too," she whispered, "only I didn't know I *could* dream this. It's crazy."

"Not crazy." The clarity of his eyes swore to it. "Just sudden. Let's get married."

She grinned. "Okay. When?"

"This weekend."

"Perfect," she said. "Makes total sense." It was way *way* crazy. "We've never been to a restaurant together, never celebrated a holiday together, never talked about what we want for our boys in two or five or eight years, never discussed work, like what we do in a day, never even met each other's families—"

He stopped her mouth with gentle-giant fingers. "Don't overintellectualize this, honey. Just feel."

Intellectualizing versus feeling. It was a potent choice for someone whose life had been dominated by deliberate thought—at least, before Chip. Since meeting him, it seemed, feeling had been major. Still, she heard her father's words and felt chastened.

"I'm trying to think like a grown-up."

"We are," he said in a measured voice. "But things happen—like death, like instant parenthood. I'm thirty-three. There are times when my knees don't work and my past makes me old, but I *see* better than I ever did, and I know what I want. Besides"—he gave a half-smile—"I did meet your father, more than once. He used to come up to me at Fiona's to talk sports. I'm sorry he's dead, Jamie."

"So am I." With each day that passed, she remembered more of the good and less of the bad. "There is an irony, you know." When he raised questioning brows, she said,

"If it hadn't been for that car accident, we wouldn't be here now. If I hadn't inherited Tad, I wouldn't have been a basket case at the playground that day, you wouldn't have rescued me, we wouldn't have shared the parent thing and dealt with lice and had sex." She considered. "Dad would like you."

He made a dry sound. "You think? Talking sports with an ex-jock is one thing, letting one marry your daughter is something else."

She studied his face. "Are you serious about that?"

"Getting married? Completely."

"How can we? We just met."

"Only in the most narrow sense. Big picture, we've known each other for years. We're both Williston—grew up here, went to school here. We work here, shop in the same stores, know the same people."

Jamie was desperate enough to rationalize along with him. "Maybe we were totally aware of each other in high school and didn't know it. Maybe we were attracted back then. Maybe we were imaginary lovers. Did you dream about me back then?"

"I didn't dare. You were a MacAfee. Did you dream about me?"

"I didn't dare. You were too cool. I'm not sure I'd have known what to say to you if we'd ever come face-to-face. I don't even know what to call you now. I can't get used to Charlie."

His handsome mouth curved up. "Chip is fine."

Distracted, she touched a tiny white scar at the corner of his upper lip. "You don't have many of these. Aren't hockey players supposed to be missing teeth?"

He chuckled. "Face masks and mouth guards work when you use them. I got this baby playing street hockey when I was eight."

"Was it fun, playing street hockey?"

"Very. There was a whole group of us. I still see a lot of the guys."

"I'm envious. Tennis was solitary. But I can't call you Chip. You hate that name."

"It's different coming from you. Kind of unites past and present."

He was so easygoing, so sensible. She might have remarked on that if the monitor hadn't made a sudden noise. She froze, listening.

"It's Buddy," Chip murmured. "He's a noisy sleeper. Give him a minute."

That was exactly how long it took for silence to return, but for Jamie, the brush with reality lingered. "Being responsible for a child is huge. Whatever we do, it isn't just us." Caroline had said that, but Jamie felt it firsthand now. Marrying Chip on impulse was totally off the wall, even more frightening than stashing Tad in a strange bed so that she could have sex.

Have sex? Make love? If she was *feeling,* as Chip wanted, given the richness and depth of what they had just done, it was the latter. Still. "I've never been as impulsive as this."

"Me neither."

She felt a stab of self-doubt. "You've been with ten times as many women as I've ever had as friends."

"*Big* exaggeration."

"You know what I mean. Women chase professional athletes."

"They're called puck bunnies, and there weren't that many for me. For the record, I've never been with a woman like this."

"You mean totally crazy with two children down the hall?"

"I mean *meaningful.* I mean thinking about what I'm feeling and being humbled by it. Are you on birth control?"

"Yes, pills. 'Humbled' how?"

"Knowing you're a gift I may not deserve. I want more kids."

"So do I," she said with fervor. Brad had always limited it, another SLOW sign she should have seen. "I want *lots*."

"See, there's another thing we share." And it was like he was in her mind. "What happened with your fiancé?"

She returned her cheek to his chest. "He only wanted two kids."

"Tell me about him."

"Not in this bed."

Gentle hands raised her head. His eyes were positively cerulean, earnest and clear. "I need to know, Jamie. My heart's at stake here. Are you and he really over, or are you just taking a break?"

She wanted to be offended. But how to be that in the echo of *my heart's at stake here*? Besides, he was only asking what any normal man would wonder. For all their talk about marriage and kids, they didn't know each other.

Wanting to change that, she sat up and wrapped a corner of the sheet over her breasts. "For the record, Checker Chip, I would never, *never* have been with you if Brad and I weren't completely done. It probably ended the day my father died, only I didn't see the writing on the wall until I wanted you so much. I'm actually amazed Brad and I lasted as long as we did. At the first sign of trouble . . ." Her fingers exploded into the air from a fist.

"Is it a problem that he's part of the business?"

"Only short-term. He's leaving. We'll hire another lawyer." She considered. "His being with the company may actually have been why we got engaged. I mean, he's a nice guy in every respect, but the office was watching. It became a game. Once we were dating, getting engaged was the next step." She reflected. "I couldn't get myself to plan a wedding. My mom thought I was afraid to commit because my parents' marriage failed, but I think it was because I must have known deep down he wasn't the one. We come from different places, Brad and I."

"Maybe you and me, too," Chip cautioned. "You're a MacAfee."

"Don't keep saying that."

"But it's true. You're out of my league."

As often as she had seen, or imagined seeing, vulnerability in Brad, what she saw on Chip's face rang true. There was nothing innocent and pure about Chip. She knew his past. But it didn't make a bit of difference.

No. That was wrong. His past gave him depth, which made him more attractive to her.

Rocking forward on her knees, she pressed a hand to his mouth and whispered, "We are *so* in the same league. I feel connected to you like I've never felt to anyone else." And completely comfortable, though he was sprawled naked on top of the sheets and she had her legs folded in a nonladylike way. When an inner stirring flared, she remembered the caution thing and sputtered a laugh.

"What?" he asked.

"All last night and today, I told myself to go slow. Like that was possible. What will Buddy say if he finds me here in the morning?"

"I don't know. It's never happened before. There's no way I would have had a woman in here with Buddy around."

Yet here Jamie was.

"Does that scare you?" he asked.

Scare. Funny. Had Chip Kobik looked at her back in high school, she'd have run in the other direction. *Anything* about him would have scared her, from his size to his looks to his radiating sexual appeal. Now? The grown-up Jamie had her own confidence. She could see substance, brains, a caring teacher, a loving father. The grown-up Jamie had more deep-down, visceral faith in him than in any other man she'd known. He had been tested and was a better person for it. The grown-up Jamie wanted to stake her future on him.

"Scare me? Are you kidding? It makes my heart sing."

He smiled and, reaching for her hand, wove his fingers through hers. "Heart sing, huh? I'm not telling the Budman that, but he'll have to get used to having you guys here." He was suddenly serious. "You okay with that?"

Chapter Twenty

Caroline was in the garage shaping rosewood slats with a molder when Dean came from the house. She didn't see him enter, she was that focused on the wood. It was only when Champ, who had been sleeping against the cool wall, roused to greet his master that she silenced the molder and raised her goggles.

Thanks to the dog, she shouldn't have been startled to see Dean. But she was. Bare-chested, wearing jeans that were zipped but unsnapped, he looked like he had just rolled out of bed. Which he had. Which was still stunning to her.

"Will I ever get used to this?" she asked without asking.

He bent to rub Champ a greeting. Straightening, he approached her on bare feet, wrapped an arm around her chest, and gave her neck a smacking kiss.

She had to smile at the affection in the gesture. "Just wake up?"

"Pretty much." He nuzzled her hair for a lingering minute before releasing her and moving around the table to admire a dozen more slats. "You've been busy."

"Plantation shutters for multiple windows in six rooms makes for lots of work."

"Boring?"

"You know it is. I've long since finished the control rods and frames, but I've been putting these off." She ran her fingers over the newest slat. "Look at the veining here, Dean. The brown is so rich."

"It is. You've always liked rosewood," he remarked, then asked, "What time did you get up?"

"Five."

"If I were to guess from how focused you were just now, I'd say you're trying not to worry about Jamie. Ease up, sweetheart. It hasn't even been a whole day since you two talked."

"Well, I keep telling myself that," Caroline said, adding the new slat to the pile, "but right now, her life is— how to even describe it?"

"Busy is fine."

"Busy is inadequate," she countered and, checking to see that everything electrical was turned off, went out the door. "Try new. Or changing daily. Or *precarious*."

Closing the door, Dean fell into step beside her while Champ bounded ahead. "Why precarious?"

"Because she's stressed, and when people are stressed, they sometimes do things they come to regret."

"Precarious means dangerous, but you don't regret her breaking up with Brad, which means you're seeing danger in Kobik. He's a good guy, Caro. I asked around."

She stopped walking to looked up at him in horror. "You didn't. Oh, Dean. If Jamie thinks I'm snooping behind her back—"

"—you'd only be doing what any other mother would do. But this wasn't you, it was me, and I was subtle."

She sputtered a laugh. Dean Brannick was good at many things, but subtlety wasn't one.

"I *was*," he insisted and, taking her elbow, got her moving again. "Some of our guys' kids play hockey, and

Kobik's camp is starting soon. They were talking about it, so I stuck in a few innocent questions. These guys think Chip Kobik is a god."

Of course they do, she mused as they reached the stairs. "Because he was a professional athlete."

"No. Because he's so good with their kids."

She considered that and sighed. "Given that Jamie has one now, that's a good thing, but still, he was a party boy for a while. I don't want her hurt."

"She's a big girl. And a sensible one. Besides, I don't see you rushing to tell her what *you've* been up to."

"I'm fifty-six. She's twenty-nine."

"Twenty-nine is adult."

"Fifty-six is more so."

"You're grasping, Caro." He opened the screen door. Champ scooted through. "Who was telling me that a mother raises her children to let them go?"

Caroline grunted as she went inside. She had told him that in a philosophical moment of self-restraint the night before.

"The same argument stands today, sweetheart. Don't call her."

"Fine for you to say. You aren't the one trying to repair a relationship. So I'm giving her space now, but I'm worried she'll think my not calling her is from lack of interest or, worse, anger, like I'm still blaming her for the *Gut It!* switch."

"Are you?"

"Only when I think about it." She opened a cabinet. "I've had other things on my mind."

"Me," he said sweetly, and her mood lightened, which was why she was pulling out pancake ingredients for a second day in a row. She had promised. And he had been very, very good.

"Are we arrogant?" she asked.

"Shouldn't we be? Last night was pretty damned amazing."

"Who *was* that in bed with you—"

"—she asks for the hundredth time." He opened the fridge.

"I'm sorry. The whole of me remains a puzzle." She was trying to settle on a self-image as safe as the one she had relied on for the past dozen years, but it seemed to change each day.

"Here's a clue. Who used her tongue last night—"

"*Dean.*"

"Just asking." He had a block of cheddar cheese and a slicing knife. "For the record, sweetheart, the answer is one hot lady who should be eating crow by now."

"Gloating is not nice," she chided but without true bite. The sex kept getting better. She still wasn't ready for prime time, as in going naked in daylight or, more immediate to her needs, soaking her aching thighs in a hot bath while he looked on. But she was growing more confident. "Uh . . ."

He was feeding Champ her organic cheddar.

"He's hungry," Dean reasoned. "You can't begrudge him this after making him sleep in the garage."

"He upsets my cats."

"I upset your cats."

"Only Master. He has this alpha thing."

Snorting at that, Dean leaned down to scrub Champ's ears and told the dog, "Caro really does love you. She's just between a rock and a very hard cat." Leaving the dog, he came up behind Caroline as she put the skillet on the stove. Sliding his arms around her waist, he put his chin on the top of her head with a quiet intimacy that had her melting.

In a flashback moment, she remembered what Annie had said about being touched. She had been right. There was something about a man's hand moving over your skin that was special. Had she not missed this? Perhaps never had it with Roy, or simply been without for so long that it was new now? Or did age enhance the appreciation of little things, like a hand on an arm or fingers on a cheek?

Again she wondered how she could have been so close to Dean all these years and never wanted this. *Again* she wondered who she was.

A high bark came from the parlor, followed by a feline snarl.

"Champ!" Dean hollered. "Get back here!"

The dog came running. Freeing one arm, Dean pointed him to a spot by the door. With a shamefaced look, he slunk there and sat.

"At least he obeys," Caroline observed.

"More than Master ever will."

"Master is a cat." As far as she was concerned, that said it all. "Do you want pancakes?"

"Absolutely."

She could not cook with him plastered to her. There were some things that begged for space. "Then back off and let me cook."

He did. But his mind must have been hard at work the whole time she was making breakfast, because they were no sooner finished eating firsts under the watchful eye of her grandmother's smug-seeming lace than he said, "Marry me."

She nearly choked on her tea. Pressing her chest, she shot the lace a frown and caught her breath. "Where did *that* come from?"

"The heart."

Breath left her again. He couldn't have given a better answer. Still, *marriage*? "My *God,* Dean. How can you even *think* that word so soon?"

"Twelve years is too soon?"

"You know what I mean. Being friends is different from being lovers. That's a sea change."

"Not a sea change. An evolution. It's been brewing. Sex was the clincher. If we weren't compatible in bed, it wouldn't have been any good."

"Sex was a *test*?"

"Not for you," he said with a self-conscious look. "For me. I needed to know I could satisfy you in bed."

Put that way, as if the potential deficiency were in him and not her, she was more touched than she could say. Dean was taking responsibility for making her happy. Roy had *never* done that. "But why marriage?"

"Why not?"

"Uhhh, take the little thing about marriage being for-ever, with both of us having failed once, and what about love?"

"I've loved you forever. And you love me."

She might have argued that there was love and there was LOVE, though in truth, since they'd had sex, since he had been so caring of her in bed, since physical intimacy had deepened the emotional intimacy that had always hov-ered, the lines had blurred. "But why get married?"

"I want to know you're mine."

"I am yours."

"I want the *world* to know it." He scratched the back of his head, dropped his hand, and scowled. "Call me a throwback, even a Neanderthal, but it's how I am."

Caroline actually understood. She had grown up with a similar mindset, assuming that marriage was what women wanted in part to let the world know they were loved and taken care of.

But times had changed. Marriage didn't have to protect women. In this new world, Caroline could protect herself. She was single and proud.

At least, she had been proud until the hosting issue

cropped up. She thought about the age issue through break-fast. Later, buttoning a blouse over her bra while Dean showered, she went into the bathroom and, speaking loudly enough to be heard over the water, tried to explain. "Here's where I'm hung up. We don't need marriage. We're not having kids, and we're both financially independent. We don't need a piece of paper tying us together. And a wedding—flowers and fanfare? I can't picture it."

When he turned off the shower and drew back the curtain, she passed a towel through the steam. The towel was pink, like her sheets, but it was plush.

He began drying himself. "It doesn't have to be fancy. We can go off, just the two of us, and get married at a little inn. Lots of them have elopement packages."

She drew back in alarm. "How do you know?"

"I looked."

She didn't want to hear more. The fact that he was bending and stretching to dry himself, casual with nudity in ways she was not, only added to her dismay. "There's something evasive about eloping. It's for people who either need speed or have secrets."

"You're afraid people will start counting months?"

"Cute. But what about Renny? If you want a closer relationship with him, how can you do something as momentous as get married and shut him out of the ceremony? Don't you think he'd be hurt? Jamie would be."

He wrapped the towel around his waist, his body all the more masculine against pink terrycloth. "So we'll invite them."

"But then it becomes something bigger, so what's the point? I don't want to elope. I don't want to get *married*."

He was quiet as he went into the bedroom to take clean clothes from a gym bag. Then he turned. "Are you afraid to commit?"

Brad had accused Jamie of the same thing. Caroline

wanted to think her daughter had sensed the relationship would sour before they made it to the altar. That wasn't the case with Dean and her. If Caroline was involved with anyone, Dean would be it.

But she was used to being on her own, cooking without a shadow against her back, coming and going as she pleased without reporting to anyone. *I'd give my right arm to be as free as you are,* Annie had said. Caroline liked that freedom.

She also liked knowing that no one could put her down for her age as Roy had done Fine, Dean said he didn't mind that she would be sixty well before he was—but once the novelty of their relationship wore off, would he feel the same? Roy had divorced her for being too old. Claire was firing her for being too old. She would be crushed if Dean changed his mind after a few years and was turned off by liver spots or varicose veins. At least if they weren't married the breakup wouldn't be quite so hard.

Here he was right now, though, waiting for her answer with his shorts in his hand, naked and exposed with his scars and his crooked finger and shots of gray through the hair on his chest, and well and heavily hung. Oh my. But she couldn't dwell on that, or even on her own fears, when his eyes held such vulnerability. That vulnerability touched her deeply. It made her want to protect *him,* which in turn made her realize just how much he did mean to her—and in ways that had less to do with sex than with the person. He might be a throwback, but he was honest and steady. He had been in her corner for years without wavering. She knew the truth about his marriage and divorce, knew how he agonized over his son. She didn't doubt that he loved her. And yes, she loved him.

"I'm not afraid to commit," she said. "I am totally committed to you."

"You are?"

"Would I have slept with you if I wasn't?" She tucked the tails of her shirt into her jeans. "And, for the record, sex is not overrated." She owed him that. "But at our age we don't need a piece of paper. No one will approve or disapprove if we sleep together."

"Not old-world Theo?"

"Theo doesn't matter. I'm a carpenter, and if my morals prevent him from naming me as his successor, I'm good with that."

"What about the show? Will Claire be happy if her host is sleeping with the GC?"

"I'm not her host, remember? She booted me out. So she may be jealous that an old lady like me can attract—"

"Old lady—"

"—a hunk like you, but the fact is, a romance on the set would *boost* ratings."

"You are no old lady. Would you wear my ring, at least?"

"A wedding ring without the wedding?"

"An engagement ring."

"To mark me yours."

With a growl of apparent frustration, he tugged on his shorts and jeans. By then, Caroline was feeling awful. Closing the distance between them, she ran an open hand down his chest. As gestures went, it spoke of intimacy in ways words could not. "It isn't you, Dean. I do love you. It's the institution I don't love."

"If I gave you a diamond, would you wear it?"

"Too *soon*," she begged. "Can't we take it slowly?"

"Does that mean you won't rule it out?"

"Yes. It means I won't rule it out. Ask me again in ten years." When his eyes went wide, she pinched his middle. "Just kidding. Ten years is as ridiculous as two days. But haven't I been good about your country place?" She tried lightening things up. "I agreed to spend tomorrow helping you build a deck, though I still think that house is more trouble than it's worth."

His hazel eyes were chiding. "You agreed because you like the place. Admit it. It has sentimental value for you now."

She heard a distant ding. "Is that my phone?" As she headed for the stairs, she heard a soft "Coward" behind her, but she kept going, following the sound of the phone into the kitchen. She didn't want to miss the call if it was Jamie.

It wasn't. Nor did she recognize the number. Since her own was unlisted, though, it had to be someone with a personal connection. A new client, referred by a friend?

"Hello?"

"Caroline MacAfee, please."

"Speaking."

"This is Zoe Michaels, from the *Globe*." The words came in a rush. The woman sounded young and nervous. "Since *Gut It!* is homegrown, I'm doing a piece on Roy MacAfee's death and its impact on MacAfee Homes and the show. I was hoping we could talk."

Caroline had done many interviews. They didn't intimidate her, especially when the interviewer was as young as this one sounded. But the last thing she wanted was to talk about Roy. "I think you ought to call Theodore MacAfee. He's the head of the company." On one hand, she hated burdening Theo. Outweighing that, though, he could be a charmer when he wanted, and it would give him an outlet, even be a distraction. He was certainly an expert on Roy.

"He was the one who gave me your number," replied the reporter. "He said you were his spokesperson. My mother is a total fan of the show, so I know exactly who you are. You'll be perfect for me to talk with, seeing as you're the host."

Then word hadn't spread. That was something. It struck

Caroline, though, that Jamie would be a better spokes-person. If she was taking over as host, she had to learn to handle the media, and as for handling Roy's death, as his daughter, she was in a better position to speak of it than his ex-wife.

Here was a perfect reason to call Jamie. But Caroline wasn't sharing her number with a reporter without check-ing first. "Can I call you back, Ms. Michaels?"

"I need to do this as soon as possible. My editor wants to run the story on Monday."

"Give me your number," Caroline said with authority, "and I'll get back to you." A minute later, she called Jamie, who picked up sounding breathless.

"Hey, Mom."

Breathless could mean busy or excited or just late. "Everything okay?"

"Everything's great. I'm just trying to get out of here."

Late, then. Perhaps the others, too, but if her tone said she didn't have time to talk now, Caroline couldn't very well ask. Quickly, she told Jamie about about Zoe Michaels. "You'd be perfect for this interview, Jamie. Should I give her your number?"

"God, no. Thanks, Mom, but you can do the interview."

"If you're the next host—"

"I'm not."

"Has Claire changed her mind?"

"I haven't talked with her. But there's no way I can take it on right now."

"Well, the reporter needs one of us ASAP. They're run-ning the article on Monday. If I do the interview, Claire may be annoyed."

"*Good.* Do the interview, Mom, please?"

"Are you sure?"

"Absolutely. Thank you. You're the best. We'll talk an-other time, okay?"

Caroline knew when she was being rushed off the phone. Fearing Jamie might have even less time if she was with Chip and his son over the weekend, she asked a quick "Is Tad okay?"

"He's *great*."

"Have you seen Chip?"

"He's great, too." The voice was higher and more breathy. "But I have to run, Mom. I'll give you a call, okay?"

Seconds later, Caroline held a silent phone, the sense that what she had heard was extreme excitement, and no clue whether to be pleased or worried.

Chapter Twenty-one

*E*xtreme excitement didn't quite cover it. Jamie was so totally in love—so *impossibly* in love—that she didn't dare tell Caroline lest her mother have her committed. What she was doing with Chip was crazy. *Crazy.* She kept coming back to that word.

But it didn't feel crazy when Tad began to cry at three in the morning and Chip bolted out of bed and carried him to her. Or when she woke up in the morning to hot coffee served in bed by a guy who already had the boys eating breakfast downstairs and was looking at her now as if she were priceless. Or when they met at First Unity later that afternoon and drove in a caravan to the pediatrician's office to discuss what Tad would be feeling about his parents' death and how best to ease both boys into a new relationship. Chip had arranged the meeting. He seemed determined to make their family work. She kept looking for signs of crazy in him but only saw commitment.

Stopping back at his house, they put Tad's seat in the Pilot and drove to Jamie's condo, and there, for the first time, a problem arose. As if Tad had actually heard their discussion with the doctor—which he could not have, since he and Buddy had been in the playroom down the hall—he was suddenly and fiercely possessive. Buddy picked up a toy; Tad grabbed it out of his hands. Buddy went for another toy; Tad started to cry.

"He's feeling loss without understanding it," the doctor had said. "He's at the age when sharing is difficult anyway. Let him cling to things that mean most to him—a stuffed animal or a blankie or a favorite toy—but teach him to share others. Be consistent. Be patient."

Wrapping her arms around him now, Jamie held him until he finished kicking and grew quiet, then softly explained that Buddy wasn't taking anything away, and he wasn't touching Moose. Didn't it feel *good* to share other toys, she asked, especially since Buddy would always give them back? "See, Taddy, he's already done with the farm."

Chip snickered from the sidelines. "Not a great attention span on my boy."

Jamie disagreed. "There's just a lot to see here. This is like a toy store to him, and he's been so good about sharing with Tad. Which of these should we take to your house?"

They picked a few. Chip played with the boys while she packed what she wanted for herself; then he joined her in the office to gather Tad's things. He ran a hand over her sleek white desk, admired her huge computer screen, studied drawings tacked to a corkboard, and flipped through design books—all the while asking questions about her work. He described the small office he had in a spare bedroom and vowed that any new house they built would have a large one, which got her thinking. She rather liked the connection he had with his childhood home and was inclined to stay there for now. Adapting it would be easy, starting with a simple addition. Her artist's eye saw modifications that would give the place a vintage-modern look inside and out.

Moreover, staying at Chip's would minimize change for the boys, and that was the responsible thing to do. His house wasn't pristine. But nor, any longer, was hers, and she was surviving just fine.

She was deciding that pristine had a sterile side when Tad wandered in, slid his little arms around her leg, and held tightly.

"Hi, monkey," she said. Kneeling, she cupped his face. "All done playing?"

He didn't answer, just looked up at her with such mournful eyes that she knew what he was thinking. They were the same eyes she saw when he woke at night needing to be held. He was a smart boy. Having gone through one life shift, he sensed another coming. One too many?

His lower lip trembled. "Where Mommy?"

Be honest, the pediatrician had said. "Mommy's in heaven."

"Wanna see her."

"I know, monkey, I know."

"Where my daddy?"

Jamie teared up. "He's in heaven, too."

"Taddy wanna go there."

"Someday."

"Now," he demanded, but he didn't resist when she hugged him close.

"I miss him, too," she whispered against his warm curls, rocking him as much for her own comfort as his. Despite their differences in those last days, Roy had been her father. So much had happened in the two weeks since his death, so much filling her mind, that she hadn't really had time to mourn, but right here, right now, emptiness hit her hard.

She might have wept if Chip hadn't suddenly hunkered down close, making her feel less alone. Cupping her head with one hand and Tad's with the other, he said in an exquisitely gentle voice, "Since we can't visit heaven right now, we ought to do something else. It's pretty warm

outside. I have a sprinkler with Mickey Mouse on it
How about we play in the water before dinner?"

Jamie came forward just enough to press her face to his
neck and breathe in his scent. That quickly bolstered, she
faced Tad, who likely had no clue what a sprinkler was but
would take his cue from her, and said an awe-filled
"Mickey Mouse? Oh, Taddy, you *love* Mickey Mouse
Let's *do* it!"

Not only was the sprinkler a hit, but when Chip unscrewed
the hose to spray the boys directly, he had them shrieking
and running and tumbling over each other *and* over Jamie
when she tripped, which she did repeatedly trying to escape the spray. Chip kept at it long after she laughingly
retreated—kept the boys racing back and forth and around
for such a long time that they could barely hold their heads
up at dinner and were asleep soon after.

He checked on them while she showered. She checked
on them while he dressed. When they were sure neither
boy would wake, they headed out. Not only had Chip hired
the trusted babysitter he used for school events, but he
had made reservations at a restaurant on Beacon Hill, had
brought along a bottle of champagne from his first pro
signing, and seemed determined to learn every last thing
about Jamie.

It started in the car—Jamie's convertible, so *cool* with
Chip at the wheel—when the origin of the champagne go
them talking about sports. What had Jamie felt when she
won a tournament? When she lost? Where were her trophies, why were they packed away? Where were *his*? Had
Chip regretted dropping out of college to go pro? Did he
want Buddy playing hockey? Did she want Tad playing
tennis? How to minimize the pressure of competitive
sports? In what ways did sports ethics affect their current
work?

Many answers were of the yes or no variety, because here were so many questions, *so* much to learn. By the ime they pulled up at the restaurant, they were on to their obs. What was Chip's favorite age group at school, favorite season, favorite sport? Were school parents a problem for him? How did Jamie choose between projects? Did she prefer commercial to residential? How did she keep up with the latest in technology?

Jamie learned that Chip blamed his early stardom for the arrogance that had led to women and booze, and that he dreamed of coaching hockey at the high school level to help ground budding stars. He talked about the growth of his summer camp, how it emphasized skills and teamwork over competition and partnered with a reading program at the local library. But he was as eager to know Jamie's dreams as share his own. So she talked of the drawings she had made for the Weymouth estate and her fear that the Barths would steal it away.

She had never been as thoroughly comfortable with anyone in her life. For all Chip's warnings about her being a MacAfee to his Kobik, the way he described his childhood made it sound identical to hers in terms of values. His family was firmly grounded—sisters functional professionals, one married, one not, parents still together after forty-some years. Could he be crazy, coming from that?

As they talked, they sipped champagne, split an appetizer salad, and munched on warm zucchini bread. Did Jamie see the restaurant's decor? Barely. She couldn't look at anything but Chip, which was why she was taken by surprise when a couple stopped at their table on their way to the door.

"We love your show," said the man, to which his wife added, "We watch it every week, even reruns now. Can't wait for the new season."

Much as Jamie resented the interruption, she couldn'
alienate a viewer. Managing a polite smile, she said, "W
just finished taping it. They're in the process of editing."

That led, when the couple moved on, to Chip wantin;
to know everything about *Gut It!* and Jamie telling hin
how the show had begun and what it meant to MacAfe
Homes, but also about Claire's decree on switching host
and Jamie's resulting rift with Caroline.

"Is hosting something you want?" Chip was careful t
ask first.

"I thought it was. *Assumed* it was. But under these cir
cumstances?" She shook her head. "Maybe someday, bu
not now. Especially not now," she added, reinforcing th
especially with a meaningful look.

"I feel for your mom," he admitted. "Mine lost her jol
when the hospital where she worked was bought by
for-profit corporation. They said the cuts were part of th
takeover, but it was mostly older women who were let g(
Mom liked her job. Suddenly it was gone, and she was too
old to find another."

"So she retired?"

"If you can call it that. She's a professional volunteei
her current passion being the library in the Vermont tow1
where they summer. She's busier than ever."

They continued to talk over grilled snapper and rack o
lamb, and when Chip ordered a side of sour-cream-and
chive fries, Jamie was in heaven. They lingered over cap
puccino until thoughts of getting back for the sitte
intruded, but they hadn't made it out the door when it wa
his turn to be stopped.

"Buffalo blew it when they sent you to Pittsburgh," saic
a man who was clearly a hockey fan. "You were the bes
right wing they had."

Less indulgent than Jamie, Chip thanked him, no con

versation, and guided her to the car. "I always hate that," he muttered as soon as he slid behind the wheel.

"Why?"

"Buffalo traded me because I was a problem."

"You were a great player."

"Yeah, when I was on."

"You think of the bad behavior, Chip. People like him are thinking of the good stuff."

Taking a deep breath, he grabbed her hand and held it tightly as he drove off. "Keep reminding me, please?"

By mutual, unspoken consent, they avoided PDA at the restaurant. The fact that both of them were recognized validated that decision. The last thing either of them wanted was to find a cell phone shot posted somewhere online.

After the restraint, though, they touched constantly during the drive home. When Chip wasn't holding her hand, it was on the back of his neck or his thigh. He kissed her with promise when they pulled into his driveway, and made good on the promise after taking the babysitter home. She fell asleep in his arms, well and fully satisfied.

Jamie had trouble thinking about designing when she was with Chip, but she had fallen behind after Roy's death and was nowhere near catching up. She had always been focused on work, always. So it was near-compulsion that had the wheels in her mind spinning when she woke at five on Saturday morning. Naked beside him, she lay for a time just taking in the sounds and smells of the house. Her condo had few. Well built and new, it smelled nondescript, it didn't creak underfoot, and its systems were silent. This house was different. She smelled Chip, of course, all clean male, on her skin and his as he slept beside her. She also smelled wax on aged wood floors and heard the rattling

of cool air through heating vents that had been adapted fo
AC only four years before.

Absurdly, she thought about flying. She was alway:
more comfortable when the plane was hitting a steady
stretch of gentle bumps. They gave her the illusion of be
ing on the ground.

Likewise, the sounds in this house were grounding. O
maybe what gave the house roots were silent echoes from
Chip's parents' time. They had raised a family here and
had been happy. Jamie could *feel* that, as if the house had
a character that lived beyond its inhabitants. It wasn't un
like Caroline's house in that sense. For the first time, she
understood why her mother loved the Victorian so. Espe
cially at a time when one's life was new, roots helped.

The AC cycled off, and Chip's rhythmic breathing wa:
more noticeable. Turning her head on the pillow, she stud
ied him—dark hair, shadowed jaw, broad shoulders, and
good heart—and felt such a swell inside that she was be
side herself. His body warmth was welcome in the air
conditioned chill he liked, but he wasn't physically holding
her down. Rather, he had a hand tucked to her hip, as i
the reassurance of her presence was all he needed.

But those wheels in her mind continued to whir, now
joined by a little voice that cried, *Work!* That voice had
been silent, not a peep since she had broken her engage
ment with Brad. And it wasn't snide now, just insistent.

With care, she gently slid away from Chip, but as soo
as she sat up on the edge of the bed, he mumbled, "Wher
are you going?"

Miming writing, she whispered, "Work thoughts." She
returned to kiss his cheek, then reached for a robe and
crept down to the breakfast nook, where she sat with a pa
per and pencil making a list, by client, of work to be done
When the list grew daunting, she began shifting tasks to :

second list, this for her assistant, and when that one grew daunting as well, she sat back.

Caroline was right. They needed to hire another architect. Jamie could still do everything herself, but did she want to? *No.* She loved designing homes, offices, and stores. But she had to learn to delegate, and some parts of her work couldn't be done by an intern. Oh yes, she might have trouble finding a licensed architect willing to take her runoff. Or not.

This would be a lifestyle change for Jamie. She had always been narrowly focused on one thing, first tennis, then architecture. She didn't go out with friends, didn't cook, and, other than yoga classes and the occasional tennis game with a local pro, didn't have any hobbies. But life wasn't all work. For the first time now, she wanted a mix.

Oh, and one more thing? She was absolutely, definitely, bottom-line not hosting *Gut It!* in the fall—didn't have the time, interest, or energy. She was thinking how best to break this to Claire and what the consequences might be when Chip slid into the booth snug beside her.

"The boys are up," came his deep, early morning voice. "I want a kiss before I go in there."

She kissed him—so natural, so sweet—then said, "I'll get them."

"No. You're working." He glanced at her lists. "Productively?"

She shrugged. "It helps when I organize things, but I need to hire another architect." Suddenly, though, she wasn't thinking about work. Laying her head on his shoulder with an ease that should have been years in the making, she said, "How can something so new feel so right? I keep waiting for a hitch."

"I like my house cool."

She smiled against his warm skin. "I noticed."

"And I leave the toilet seat up. Do you hate that?"

Still smiling, she raised her head to meet his gaze. "I might in the middle of the night, but hey, I like my bottles of hand soap, body lotion, and cologne lined up just so."

His blue eyes grew mischievous. "I noticed. I knocked them out of line last night when I was shaving, I think."

"It's probably good for me. I'm not exactly OCD, just organized. And clumsy? That's plain embarrassing."

"It's plain adorable. Like your freckles."

She spread a hand on her face. "I hate them."

He removed the hand, threading his fingers between hers, just as a call came from upstairs. "I need another kiss."

The second one was as sweet and satisfying as the first. It held comfort and ease and promise and love—yes, love. So bizarre, the speed of that.

"Can I make breakfast?" Jamie asked as he slid out of the booth.

He trailed his thumb along the line of her jaw. "I like cooking, you don't. I'll do breakfast, you do laundry."

Breakfast and laundry. They were mundane things to begin a day of mundane things that kept Jamie busy enough not to think once about work. When they hit the supermarket, she learned that Chip hated Brussels sprouts, liked his peanut butter chunky rather than smooth, and bought only organic milk. When they hit the drugstore for Buddy's allergy medicine, she learned that he refused to wear sunscreen himself but wanted 70 SPF on the boys. And when they hit the children's room at the library, she learned that he preferred nonfiction and read his books on an iPad.

Wherever they went, they were physically close. He seemed to need it as much as she did, which stunned her when she stopped to think. As touchy as she and Caroline

were, she had never been this way with Brad. She hadn't
thought it was in her nature to want to crawl all over a man.

That said, they were discreet. Seeing people they knew
went with the territory in as small a town as Williston.
Each time it happened, Jamie thought of Caroline. By
rights, Caroline should be the first one to see her with
Chip.

But how to see Caroline and not mention marriage? Because that was where they were heading. Once the boys
were down for a nap, Jamie perched beside Chip on the
arm of his living room chair. While one of his own arms
steadied her, the other worked his laptop, which was open
and searching. They found an inn in New Hampshire
whose proprietor would issue a marriage license, officiate
at a short ceremony, and provide music, flowers, and food
for a wedding celebration, all on a Sunday.

"A gazebo," Jamie breathed in delight when the picture
appeared on the screen. "I want it there."

"Then we're doing this?" Chip asked softly.

Sliding an arm around his neck, she searched his eyes.
On level with hers, they held the same bits of terror, excitement, and determination that she felt. "I want to," she
whispered. "I shouldn't. It's insane. But I want to. You?"

"More than anything. I love you."

She returned the words in a kiss, lingering with it until
she couldn't any longer put off the only other major decision.
"What do we do about our parents?"

Chip frowned, clearly struggling with that, too. "I'm not
sure. They'll put a damper on this."

"The voice of reason," she remarked. By all standards,
what they were planning was rash.

"They'll say we're rushing into this without thinking it
through. They'll say it's infatuation, not love."

"They'll say I'm on the rebound from Brad."

"Or that I'm after your money," which he wasn't. He had

shown her an investment statement in Friday's mail. He had way more money—and growing—in his name than she had in hers at the moment. That would clearly change once her inheritance came through, and Tad's inheritance would cover him for life.

"They'll worry that I'm desperate for a co-parent," she said.

"Or me a live-in maid."

"Or that I'm reacting to my dad's death and not thinking clearly. But I am. I feel like I'm thinking more clearly than I ever have, like I understand more what I want *because* of everything that's happened. We're not eighteen, Chip. We're fully grown, sensible, down-to-earth people."

He smiled. It was a sweet smile that matched the adoration in his eyes. "We are," he said, but his smile faded. "They'll still tell us to wait. They'll say we should take the time to plan a traditional wedding."

"Do you want a traditional wedding?" Jamie asked and caught the tiny shake of his head. "Me, neither."

"But if we elope, they'll be hurt."

She exhaled. "Yes." If there was any reason to wait, this was it. She had never met Chip's parents, but everything he said pointed to solid, loving people. He was as close to his family as Jamie was to Caroline, and then there was Theo. They would all be hurt.

Taking her hand, Chip pressed it to his mouth. His breath was warm against her skin, his eyes earnest. "All I know is that I've been happier in the last week, even when we were just talking on the phone, than I've been since I can remember. I love my son, but it isn't the same. I know what I want in a life partner, and it's you. We can rationalize this nine ways to Sunday, and it won't change how I feel." He kissed her knuckles, brushed them with his thumb. "We could wait."

"We could."

"We could get married in a month or two and have them there. It wouldn't be so awful."

"No," Jamie supposed, though everything in her objected to the idea. "On the afternoon he died, my father called me selfish and shortsighted. He may have been right about selfish, but our eloping wouldn't be shortsighted. It would give Tad a stable home with an amazing dad and brother, but even aside from that, this is *our life*. There would be something poetic about getting married so fast, given how we first got together. And the boys would be involved in the secret. They'll love knowing that."

"We're already living together," Chip added. "Done deal there. Do you have any doubts that we're meant for each other?"

Jamie did not. She had led a studied life, but not once in the shockingly brief time since she'd met Chip at the playground, not once since they'd become lovers, started living together, and talking marriage, had she had a second's doubt that he was her future. She had never been overly romantic, but if there was such a thing as a soul mate, Chip was hers.

Doubts, he had asked? "None," she replied and then, knowing that (A) she loved her mother and (B) she might be jeopardizing their already tenuous relationship but that (C) she was finally an adult and had to do her very own thing, on her own initiative, for the first time, she gave a definitive nod. "Let's book it."

Chip exhaled. "Consider it done," he said gallantly and clicked through for the phone number of the inn.

Chapter Twenty-two

Caroline breezed through an hour with Zoe Michaels. She had done many other interviews, and while none of those media outlets had the prestige of the *Globe,* other reporters had been tougher. Perhaps the newness of Roy's death weighed on this reporter, or perhaps her age kept her intimidated. Perhaps Caroline was simply adept at answering questions she liked, sidestepping ones she did not, and religiously staying on message—message, in this case, being that while the MacAfee family deeply mourned Roy, he had set them up to succeed, which they would do. Though Caroline confirmed, when asked, that Roy had been one of the founding voices of *Gut It!,* she said that the show would continue on, starting with the fall season, in the manner viewers had come to love.

The interview was held in the courtyard behind the MacAfee Building, otherwise deserted early on a Saturday morning, and as soon as it was done, Caroline met Dean at his country place, where, in work clothes, goggles, and gloves, she sawed, hammered, and shaped wood for the bench that would curve in a corner of his fast-forming sundeck.

At least, she started out doing that, but there was something about Dean in motion that caught her eye and stilled her hand. Too often of late, he managed schedules and crews rather than doing physical work. But he was a skilled builder, not to mention an impressive sight in the midday sun with his shirt off and his skin moist. As always during hands-on moments, he poured himself into the work. This was nothing new to her. His intensity attacking personal projects was what had initially invited her questions, which was how she had first learned of his struggling marriage. Later, in the darkest days of negotiating his divorce and dealing with his increasingly distanced son, he had been most able to articulate his feelings to her when he was pounding nails into wood.

There was something different about him today, though. She saw intensity without darkness, simply a man enjoying his work. Wanting to believe that their relationship was behind his lightened mood, she watched for a while.

He caught her at it, looking up absently, then doing a double take and sliding her a self-conscious smile. "Am I doing it right?"

"Absolutely," Caroline said and waved a hand. "Go back to it."

She did the same herself, but before long, she took another break. This one was for a cold drink, which she carried back outside in a single large travel mug. She had thought to bring lemonade but not insulated cups, and since she found only one of those in what could still barely be called a kitchen, they passed it back and forth.

They didn't have to talk. The companionship was just fine without sound—so fine, in fact, that when Dean returned to hammer and saw, Caroline grabbed her e-reader and sat on the grass nearby.

"Not a real book?" Dean called over at one point.

She held up the device. "A gift from Jamie last Christmas."

"Ahhh." His hammering resumed.

At some point it stopped again, which she realized only when his voice came from close by her ear. Hunkered down behind her, he read over her shoulder in a voice that was naughty and low.

" *'I am naked and hot, nearly orgasmic, and he hasn't even touched me yet.'* Jesus, Caro. What book is this?"

It was the same one the woman on the sidewalk had been reading that day after lunch. Caroline was embarrassed for all of five seconds before realizing how ridiculous that was. Recovering, she said, "If you're not wearing glasses, how can you see the words?"

"They're pretty big." His voice lowered, intimate and teasing. "I take it you don't want to miss a one?"

"I set the font bigger so that I could read in the sun."

"I'll bet."

"I did," she insisted, struggling not to smile.

It grew harder when his stubble brushed her cheek. "But you don't want anyone knowing what you're reading."

"Of course not. That would compromise you."

"Really."

"Really. I'm only reading this now to find out what the appeal is of these books."

"You didn't want to know before."

"No. I didn't." She hadn't quite analyzed the why of that, only knew that the woman she was back then hadn't been the least bit curious, while this one was.

He moved a bare shoulder against her back. "And?"

"And what?"

"Is the book as hot as we are?"

"Hotter," she said, unable to resist, and, laughing, caught the hand that slipped inside her shirt. "I'm just kidding, Dean. It's a pale imitation—*oh no,*" she cried when he flattened her to the ground and came over on top, "I am not doing this here, not in broad daylight where anyone can see, not with rocks digging into my back and that air compressor going on and off, and both of us sweaty as hell."

He slid his bottom half to the side but left his bare chest hovering. "Can we read the book together tonight?"

She made a show of considering before saying, "Only if we finish this deck first. Think we can?"

By way of answer, he quickly pushed himself up and went back to his tools. Joining him, she finished her part first and then lent a hand with his. As midday moved into afternoon, though, she wasn't thinking about sex with Dean. Increasingly, she felt a nagging unease. She hadn't talked with Jamie again, and yesterday's call had been too breathy.

No cause for concern, she told herself. *She's having fun. This is good.*

She kept thinking up reasons why the silence might not be good, though—notably, that Chip wasn't the great guy Jamie had thought but that she was too embarrassed to tell Caroline that, after the buildup she had given him. Caroline didn't want her daughter hurt. So she worried.

Dean wanted to cook out for dinner, but she wanted something more distracting, like milling crowds at a sidewalk café in Boston. They compromised on a suburban restaurant overlooking the Charles River that was popular enough to be packed without requiring a trek through city traffic. The last meant that Dean could take the Harley, which he claimed he badly needed, given the workweek that had been.

Caroline knew about that week. Cell constantly dinging, he had juggled crises ranging from the mundane to the not so, including a shipment of cracked marble, a surprise raccoon den with kits, and a framer suffering a major heart attack on-site. For Dean, working at the country place, where the sounds of their tools were solitary and he was in control, was therapeutic, too, but the Harley was his joy. She couldn't begrudge him this.

First, though, she was having a pedicure. The nail shop had started to empty when she arrived. Preferring it that way, she and Annie always took the last appointments of the day, customarily on Saturdays to enjoy their toes without work on Sunday. Linda Marshall often joined them, though there was no sign of her today.

For a time, they talked about nothing—a new varietal of peony, a summer salad at Fiona's—while they sat side by side in pedicure chairs, backs vibrating, feet soaking. Only when the whirlpools went off and their feet were taken over by practicians who spoke little English, ensuring privacy, did Caroline ask about Jordan.

Annie shrugged. "I finished the job Tuesday, so I haven't seen him much."

Her voice was predictably high, but something about the way she kept her eyes on her toes made Caroline ask, "You opted for prudence?"

A soft snort. "You could say that."

"Oh dear. What happened?"

Annie sank deeper in the chair, moving her silver hair against the headrest to stretch her neck. "I think my imagination got the best of me."

"How so?"

She shot Caroline a look of chagrin before refocusing on the pedicurist's work. "The last time I was there, I went inside to let him know I was leaving. A crew was installing draperies, so I knew he wasn't alone, but that made it safe to talk—you know, maybe arrange another time to see each other. I called his name and went looking, and there he was, testing the new Roman shade in the itty-bitty little first-floor powder room with the only female member of the crew. They weren't doing anything improper, and he wasn't embarrassed or awkward seeing me. He didn't take

his hand off her arm, just gestured me in with his head.
He touched my shoulder when he introduced me to her,
and he touched her hair when he introduced her to me. He
thumbed my chin when he talked about his shrubs and
tapped her cheek when he praised her shade. Apparently,
he's just a toucher."

"All touch, no action?"

Annie looked wounded. "It isn't funny, Caroline. I felt
desired when he touched me, and I thought it meant something." She took a self-deprecating breath. "I thought it
meant something—because I wanted it to, because I miss
being touched."

Caroline twitched as the pedicurist hit a ticklish spot
near the dry skin on her heels. She hadn't wanted Annie
fooling around with Jordan in the first place, but her
friend's disappointment was real.

"I'm sorry," she soothed.

"I told Byron."

"About *Jordan*?"

"Yes, because nothing happened, but it made me realize what I need and how badly I need it. If it isn't Jordan,
it'll be someone else."

"You told him that?"

"I did," Annie said in a voice devoid of regret. "Byron
needs to know I'm not just blowing off steam when I tell
him I'm lonely."

Okay, Caroline realized. Annie wasn't giving up on her
marriage yet. That was good. "Did he hear you?"

"He heard. Whether he can do anything about it is
something else."

"I'm sure he can."

"I'm not, but we have to try. We're going on a 'date' this
weekend. Overnight."

"Good move. I know a really romantic place if you want
one." She snickered. "Dean's country house."

Annie eyed her curiously. "The house you say you hate but seem to be working on a lot?" She paused, frowned. "Romantic?"

"Well, aside from the ghosts, but if a man can't protect you from those, what good is he?"

"Romantic," Annie repeated, clearly suspicious now. "Am I missing something?"

Caroline wouldn't have chosen this particular time to tell Annie this particular bit of news, but something subconscious must have been at work, a tiny little imp of excitement craving expression. Denying it now would be lying.

Romantic? "Oh yeah."

"Dean?"

She nodded.

Seeming not in the least jealous or disturbed, Annie angled into the seat to face her more fully. "Oh. My. God. Tell me all."

"No one else knows."

"Or will." Annie's fingers locked her lips. "Tell me *all*."

Caroline wasn't about to do that. Much as she treasured the honesty between her and Annie, some details were too personal to be shared. What she had with Dean was special. She didn't want to dilute that. "One thing led to another," she said simply. "It's been nice."

"Nice," Annie echoed.

"Fun."

"*Fun*? I can't believe you are talking so calmly about being in bed with Dean Brannick."

Caroline shushed her with a glance toward the women who were now rubbing cream into their skin. For all she knew, despite assumptions to the contrary, they understood every last word. First names were one thing, but first and last could incriminate.

Annie's only concession was to lower her voice. "Do

you know how many women daydream about that? How many see him on TV and take him to heart? How many women think of him while they're making love with someone else?"

"You don't know that," Caroline chided, though the possibility of it gave her a little thrill. Dean was hers. She still had doubts about her body, but it seemed to please him. He had said it enough—*touched* it enough— that she was starting to believe.

"Is he good?"

"Very good," Caroline said softly. He deserved that credit.

"And it worked? Everything you were worried wouldn't?"

Caroline blushed. She remembered their discussion— *so* hard to believe it had been only one week before, given all that had happened since. "He makes it work," she said now.

"Wow. Atta *girl*. Does Jamie know?"

"No, that's what I'm saying," Caroline replied with hushed urgency. "You're the only one. I don't know what Jamie'll say. She has so much else going on in her life right now, what with Tad and all." She couldn't mention Chip to Annie without mentioning Brad, and it wasn't her place to do that. No one at MacAfee Homes even knew the engagement was off. "I worry about her. I can't help it, Annie. I get nervous when I don't hear from her."

"When was the last time you talked?"

"Yesterday morning." At Annie's dry look, she added, "I know. Not so long ago, but we used to talk all the time." That was, of course, before the *Gut It!* crisis, but Annie didn't know about that either. "Most women have nine months to get ready for a baby, plus whatever time they spend thinking about getting pregnant. Even those who adopt think about it beforehand. Jamie had no warning.

Overnight, she became a mother. She must have constant questions about dealing with Tad. I want her to call me with those."

"Her generation goes to the Web."

"I don't want Jamie doing that. I want her getting answers from someone who sees the world the way she does."

"Meaning you, but parenting has changed since we had kids. When my assistant talks about equipment or food or discipline, it's like another language to me. Jamie speaks that language. She needs current sources."

Caroline grunted. "That's what Dean says." Strong hands worked at the tension in her calves, her heels, her soles, her toes. "I'm trying to give her space, Annie, really I am, but it's hard. When she was playing tennis, I had to be involved, because Roy wasn't about to do the driving to practices and all. I was her on-call therapist when she was in college, and we see each other now at work and even more during *Gut It!* tapings. She's my daughter. I love her."

"This has nothing to do with love. She needs space to grow."

The sensible, down-to-earth, intuitive part of Caroline knew that was true. The part that worried continued to worry.

"Sometimes," Annie went on, "out of sight, out of mind is better."

"That's easy for you to say. You have sons. It's different with boys. Jamie isn't only my daughter, she's my friend. And right now, she's going through the biggest change of her life."

"If she needs you, she'll call. In the meantime, she may be wanting to do things her way."

Caroline thought about Jamie's broken engagement and now her infatuation with Chip, and sighed. "Dean says that, too. He reasons it all out, and then gets me doing something distracting."

There were more subtle things going on, too. Being with Dean made her feel good about herself. Not that she had been aware of feeling *bad*, though Claire had given her moments of late. But being with Dean, being sexual for the first time in years, was adding a *glow* to her life. Claire might have told her she was old, but what she did with Dean proved she wasn't dead yet. It said there was more to come.

Which didn't mean sex was the be-all and end-all of life.

It absolutely was not.

But it was nice.

"I'm glad you're with him," Annie said. "It means you're finally making a life for yourself beyond Jamie."

"What if she makes a mistake?" Caroline asked. This was her greatest fear. There were so many potential pitfalls in Jamie's current path.

"Then she makes a mistake. We all do."

"What if it's a big one?"

Gently, confidently, Annie said, "Then you'll be there to help her pick up the pieces. That's what mothers do."

"Dean said that, too. Did you talk with him?"

"I did not, but if he said it, he's both sexy *and* smart. Speaking of smart—" Her eyes went to the door just as Linda breezed in.

"Oh, good," the Realtor said with visible relief. "You're still here. I was hoping to catch you before you left."

Caroline surveyed the back of the shop. "I think Van is gone." Van was Linda's usual pedicurist.

"I'm not here for toes." Perching sideways on the next pedicure chair, she bent toward Caroline with her elbows on her knees. "This may be nothing, but I just overheard talk at Timmy's lacrosse game. Two guys were discussing the market, one telling the other that if he wanted a really good house he should wait until the Barths start building on Weymouth land. When I asked him about it, he said he had just met a local Barth and was talking with him. Their kids are playing summer soccer together. On my way here, I called friends from two different brokerages. They hadn't heard about any deal, but they've both been approached in the last week by the Barths asking about available property."

Caroline felt a twinge of anger. What else to think but that the Barths were taking advantage of Roy's death to move while the MacAfees were down? She had no trouble losing a few houses to them, but losing the Weymouth acreage was unacceptable. Even beyond what it would say about MacAfee Homes without Roy, it would be a blow to Theo, who had worked hard and long to own Williston and the surrounding MetroWest suburbs, and a blow to Jamie, who had already sketched out dream designs for that land. And *Gut It!*—hadn't Claire told Jamie she was considering a Barth season? The Barths buying the Weymouth property would ensure that.

Caroline had never been anywhere near as competitive as Roy and Jamie, but she felt a personal drive now.

"Well then," she told Linda with new determination, "we need to shop aggressively ourselves, and if that means playing dirty, so be it. We can start with the local connection. Weymouth roots run deep in Williston soil. So do MacAfee roots. Barth roots do not."

"My understanding is that only one of Mildred Weymouth's three sons is still in Massachusetts."

"John," Caroline confirmed, "in Boston. I never knew him personally." She turned. "Annie? You grew up with them, didn't you?"

"That was years ago, and we weren't exactly close."

"Why not?"

"I was beneath them," Annie said, and while another person would have heard upset in that high voice of hers, Caroline knew better. Annie was fiercely proud of her roots. "My dad cut grass for a living," she said with her chin up. "He didn't speak English well, just drove around town with a cigar in his mouth and a mower in the bed of his truck. Needless to say, he never cut Weymouth grass, though, in fairness, neither did any other locals. The Weymouths had a full-time gardener on staff. Clearly, those days are gone. From what I hear, most of the trust money has been spent, hence their need to sell the estate. That land is their only remaining asset."

"So they'll want top dollar," Linda warned, "which is why we can't risk driving the price even higher by getting into a bidding war with the Barths."

"What's their idea of top dollar?" Caroline asked.

The Realtor speculated. "Thirty acres of prime wooded land, with twenty-six of those acres able to support a new build to sell at a million, plus or minus? That's allowing two acres for a rec area and two for the manor house, which needs work but has good bones. The manor could be fixed up and sold as a single for two million, or broken into four condos selling for five hundred each. You do the math. The Weymouths will."

"And the Barths," Caroline murmured. "Bottom line for us to buy?"

"I'd guess a million for the house and three for the remaining land."

Four million to buy, with turnaround potential approaching twenty-eight million? Granted, building costs would be high on high-end houses, which these would be. Still, Caroline had lived long enough in the right circles to know a good profit margin when she heard it. She would have to talk with MacAfee Homes' banker and with Theo, of course, but, totally aside from the political advantage of developing the Weymouth property, she couldn't see them ignoring the money.

"That's assuming the Barths don't bid," Linda warned. "Right now, I don't see any other competition, but that could change once word gets out that the property is on the market. Inventory is low in all of MetroWest. Interested parties may appear out of the blue."

"Then we'll act quickly," Caroline vowed. "That means making the Weymouths an offer they can't refuse. How high do we have to go for that?"

"I'm not sure. Let me do a comp study. The key will be getting the brothers in a room with you and making a presentation. Do you have plans you can show them?"

Caroline thought of Jamie, who was off doing whatever she was doing with Chip Kobik and certainly not home designing for a project that had been hypothetical until now. What sketches she had were rough. That said, Caroline knew Jamie could embellish them. She would pull all-nighters if necessary. She wanted the project as much as Caroline did.

"We'll have plans," Caroline assured Linda and turned to Annie. "Do we assume we'll be dealing with John, since he's the one who's here?"

"I wouldn't. The three of them don't get along. One won't trust the other to make the final decision."

"Where are they now?"

"The oldest, Ralph, is a turnaround specialist in San Francisco. He buys companies, builds them, sells them. He keeps insisting that one of his companies will develop the land, though he's strictly West Coast and hasn't been able to get an operation going anywhere near here. The middle brother is Grant. He's an impoverished artist."

"Needs money."

"Big-time. And our local yokel, John, is a hotshot plastic surgeon."

Caroline knew that. His name consistently appeared on the Best of Boston lists, more often associated with Botox than with surgery.

"He rakes it in," Annie went on, "but spends it as soon as he makes it. He keeps telling the brothers that he wants the estate for himself. I heard something about his wanting to run a clinic out of the house, which the town would never zone for, but John hasn't given up on the idea. My guess is that Herschel Oakes is key. He's the family lawyer, more likely the family referee. I'd start with him."

Caroline agreed, though reluctantly. She knew Herschel Oakes, had actually dated him once after her divorce. Once was enough. The man had been thoroughly self-absorbed. There was zero chemistry then and would be zero now, but if she could play on the local connection to make an inroad to that land, she would.

Time was, Theo would have done it, and after him Roy. Her own experience had taught her that a male might be more successful talking business with a male, but she didn't want to involve Brad.

Dean would help. But he wasn't a MacAfee.

Jamie could do it. But she was both female and young, two strikes against her, and she was a designer, not a salesperson. Not that Caroline was an expert in sales either, and she certainly didn't have management experience. But who else was there?

The buck stops here.

How often had she thought that when she was raising Jamie, and Roy dropped the ball on one parenting event or the other?

Time didn't change certain things. Or maybe it did. She was fifty-six. If she could corral the cachet that came with age—the brains, the poise, the guts—she might be able to play the MacAfee champion as she couldn't have done even ten years before.

She wanted the Weymouth project—wanted it for Jamie, for Theo, for MacAfee Homes. She wanted it for *Gut it!* And she wanted it for herself. The carpenter in her dreamed of creating some of the effects Jamie had put in her sketches. Add the challenge of winning at her age—of showing *all* of them what she could do?

In light of recent events, that was suddenly very important to her.

Caroline actually hesitated before calling Jamie. It was Saturday evening. If she didn't have plans with Chip and the boys, she would have called Caroline, wouldn't she have? And Annie's warning was fresh in her mind's ear. *She may be wanting to do things her way.*

But that was personal.

This was business.

Hesitation overridden, she thumbed in the call on her way home from the nail shop. When it went to voice mail, she said, "Hey, baby, sorry to bother you, but something's just come up. Linda Marshall has the distinct impression that the Barths are working behind the scenes to ink a deal on the Weymouth land before we even have a chance to bid. If we want to beat them to it, we have to act fast. I can coordinate everything except design plans. They're yours. Give me a call?"

Waiting for the callback, she held the phone palmed against the wheel during the drive home, and though that took barely five minutes, she was impatient. As soon as she pulled into the driveway, she sent a text.

Just left voice mail. Let me know you got it. Kinda urgent.

Fifteen minutes passed. Her phone was balanced on the

rim of the sink as she stepped out of the shower when a reply finally came.

This is happening right now?

So Jamie wasn't pleased with the timing. Well, hell, neither was she. *We have to arrange a meeting with the Weymouths for early this week,* she typed back. *Where do your plans stand?*

Long minutes passed. Caroline had a helmet on her head and was about to climb on the Harley behind Dean when she felt a vibration against her thigh. Pulling out the phone, she read, *They're just sketches.*

How long before they can be more? she typed back. She didn't want to pressure Jamie, but she needed something of presentation quality.

The answer came more quickly this time, actually while they were on the road, and though Caroline was anxious to read it, she wasn't yet comfortable enough on the bike to take one of her arms from Dean's. The minute he parked at the restaurant, though, she accessed it.

Wednesday, maybe?

Any chance of Tuesday? The Barths are breathing down our necks.

I'll try.

Chapter Twenty-three

S unday dawned warm and heavily overcast, but not even the occasional drizzle could dampen Jamie's spirits. She refused to think of the promise she had made Caroline and the juggling she would have to do to be ready for a Tuesday presentation, *refused* to think about how much she wanted that project and feared losing it.

Today was her wedding day. Even the brief text exchange was foggy now, seeming to dissipate along with the mist. By the time they hit the New Hampshire line, the sky held patches of clear, and the sun was positively beaming on the small Colonial inn by the time they pulled up.

As omens went, it was a good one. Jamie vividly recalled the rain on the night her father had died, and suspected thunderstorms would shake her for the rest of her life. But sun, here, now? She chose to believe Roy was smiling, knowing with a heavenly wisdom that her marriage to Chip was right.

The innkeeper was waiting. True to his word, he had the appropriate papers ready to be signed, and within the hour, with Chip and the boys in pressed shirts, shorts, and sandals, and Jamie in a sundress, the ceremony began. The gazebo was woven through with wild roses that matched those in Jamie's bouquet, and while a violin-cello duo played softly, she and Chip exchanged the simplest, sweetest, most heartfelt of vows.

It barely took five minutes, which was a good thing, since the boys wanted no part of standing still when lush gardens beckoned, but those five minutes were still beautiful and extraordinarily emotional for Jamie. She didn't know whether it was all that had happened of late, or whether she would have cried at her wedding even if they had waited a year, but her throat was tight and her eyes moist as they held Chip's, and her heart was filled to overflowing the entire time.

There were pictures taken by Chip's camera—a sophisticated digital SLR that he proved expert both at using and at telling others how to use. There were toasts with champagne for adults and apple juice for kids, even a dance for the newlyweds. There was an elegant picnic by the brook, with the innkeeper's wife arranging plates on a fine linen cloth and serving a hearty peasant bread, sliced filet mignon, and an asparagus and endive salad to die for. When the boys balked at the meat, she produced peanut butter sandwiches from her cart. None of them had trouble devouring freshly frosted wedding cupcakes.

They spent the afternoon between the garden, the brook, and the hot tub, and when it was time to head home, there were sandwiches for the car.

Jamie couldn't imagine a more perfect day. She had roses to press, pictures to frame, and memories to last a lifetime. Most important, she had a husband she adored and who adored her. He was forever lifting her hand to his lips as he drove, forever glancing at her with the same stunned pleasure she felt, forever citing one part or another of their wedding day as being *the* most special.

The boys fell asleep in the car on the way home, which meant that they were up later than usual into the evening, but Jamie loved even that. And when the house was finally silent, she had Chip. They didn't have to speak, were of like mind in what they wanted. Their lovemaking was slow and sweet, deeper and more meaningful than ever before.

She fell asleep in his arms and woke up feeling blessed. Eyes wide, she lifted her hand and looked at the ring he had produced in the middle of the ceremony. It was a total surprise; they hadn't talked rings at all, neither of them needing the physical symbolism. But the emotional one? When Chip was in Boston buying shirts for himself and the boys, he had gone to the Cartier boutique—not that she needed that either, but he had.

Three entwined gold bands, white for friendship, yellow for fidelity, rose for love—he had explained this while slipping the ring on her finger. All three bands were encrusted with diamonds, and though he didn't say it aloud, she knew he wanted the diamonds he gave her to be totally different from any diamond she had worn before.

"Hey," he murmured, smiling sleepily when her eyes flew to his.

She smiled back. "Just admiring my ring." She cupped his jaw. The dark morning stubble made the ring look even more delicate.

"Did we actually do what this ring says we did?" he asked.

"We did. Are you having second thoughts?"

"Not me. You?"

"Nope."

Grinning, he scooped her close and was about to act on an impressive arousal when the boys trailed in, at which point it seemed more important to make them feel loved. And that was heavenly, too—her adored baby half brother, soon to be her son, tucked up against her with his thumb in his mouth and Moose in his arms, grinning around that thumb as he watched Chip tickle Buddy, who squirmed and contorted.

As an only child in a house that had grown even more quiet after her parents' divorce, she had always dreamed of having a large family. This, here, now, was what she wanted. She didn't fear that Chip would tire of her, that Buddy wouldn't accept her, or that the children she and Chip had in the future wouldn't be wonderful.

Her only fear was what Caroline was going to say when they showed up at her house that morning.

Caroline was on the front porch with Champ and her laptop, researching Herschel Oakes's recent activity, when a Honda SUV turned into her driveway and parked behind Dean's truck. It was a minute before she realized that it was Jamie with Chip and the boys. Excited, she glanced at her watch. Not yet seven thirty? The implication of that didn't sound like the caution she had urged for Jamie, but she was so hungry for contact that she was relieved nonetheless.

Closing the laptop, she returned Jamie's wave, motioned Champ to stay on the porch, and started down the walk. Her eager eyes were first and foremost on Jamie, who was dressed for work, summer chic in a skirt and silk tank, auburn hair daring to curl past her shoulders. She took Tad out of the backseat, shifting him to a hip as Chip and his son rounded the SUV. And how could Caroline not stare at the man? More casual than Jamie in sneakers and jeans, he was also taller and darker, but if looks were the basis of a relationship, her daughter couldn't have done better. They were a striking couple, a *modern* couple dressed for different jobs.

Taking his hand, Jamie drew him alongside her, and in that instant Caroline saw beyond a handsome pair to a tight foursome, the quintessential all-American family. Her gut said that there was commitment here, though whether it was infatuation or true feeling she didn't know. Her gut also said Jamie wasn't here to talk about the Weymouth land.

They seemed nervous. But so, in her own more mature and experienced way, was Caroline. Anything Jamie was committed to, whether brief or long-term, mattered to her.

Meeting them at the head of the walk, she smiled and extended a hand to Chip. "I'm Caroline. I'm sure our paths have crossed at some point."

His handshake was firm. "Charlie Kobik. I'm honored. You've raised an amazing daughter."

"I think so," Caroline said in faint warning that Jamie was hers, would always be hers, and that Charlie Kobik could go by whatever name he chose, but it wouldn't change Jamie's parentage.

Lowering Tad to the ground, Jamie said a breathless "Mom—"

She had never been breathless where Brad was concerned, yet here it was again. Unsure of the meaning of that, Caroline bought time by dropping to a knee. "Hey, Tad," she said and was pleased that the child didn't resist when she drew him close. She reached out to Buddy. "You must be this handsome man's son. I'm Caroline, Jamie's mom."

"Where da cat?" Tad asked.

"You have a cat?" Buddy asked.

"Three," Caroline admitted.

"Mom—"

Caroline rose with a hand on each boy's head and her eyes on Chip. "I'm not one for formality. Do you mind if I'm on a first-name basis with your son?"

"I'd like that."

"*Mom,*" Jamie demanded with too much force to be further denied, and held out her left hand. The fact that it was shaking gave Caroline a feeling of déjà vu. Last time, the ring finger had been bare. This time it was not.

Meaning? Caroline wondered uneasily. Three days after breaking her engagement to one man, her heretofore prudent daughter was engaged to another?

"We got married," Jamie said, visibly holding her breath.

Caroline's eyes flew from the ring to Jamie and Chip. Neither was laughing, winking, or taking it back, and there was nothing remotely bogus about the diamonds in those three entwined rings. She didn't have to be a jewelry buff to recognize the design. It was stunning, high end, and authentic.

But *married*? After knowing each other, what, *half a day*? And . . . and without a word to her mother?

Jamie wouldn't do that. They were more than mother and daughter. They were best friends.

"Where da cat?" Tad repeated, standing inches in front of Caroline, looking up at her.

"Uh, oh, sweetie, he's inside. Upstairs, actually. I believe he's sleeping." She didn't know for sure. Having ceded the front porch to Champ, Master could easily be hiding in the parlor, waiting to attack when the dog invaded that space, too. Whatever, Caroline couldn't let anyone in the house, certainly not to the second floor.

"Is there a ball in the car?" Jamie softly asked Chip, who immediately loped off. Her eyes followed. Caroline couldn't miss the way they clung, seeming to take strength from just looking at him.

But still, marriage after knowing each other such a short time?

Chip returned with two kickballs, rolled them off across the grass, and leaned over the boys, who took off seconds later. As Jamie's vigilant eyes followed, Caroline struggled to find words, but she didn't know where to begin.

Helplessly, she listened as Jamie listed the arguments against what she and Chip had done, preempting Caroline's raising them, but insisting that their marriage was right, that they loved each other and the boys, and that, *believe it or not, Mom,* she knew Chip better in this short time than she had known Brad in four years.

Caroline could believe it. She had never been able to open to Brad, in part because he hadn't opened to her. Charlie Kobik looked like a different sort, stronger and more dynamic, but either of those traits could have a dark side.

She was thinking he might have somehow enthralled Jamie, forcing her to act in a way she would never have done on her own, when he said in too normal and sensible a voice, "For what it's worth, my parents will be as shocked as you are. They'll have heard of Jamie, but they'll be upset that they've never met her, and they'll be hurt not to have been included in the wedding. I apologize to you, and I'll apologize to them. I know this is sudden, but I know my own heart. I also know what I want in a family, because I grew up in a good one. Jamie's the first woman I've ever been with who wants the same thing. I love her, Caroline. She's it for me."

Caroline fought liking him, but the words resonated. His family had an outstanding reputation in Williston—which she knew how? Quickly she remembered. When Chip made a mess of his hockey career, the buzz around town had been what a shock it was, given his parents' goodness.

Did that make him the black sheep with emotional problems?

Champ had come off the porch, apparently as impervious to Caroline's authority as Jamie, and was eying the kickballs. Tad inched away. Buddy simply froze.

"He'll want to play," Caroline called gently. "Try rolling him the ball."

"Why is the dog here?" Jamie asked. "Why is *Dean*

here so early? I thought he wasn't a morning person. Is he working in the garage?"

Caroline could not go into that. When Chip trotted toward the boys to show them how to befriend the dog, she turned to Jamie. "I'm just stunned, baby." Her voice was hushed. "I never expected you'd run off to get married. When did this *happen*?" There weren't many choices, but she needed to know.

"Yesterday, at an inn in New Hampshire."

More pain. "You knew you were doing this when we texted Saturday night?"

"We had just decided, like a few hours before. The innkeeper is a justice of the peace, and there was a beautiful gazebo covered with roses. His nieces played violin and cello, and his wife served a picnic lunch."

Something felt familiar to Caroline. She gasped. *Dean.* Hadn't he said they could avoid a wedding? That there were elopement packages? Had he put them up to this?

But no. That thought was nearly as preposterous as the one saying her daughter had just gotten married.

Needing a visual—something, *anything,* to make the unreal more real—she asked in an aching whisper, "What did you wear?"

"My pink sundress."

"From J. Crew?"

"It's my favorite."

Yes. Caroline knew that. The dress was adorable. "But we were going to shop for a gorgeous gown. You wanted a big white wedding."

"Not me, Mom. Brad, Dad, and Theo. Did *you* want that for me?"

"I only wanted what you wanted."

"Which is Chip," she pleaded softly. "I love him, Mom. He's everything I could have asked for."

Caroline told herself that Jamie was a good judge of

people. But all she could think was that her only daughter was now legally tied to a man she had known for too short a time, that marriage was hard enough without this kind of rush, and that Roy would *die* if he knew.

Which was a ridiculous thought, of course.

Needing to blame him somehow still—Caroline had never set this kind of example for her daughter, had agonized for years before getting a divorce—she asked in the same hushed voice, "Does this have to do with your father's death?"

Jamie's voice was as hushed. "No. Chip and I discussed that, too. I'm telling you, we looked at every angle to find one that would tell us to wait. It wasn't Dad, per se. He and I were close, but he wasn't my best friend." *You were,* her eyes said, but the compliment stung.

"If I was the close one, how could you not tell me what you planned? How could you keep the most important thing in your life a secret? We talked Friday, and you said nothing. We talked Saturday night, and you said nothing. You could have come over any time in between, and you didn't. I could have kept a secret, Jamie."

"I know that, Mom, but I knew you'd tell me not to, and I didn't want anything spoiling my joy. I love Chip. I want to be with him."

"Couldn't you just live together to make sure it would work? Couples do that all the time."

"We could have," Jamie conceded. "But we know it will work. There's no question. Plus, we have kids. We didn't want anything tentative for them, and Tad, especially, has gone through so much. He needs permanency."

"Knowing someone for three days guarantees that?"

"I've known Chip more than three days," Jamie argued. "It feels like *forever,* like he's lived through the same things as me, like our lives ran parallel for years until last week, when they finally intersected and fused." She held out a hand to Chip as he returned, and when he wrapped an arm around her neck, she brought their linked fingers to her throat.

As lovely an image as her words produced, as sweetly as she was tucked into him, as truly connected as they seemed, Caroline ached inside. The rift Claire had caused over *Gut It!* had been bad. Jamie had sworn she was simply a pawn in that, but she had withheld information. This time, she was no pawn. This time, she had actively done something she had known would hurt.

Speechless, Caroline wrapped a hand around her own neck in an effort to get a grip.

"My son means the world to me," Chip told her—and though she wanted to shoo him away and say this was between her and Jamie, it wasn't. He was a key player. "I would do nothing, *nothing* to harm him. If I'd had any doubt that this marriage wasn't right, I'd have waited. And this isn't about my getting a live-in sitter. I love spending time with Buddy. It's what my dad always did with me and what I always dreamed of doing myself. I always knew I wanted a wife, but there was too much at stake for me to risk it all with the wrong woman. I never even brought a woman home before Jamie. I love that she has a career and that my work hours conform to the kids' schedule, so that I can be at home with our kids when she can't. I love that she considers Tad hers and that I have two kids now, and I want as many more as she does. Getting married may be sudden, but I knew from the first time we talked that she was the one. If we'd gotten together in high school, I might have saved myself a lot of grief."

"No," Jamie responded as if they were alone, "it wouldn't have worked back then. We weren't ready. We were both one-dimensional and self-focused."

"And you think marrying on a whim isn't self-focused?" Caroline asked, immediately regretting the words and their tone, but lacking control.

Jamie eyed her sadly. "(A) we didn't marry on a whim. Sudden doesn't necessarily mean on a whim. We considered it from every angle. And (B) I'm not afraid of marriage. You are, and I understand why. You're afraid of it not working. But Chip is not Dad."

Caroline gave a self-deprecating huff. "I didn't think Dad was Dad when I first married him either. That's my point. It's hard to know a person deep down in the best of circumstances." She didn't finish. Jamie was suddenly focused behind her.

Even before Caroline turned, she knew what she would see. There was Dean. Trotting down the steps. Striding down the walk. "Hey," he said to the gathering in general with a nonchalance totally at odds with the situation.

Jamie's startled eyes flew to hers.

Caroline might have denied it if he had been wearing a shirt and boots, but coming from the house rather than the garage, in jeans, a coffee mug, and little else, was incriminating. But—*whoa*—cause for shame, given what *Jamie* had just done? Absolutely not! "I'm fifty-six," she told her daughter, "and I'm *not* getting married."

"So she says," Dean injected as he shifted the mug to his left hand and offered his right to Chip. "Dean Brannick, and I sense something intense. What did I miss?"

"They got married," Caroline cried. "Eloped." She folded her arms, trying to cushion herself from the hurt.

Dean had the audacity to put a comforting hand on her back. She would have stepped away, if that hand hadn't made her feel less alone.

"You're *sleeping* with Dean?" Jamie asked. She looked surprised, but far from scandalized.

Caroline gave a dismissive wave. "It's very new."

"How new? Like, last night? Saturday night?"

"Honey," Chip cautioned, seeming to sense her point at the same instant Caroline did, but Jamie didn't listen, which probably was a strike against enthrallment.

"You didn't tell me, Mom. You could have, but you didn't." Her eyes went wide, dawning. "Last *Thursday.* I was driving here to tell you I'd broken my engagement, and it was early enough so that there weren't many cars on the road, only a few work trucks. And. A. Harley. He was heading out after spending the night, wasn't he?"

"It doesn't matter."

"It sure does," Dean argued. "Wednesday night was the beginning of the rest of my life."

"*Dean,*" Caroline cried in exasperation.

"There you go, Mom," Jamie declared. "You've been sleeping with Dean longer than I have with Chip, and you didn't tell me."

" 'Sleeping with' is not the same as 'married to.' "

"If you and I are best friends, it is. But you said nothing. Omigod," she cried, clearly seeing even more, "we talked about sex. About whether it's important. You acted like you had no idea. You said you weren't the best one to ask, which was a total *crock*—"

"No, I *had* no idea—"

"It was the perfect opening, but you said nothing. Why is it okay for you to withhold vital information but not for me to do it?"

Caroline was upset enough to mimic her daughter. "(A) I'm your mother, and (B) I'm old enough not to have to report in."

"*So am I,*" Jamie argued. "I'm older than you were when you married Dad. Did you ask your mother's permission before you accepted Dad's ring?"

"No—"

"And you were married within weeks."

"I was pregnant. You're not." She had a sudden, awful thought.

"No," Jamie confirmed, having one right answer, at least, "but Chip would have treated it like his if I was, which is only one of the reasons I love him. Look at his family. Look what he does for a living. He has the biggest heart in the world—but even if that weren't so, you need to respect my choice, because I'm an adult and now a parent and this is *my life*. Marrying Chip is probably the very first thing I've ever, *ever* done without consulting you, but he and I knew that what we had was real, and we wanted to act on it. Yes, it was fast, and people will talk, but we don't care." Her brow furrowed, eyes suddenly reflective. "So . . . so maybe Dad's death did have something to do with this. He died too early. Maybe the message is that if we put off the things we want, we may die before we get them."

"That's a recipe for disaster."

"My marriage is not a disaster."

You could always get it annulled, Caroline thought and might have said if not for Dean.

"Caroline," he warned, a single low word.

But Jamie seemed to have heard, too, because she was suddenly emotional. "Mom, *listen* to me. In other circumstances, we'd have wanted our families there. But this— here, right now," she wagged a finger between them, "is exactly why we didn't. Yesterday was beautiful. It was meaningful and intimate. Other than being with our families, I wouldn't have changed a thing." Her eyes grew moist. "Be happy for me, Mom."

Caroline had always wanted that, and she did hear shreds of common sense in the arguments, but it was overshadowed by a sense of loss. "I wish I could be," she whispered. "This is just so not what I expected from you."

"Nor is this," Jamie said with a look at Dean, "but it's

okay, Mom, because it's clearly what you want, which is the lesson you always taught me. You know, if we're talking about who's the most honest, you or me, it's kind of a draw."

Still Caroline fought. At some level, she knew she shouldn't, knew that she didn't fully understand her own reaction, but Jamie's actions hit at the heart and soul of the stability she had always tried to provide. "What about Brad? What about everyone at work? Marrying this fast after breaking up with him, you'll be called a cheater. Do you care?"

"Yes, I care. I've always cared about MacAfee Homes, but this is my life, and it's right, and they'll just have to accept that. If they want to think the worst, I can weather it, because I'll be with the man I love and our kids, and, by the way, that man will be covering for me at home while I work up designs for the Weymouth land, so you owe him for that, and as for Brad, he's outta here. He texted me last night—*after* I got married—to say he's accepting the position he wanted in Minneapolis. So who cheated? He was looking to change jobs and leave town while we were still engaged. I wasn't looking for anything, and broke my engagement the minute I realized I *wanted* to look. I'll talk with Brad this morning. But he's giving his notice today, so Theo has to be told."

Caroline held up both hands, palms out. "You're on your own there."

"I need to work on the plans."

"Sorry."

"You said you'd handle Theo."

"That was before this. I'm not *touching* this."

Chapter Twenty-four

Normally, Caroline would cling to the sight of Jamie's car until it rounded the curve, but not today. For one thing, it wasn't Jamie's car, for another, she was furious with Dean, and for a third, her cell was ringing in the front hall. Entering the house, she snatched it up. She knew who was calling even before she glanced at the screen. She had seen the *Globe* piece herself first thing and had actually thought it quite good, but the *Gut It!* EP would not.

Phone in hand, she strode barefoot deep into the parlor and looked at her mother's Victorian lace as she clicked into the call. Even with the reassurance of the lace, she was feeling ornery enough to dispense with pleasantries. "Yes, Claire."

"What possessed you to do that interview?"

She imagined that the Victorian lace had just stiffened, like her spine. "I got a call from the reporter and thought the publicity would be good."

The screen door slapped a second time. Dean. Turning her back on him, she went deeper into the parlor until she came up against the hand-hewn walnut of the dining table.

"You couldn't have called me?" Claire asked.

"Why would I do that? The reporter wanted to talk about Roy's death and MacAfee Homes."

"And *Gut It!*"

"Oh, Claire. That wasn't the purpose of the interview."

"Of course, it was. *Gut It!* put MacAfee Homes on the map."

The show had certainly given the company good exposure, but a little perspective was in order. *Gut It!* wasn't the be-all and end-all of life. Hosting it had boosted Caroline's self-esteem, certainly in her post-Roy years. But she could live without it. She saw that now—actually *felt* it, perhaps for the first time since the threat of losing it had arisen. Moreover, MacAfee Homes had been in existence long before *Gut It!* and would definitely outlive it.

Feeling remarkably calm, Caroline said, "The *Globe* covers local businesses. That was the context of the interview. This was about business, not entertainment."

"Jamie should have done it."

"Actually, I called Jamie. I felt that since Roy was her father, she might want to comment on his death. She was busy"—and didn't *that* suddenly take on new meaning—"so she opted out, and since I'm more into MacAfee Homes management right now than she is"—which actually felt quite good to say—"it made sense for me to do it. The reporter was on a tight schedule."

" 'Tight schedule' " Claire scoffed, in rare form for so early in the day, "means either 'I screwed up and forgot about this assignment,' or 'I need to do this interview now to be free later for a more important one.' Reporters can be handled, Caroline. We have professionals who know how to do it, which is another reason why you should have called me. That interview was a golden opportunity, and now it's lost. A *Globe* piece would have been the perfect vehicle to start shifting the show's leadership—"

While she ranted on, Caroline held the phone away from her ear and stared at Dean, who, incredibly, was finishing getting dressed in the clothes he had deliberately chosen to leave on the newel post on his way down the stairs earlier.

"—and you didn't even mention Jamie's name," Claire concluded.

"Oh, I mentioned it. I mentioned it plenty. The reporter chose not to print it."

"You made it sound like *Gut It!* was all about you."

"No, Claire. I am simply the MacAfee Homes spokesperson, which is clearly what's pissing you off."

"You didn't *mention* the station, but the station is crucial here."

"Not for this interview," Caroline insisted with renewed defiance, "and, in fact, maybe not at all. If not your station, another station"—which Dean had suggested and subsequently vetoed, though his judgment was *lousy*—"but you know something, Claire? I have more important things to deal with right now. I'll have to talk with you another time." She pressed END, tossed the phone onto the table, and swung her irritation on Dean.

He was beaming at her. "Well, *that* was impressive," he crowed. "Good for you!"

"Flattery won't work," she declared, further annoyed by the tingle she felt seeing him there with his belt hanging loose. A week before, she would have been mortified if his jeans had been unsnapped, but she knew now what was under his clothes—or *someone* did, though she still wasn't sure who that woman was, especially when he irked *this* woman so. "And there you were, barely dressed, trotting down the front walk bold as brass. Why did you do that? It was *my* place to tell Jamie about us, at *my* time, in *my* way."

He tucked a black tee into his jeans. "Given how you were dragging your heels, I'd have been dead before you got to it." He zipped his fly.

"Dean. It's been *five days.*"

He grinned, unrepentant as he sank down on the ottoman to put on his boots. "Counting, are you?"

"Did you have any inkling what Jamie was telling me?"

The grin faded. He paused and braced an elbow on his knee. "Actually, I did. Since you don't have AC, your windows were wide open. I heard what was happening and heard it heading nowhere good, so I figured it wouldn't hurt if I came down."

"Looking like you just rolled out of my bed."

"Which I had."

"*Dean.*" She wanted to strangle him. "You changed the whole dynamic of the discussion. I was making headway, and you gave her what she needed to turn my single best argument against me."

"The friendship one?" He went back to lacing his boots. "Oh, come on. It's not like she waited a year to tell you. They went off for the day yesterday, and she came here first thing today."

"She could have come over last night. She should have come yesterday morning, *before* she went off for the day."

"And given you a chance to say no?" He snorted. "She wouldn't have listened, Caro. All you'd have done would have been to rain on her parade, and please, *please*"—he speared her a quelling look as he reached for the second boot—"don't go on about her rushing into marriage. Yes, she rushed, but it wasn't just her, it was him, and it was their thinking about two little boys who they thought would be best off with two parents. They're adults, Caro. You might have acted differently had you been in her place, but this isn't your life, sweetheart, it's theirs. Besides, do you think time guarantees success? You took your time with Roy, Jamie took her time with Brad, I took my time with my ex, and God knows none of those relationships worked, so maybe time isn't the answer. Maybe it's about gut instinct and basic animal attraction."

Sex. "Why did I know it would come to that," Caroline muttered.

Both boots on, he stood, seeming too large and too right. "You didn't. You're just spoiling for a fight. You want to argue with Jamie, only she isn't here."

"Well, do you blame me for being upset?"

He held up a crooked-pinkie hand. "No, I do not. Being upset is normal. She's your daughter, you love her, and she did something that shocks you. But stop for a minute, Caro. Think about how she looked and how she acted."

"I don't know him."

"You don't have to. She does. And Williston does. He's a known entity here."

"Not all good."

"Pretty damn close, of late. So I repeat. Think about how she looked and acted just now. Think about the life she's making for herself. Is it all bad?"

He sounded so rational that Caroline couldn't ignore what he said. Jamie had an instant family—not just Tad now, but Chip and his son. Even without the Weymouth project, her life would be ten times busier. And richer? Maybe. She had always wanted a slew of kids, hadn't made any secret of that. If Chip's words were to be believed, he wanted the same and would carry his weight.

So, had she looked happy? Not when she faced Caroline. When she looked at Chip, though, or held Tad or said Buddy's name, she was happy. And she hadn't blown her hair stick straight, unintentional if she had run out of time. Or symbolic? It had looked prettier. Softer. Natural.

Dean's eyes were knowing. "Not bad at all," he confirmed, "but it is a life she's making for herself. If any one thing has you upset, it's that. She took her life in her own hands and acted without consulting you. So for you it's about control."

"It is not," Caroline argued. She *refused* to think she

was a controlling person. "It's about closeness and trust. And—and *respect*. If she respected me, she would have told me what she was doing."

"It's about control," he insisted as he approached. "Why do you need it, Caro? You have your life, and she has hers. She's twenty-nine. Why can't you let go?"

Feeling personally attacked, not only by Dean but belatedly by Annie, who had said much the same thing Saturday at the nail shop, she raised her chin. "Maybe because I'm a difficult person who wants to rule people's lives. So now you see the real me. Now you can just"—she gestured toward the door—"just walk out of here and never look back and be all the better for it."

That quickly, he was inches away. "Oh-oh-oh no, you don't get rid of me that quick. I'm not leaving, Caro. You're making a mountain out of a molehill, but I'm not running away, because I am not the problem. So what if Jamie knows we're sleeping together? You've always wanted her happy. Don't you think she wants the same for you?"

Caroline opened her mouth to answer, but thought twice.

"Are you happy with me?" he asked, suddenly vulnerable.

She supposed.

"I'll take that as a yes," he decided, his hazel eyes warming in relief, voice dropping, "because I *do* like sleeping with you, and it isn't just basic animal attraction. I like touching you in the middle of the night—just touching—and if you didn't like it, you'd move away, but you don't. There are times when I'm awake watching you, and in your sleep you scootch closer, like you want to make sure I'm there. Know how that makes me feel? Like a million bucks! So I don't care if the world knows we're together, and that starts with your daughter. She's not going to think less of you for it, unless you're with me for some other reason that I can't figure out, when deep down inside you're really miserable."

"You know I'm not," Caroline grumbled.

He brushed her cheek with a gentle fist. "So what's really bothering you? It isn't just that Jamie got married without asking permission. You're not that small a person."

His gentleness did it, stripped away her fight. She was horrified when her eyes filled with tears, but she couldn't will them away. "I feel like I've lost her."

"Because of her tie to Chip or your behavior just now?"

Wrapping her arms around herself, she confessed a soft "Both. You said it. She made her own life. I'm not part of it."

"Of course you are."

"She doesn't need me. Certainly not like she used to. So where does that leave me? If I'm not a mother, who am I?" *Who am I?* How many times she had wondered that in the last few weeks. After years of stasis, so much had changed.

He grasped her elbows. "You're her mother, her friend, her confidante. You'll always be those things."

"Her confidante? Like she confided in me this weekend?"

"Oh, Caro," he breathed and, drawing her in, wrapped his arms around her, "you're confusing confidante with consultant. She didn't consult with you beforehand, but she confided in you as soon after as she could."

With his chin on the top of her head, her face fit his neck just under the stubble that was his salt-and-pepper not-quite-scruff, not-quite-beard. His skin was warm and his pulse strong, and though he didn't speak, she felt a dense emotional support. Having always been her own best backup, she had never leaned on anyone quite this way.

Daring to let down her guard, she said a self-conscious

"So maybe it is about control. But it's hard, Dean, hard letting go."

"Is that why you won't wear my ring? Afraid of sharing something with someone? Of losing a little of that autonomy?"

She considered that, trying to figure out if it was true and, if so, where it came from. "I've just been the one in charge for so long. My parents were Poughkeepsie-centric, so I was on my own once I left, and Roy—well, Roy opted out soon after Jamie was born. When he was around, he ruled, but the rest of the time I was on my own. Jamie was mine. But I swear I didn't push her. The whole tennis thing came from her. I was just her manager."

"And cheerleader."

"Of course. What kind of mother would I be if I wasn't? But I tried to give her space, honestly I did, especially when she was at RISD, and still I was the one she came home to. So now she's going home to a *husband,* and the powers that be say I'm too old to host *Gut It!*"

"The powers that be don't know their ass from a hole in the ground," Dean said with such fervor that she had to believe it. "You're not too old. Jamie's too young to do what you do with the show, but she's better suited than we are to chase little kids around 24/7. Would you want to be in her shoes, starting out raising a family?"

Caroline thought about tired muscles and wrist tendonitis. She thought about quiet time with her computer each morning, minimal cleanup after breakfast, pedicures with Annie, and quality time with her cats. She thought about what she was doing this very instant, arms around Dean, deep breathing, quiet comfort, no interruptions.

Would she want to be starting out raising a family? "No *way.*"

He chuckled. "Me neither. I kind of like being near the

top of the MacAfee Homes food chain. You're higher'n me, and you'll go even higher if Theo has his way."

"Oh, Dean, I'm not sure . . ."

"If you want to run the company? You keep saying that, but it isn't so much filling Roy's shoes as paving your own way. What you did with the *Globe* was great. Jamie couldn't have done that—no offense, sweetheart, but she doesn't have the experience or the gravitas. She will some-day, but not yet. And what you're doing with the Weymouth acreage? Look how you've approached that."

"It's only one meeting." Later that morning with Herschel Oakes in his Boston office, and she was not looking forward to it. She was actually surprised he had agreed to meet—surprised he had even returned her call on a Sunday afternoon. If he thought she wanted to try them again as a couple, he had another think coming. She was perfectly happy where she was.

Dean's throat moved, sound vibrating past his Adam's apple. "I'm talking about the way you've taken the lead."

She sighed. "There's no one else to do it."

"I'm talking about you, Caro. You know what you're doing."

"I'm flying by the seat of my pants."

"You have good instincts. You make decisions. You act."

Letting the argument go, Caroline was quiet for a time, listening to the dove in the maple, to the patter of kitty paws overhead and Champ nosing at the front screen, wanting in. Superimposed on it was the steady beat of Dean Brannick's heart, not a bad moment at all, when removed from the rest of her life.

She tipped her head back so that she could see his eyes. "I made a mess of things with Jamie again, didn't I."

Wisely, he didn't respond.

"Only it's worse this time," she added, "because it isn't just Jamie, it's Charlie Kobik, who is now her husband, and

the two little boys who will be calling her Mommy before
long." She took a deep, resigned breath. "One bad thing
about age? Hard to accept change."

"One good thing about age?" Dean, her hero, pointed
out. "Realizing you need to do it."

"Well, *that* went well," Chip remarked.

"It was a *disaster*," Jamie cried, only then shifting her
eyes from the windshield and catching the grim look on
his face. The fact that he agreed with her was small con-
solation for how upset she was.

"Consider it a dress rehearsal," he warned. Indeed, now
that the hour was more reasonable, they were heading
home to Skype with Donald and Helene Kobik before Chip
dropped off the boys and headed for school. "My parents
won't be much better, and there are two of them."

Chip's parents actually were better precisely because there
were two of them. Don calmed Helene when she got caught
up in many of the same arguments Caroline had. Jamie
couldn't help but think, slightly hysterically, that the two
moms would get along just fine if they could get past the
suspicion that their son or daughter had been bewitched
by the other's daughter or son.

Presenting a united front beside Chip during the video
call, Jamie tried to look as unbewitching as possible. She
tried to look as *together* as possible, when her insides were
a tangle of nerves. She tried to reassure Helene as Chip
had done with Caroline, and while there was no Dean to
compound the argument, the call ended only marginally
better.

"Should we have waited?" Jamie asked the instant the
live feed ended.

Still bent over his laptop, Chip looked back at her. "Do
you think so?"

"I asked you first."

He straightened. "My answer is no. What's yours?"

"No," she said, relieved that they agreed here, too, especially considering the big deal her mother had made over needing time to know a person. She hated that Caroline had planted even the tiniest seed of doubt. "I like your parents, Chip."

"You do not," he muttered and pushed a hand through his hair. "Hell, you'd think I was twelve."

"You're the baby of the family. Your parents worry."

"They had cause once," he said, seeming momentarily lost in that old regret. His eyes held sincerity when they focused on Jamie again. "They really are good people. They'll love you once they get to know you."

"So will my mom once she gets to know you, but I'm sorry about earlier, Chip. She came across as a bitch."

He arched a brow at her leg, to which Tad was clinging. Whispering, "Ooops. Gotta work on that," she knelt to give her baby a hug. His warm little body was reassuring. Funny, given how recently he had become hers, but he was now a constant in her life. She was still trying to decipher his reactions and moods, but even his little tantrums were easier to deal with than, say, Caroline's right now.

Putting her chin on the top of Tad's head, she looked up at Chip. "She isn't usually so rigid. If she was talking about anyone else, she would have been more forgiving. I'm her daughter, so the rules are different. I get that. Still, given our ages, you'd think she'd be less uptight."

"Same with my mom. At what point do they ease up?" he asked rhetorically, then called into the other room, "Buddy, use the potty before we leave!" Back at Jamie, he said, "At least the men kept the moms sane."

Jamie frowned. "The men."

"My dad and Dean." He paused. "What?"

"(A) that remark borders on stereotypical, and (B) Dean

didn't quite keep my mother sane." When Tad squirmed for freedom, she kissed his head and let him run off. More pensive, she said, "Dean and Mom—why didn't I see that coming?"

"Maybe because they've known each other so long. Do we like him?"

"Yes, we like him, but why in the world she needed to keep it a secret is anyone's guess." She considered, then added a meek "It is a little weird, though."

"Imagining your mother with Dean?"

She stood, sighed. "Imagining my mother with *anyone*."

Sputtering a laugh, he slid an arm around her waist. "I can't *begin* to go there with my folks. As far as I'm concerned, they've had sex three times. Period."

Thinking that he knew so well how to handle her, she locked her hands at the small of his back. "They have a right to do it."

He snickered. "You think?"

She did, which was why she wasn't truly upset thinking of her mother and Dean together. It actually made her feel better to know Caroline wasn't alone, since now she herself had Chip. She had never felt that way about Brad, probably because he had never fully occupied her the way Chip did. Even now, with so much urgency on her mind, he took her away, if for only a minute or two.

"Anything beats thinking about telling Theo, but I do need to do that, seeing as he's my first stop. Not that I have time for this right now." Chip had already offered to drop off the boys, so that she could see Theo and then go on to the office. Presentations were crucial. If she had a prayer of having something done by tomorrow, she needed every possible minute.

Chip drew her to him, his eyes the riveting blue that never failed to send a little thrill through her. "Are you sure I can't go with you?"

"I'm sure. Mom was right. I need to do this myself." The thought of it tied her in knots all over again. She would love to have her husband with her as backup. But her grandfather could be unfiltered when it came to pithy remarks. She didn't want Chip hearing that.

Knowing where Theo would be and that he would be softer there, she drove to his house. Though the Tudor structure was totally old-world, with its half-timbers and stucco over a fieldstone skirt, its second-floor gables, its grand portico and broad stone steps, the house had always called to Jamie. She had never once dreamed of redoing it, though many of her recent designs involved updates on the Tudor style. Theo's house was Theo's house.

More to the point, Theo's house was Jamie's grandmother's house. Though Patricia was long dead, her generous spirit lived in the antique furnishings and exquisite art she had personally bought. These things evoked her memory at every turn, but nowhere was that more true than on the back patio.

That was where Jamie headed. Circling around, she walked over well-mown grass, passing beds of heirloom flowers in staggered states of bloom, a stone chimney, and shrubs of varied greens. The patio was soapstone. Patricia had herself set the stones, which were a richly veined gray and held enough of a pattern to delineate three large vaguely circular shapes, one each for lounging, grilling, and eating.

Surrounded by an outer yard of ancient trees in full leaf, the patio itself was lush. Jamie vividly recalled Patricia on her hands and knees, weeding the gardens that bordered the stone. A subservient woman doing her husband's bidding? Only the ignorant would think that. Patricia was strong and quiet. She was also insistent when she believed in a cause, whether that cause was building a pergola,

which was right now covered with lilacs, or raising money
for the church. Though she had never been directly involved in the operation of MacAfee Homes, she took joy
in the house her husband had built her. That joy shimmered
over the gardens even now.

By contrast, Jamie's first glimpse of Theo so alone
squeezed her heart. Wearing suit pants and a shirt, he
would add a tie and jacket before heading to the office. For
now, his neck was open, sleeves rolled to expose forearms
whose skin was marbled and loose. A creature of habit,
he was drinking orange juice, eating the last of the scrambled eggs and toast that his housekeeper had made, and
reading the newspaper.

He didn't see her until she slipped into the chair closest
to him, at which point he looked up with a start, then came
alive. Gleeful, he slapped the paper.

"See this?"

Jamie had seen two things that morning. First, she had
seen Chip, the boys, and the beautiful wedding ring that
she kept looking at in amazement but that Theo hadn't noticed. The ring was stunning and held a world of meaning
for her, but the subtlety of it would camouflage its meaning. Second and haunting now, she had seen Caroline's
disappointment.

"What's there?" she asked.

"Your mother's interview. She did a damn good job,
damn good job. She keeps saying no to it, but she's a
fine spokeswoman for the company. You need to tell her
that, too." He pushed the paper aside. "So, little girl, if
you aren't here to talk about the *Globe* piece, why'd you
come?"

Jamie tried to still her nerves. "I have news, Granddad,"
she said. Spotting the housekeeper approaching to offer
food, she shook her head. The instant they were alone
again, she faced Theo. She hated doing this to him when

his spirits were high. She hadn't seen him animated since Roy's death. But her news wouldn't wait.

His creased face grew progressively drawn as she told him about her broken engagement, about Brad's plans to leave the company, and finally about Chip. By the time she finished, he was frowning, his blue eyes confused. Seeming older, he turned away for a moist cough, then shifted gingerly on the cushions of the iron chair to face her.

"Brad is leaving?"

"Yes. He misses his hometown."

"I thought Williston had become his hometown."

"Apparently not."

"What about loving you?"

"I'm afraid we were both wrong about that. I'm sorry, Granddad. I know the last thing you need right now is having to hire a new lawyer."

Theo's mouth was a pale line. "Bad timing, so soon after . . ." *Roy's death.*

"Yes," she said and waited. Brad had only been half of the news she had delivered. She had no clue what Theo was thinking about the other half. Giving him time to process it all, she remained quiet.

Finally, screwing up his face, he asked, "The washed-up hockey player?"

"But he's not washed up," she rushed out with a promising smile and sat straighter. Earlier, with Caroline, she had felt like the little girl Theo always called her. Now conviction gave her new force. "He teaches here in town and runs a successful hockey camp for kids each summer. He has a three-year-old son he's raising himself, lives in the house he grew up in—"

"Living back home?" Theo broke in. His implication was clear, made all the more so by the disdainful tone of his gravelly voice.

"Actually," she countered, "he bought his parents two homes to retire in. He has plenty of money."

Theo gave a guttural grunt. "He made a mess of his life."

"He knows that. Trust me, he does. He hit rock bottom but pulled himself up. He's gainfully employed, has a family behind him and a son needing him, and his instincts are good." She hurried on, unable to resist the argument. "We all liked Brad. But Brad didn't want a child, couldn't even open his heart to an orphaned one, who happened to be your namesake grandson. So we can intellectualize his merits all we want, Granddad, but on the things that matter most, he fails."

Theo continued to scowl. "You could've raised Tad yourself."

"I could have. And I would have. I had a good example of single parenthood in Mom." It was a slam against Roy, but it was the truth. Theo didn't deny it with so much as a raised brow. "Believe me, I was in no rush to get married, certainly not on the heels of breaking up with Brad. Tad is not the reason I married Chip."

From inside the house came a distant phone.

Theo seemed not to hear it. His eyes didn't waver. "What is?"

"I love him."

"That quick?"

"That quick," she replied, driven by determination, even a smidgeon of anger. If the ringing phone meant Caroline wanted to share her feelings about Jamie's marriage, grit was needed. "Call my behavior impulsive, Granddad. Lord knows, Mom did. But when it comes to Brad, at least, he was happy to let me go and take a job halfway across the country—a job, PS, that he'd apparently been considering for a while."

Guilt stopped her. She hadn't meant to sound resentful. "I'm sorry. That was unnecessary. Brad served MacAfee Homes well. But he has an assistant who can cover until we hire someone else, and in the long run, the company will be stronger for it. As for Chip, I've never been so sure of anything in my life. He and I think alike. We've both done the superstar thing and understand about passion and focus. Right now, his focus is on his son, and on me and Tad. That said, I understand your caution. I shouldn't have snapped at you. I'm sorry."

Theo surprised her with a sly grin as he sank back in the wrought-iron chair. "I always wondered if you had it in you."

"Had what in me?"

"Your father's spunk. It makes me feel like I haven't completely lost him." His gaze shifted as the housekeeper came toward him with the phone.

"Brian Leavitt," she murmured apologetically. "He said it was urgent."

Jamie was still trying to grasp what had to be a major compliment—at least, she thought it was—when the identity of the caller sank in. An urgent call from Brian could only mean that Claire was up in arms about the interview Caroline had given the *Globe,* and if Claire was upset about that, she would retaliate by upping her demands about *Gut It!*

Jamie took a deep breath to still her racing heart, but it made barely a dent.

"Yes," Theo barked into the phone. He listened, then said reasonably, "I thought it was a good piece," then, without remorse, "I'm sorry you feel that way," then, watery eyes meeting Jamie's, "A meeting is an excellent idea." She saw him sit straighter, as if his spine had had an infusion of steel. "No, tomorrow won't do, or Wednesday . . . Yes, Brian, I understand that time is of the essence, but I run a business . . . Thursday morning is fine." His eyes warmed. He was enjoying himself. "No, not at the station, at my office . . . Yes, that's all well and good, but I'm eighty-two, so you can just come to me." *Home field advantage,* he mouthed to Jamie and winked. "MacAfee Homes is my major concern. Yes, Brian. Yes. I know Claire is upset, you already said that. A word of advice? Have her tone down the rhetoric before she gets to my office. I don't do well with ultimatums." A final pause, then a nod. "Thank you."

Jamie didn't know whether to be excited or nervous. "A meeting with Brian and Claire?"

"And your mother and Dean and you."

For an instant, Jamie wondered if Theo knew that her mother and Dean were involved. Then she realized that (A) Theo would have probably assumed they had been involved long before this, and (B) Brian would have requested Dean be there, so what Theo thought was moot.

"What did he threaten?"

Leaning on the arm of his chair, Theo came closer. His eyes, remarkably clear, held both challenge and amusement. "He threatened to cancel *Gut It!* What he doesn't know is that I don't *care* if he cancels *Gut It!* It was my son's baby, not mine. And that's a message for you, too. If you and your mother want it, you'll have to fight for it." He sat straight again, watching her closely. "Married?"

"Married. I love him."

He was silent.

When she couldn't take the suspense any longer, she coaxed softly, "Say something, Granddad."

"Do I know his parents?"

"If you're asking whether they run in the same social circles we do, I'd say no, but they're well thought of in town."

"Tad is named after me. I don't want him called Kobik."

She felt a tiny breath escape. The beginning of acceptance? "He won't be. Chip and I talked about that. I'm keeping MacAfee, too."

Again he was quiet. Then, his voice more gentle than she'd ever heard it, he asked, "Is this what you want?"

Jamie's throat tightened. Given how brusque her grandfather typically was, she had driven here fully prepared for a dressing down peppered with lots of *little girl* this and *little girl* that. Now, though, he was different, perhaps mellowed by age or by the death of his son. She almost imagined he was standing in for Roy. That was enough to bring tears to her eyes—and if not that, then the fact that Caroline had always been the one who wanted for Jamie what she wanted for herself, but was closed off to it now. Theo's gentleness couldn't have come at a better time.

"What?" the man asked gruffly, clearly unsettled by the tears in her eyes.

"That's the nicest thing you could have said. Yes, it's what I want, and yes, it's going to make me happy, and yes, I've thought of every reason why someone who doesn't know the situation may call it crazy, but I love him, he adores Tad, he's a fabulous father, and he treats me like gold. Tad will always be my first priority. He has to be. But this will give him a stable home with a mother and father who want him." She paused and chanced a tentative "Mom is pretty upset—the speed of this and all."

Theo made a dismissive sound. "I proposed to my Patricia the day we met. We married a week later."

Jamie had known that but hadn't seen a correlation. "Times were different back then."

He did a thing with his white brows that said he didn't think that was important either. And since he didn't, she had a thought.

"Maybe you could remind Mom about you and Grandma? What with everything that's happened, she's probably forgotten. I would greatly appreciate your help with her."

"It doesn't come without strings."

"What strings?"

"Convince her to take my job when I retire."

Blindsided by how serious he was, Jamie was momentarily without words. There were so many reasons why she might not be Theo's best advocate, the most immediate being that Caroline would assume Jamie wanted her anywhere that would get her off the set of *Gut It!* so that Jamie could host.

"I've been testing her," Theo said with that same earnestness. "She's good at what I do."

"I'm not sure she agrees."

His smile was wily. "Then it's your job to convince her."

Chapter Twenty-five

Caroline's outfit of choice for her meeting with Herschel Oakes would have been armor. He had never taken pot-shots at her directly, but she had seen him target others enough to know to beware. He wasn't a trial lawyer; his smooth zingers rarely reached a judge. They were aimed at everyday people, especially family members who were thinking of contesting a will for which he was the executor. Whether Mildred Weymouth had filed her estate plan with him to discourage one of her sons from doing that, or simply because Herschel had Williston roots, Caroline didn't know. All she knew was that he was a serious hurdle to cross in making a deal for that land.

Lacking chainmail, she went with the black flared skirt, peplum jacket, and ivory tank that she had bought for Roy's funeral. The outfit was as close as she owned to clothing that was both executive, as in I-am-MacAfee-Homes-take-me-seriously, and feminine. She did own slacks and blouses that she had recently worn to meetings calling for more than carpentry gear. But she thought the funeral outfit stylish and young, and Dean thought it sexy—not that that counted for anything other than making her feel attractive.

Actually, it did count for something.

Actually, it counted for a lot. The more attractive she felt, the more confident she would be. There were moments—fleeting, here and gone, back in an hour or two—when she still wondered what in the devil she was doing with her life. She was a carpenter. Her specialty was working with wood. She was happiest under a veil of saw-dust in the quiet of her garage, not negotiating Boston traf-fic in Theo's Caddy sedan, which he had insisted she drive. Yet here she was, dressed for business, following a GPS in a spanking clean and quite comfortable car, and it wasn't all bad. Interspersed with those moments of doubt were ones that said she was growing, trying new things, evolving. The terror she would have felt doing Theo's bidding even a month or two before was now mixed with anticipation.

She hadn't seen Herschel Oakes in more than a decade. After he had sold his Williston house and moved to Boston, there was no more running into him at Fiona's or the town dump, and while she had absolutely no personal interest in the man, she wanted him to think her a powerful woman. Powerful women who were also stylish, youthful, and sexy were impressive. If he was impressed, he might be inclined to help her.

Call her backward. Call her politically incorrect. Call her an embarrassment to every feminist in New England.

But she wanted the Weymouth land.

Herschel's firm occupied two floors of office space in the Financial District. The elevator that zipped her up had a brassy gleam, the twelfth-floor lobby was done up in a handsome navy lit by a wall of windows overlooking the city, and once her presence was intercommed through, the man who came out to greet her was as impeccably dressed as ever. His suit was Italian, making him look slimmer than she recalled, and his salt-and-pepper hair remained thick. But he looked much older. His skin didn't have the high color it used to, and his eyes, though still dark brown, were tired.

Older didn't disturb her, but something about him did.

After giving her a light hug, he guided her back to his office. A large mahogany desk dominated the space, but he passed up its high-backed chair—his throne, she thought dryly—and took the companion armchair to hers, where he folded one knee over the other and sat back. Surprisingly polite, he asked about Theo and Jamie, and congratulated her on her the success of *Gut It!* When he expressed condolences on Roy's death, adding as a caveat that he hadn't known Roy well and had never particularly trusted the man, she didn't reply. But when he told her how good she looked and tacked on "Roy's death must be agreeing with you," she couldn't be still.

She opened her mouth to protest.

He beat her to it. "I'm sorry." He actually looked sheepish. "That was mean-spirited. It's hard to change a lifetime of crass remarks. But I am trying."

"Why?" she asked, still startled.

He did a thing with his mouth that said it wasn't important and moved on. "So. You're interested in the Weymouth property."

Three times in the course of their one failed date he had complained about people wasting his time. She remembered it clearly, in part because he had been so focused on himself the rest of the evening that she had gone home convinced her own time had been wasted. So it didn't surprise her when he cut to the chase now. This was the man she remembered, and this was why she had come.

"MacAfee Homes would like to buy it."

"Before someone else does."

"If that's the case. We've been eying that land since Mildred died. We hoped we'd get a fair shot at it once the brothers decided what they want to do. Lately, the name Barth is cropping up a little too often. Is there a deal?"

"No."

"Would you tell me if there was?"

"Yes. I wouldn't share details, of course."

"Of course." More lightly, she added, "But can you tell me if anyone named Barth has sat in this chair in, say, the last six months?"

"They've tried. The Weymouth brothers aren't ready to act yet."

"Is it just a matter of waiting for the right offer?"

"I don't know," he surprised her by saying—surprised, because it seemed too honest an answer for the wily lawyer she remembered Hersch Oakes to be. That man would have hedged, simply to imply that the right offer would have to be high. If he were on top of his game, the man she had known would mention a recent golf outing with one of the Weymouths, to let her know how close they were.

If he were on top of his game, came an echo.

Her gut said he wasn't. Something about him was muted, as if he were a windup toy whose key needed turning. Perhaps he had just mellowed, but if so, it was unexpected.

"Are you okay?" she asked gently. "You seem—" She hesitated, not wanting to offend.

"Seem what?"

"Tame," she sang out, deliberately making it sound like a high compliment.

His brown eyes were steady. "Isn't that what life does as you age? You're aging. Aren't you more tame?"

She didn't have to weigh that for long. Strength, daring, passion—all had been front and center in her mind of late. "Actually, I think I'm bolder. But if I'd been as brash as you fifteen years ago, maybe I'd be tame by comparison now, too."

"Brash, huh?" His smile was wry. "I should have expected that from you. It was one of the reasons we were wrong for each other. You were totally honest and I was totally not. You saw right through me."

"Only partly this time. Something's different with you."

"And with you."

"If not now, when?" Caroline quipped in offhanded explanation, realizing only after she said them how true the words were. Wasn't she at an age where if she didn't try something, didn't do something new, didn't dare to push the envelope, she never would? Hosting *Gut It!* had been a challenge. She hadn't dreamed she could do it until she actually did it. Now that she faced losing it, she was discovering other things she could do, like pleasing Dean Brannick in bed. Like playing CEO. Even like arguing with Jamie.

Thinking of the last, she felt a painful curl near her heart. Needing to get back to the here and now, she eyed him and said, "Menopause. That's my excuse. What's yours?"

He huffed a soft chuckle at her response. When she didn't add anything, he said, "Ach," and waved his hand though his wrist didn't leave the arm of the chair, "just tired."

"Just?"

"Cancer, actually." She gasped, but he went on. "I was diagnosed three years ago. The treatment was aggressive. Right now, I'm in remission. It will kill me eventually, assuming a client doesn't kill me first."

"I'm sorry," Caroline breathed. "I had no idea."

"No one did. That was the point. It was important to maintain the appearance of strength. Unfortunately, my energy level has never quite gotten back to where it was."

He grimaced, bared his teeth, shook his head. "Now, there is another not quite honest remark. My conscience is what took the hit. When you face mortality, you start looking at your life, and when you overhear things like 'Couldn't happen to a nicer guy,' or 'I want his office the minute he checks out,' you start taking stock of where you've been."

Caroline didn't have to like the man to feel compassion. "People can be cold-hearted."

"If that's the example set for them by their mentors," he said with audible self-recrimination. "But the slowing down hasn't been a total waste. I've gotten to know my daughters. I have five grandchildren now."

"Five."

A smile softened his fatigue. "Two boys and three girls. They're pistols."

She eyed the photographs on the credenza. Most were of young children caught in spirited moments. "If they're pistols, they take after their grandfather," she remarked.

"Their grandfather made it work only to a point." He shot her an amused frown. "Why am I telling you this?"

"Maybe because we go back."

"It won't get you the Weymouth land," he warned smoothly. "I don't care how hard up MacAfee Homes is—"

"We're not hard up."

"Then why fight for that land?"

"Because it's a breathtaking parcel."

"It'll cost you a fortune."

"It'll make us a fortune."

"Well," he said and took a minute, seeming energized now as he regained command, "you may be barking up the wrong tree, because I'm not the one who owns the place. If I was, I'd have sold it months ago."

"It's that much of a drain on the trust fund?"

Lacing his fingers over his middle, he studied her with amusement. "I didn't say that. I said if I owned it, that's what I would do. I sold my place in Palm Beach—you knew I had one, didn't you? I held it longer than I should have. It was a greedy mother that cost a bloody fortune to keep looking good even when there was no one there, which was most of the time—but it had the right address and was just off the fifteenth hole. It was a great place to entertain. Evening guests, weekend guests, I'm telling you, you have no idea what you missed. I had a live-in cook who could prepare gourmet dinners for twenty, hell, sometimes thirty. When you offer guests a free meal that's better than the one they can get at the club—" He stopped, closed one eye, grunted. "There I go again."

Talking about himself. She smiled kindly, remembering that long-ago date.

He tipped his head. "If you owned the Weymouth estate, what would you do?"

Caroline didn't mistake his casual curiosity for anything other than what it was, namely an invitation for her to make her case for MacAfee Homes buying that land. So she began with the company's roots and ended with its love of Williston, and in between she spoke of Jamie's award-winning designs, other local projects they had done, the roster of local craftsmen they used, and the possibility of *Gut It!* involvement. "If the Weymouths choose MacAfee Homes," she concluded, after covering all of her major points, "they'll be guaranteed a quality product that will preserve the spirit of their childhood home."

"What spirit is that?"

"Elegance. Success. Beauty. Warmth."

"The Weymouths aren't any of those things."

She smiled. "But I bet they wish they were. Home development is about wishful thinking. It's about capturing a dream."

"That sounds very pretty."

Turning mockery to her advantage, she said, "It will be

very pretty. We've done this before, Hersch. We know this land, we know this town, we know this business. We get things done, and we're willing to work with your clients to make them comfortable with everything we do. We'd like to meet with them. Can you arrange that?"

She imagined she saw a glimmer of admiration before he put on his game face again and clicked his tongue. "That may be tough. Like I said, they're not ready to act."

"*That,*" she said, coming forward, "is because they haven't talked with us yet. You said it yourself. The trust fund is taking a hit."

"I didn't say that. You did."

"And you didn't deny it," she countered. Facing this man who, regardless of its cause, wasn't quite the demon she remembered him to be, she felt surprisingly strong. It struck her that she was almost enjoying herself. "You just told me about your place in West Palm. Given the weather up here, the Weymouth house has to cost far more than that one to heat. Throw in electricity, the cost of a live-in caretaker, the standard lawn cutting and snow plowing, homeowners insurance, alarm company fees, and property taxes—should I go on?—and it adds up."

He whistled softly. "You're good."

Studying him, she sat back. "*Are* you mocking me?"

"No," he said. "I'm thinking that I may have missed something in you."

It was high flattery, she supposed, though she couldn't return the compliment. Even mellowed, the man held less personal appeal for her now than he had then. Zero chemistry was an understatement, now that she knew what real chemistry was. Dean was such a total *man* compared to Herschel Oakes.

But that counted for nothing when it came to the land she wanted. Herschel was the man here, and she couldn't offend. Laughing softly, she raised a hand. "Oh, I am not touching that, but trust me, when it comes to the company that will do the best job in developing the Weymouth acreage, I'm right. The Barths don't have a feel for this land or this town, and as for your clients not being ready, Ralph hasn't gotten his act together enough to send a crew out to even look at the property in the year since his mother died, John may want the house for himself but will never be able to pay the trust as much as we can, and Grant is so desperate for money that he'll take *any* sale."

She wouldn't have dared be this blunt with a nonfriend, but her knowing all this told Herschel Oakes that she hadn't come on a whim.

"Here's the thing, though," she went on, striking while the iron was hot. "We want to act quickly. Arrange a meeting, and we'll talk money and designs and whether the brothers want the land featured on our show, but now's the time, Hersch."

"You want a preemptive deal."

She nodded. "We do."

"Why right now? Is this a play to show the world that the company can survive without Roy?"

"No. We know others are interested in it. We want that land before someone else gets it, because we know we're the best ones to develop it."

"Why are *you* here? Last I heard, you were a carpenter. Isn't that what you are on the show?"

Ignoring the put-down, she smiled. "Ever watch it?"

"Reality TV? I think not."

"You should watch ours. It's good."

"You didn't answer my question," Herschel countered smoothly. "Why you? Is it because we have a little, uh, itty-bitty little bit of history together, so Theo felt you could sway me for old times' sake?"

She actually laughed. "You and I both know that would

never have worked, though I have to say I like the new you better than the old one, cancer and all."

"Cancer is no laughing matter."

Studying his earnestness, thinking about his reformed manner, and having the sudden thought that other things in his life might have changed as well, she glanced at one of the photos on the credenza. No family shot, this one showed a woman who was dark-haired, middle-aged, and seemingly down to earth. She wasn't his ex-wife or either of his daughters. Her face was kind.

Caroline hitched her chin toward the photo. "Is that someone special?"

"She's my therapist."

She might have laughed at the idea of one's therapist holding a prime spot among family photos, if he hadn't remained so serious. "Literally?"

"Yes. She helped me when I was first diagnosed. Not my usual type. She works."

"Works, present tense—as in continues to treat you?"

"Works as in goes to work every day. I always liked my women to be available. That was one of the problems I had with you. You kept me waiting an hour for our date while you finished a job."

Caroline smiled. "And here I thought you were going to say I had dirt under my nails."

"I could never see that," he mused with a glance at her hands. "You kept them polished, even back then."

"There's no dirt."

"And Alice isn't my therapist anymore, at least, not in any official capacity."

"Ahh." A romantic link, hence her presence on the credenza. "That's nice, Hersch. I'm glad for you." And she meant it.

"So, I ask again, why you?"

She could have said that Theo wasn't as mobile as he used to be, or that they hadn't yet picked a replacement for Roy. She could have even admitted that yes, it was because she and Hersch sort of had a past. The truth held bits of all these things. It held other things as well, like Theo wanting her in management and Dean wanting her in bed and the money behind *Gut It!* wanting her fifty-six-year-old face out of the limelight, meaning that she had something to prove by orchestrating this deal, but Herschel Oakes didn't need to know those things.

For now, she simply said, "Because I care about that land."

"If you care so much about a piece of land," Dean responded the instant Caroline finished her blow-by-blow over a late lunch at Fiona's, "then you need to care more about Jamie."

Startled, Caroline held her chicken-breast-on-focaccia midair. "Whoa. Where did that come from?" She had been feeling good. Suddenly, she wasn't. The little nagging that had been hovering just beyond the periphery of her consciousness sprang forward and squeezed her heart.

"Have you called her?"

Carefully, she replaced the sandwich in its wicker basket. She looked at her watch, then across the booth at Dean. She had been expecting praise for having held her own with the lawyer. Feeling defensive now, she said, "It's barely one o'clock. My morning was busy."

"You said you'd call her. Things weren't left well, and if you've taught me anything about handling my son, if you've learned anything since the last fight with Jamie, it's not to let moss grow on a festering stone."

A *festering* stone? "Did I ever use those words?"

"Fine. Not those, exactly," he conceded without backing down, "but you get my drift. You said you'd made a mess of things with Jamie. You said you were going to call her while you were driving to Boston."

Sitting back in the booth, she kept her eyes steady on his. "I thought I would, but then I wanted to stay focused on my meeting." She was challenging him straight on, having found that when she did, he was slower with barbed replies. She wanted him to think before he said more. Jamie was her point of greatest vulnerability.

Lifting the last of his ham-and-cheddar-on-focaccia, he studied it before dropping it again. Pushing the basket away, he wiped his mouth with a napkin, set it down, and met her gaze. "You could have called her on the way home. It's important, Caroline."

He wasn't letting it go. Frustrated, she shot back, "You think I don't know that?" Planting her elbows solidly on whatever newspaper article was under the glass that covered the table, she said, "Please don't lecture me, Dean." She lowered her voice. "Just because we're sleeping together doesn't give you the right to tell me what to do." She had been a free agent too long for that. "I'll call Jamie when I get my thoughts together enough to do it. Besides, she hasn't called me. And don't make a comparison between your son and Jamie. He's fourteen. She's twenty-nine. If she's old enough to decide to get married one day and do it the next, she's old enough to know that she hurt her mother and needs to make amends—*and* that she has no right to judge me for what *I* do in bed." She knew she was getting wound up, but couldn't stop. He had hit a nerve. "Did I cheat on her father? No. Did I have men in the house after my divorce? *No.* But all these years later, she wants me to stay chaste?"

His hazel eyes chided. "That's not what she meant, Caro. As I understand it, the argument was about your not telling her."

"I don't *need* to tell her."

"And she doesn't *need* to tell you. So you're even."

"Which is why she can call me," Caroline said, sitting back. "I have a lot on my plate right now."

"So does she," he said so reasonably that, perversely, she had to keep up the fight.

"Of her own choosing."

"Not all. You were the one who asked her to have preliminary Weymouth drawings done for tomorrow. And you're right, she's older than Renny, but you're older than she is."

"I'm older than you, too," Caroline said. Her anger was starting to fade—it had been stupid all along—leaving her embarrassed and, to cover that, hurt. "How about a little respect?"

He took a drink of his Coke and set the glass down, then, coming forward, put ropey forearms on the table. His brow was furrowed, his eyes puzzled. "You express your opinion of things that I do or don't do. Can't I do the same?"

"I don't attack you," she said quietly.

"I wasn't attacking."

"It felt that way."

"Then I used the wrong words or the wrong tone or the wrong look. And don't give me that bit about being older than me, because at our age months don't matter."

"It's years," she corrected sourly.

"It's twenty-nine *months,* and the only time I'm aware of that is when you remind me." He sighed and said in a conciliatory way, "All I wanted to do was remind you that Jamie is a priority. The longer you wait to call, the harder the call will be."

Caroline said nothing, simply listened to the surrounding blur of voices, the tick of utensils on china, the calls from the kitchen. A woman she knew approached and introduced a star-struck friend from out of town to her and

Dean. Too soon they moved off, and the flash of pride she felt broke apart.

She looked at Dean. He was fingering the knife he hadn't used, turning it this way and that. Seeming to feel her gaze, he raised his eyes, showing her the vulnerability that never failed to touch her.

"I'm sorry," she said quietly. "I overreacted."

He reached for her hand. Usually they were careful, but now he wove his fingers through hers in plain sight on the table. "I don't want us fighting."

As uncaring as he was about who was watching—getting things right between them was suddenly more important—she squeezed his hand. "We've been fighting for years. It's who we are."

"Bickering is different from this." He seemed worried. "We were doing okay on the bigger things, weren't we?"

The bigger things. Like Champ. And the country house. And action movies that she couldn't stand and for which he now wore headphones when he watched in bed late at night. And even her baths, which she preferred to his showers, but for which she still liked privacy.

"Yes," she acknowledged. "And we are. We're doing good. It's just . . ." She tried to figure out what had set her off and explain it to him. "I was feeling triumphant."

"And I burst your bubble."

"I will call Jamie."

"I'll try not to attack."

"She really could call me, too, you know. She was pretty judgmental."

"You were judgmental on the bigger issue. Her husband is her life now. If you don't accept that, your relationship with her is screwed." He paused. "You're the adult."

"Seems to me you said she was one. She certainly said it."

"So who'll be more adult?" He stared at her and waited.

Caroline let out a breath. "We'll see."

"That's the best you can do?"

"Yes. This is still raw."

"Want to go back to your place for a little—"

She cut him off with a sharp stare.

"I can't help it," he said, eyes touching her torso. "You're wearing my favorite outfit."

"The one I buried my ex in?"

"Exactly."

"You're bad."

"But you love me anyway."

She sighed. "I do."

"Enough to marry me?"

"Please. That is one more thing I can't deal with right now. Theo's waiting. He wants to know about the meeting."

Relenting, Dean smiled. "You did good, sweetheart."

"Did I?" she asked. "For all my brilliant campaigning, Hersch wouldn't commit."

Chapter Twenty-six

*E*ncouraged by Theo's blessing, Jamie might have made progress with the Weymouth plans if she'd had nothing else to do at the office, but first there was Brad. Less than a week before, she had been wearing his ring. Her grandfather might not have noticed this new one, but someone else at the office was sure to. She owed it to Brad to tell him herself.

He was in his office when she arrived, and his anger when she told him about Chip shook her. She had hoped he would be as detached as when they last talked, but no such luck. Gray eyes cold, voice low in a way she had never heard it before, he accused her of cheating on him, didn't want to hear her denials, and went on about it way too long, so that she grew angry herself.

"You're a lawyer," she interrupted with enough force to make him listen. "There's all kinds of evidence in phone and text records to show that I didn't *know* Chip Kobik until he gave me advice on Tad, and there's an e-mail trail a mile wide proving that I was never alone with him until after you and I broke up. But if it makes you feel less guilty—"

"Guilty?" he cut in, pushing at his glasses with a slim finger. *"Me?"*

"For job-hunting months ago, for considering a huge move on the sly, for not being able to give of yourself to a *child,* Brad—that was the real eye-opener for me—then, fine. Believe what you will." Shaken as she was, she forced calm into her voice. MacAfee Homes needed Brad for one last task. "Theo knows you'll be leaving. All we ask is that you honor the two weeks' notice your contract allows. There may be action on the Weymouth property this week. It would be much easier if you were to handle it for us. If you ever had any feeling for me, I'd appreciate your help there, and if you can't do it for me, do it for Theo or for Roy. They treated you well."

To his credit, he remained silent. She wasn't sure if he would do what she asked, but she didn't have time to press him on it. Too much was weighing on her. Thinking about the work she had to do, she hurried upstairs to her office.

She might have made progress on the Weymouth plans then, if the phone hadn't started to ring. Each time it did, her pulse skittered on the hope that Caroline was calling. The morning's argument was like a paper cut with a constant little sting. If being a daughter was the only role she had to play, she might have been better able to deal, but being a wife, a mother, and an architect who was falling further behind each minute, she was raw. Caroline could make it better if she called.

But no. Not Caroline. Clients. They wanted progress reports, of course they did, and sending e-mail that Jamie might put off reading was too easy. How to tell them that their projects weren't her first priority just then? She did her best to reference details of each, pulling up the applicable screens on her computer, trying to make it sound like she was on top of things, when all the while she was thinking that she was losing precious time.

One call ended. She returned to the Weymouth project. Another call came in. Had Caroline been on the phone,

Jamie would have happily talked, but designers and contractors, even a town official with setback concerns? Seeming of one mind, they had decided that she'd had enough time to mourn Roy and was now free to work.

They had *no clue.*

At the end of another nonproductive hour, she asked her assistant to hold her calls. That was when the woman noticed her ring. Jamie considered dodging the issue by saying it was her grandmother's ring or even her mother's, but a bigger part of her wanted the world to know about Chip. She was proud of him, *proud* that she had recognized how perfect he was for her and had acted on it. Just picturing him now brought a soothing wave into her turmoil.

But that was a lot of dirt for her assistant to handle, between a broken engagement and a wedding. The woman asked if she could tell people. Figuring that word had to get out sometime, Jamie didn't say no.

Big. Mistake. Her assistant told the receptionist—that was all, she swore afterward, but it was enough. Jamie was finally getting into the Weymouth plans when MacAfee people began texting her. Texts she could ignore; physical bodies, strolling into the design department and right up to her desk, wanting to see her ring? Most had no idea that she and Brad had even broken up.

"Nightmare," she told Chip when he called after his last morning class. "There are too many interruptions. I can't focus."

"Did you make any progress at all?"

"Not much," she said, trying to stay calm. She didn't want her new husband thinking she was prone to hysterics. And she wasn't. Not normally, at least. Of course, she didn't normally have as little time to prepare for something she wanted as much as she wanted the Weymouth job. "You saw my designs. They're dreams, that's all, dreams. My mother wants me to do something in two days that I would normally spend two weeks on, and it isn't all CAD work, it's imagination. You can't force that."

"Call her. Discuss it with her."

But Jamie knew how things worked. "There isn't much to discuss. We need the Weymouth project to undercut the Barths and be able to go into the *Gut It!* meeting Thursday from a position of strength. I just have to get going. Normally, I'd do a ton of site work beforehand, but it wasn't like I could hire a surveyor or walk the property taking pictures and measurements when the land isn't even formally for sale, and now, well, I just don't have time. The town assessor's office is faxing me a land plot, but it'll be primitive."

"How much detail do you need?"

He was right. She didn't need much. But detail wasn't the problem right now. "I need enough to convince them that we love the place and have a vision for it, and they'll want that vision to be beautiful and innovative and still preserve some kind of old-world feel—at least, I'm guessing that's what they want. I don't know them."

"I do."

Jamie caught her breath. "You do?"

"I played hockey at Harvard with Alex, son of Ralph. He was two years ahead of me, but the team was pretty tight. His dad used to fly in for games all the time. He was every coach's worst nightmare."

That didn't bode well for Jamie. "In what sense?"

"Egotistical. Larger than life—a big man with a big voice and big expectations. You won't need details with him. All he'll want to see is the big picture."

"Luxury?"

"I'd say so. As over-the-top as your dreams go."

"Ralph is one of three. Will the other brothers want that, too?"

"Not necessarily, but it'll stroke their egos to see something grand. I haven't seen Alex since I left Cambridge. I could call. If his dad thinks I'm a loser, the contact might backfire. Should I try anyway?"

"Not yet. And not because of that," she added quickly lest he worry. "You're no loser. You made the pros, Chip. That's phenomenal. It's just . . ." She tried to express it. "Old habits die hard, I guess. I really wanted to do this myself. The problem is that when I feel so scattered, I can't concentrate, and when I can't concentrate, self-doubt moves in. Maybe my vision isn't grand enough. Maybe they'll think I'm too young for the job."

"Age is just a number, honey. We've talked about that. Look at your portfolio. It's top-notch. Besides, if there's a meeting, Caroline will be there. And Theo and Dean. They'll add the element of age."

"But I'm the designer."

"With impressive designs."

She wanted to believe him, wanted it badly. "You think? I've only shown you dreams."

"Impressive dreams."

"You're biased."

"Absolutely," he said with a smile in his voice. "So here's an idea. Your condo is quiet. Could you work there?"

She could. The room where Tad had slept was a home office. When she thought of the place, though, she felt cold and alone.

Seeming attuned to her thoughts, Chip said, "How about I get someone to take lunch duty for me here. Meet me at the condo now, and we'll move your office to the house. My old bedroom already has a desk and Internet hookup."

"You need to work there. Student evaluations, all the paperwork for camp—"

"If I push my stuff to one end, there's still room for yours. We can pick up another table tomorrow at Home

Depot and in the meanwhile put the printers on night-stands. The room'll be thrilled. It's getting bored with my work."

She laughed. "Like the room has a mind? You sound like my mother. Her house is always telling her not to renovate. She claims it wants its history intact."

"Wise woman," he said, but he didn't ask that she call Caroline again, for which she was grateful. More than any other distraction, her mother hovered in the periphery of her consciousness, a little ache that wasn't debilitating, just always there.

"I mean it," Chip insisted. "We talked about you working in that room until we could build on. It won't take us more than an hour to get the basics moved from your place and hooked up in mine if we do it together." He was a whiz at technology, from what she had seen of his Wi-Fi setup, which included not only Internet but music, television, and wireless heat control.

Feeling a glimmer of excitement that came as much from the idea of seeing him as from being able to work in a place that was emotionally warm, Jamie glanced at her watch and calculated the amount of time it would take her to collect what she needed and drive to the condo. "Ten minutes?"

She heard another smile. "Ten minutes."

Thirty minutes later, he said in a voice that rumbled, as intimate as nakedness, body heat barely cooled, and the mess of sheets on Jamie's bed, "We need to keep this place. It sure beats a motel for a tryst."

Jamie was logy in the wake of two mind-blowing orgasms, and if those hadn't done it, breathing him in would have. He had a unique scent, very male, now tinged with sex. "Tryst?" she managed to tease.

"That one word is the grand total of what I got from

the literature course I took at Harvard during my abbreviated tenure there," he drawled in self-deprecation, but his eyes were on her mouth. Rolling on top again, he wound his fingers through hers, anchoring them on the pillow on either side of her head, and gave her a lingering kiss that ended with one to her freckles, which he claimed to love. "But you have to work."

Work? What was work? She hadn't been thinking sex when she drove over—well, maybe a kiss or two—but one look at Chip in gym shorts that hung from lean hips, with his dark hair spiked over his brow and his blue eyes hungry, and she was lost. Easy to subdue the attraction when they were preoccupied with getting the boys to dinner or bed or daycare, but the chemistry between them remained potent. Tryst? He might be onto something. *Thank you, Harvard.*

But yes, she had to work. The sudden twist in the pit of her stomach had nothing to do with arousal. Reluctant, she checked her watch. "So do you. Do we still have time to move the office? I should probably work here today."

"Are you okay with that?"

"No. But I'll suffer."

Grinning, he stretched over her again, moving a certain part of him against a certain part of her to remind her exactly *why* they hadn't had time to move her office. She arched up to catch his mouth a final time before giving in to that other shrieking need.

Several consecutive hours of quiet helped. Shifting between an old *Williston News* photo, Google Earth, and her memory, she made a computer rendering of the main house, which, in its heyday, had been a grand French country estate built of stucco and brick, with tall windows that rose from the second floor into the eaves, drawing attention to three high, steep hip roofs, each with a large chimney.

Time had taken its toll on the real thing, but her drawings depicted a restored glory, which was how her mind's eye had always seen the place. Refining the image that had taken shape on her screen, she cleaned up the stucco and repointed the stone, pruned back ivy and overhanging trees, replaced rotted wood framing the windows, and added gables to lift the entire facade.

Lost in the work, she didn't notice the passage of time until she reached for her liter of Poland Spring and found it empty. Grasping the bottle, still in the kind of semitrance that came when she worked on something she loved, she stood back from her desk and studied the screen. She did adore this house. It had always seemed lonely to her, perhaps because for as long as she could remember Mildred Weymouth had lived by herself, perhaps because it had been so sadly neglected. Working on these designs reminded Jamie why she had dreamed for so long of this project and why she had to do it right.

When she went down to the kitchen for more water and glanced at her watch, though, she realized it was almost pickup time at First Unity. Chip would get the boys. But what would Tad be thinking when she didn't show? He knew Chip, but she was the one who had seen him in the hospital within minutes of his birth and been a fixture in his life since. If she wasn't at pickup, he might fear that she was gone, like his mommy and daddy. He seemed like such an easy kid, taking to Chip and to Buddy, adapting to two new homes in quick succession. She wasn't sure, though, if he was happy or simply on change overload—whether he was so lost without his parents that, other than the occasional crying jag, he just went along.

She needed him to see her. And she needed to see him. As priorities went, Tad came first.

That was why, when Chip pulled up in the silver Honda,

wanting to see how she was doing before he went for the boys, she said, "I'm coming."

"You owe me for this," Herschel Oakes announced straight out when Caroline picked up her phone. "Wednesday at one. We'll videoconference from my office. John will be here in the flesh, Ralph and Grant on the screen."

Yessss. With the passing of the afternoon, she had grown doubtful. But he had come through! "Wednesday."

"At one," he repeated. "Will you be prepared? I'm going out on a limb here. I don't want to waste anyone's time."

Of course he didn't, but Caroline forgave him that. The timing was perfect, or as perfect as it could be given the meeting Thursday morning with Brian and Claire. If they had even a preliminary deal with the Weymouths before then, they would neutralize the Barths.

Tomorrow would be hectic. She wouldn't get much carpentry done, what with meeting with Theo and the MacAfee finance people. While Linda compiled a comp study, Caroline had to bring Dana Langham into the loop. She also had to talk with Brad, which might be fine, since he was likely as shocked by Jamie's marriage as Caroline was. Well, maybe. Actually, probably not quite. But Brad was still on payroll. Marketing presented a problem, since they hadn't hired a replacement for Roy. Well, between Theo, Dean, and her, they would come up with something. She would drive Theo into Boston herself.

"We'll be there," she promised. "And yes, I owe you. Anything, Hersch. This is a huge help to me. It's the act of a loyal friend. Thank you."

As soon as she ended the call, she texted Jamie.

Jamie might have ignored the phone if she hadn't suddenly realized it was still on vibrate, which was the only way she had been able to get any work done. When she saw Caroline's name, she sorted through a score of messages to this one.

Just got call. Meeting with Weymouths 1 PM Wednesday. Work for you?

No, it did not work for her. She needed twice as much time, *four* times as much time, to get the designs right. But if she wanted to show Caroline that she could do it all—marriage, motherhood, work—she would manage it somehow.

No problem, she texted back and broke out in a cold sweat.

"Everything okay?" Chip asked, darting her little looks as he pulled into the First Unity lot.

"Yup, yup, everything's fine," she said in a high voice and pushed it out of her mind. She was going to be with her boys. Her eye was already scanning the playground.

When Chip stayed behind to talk with one of the teachers, Buddy spotted her and came on the run. Bending over him, she slipped an arm around his shoulders. "How was your day?"

"Good." He pointed. "Taddy's there. He was crying during rest."

"Uh-oh."

"I think his stomach hurt him." He looked past her. "Where's Daddy?" When he spotted Chip, he broke free and ran.

Jamie turned her attention to Tad, who was standing off to the side, watching three kids on the seesaw. His aloneness broke her heart.

She was on her way to rescue him when she was waylaid by one of the teachers. "Don't let this fool you. It took him a while to settle down during quiet hour, but he's had a good day."

Watching him now, though, Jamie worried. "Is he afraid of the seesaw?"

"A little. He climbed on earlier and fell off. He didn't hurt anything but his pride. But this is how they learn. He'll get the knack."

He spotted Jamie then. Face lighting in recognition—breath-stopping, *that* was—he forgot the seesaw and ran to meet her, little legs churning so fast that he tripped, sprawled on his belly on the dirt, and began to cry, breaking her heart for a second time in as many minutes. Rushing to him, she scooped him up and buried his face in her neck, finally holding him back to wipe the streaks from his face. "Hey, monkey," she crooned, as she brushed at his clothes, "you run so well." It was true. He was fast like Roy, maybe prone to tripping like she was but the way he had lit up when he saw her made her day.

When he babbled something or other, the teacher interpreted. One of the children had a birthday, and the mother brought cupcakes.

"Rainbow sprinkles?" Jamie asked, brushing a crumb of one from the corner of his mouth.

"Wainbow," he cried with a big smile, tears lingering on his lashes but forgotten. He was that easily distracted.

As was she, she realized. She loved being with these guys. Oh yes, work lurked in the background. When she let her mind go there even for a second, her stomach clenched. But she wanted to be here with Tad, needed to be here. Determinedly, she stashed that other part of her life in its own little box as they started back to her condo for her office equipment.

Two minutes into the drive, Tad fell asleep with his chin on his shoulder, his cheeks pink, chocolate curls sweaty. The heart-melting sight of him was further distraction, along with the finger painting Buddy pulled from his backpack. When they turned into her condo complex, whose entry bore a *Family Built by MacAfee Homes* sign in blatant reminder, she felt a twinge of guilt. In the next breath, she banished it. Relocating her office to help her work was a form of work, wasn't it? Soon enough, her office equipment was packed, half in her car, half in Chip's, and they were on the road again.

This time, passing a MacAfee truck brought back the guilt.

Again she pushed it away. But it made her think. Compartmentalization was apparently a learned art. Like a backhand slice on the tennis court, like Tad on the see-saw, it would take practice.

"Like deking," Chip added as they talked on the phone, car to car.

"What's deking?"

"Short for decoy. It's when a player handles the puck in a way that misleads his opponent—you know, feints left, moves right, that kind of thing. The opponent gets out of position. The player moves past."

"Clever. How long did it take you to learn?"

"Years." He turned the corner onto his street.

Putting her blinker on, she followed. "I don't have years. I've never had to wear so many different hats."

Chip didn't respond at first. Then came a low "Oh shit" and an aggrieved sigh. "Brace yourself. You're about to try on another."

Chapter Twenty-seven

Jamie was about to ask what he meant when he pulled into his driveway beside a black BMW. A woman was leaning against it, hands flanking her hips, eagle eyes tracking the Honda. Jamie's first thought was that it was Buddy's mother. As she got closer, though, she realized the woman looked exactly like Chip.

Jamie barely breathed. "Which sister?"

"Samantha," he murmured and, ending the phone connection, called out his window, "Hey, Sam."

Samantha Kobik was the sister who lived in Manhattan. Black leggings covered slim legs, and though her tunic top was stylishly voluminous, her arms and face were lean. Her hair was long and caught in a high ponytail, but it was as dark and thick as Chip's, her eyes as blue, her jaw as square.

Jamie knew other things about her from stories Chip had told her, but could she remember them now? No! All she could think, with an edge of hysteria, was that she had promised Caroline a presentation on Wednesday—*No problem!*—and that being with Chip and the boys alone would eat up more time than she had. She couldn't be meeting a sister-in-law right now, much less a hostile one, to judge from the sharpness of those eyes.

But what choice did she have?

Parking behind him, she climbed out in time to hear Chip say a facetious "That was fast."

Samantha had straightened. "Look who's talking."

He kissed her cheek and gave her shoulder what Jamie thought to be a conciliatory squeeze. "If you're here to do Mom's bidding, save your breath."

"Do I ever do Mom's bidding?"

"Always."

"I do not. I do my own thing."

"Which is always on Mom's approved activities list," Chip said. "You're her first child. You don't break rules, and you strive to succeed. You're her dream child."

"Who isn't married."

"Who has two graduate degrees and a choice job, who travels all over and earns a ton of money."

"Who isn't married," Samantha repeated, only then shifting her gaze.

Opening an arm, Chip drew Jamie close. "Wife, meet sister Samantha. Sister, meet wife Jamie."

Samantha held out a hand—no hug offered, for which Jamie was grateful. "Sister-in-law" was a technical term. A hug would have suggested a relationship, which they didn't yet have. No, a handshake was fine, and Samantha's was firm. Jamie returned it in kind. If her father had taught her anything, it was that.

"I'd say I'm pleased to meet you," Samantha said, "but right now we're all stunned."

Jamie said the first thing that came to mind. "You should talk to my mom."

"She should talk to *my* mom, or maybe not. Mine was pretty steamed, and not only at Chip."

"If she's angry at Jamie," Chip said, "she's totally off base. Jamie's my other half."

"A little advance warning would have been nice."

"We didn't have advance warning."

"Exactly. *That* reassured her. Did you not upset her enough back when you were boozing it up?"

"Sam—"

"Or when you kicked them out of this house?"

"I did not kick them out."

"You said you could raise your child alone. You said you didn't need them."

To Jamie, Chip muttered a tight-jawed "That's not what I said. I'm getting the boys." He strode off.

Jamie wasn't sure she wanted to be left alone with Samantha. Little things were coming back, like the fact that this oldest sister was a perfectionist, which would be a disaster for Jamie, who wasn't sure she was doing *anything* right just then. But she couldn't move. Piercing blue eyes were pinning her in place.

"You're an architect."

With a serious deadline. "I am."

"Dressed like that?"

"I was working at my condo."

"No wonder. In a town like Williston, no good deed goes unnoticed."

Jamie laughed. She couldn't help herself. Broken engagement plus sudden wedding equals town gossip. The woman did know her Williston.

"I'm sorry about your father," Samantha said in a way that wasn't soft or sympathetic, just fact. "I read about it on the company website. MacAfee Homes was an institution when I was here. If half of what's on the website is true, it still is. I haven't watched your TV show. Is it any good?"

"I think it is," Jamie said. Just then Chip approached holding Tad, and she took him and made the introductions. Tad just stared at Samantha, clearly not knowing any more than Jamie did whether the woman was friend or foe.

Buddy, on the other hand, was no sooner released from the car than he made a beeline for his aunt. Stopping short inches away, he rocked back on his heels and grinned up.

Samantha gave him a thoroughly Chip grin, which made Jamie warm to her a little. "Hey, big guy," she said with genuine enthusiasm and bent for a hug. "I'd pick you up, but . . ."

"But what?" Chip said, approaching with Jamie's computer in his arms.

"He's too heavy."

"Then I won't give you this. If you want to make yourself useful, take the boys inside and make dinner. There's ground beef in the fridge." To Jamie, he said, "She likes to cook. Mom molded her."

"Taught her," Samantha corrected, "and it's a good thing someone learned something from her, because my brother sure didn't. Marriage is a major thing."

"Sam—" Chip began.

"You could've called me, y'know." She swallowed once, then again, and seemed to be taking a deep breath even as she asked, "Why did I have to hear this from Mom?"

"Because Jamie's mom wasn't happy, and our mom wasn't happy, and I didn't want more not-happy from you and my sisters, and Jamie and I had to get to work. She has a killer deadline on a major project, so I need to hook up these machines ASAP. Are you staying the night or driving right back?" As an aside to Jamie, he said, "She does that sometimes. Important people don't take time for family, which may be one of the reasons she isn't married."

"Chip," Jamie scolded softly. Marriage was a touchy subject for some unmarried women, and his sister seemed to have gone pale.

But she didn't back down. "Actually," she said, "the reason I'm not married is that I've never been able to find a guy who was anywhere near as solid as Dad. I've been looking. Trust me, I have. And yes, I'm staying the night." She swallowed again. "But I didn't bring my key, so if one of you could unlock the door, I could use a bathroom."

She was looking a little green. Jamie wondered if she was sick. Shifting Tad on her hip, she went to the side door, unlocked it, and stood back. Samantha had grown up in this house and knew her way around. She made a beeline for the closest bathroom.

When Tad squirmed, Jamie set him down near the fridge. Buddy was suddenly there. "Mamie, can I have apple juice?" he asked.

"That's just what I was coming to get," Jamie said with a smile. Buddy was a sweet child, and even if that hadn't been so, the fact that he had accepted Tad so readily would have endeared him to her.

Removing two juice boxes, she tucked one under her arm while she fixed a straw first in Buddy's, then Tad's. She unwrapped granola bars and set the boys up near the toys in the living room. Retracing her steps, she heard the toilet flush as she passed the first-floor lav. Wanting to give Samantha as much privacy she could, she went straight on through the kitchen and out the door. She reached the car as Chip was gathering a second load.

He straightened, looking hassled. "I'm sorry. I figured I'd hear from her at some point, but I didn't think she'd leave New York so fast. You don't need this right now."

Thinking that she was so far behind in work that a little more wouldn't hurt, she tugged at his shirt to lighten his mood. "She doesn't seem so bad to me. Do you think she's okay?"

"Okay how?"

"She got really pale there."

He snorted. "Being brilliant can be draining."

"Be kind," Jamie chided. "She's your sister. She wants you happy."

"I'll be happy if she makes dinner," he said and, carefully extracting a machine from deep in the SUV, headed back to the house.

Jamie followed with a carton of typing paper, traceing paper, packs of Sharpies, pens and pencils, and correction fluid. When she saw the bathroom door still closed, she set the box on the kitchen table, went into the hall, and knocked softly.

"Samantha? Are you okay?"

There was total silence from inside. Then the handle turned and the door cracked open.

An invitation?

Thinking that she didn't have time to accept it but that this was Chip's sister and she couldn't turn away, she gently eased the door back. Samantha sat sideways on the closed toilet with her head bowed and a damp cloth pressed to the back of her neck.

Frightened, Jamie slipped inside and shut the door to keep the boys out. "What's wrong?"

"Morning sickness is only supposed to last three months. I'm going on six."

"Pregnant?"

Confirmation came with a snicker. "Not on the approved activities list when there's no husband."

"Who's the father?"

"Donor XR 21899."

Jamie gasped. "Not an accident, then."

"Oh no. I picked him carefully. He's six-three, comes from a large family, did a Peace Corps stint, and is currently a pediatric resident at a major hospital God knows where. I was lucky. I got pregnant on the first try."

Chip hadn't mentioned a pregnancy, which meant that either his parents had chosen not to tell him or . . . "Your parents don't know?"

"No." Samantha rocked gently. "I knew they'd be against it. They'd want the husband to come first. They'd tell me I'm not that old, and they're right, but I've always wanted kids, and my life is perfect in so many ways but empty in others, and I seriously do not like the guys I see out there. My folks say I need friends." She made a disparaging sound. "Like I have time to make friends?"

Boy, could Jamie identify with that. She didn't have time for friends *or* for a sister-in-law. Yet here she was, chatting it up in the bathroom with one. And mothering Tad? Granted, she'd have chosen any other way of getting him than having her father and Jessica die—but she loved her baby. Had it not been for him, she wouldn't be with Chip, with whom she was over-the-moon crazy in love. Nor would she be stressed to the max over time demands, or setting up an office in a house she would never have designed but in which she felt totally at home, or terrified about meeting in-laws. But she wasn't turning away from any of it.

Samantha set the cloth on the edge of the sink and raised nervous eyes to Jamie. "If I don't have time for friends, do I have time for a baby? I mean, what was I *thinking*? My lifestyle is crazy. I work long days, and I'm gone overnight all the time." Jamie remembered now; she did publicity for a restaurant group that had started in New York but was spreading steadily westward. "I can't do that with a baby. My boss may can me when I tell him I won't travel."

"He can't fire you because you're pregnant."

"No, but if I refuse to do the job he hired me for? Travel was always part of the package. I signed on to the deal. So I think about that, and I think about my teeny apartment, which is a walk-up, which I love for the exercise, but which may not be cool once I have a baby and a carriage and groceries, and the nausea's been so bad that I've used up my sick time, and this is all before child-birth, which terrifies me, and I haven't *begun* to consider child care."

"You're thinking too far ahead."

"But shouldn't I have done that before I got myself into this?"

"Would you do anything different if you could go back?"

"No. Mothering is the job I want." Closing her eyes, she put a hand on her stomach and drew in a slow breath through pursed lips. Exhaling the same way, she said, "Except when I feel sick." She breathed in again, out again. "Okay. I'm good." But she bent forward again.

Not knowing what else to do, Jamie freshened the cloth, refolded it, and returned it to her neck. "You don't look pregnant."

"A mixed bag, there," came the muffled voice. "I didn't tell my parents during the first trimester on the chance that the pregnancy wouldn't hold, and once I knew it would, I kept putting it off. I haven't seen them in a while. Besides, I've always worn leggings, and tunics are in style." Moving the cloth to her throat as she straightened, she smoothed the wide tunic so that her middle showed.

"Oh my," Jamie breathed. The baby bump was small, but definitely there. "Is it healthy?"

"She is."

"A girl!" A momentary excitement caught her up. "I want one of those next."

Samantha snorted. "Mom always said she loved that her first was a girl. Wonder what she'll say about her first girl now." She grew earnest, seeming to want Jamie to understand. "It's not like they won't want the baby. They just won't like how I got her. I was waiting to tell them until I felt better, so my third month became my fourth, and now that I'm well into my fifth, I tell myself that they'll just have to accept it the more of a done deal it is."

"Like Chip and me getting married," Jamie said.

Samantha was quiet. When she finally lifted her head, her eyes were defiant and ashamed at once. "Want to know my first thought when Mom called this morning with your news? Pure glee. I kept thinking, *My being single and pregnant will be small potatoes compared to Chip marrying one of his bimbos.*" Her defiance faded, leaving apology on its own. "Only you're not a bimbo, are you."

Jamie smiled. "No. But I'm horrid in the kitchen, and I'm in a state of panic about a deadline that my mother, who, by the way, isn't speaking to me right now, set for a project she wants done by Wednesday. So if I get you crackers, will you be able to make dinner while Chip and I set up my office?"

"I could do that," Samantha said but was suddenly cautious. "Which one of us tells him about the baby?"

Jamie didn't think it was her job to do that, but she heard a tiny thread of pleading in the question, and the part of her that had never had a sibling wanted to be involved with one now. She actually felt bad for Samantha. Jamie had had Chip with her when she broke the news of their marriage to her mother. Samantha was alone.

Leaving the cook munching Goldfish as she searched the cupboards, Jamie got another armload from the car. She carried it upstairs, where Chip was just finishing the computer hookup.

He took a step back. "Try it."

She tripped on the carpet as she crossed the room and would have fallen if he hadn't caught her. "Why do I *do* that?" she cried, glaring at the carpet as he took the box.

"To make the rest of us feel better, since you are otherwise perfect."

"Hah. I couldn't hook up these machines if my life depended on it."

"Do we know anything works? Try it."

Instead, she put her back to the computer and her palms on his chest. "I need to tell you something first. I don't want you to say anything until I'm done, and before you speak then, you need to know that I think it's good."

His eyes were large and scared. "Ah hell. You want out."

She nearly laughed. "Excuse me? *Never.* This is about your *sister.*" Quickly, she outlined the facts, watching his expression go from relief to surprise to disbelief.

"Pregnant? Miss High and—"

Jamie put a finger across his lips. "Let me finish."

He struggled with that. She could see him wanting to insert editorial comments when she described the sperm donor, and when she told him told him why Samantha hadn't told her parents, she could see he was dying to speak.

Finally, she said, "I like her, Chip. She's vulnerable—"

"Samantha?"

"Yes. She did something she wanted to do, just like we did, and not everyone will agree with her choice, but I want to. It's a baby, Chip, a little girl."

"If it was a boy," he said with a grunt, "it could play with ours."

"And a girl can't do that? Hello?"

"She was wrong, Jamie. When she said I kicked them out of this house?" Clearly this was bothering him. "Mom and Dad were looking to move, so I bought them two houses in exchange for this one, and I never said I didn't need them. I said that if they weren't there, I'd have to finally grow up."

"You have." Standing on tiptoe, Jamie kissed him.

By the time she lowered herself, his arm was around her waist and his grin was smug. "One thing's for sure. This'll give the folks something to think about besides us."

"Samantha is counting on our marriage helping her the same way. That's one of the reasons she got here so fast."

"Her timing couldn't be worse. You need to work."

"I will once the boys are asleep. So, do we support Samantha?"

Chip made a no-brainer face. "Of course, we support her. She's my sister."

He was right about Samantha being a good cook. In no time, she had whipped up their mother's chili recipe, baked cornbread, and made a salad. And Chip behaved well. Granted, Jamie was standing guard, but he didn't give his sister a hard time about the baby. He was actually reassuring about being a single parent, having just gone through three years of it himself, though he described the raw panic he had felt when he opened his front door to a woman he had never thought he'd see again but who was carrying a week-old infant she claimed was his son.

Yes, he said, mostly for Jamie's benefit, since she was hearing the details for the first time, he'd had a paternity test done, though the timing of the baby's birth, vis-à-vis its conception, made that a formality. For Samantha's sake, he listed some of his early mistakes taking care of Buddy. They were hilarious.

Of course, he had had his parents to help, even long distance. Samantha didn't have assurance of that yet.

Nor, right now, did Jamie. She kept thinking about that as she watched Chip and his sister, kept thinking about her father being dead and her mother being alive and the precious time they were wasting being angry at each other. Right now, she might have asked Caroline whether Tad's clinginess during dinner was a factor of yet another new person in his life or something else. He refused to sit in his own chair, whining for her lap, and while she loved the feel of his warm little body, she imagined it was too warm.

He didn't eat much, just crumbs of cornbread and one o
two tiny pieces of chili, and by the time Samantha pulle
chocolate chip cookies from the oven, his little eyes wer
closing.

"I don't think he feels great," Jamie said, holding hir
tight as she stood. Her eyes were on Chip, who knew bet
ter than she what to do in this situation. "A quick bath an
bed, maybe?"

He started to get up. "I'll do it. You have to work."

She pressed his shoulder down. "I'll work once he'
asleep. Bath, Buddy?"

Buddy pouted. "I want another cookie."

"You go settle Tad," Chip told her, running a reassur
ing hand up her arm. "I'll bring him along in a few."

Tad took little settling. She stretched out beside him t
read a story, but he was asleep before two pages were done
Worried, Jamie rolled to her side. She knew she should ge
up and work, but she couldn't just yet. Breathing in baby
soap sweetness, she watched him for a while, listened t
his breathing, monitored the rise and fall of his little ches
She knew he was bound to get sick at some point. No chil
made it to kindergarten untouched by other kids' germs
especially not a daycare child, but that wasn't reason t
take him out, was it?

He still felt warm to her. But he slept through the soun
of the bath being run and he didn't stir when, a short tim
later, Chip deposited Buddy on the top bunk.

"*Now* you work," he whispered as they crept from th
room.

"What about your sister?"

"I'll handle her."

It took Jamie time to get organized—putting things wher
she could reach them, adjusting the height of her chai
connecting to the Web on one computer and the MacAfe

network on another, hooking up the monitor to hear if Tad
woke—and all the while, distracting tendrils of thought
came and went. Some had Tad's name on them, some
Samantha's. Thoughts of Chip soothed. Not so thoughts
of Caroline. The ache remained, along with serious self-
doubt, so when she was finally able to pull up her design
of the main house, she was surprised to find that it was actually good. If her goal was to make the Weymouths
proud of their family home, this was a solid first step.

That said, if the first glance at a presentation mattered,
and the estate was to be truly inviting, the entry had to be
more imposing than the narrow lane of cracked tar that it
was. *Natural speed bumps,* she could hear the ghost of
Mildred say, and while that might be true, there were more
gracious ways to discourage speed. Widening the drive,
she paved it with bricks made of recycled materials that
gave it a slightly uneven, almost cobblestone feel. When it
reached the house, she swung it into an elegant circle, with
a trio of river birch in the middle and ample space for guest
parking around the curves.

"How's it going?" Chip whispered from the door. An
hour had passed.

She gave him a thumbs-up. Returning to her screen,
though, she realized she couldn't show guest parking without addressing resident parking. That could be in clones
of the existing carriage house, which she would tear down.

No. Not carriage houses. She wanted attached garages.

But that meant a redesign of the back of the house, for
which she needed a rear exterior view. Turning to the second computer, she searched earth-view sites in vain. The
Williston News had photos from long-ago backyard parties, but they showed people with only slices of grass, lawn
furniture, or trees. What memories Jamie had herself were
too vague to use.

Imagine, she told herself. *Create.*

But another half hour had just passed with nothing t
show.

Frantic to draw something—*anything*—she turned he
back on the house and, on a fresh screen, re-created th
woods. She set the outline of three carriage houses alon
its rim. No, freestanding carriage houses weren't her firs
choice, but they were charming, certainly practical wit
storage space above, and if they differed from one anothe
the visual interest of the presentation would be enhanced

But three? Or four? With walkways connecting one t
the other and the house? Would the Weymouths like see
ing a circle out back with a courtyard in the middle?

Not if there was a circle out front.

A landscaped courtyard might work if it had grass
flowers, and benches.

Then came another thought. There had to be access t
the pool and tennis court from the main house. But how
close should they be? Too close and those owning the con
dos would hear noise. Too far and they'd need a friggin
golf cart to get there.

She glanced at her watch. Another hour gone, with to
many decisions, too little input, and little progress. Sh
was starting to hyperventilate when Chip appeared.

"Ignore me," he whispered, pulling a chair up to hi
own computer. "I need printouts for tomorrow."

She gasped. "The field day." She had been so obsesse
with her own work that she hadn't thought about his. "I'r
so sorry, Chip. I forgot. And here I left you alone with you
sister. Where is she?"

"Sleeping. It's after ten." He shushed her with a finge
to his mouth and pointed at her screen. "Work."

She would never have been able to—would have sa
watching him do his thing—if she hadn't been so awar
of the time. After ten? The clock was ticking.

Postponing exteriors, Jamie turned her thoughts to th

interior of the house. The Weymouths had memories of growing up there. She wanted to tap into memories, but intimate and close didn't work. She wanted the condos branching off from an impressive foyer that incorporated a grand staircase in the front hall. She had made sketches of this in her dreams.

But, again, how many condos? If four, each unit would be smaller and more reasonably priced. If three, the units could be larger, with luxury elements like his-and-her walk-in closets and a solarium. Which would the Weymouths prefer? Which would potential buyers prefer?

Roy had been the marketing genius. He would have known instinctively which route to take. In his absence, Caroline might have thoughts, since she was taking the lead in this project. But Caroline hadn't called, and design was Jamie's thing.

She went with luxury, partly because of what Chip had said about the Weymouths, but even more because three units would take less time to draw than four.

But wait. She had no existing floor plan, no starting point. She told herself that was fine, since the brothers wouldn't have a floor plan handy either, but she had never worked this way. It was disorganized. It was *messy*.

Thinking that she had *no choice,* she was about to start when she heard a gagging sound, then a shrill cry.

In a flash, she ran to the boys' room. Tad had thrown up and was sitting on his bed in a gross mess, crying pitifully. She snatched him up and cradled him, cooing softly, "It's okay, monkey, Mommie's here." But she wasn't a vomiter, had never seen Tad do it before, didn't know *where* to begin to clean up.

"The bathroom," Chip said with a calm hand at her back. "Put him in a tepid tub while I change the sheets."

She might have marveled at his composure if she hadn't been so concerned about Tad, but the bath seemed to work.

The water soothed him. Once she had him soaped and rinsed, she refilled the tub so that he could soak in clean bubbles, and all the while, ignoring her fear-filled heart, she played with him as if it were just another night in the bath.

"What now?" she asked Chip when he appeared.

He touched Tad's forehead. "He's cooler. That's good."

"What *was* it?"

"Who knows. Maybe something he ate. Maybe something going around at school."

"Do I call the doctor?"

"Nah."

"Give him Motrin?"

He considered that. "Let's wait. If his temperature spikes—"

"I don't even know how to *take* his temperature."

Chip slid her a tired smile. "Not to worry, wife. I do."

Tad's temperature was only mildly elevated, no cause for alarm, Chip assured her. She gave the child water to sip, but he seemed happiest clinging to her, arms and legs. So she brought him back to the office and let him doze against her that way while she tried to work—"tried" being the operative word. She couldn't settle into it. She was a creature who worked with facts and figures. Without them, she was groping around in the dark.

Thinking she might do better if she set the manor aside and worked on the rest of the acreage, she pulled up her work e-mail and scrolled through a fearsome list until she found the plot map that the Williston town assessor had sent. Unfortunately, it was as crude as every other assessor's plot plan she had ever seen.

Disconcerted, she bowed her head against Tad's warm curls. If construction ever became a reality, MacAfee Homes would bring in engineers to determine the location of access roads and the positioning of each house. But she had no engineers now. She had no marketing advice, no Realtor advice. She had no Caroline. She had no Chip, who had finally gone to bed. She had Tad, who woke each time she tried to put him down, and she was exhausted. It was past midnight. Fear alone kept her at her computer. But fear wasn't conducive to design.

Thinking that an hour or two of sleep might help, she tucked Tad close and climbed in with Chip, who stirred. "I don't know if this is allowed," she whispered, "but he starts to cry when I take him to his own bed, and I don't want to wake Buddy, and I need to feel you here."

His answering whisper came against her hair as he drew her back into the curve of his body. "It's good. Sleep."

An hour was all she managed. This time it was Buddy who got sick, and they were up again, repeating the drill of bath and laundry. Though Jamie felt less guilty knowing it was *Chip's* son now and that she was doing her part, she was exhausted.

The good news was that both boys settled down in their own room.

The bad news was that it was three in the morning before that happened.

Determined to work, she made coffee and went to the office, but where to start? Forget the manor. Forget carriage houses and courtyards. Forget even the clubhouse by the pool, which would double as an event room and be constructed in the style of the main house . . . or in the style of the original carriage house . . . or maybe in the style of one of several different house plans she envisioned for the outlying acres. Forget the gazebo and the trellis and the huge fire pit. That was all detail.

She needed to think big picture, bird's-eye view. *That* would impress the Weymouths. But not only didn't she have an engineers' report, she had never walked through the wooded part of the land, didn't know which sections were wet and which were not, which were underscored with granite that would require blasting, which were embedded in stands of pine or birch or beech so dense and beautiful that removing even a single tree would be wrong.

Caroline would understand this. She had a keen perspective on these kinds of issues and might have pertinent thoughts. Jamie would have given anything to call her, if for no other reason than to share the responsibility. But this was her job to do.

Just do it, she ordered herself. *The Weymouths won't know where boulders or trees or low-lying wetlands are. Scatter homes over the land in a way that looks interesting. You've done this before. Just do it now.*

Desperate, she did. She spaced houses on the computer in a way that looked plausible. Pretty. Maybe even interesting. Same with siting the swimming pool, tennis court, and clubhouse, though she hated working this way. It reminded her of the year she had tried to bake gingerbread for Caroline's birthday and, not having molasses, used honey instead. Caroline had said it was perfect. But Caroline was her mother, what else would she say? Jamie tasted the gingerbread and knew it was flawed.

Flawed was how she felt about what she had done here.

She redid it once, then looked in on the boys. Back in the office, she saw more flaws, so she redid the design. She was in the kitchen filling her third cup of coffee when Chip hurried in looking as tired as she felt. It was seven. He had showered, and his messenger bag was stuffed, but he sidled up close to her as he reached for a travel mug.

"How's it going?"

She waggled a hand and opened the fridge. "At least the boys haven't thrown up again. Will they?"

"There's not much left in their stomachs," he said as he

filled the mug with coffee. "They'll need liquid, but make it watery."

She topped off his coffee with cream. "What about milk?"

"Only if they ask. If they keep down lighter stuff, it's probably okay. If there was ever a day when I'd stay home and help . . ." He scowled. "Make Sam watch the boys."

"Is she staying?"

"Tell her if she doesn't, I'll call Mom and rat her out. And I'm serious." He screwed the top on the mug, looped an arm around her waist, and pulled her in. "Will you be okay?"

"I have to be."

"You can always call your mom."

She didn't answer, just mined his blue eyes for strength.

"I'll call in sick," he offered.

"You will not. It's the last day of school. You've been planning this field day for weeks. Go." She pulled away.

He leaned in for a kiss, started off, came back for a second, then left.

Chapter Twenty-eight

Caroline was twisting to get a rear view of herself in the cheval mirror when she saw Dean staring at her from a corner of the glass. Much as she'd grown used to having him around, there were times when it was embarrassing. Blushing, she felt the need to explain. "My hips look big. Should I tuck in the shirt?"

The outfit was new—a slim white skirt that ended in a soft flare at the knee, a fitted brown silk shirt with clingy tails, and cork wedge sandals. Jamie would approve. But she hadn't bought these things for that reason alone. She had important meetings this week, and her funeral outfit had exhausted its stay. It was black. She didn't like black. Dean did, and a good thing *that* was, or he would clash with the floral wing chair in which he was now sitting to lace his boots. Today's black shirt, already tucked into belted jeans, had its sleeves rolled to the elbows and its neck open.

Holding her eyes in the mirror, he left the chair and came up behind her. "Your hips aren't big, and leave the tails out. You look very chic. Grown up but still you."

She gave him a puzzled smile. "Grown up?"

"Sophisticated."

"Am I not usually sophisticated?"

"Yes, but in a craftsman way. This is cosmopolitan." He paused, speculative, but not quite. "It could use something, though."

Frowning at her reflection, Caroline touched her watch, then the studs in her ears. She wore a hand-carved silver ring on the middle finger of her left hand. It was a gift from her parents, marking no special birthday, but its heft so fit who she was that it she wore it often. Her mother's own filigree bangle-and-cuff set was a delicate heirloom, and though Caroline treasured it, she would no more wear it than she would wear a wedding gown of Victorian lace.

Then again, who'd have thought she would willingly buy a white skirt and wedge sandals, much less feel good in them? But she had, and she did. Who'd have thought she would be power dressing—well, as much as her carpenter side would allow—and auditioning for a role that she didn't want? Or hadn't wanted. Only it wasn't so bad. She was actually good at it, mainly because it entailed dealing with people. That was what she loved about *Gut It!*—not the eye of the camera or the public recognition, but working with people to produce something that other people would enjoy.

The woman she saw in the glass was interesting. Oh, she looked her age. Neither her neck nor her hands were as smooth as the silk of her blouse, and her bare legs no longer tanned as evenly as Jamie's did. But there was something different about this woman. With Dean's nearness evoking the memory of sleeping with him last night, she might have said that the something different was confidence. She might have even added the word "complete" had it not been for Jamie. There was nothing complete right now in Caroline's role as a mother.

But that couldn't have been what Dean meant when he said her outfit needed something. He was a literal guy.

One hand left his pocket, then both touched her nape, and suddenly something was sliding down a platinum chain to nestle between her breasts. By the time her fingers were there, he had both hands on her shoulders and was looking at their reflection in the mirror, his ruddy skin less ruddy as he waited for her response.

"Dean," she warned softly. She knew just what it was, but that didn't prepare her for the real thing when she found the nerve to pull it out and look. He had chosen an emerald-cut diamond flanked by vertical baguettes—and her very first thought was how much more the straight stones fit her than the round stone she had once had. Set in platinum, the ring was simple but elegant, traditional but new, exquisite any way she put it.

His fingers found hers inside the shirt, work-roughened skin against the swell of her breasts. "Wear it for me?" he whispered. His hazel eyes, always magnetic, were suddenly a truer green, as if the brown had been overrun by a surge of life inside. Her heart positively ached.

"Oh, Dean."

"Don't you like it?"

"I *love* it," she said, closing the ring in her fist. "But I don't want marriage. I like what we have."

"So do I. That's why the chain. It's a long one. No one needs to see the ring."

"But you want people to know. You said that."

"I changed my mind. This isn't about other people. It's about us."

That was the moment she knew it would happen, the moment she knew they were both old enough to make it work. It was the moment when she realized that the important part of growing older was the growing part, and that resisting change meant forever standing still, which was a sad way to live.

It was also the moment when she saw that holding little

grudges was as paralyzing as insisting on hosting *Gut It!* season after season.

Letting the ring settle between her breasts as it seemed made to do, she turned, looped one arm over his shoulder, and framed his whiskered cheek with the other. "Thank you."

"Is that a yes?" he asked with such boyish hope that her heart squeezed again.

Through a sudden sheen of tears, she smiled. "It is."

With Chip gone, Jamie set the monitor beside her computer. It gave her a full view of the bunk bed, and while she was desperate to creep in for a real look at Tad, she resisted the urge. One boy shifted, then the other; neither was sleeping soundly. But both were alive, and with no sign yet of Samantha, she grabbed at the chance to work.

Worried that her bird's-eye view was *BLAH* but not sure what it needed to make it *WOW,* she saved what she had, pulled up a new screen, and focused on individual houses. All she needed for tomorrow's meeting was a prototype or two to show what MacAfee Homes would build on Weymouth land.

She had dreamed of designing *six* different options for buyers, each derivative of the manor house but with its own unique personality. Among them would be an elegant miniature manor house done in brick, another done in stucco and stone, a lake cottage option, a farmhouse option—the presentation would be awesome. But which to draw first, whether to aim for luxury or charm, whether to aim for the Weymouths or the buyer, whether to site it flat or on a knoll—and how could she determine the last without detailed knowledge of the lay of the land?

Forget reality, she cried, losing patience with herself. *Reality doesn't matter. Just take an image from your head and draw it on the frigging screen.*

She was about to start when Samantha wandered in asking what the middle-of-the-night activity had been about. Hearing her voice, Buddy got up, and when Tad, still in bed, began a woeful "Mamie . . . Mamie," work was shot.

Daycare was out of the question. Both boys were still warm, unusually pale, and generally lethargic. If the constancy of the AC was any indication, it was hot outside, not that Jamie had been out to look. She could see patches of condensation on the windows where hot and humid air met cooler glass.

"What do we do?" Samantha asked. Despite her caution about lifting Buddy yesterday, she was holding him now.

Jamie had a quick vision of different-color construction paper cut in triangles, circles, and squares, with toothpicks and string, markers and glue, a perfect sick-day project for boys who didn't feel great. She had grown up on projects like this. Art was her thing. She would do this with them *in a minute* if she didn't have to work.

But she did. So in lieu of arts-and-crafts?

Pressing Tad's face to her throat, she said, "You're asking the wrong person. I've never done this before. They need to stay quiet, but we can't just hold them all morning. What do mothers do when their kids are sick?"

Samantha didn't answer. Nor did she think for long. She simply walked into the living room and turned on the TV.

Caroline's smile was gone, her eyes were dry, and while one hand touched the ring, her new talisman, the other held the wheel of the dusty MacAfee truck that should have detracted from her sophisticated look but felt right. The look was vintage modern, she decided—old car, new woman, traditional ring, new meaning. June magazines were filled with ring ads picturing two and three rows of tiny diamonds, sometimes in different colors, around a central

stone, but that wasn't for her. She liked the timelessness
of what Dean had picked.

Old, new. A person who blended the two was flexible
enough to listen and hear and grow. She wanted to think
she was that kind of person. She might have a shot at it, if
she could fix what she'd botched with Jamie.

Time worked against her. Jamie had to be feeling pressure right now even apart from being a new mom and new
wife, which Caroline was still struggling to digest, and her
own morning was booked solid. Rather than texting, *Hey,
when can we talk, ooops, no, not then,* or worse, having
Jamie tell her not to come, she figured that she would just
show up.

First, though, a breakfast meeting with the Realtor.
Over boiled eggs at a blessedly air-conditioned Fiona's,
Linda Marshall led her through a comparative market
analysis that gave Caroline a grounding on the latest in recent sales of other MetroWest properties, broken down by
the age of a house, its location, and its size. Linda didn't
notice the necklace, but that didn't mean Caroline forgot
it was there. Not for one minute. *It's about us,* Dean had
said, and the words were never far from her mind. She
pressed her fingers to the ring often, as if she were catching
her breath or suffering heartburn. In a sense, she was. With
each touch, it radiated warm little shocks of pleasure, pride,
and comfort, and while a woman who was self-confident
enough to dress chic and drive dusty shouldn't need comfort, she did.

Armed with Linda's report and a realistic grasp of the
kind of homes they could build and sell, she sped to the
MacAfee Building to see if Jamie was there.

As helpful as her sister-in-law was in keeping videos
streaming and the boys hydrated, she couldn't help Jamie
with work. And Jamie tried, really she did. Running

downstairs and back up every few minutes to check on the boys, she managed to draw the beginnings of a house on one of the acre lots. Then, when her mind skipped around, she worked the upstairs of one of the condos into an odd part of the manor house roof. Desperate to jump-start her productivity, she turned away from the computer and made drawings by hand. That was how she often began a project. But even if caffeine hadn't been making her hands shake, she knew that sketches wouldn't impress the Weymouths.

She returned to the computer, but the harder she tried, the more frightened she grew. Mothers didn't stick their kids in front of the TV when they were sick. They sang to them, played with them, held them. So Jamie was as lousy a mother as she was an architect—with one big difference. Short-term, the boys would survive. This project would not. At tomorrow's meeting, there might be negotiation over money or timing or the wisdom of showcasing the project on *Gut It!* But if Jamie couldn't get her act together and make a stunning presentation, they could kiss the whole thing good-bye.

The weight was on her shoulders. Scores of jobs and priceless publicity were at stake, as well as enough money to keep MacAfee Homes afloat while the company recovered from Roy's death and Brad's departure. And Caroline? If she was truly taking over from Theo, and Jamie's incompetence spoiled this chance for her to shine, how awful would *that* be?

Once inside the MacAfee Building, Caroline went looking for Jamie. She wasn't there, but any number of other people were, all jumping at the opportunity to talk about Jamie's marriage. Extricating herself as quickly as possible—"Theo's waiting," she said more than once—she hurried on down the hall, fully understanding why

Jamie hadn't come here. How to work in a bee's nest? The buzz would have made it impossible.

She shared Linda's report with Theo, who then added final instructions for her before she went to the bank. She might have saved time by simply phoning the banker. But Theo was insistent. "The bank is in the center of town, and Fred McDonough has been a solid adviser. He'll feel he's valued if you make time for a face-to-face meeting." The subtext, of course, was Theo wanting Caroline to begin the stroking of locals that he and then Roy had done. She would have had no problem with that if she hadn't been impatient to get to Jamie, but she figured that a few more minutes wouldn't hurt.

Besides, Fred McDonough was a convivial guy, who did seem impressed that she'd taken the time to come. He talked about Roy for a while, and asked in depth about Theo. He wanted to know when Jamie and Brad were getting married, and while Caroline was gratified to know that word hadn't spread so far so soon, what could she say? Much as she didn't want to spend time talking about this, she couldn't lie.

So she gave him the bare facts and smiled at his startled expression. "Sudden, huh? They just met. No shotgun wedding, just love at first sight."

Saying the words made them real. As she touched her own ring for the grounding it brought, she couldn't help but compare Jamie's handful of days to her own years and years. So different. Perhaps that was how it should be?

"It's been a rough month for her," Caroline said, "but she's really happy. I'm counting on you to assure people of that. Yes?"

"Yes, yes, of course, I've known that girl since she was born," Fred reminded her, "and, of course, the Kobiks have always been clients here." She waited for him to remark on Chip's past, but he did not. Rather, seeming all the more dedicated to MacAfee Homes, he gave her a vote of confidence on the Weymouth project and a promise to study the Realtor's comps alongside the MacAfee accounts, and let Caroline know by day's end how high they could bid.

Leaving the bank, Caroline drove to Jamie's condo, where there would be a fully equipped office and a guarantee of silence. But the place was deserted—no car in the drive, no gooseneck lamp in the office window.

Of course not, Caroline. She doesn't live here anymore.

Still, she unlocked the door and checked inside, only to be met by a telling heat.

She headed back to the office, needing to study Dean's cost estimates before he gave them to the banker. Then she drove to Emory Elementary. The street was lined with cars, and the playground was mobbed. Curious, she parked and approached the chain-link fence.

The entire school appeared to be there, with teachers milling around and groups of parents watching from the sidelines. The students were divided into teams. Orange shirts kicked soccer balls at a goal; blue shirts shot baskets. Greens dribbled a kickball around an obstacle course, while reds and whites competed at tetherball. The tallest adult on the field, Chip was with a large group of children who stood body to body holding the edges of a large round parachute. Purple was on the left half, yellow on the right half. Chip held a kickball ball over his head for a moment, pointing around with last-minute instructions before tossing the ball onto the chute and blowing his whistle. Instantly, the children began feverishly waving the parachute up and down in an attempt to get the ball into a hole on their side. Once it fell through, he called out the score, tapped a student to retrieve the ball, then began the game again.

She watched three cycles before he spotted her. He did a double take, eyes widening before he waved over another

teacher and trotted to where she stood. His face was
sweaty, but his look of fear was worse. "Is everything
okay?"

"Yes. No. I need to apologize to you, but this is clearly
not the time. More immediately, I need to see Jamie. The
silence between us is deafening, but she isn't at the office."

"She's at my house, and she really needs you," he said,
seeming suddenly very young and as frightened as he had
been in command with his students seconds before. "The
boys were throwing up all night, so Jamie couldn't sleep
or work, and my sister showed up unannounced, which
may be good or bad, I don't know." He swabbed his
forehead with an arm that left his hair sticking up. "I need
to be there with them, only this is the last day of school,
and field day is my thing, it's becoming a tradition. I'm
texting her, and she says everything's okay, only I know it
isn't, and I can't leave here for a couple more hours. Not
that there's a whole lot I could do to help her. I'm just a
meathead, she's the brains. She knows what she wants to
draw, but she's second-guessing it all and looking at the
clock and panicking. This is the first time she's had to deal
with illness, so she's worried about the boys. She may be
furious I'm telling you all this—she's so damn independent when it comes to work, and the whole thing with you
is eating at her. I'll be home by four, but if you could stop
off before then, I'd be forever grateful. Do you know the
address?"

Of course she did. She had looked it up in the town
directory the first time Jamie mentioned Chip. Gently
nudging him back to the field, she returned to her truck,
called Dana MacAfee Langham to delay their midday
meeting—*No, Dana, it can't be helped, I know you don't
like rush hour traffic, but two isn't terribly late, yes, that's
fine, if you can't make it I'll understand*—and headed for
403 Beech.

* * *

Jamie felt sick to her stomach. She did not have, could not have, *refused* to have what the boys had. There were plenty of other reasons why her insides were jangly, like lack of sleep, lack of food, lack of faith that she was heading anywhere good with the plans she had drawn. Just thinking of that made her sweat, so she lowered the thermostat again.

Tad was napping against her with his thumb in his mouth, his small legs straddling her hips, and Moose's head sticking up between his arm and his ear. She touched a tiny swell of baby fat that lingered at the crease of his elbow, then uncoiled a long curl from his forehead. He needed a haircut. She kept putting it off, letting the summer air simply tighten the curls. This was all hair that his parents had seen and touched and kissed. Cutting it off would be severing a part of that tie. She knew she would have to do it eventually, but not yet, not yet.

She kissed his forehead; he cuddled deeper. In that instant, she wished she could walk away from the computer and just be a mother for the rest of the day.

But her empty screen haunted, *taunted*. Desperate to fill it, she kept Tad framed by her arms while her hands worked between keyboard and mouse, constructing the house to which, in her dreams, she would take the boys for quiet soothing the next time they were sick. It would be in a secluded corner of the property, maybe a hilly spot surrounded by hemlock and pine, with thick grass for rolling here, boulders for climbing there. She gave the house vertical interest, with tall windows, gables, and a steep-pitched roof reminiscent of the manor, but then, tired enough to be foggy, she just let go and tossed in features that she loved.

She was horrified when Tad's stirring woke her from her own stupor and she saw what she had built. It was *all wrong*—looked more *Victorian* than French country, which was not at all a style that would work for the Weymouths. Realizing she had just wasted an hour of irretrievable time basically *playing* with design, she felt her heart begin to pound.

That was when the computer went dead. And the TV. And the AC. After only the briefest winding down of moving parts, the house was completely and utterly silent.

Panicked, she raced down the stairs with Tad in her arms and a hand on the rail. She could *not* afford to stumble on the stairs, not with Tad, not with a deadline.

The thermostat in the living room was blank.

Convinced that she had just pushed the AC unit too hard, she lowered Tad to the sofa beside Buddy and ran first to the kitchen, then the laundry room in search of a fuse box.

"Not a fuse," Samantha announced, dressed in a shirt and shorts as she rose from the basement. "It must be something bigger."

"Oh God," Jamie breathed, frantic. "I can't afford to lose power right now. My condo was always okay." Of course, it hadn't been on the night Roy and Jessica died, a thought that gave her a chill but did nothing to cool her body heat. "Do you lose it here often?" If so, the power company would immediately know what to do.

Samantha shrugged. "Beats me. I haven't lived here in almost twenty years. Back then, not as many houses had AC, so the grid wasn't strained."

"And Chip has no generator." If he had, it would have already gone on. A generator was a *must*. MacAfee Homes *never* designed a house now without one. She couldn't believe it. Could. Not. Believe. It.

"What happened to the TV, Mamie?" Buddy asked.

Fighting terror, Jamie pulled him close. "I'm going to try to find out," she said and, cell phone in hand, searched the kitchen board for the emergency number of the power company. "It's not even eleven," she murmured mostly to herself as she tapped in the numbers, "*not* the heaviest usage time." An automated voice. "*Gah.*" A menu. As she worked her way through it, she muttered, "It has to be routine maintenance, though why they had to pick today . . ." She listened. Not routine maintenance; an outage in the area, a crew was on its way, that was it. "*When will the power be back?*" Jamie yelled into the phone, though, of course, the recording didn't hear.

"*Mommy,*" Tad shrieked in a way that said he wanted his mother, his *real* one, not Jamie but Jessica.

Racing back to the living room, she found him on all fours facing the sofa back, clearly having dozed and woken with no idea where he was, but stuck, neither here nor there, not knowing which way to go or how to get a foothold and save himself, which was exactly how she felt. And suddenly, as she closed convulsive arms around him, the fact of no power, no computer, no work, no mother was too much.

That was when the doorbell rang.

Chapter Twenty-nine

Jamie took one look at Caroline on the other side of the door from Samantha and burst into tears, just stood in the living room sobbing above Tad's head, unable to move or think or speak. There was little relief until she felt her mother's arms wrap her up in the scent of spring and the earth, and then the comfort was too visceral for words.

"Oh baby," Caroline murmured against her hair the way she had done since Jamie could remember, "it's okay now, everything's okay, you're going to be fine."

"I don't . . . know . . . *how*."

As broken as Jamie's voice was, so Caroline's was whole. "You do. You've always known. You were born with an instinct for knowing how things work and what to do when they break. Isn't that what you did for me when my marriage fell apart?"

"I didn't fix anything."

"You did, you fixed me. You gave me a reason to hold my head up. And now, here you are, with a wonderful husband and a beautiful son and *another* beautiful son who is now clinging to a person I'm guessing is his aunt because she looks like his dad, and he said she was here."

A faint chuckle came from the door.

"He called you?" Jamie asked, too tired to be angry if he had.

"No, but I think he would have if I hadn't shown up on my own. This has gone on too long, Jamie. We're not meant to be on opposite sides of anything, especially not now, when there are so many good things going on. I was wrong about the wedding, baby, not about keeping secrets or wanting a wonderful celebration for you, but about suggesting that your judgment wasn't good. Only a guy with a big heart can do what Chip is doing right now with a gazillion kids running around and him worried sick about you." She held Jamie back and grimaced. "Is it hot in here or is it me?"

"It's *hot*," Jamie wailed, because though the temperature hadn't had a whole lot of time to rise, between Tad's heat, her own heat, anticipation of heat, and stagnant air, the place felt stifling. In a hysterical burst that included her abysmal designs, she led Caroline right up to the loss of power. "My computer's gone, the kids are sick, and I am so far behind—"

"*Shh.* Wait." She pointed her finger and voice in the direction of the now-closed front door. "I'm Caroline, Jamie's mom, and I don't know your name—"

"Samantha."

"Samantha, I need my phone. It's right there in my purse. Would you dig it out for me, please?"

When Samantha knelt to forage, the absurdity of the instant hit Jamie. "Purse? Why are you carrying a *purse*, Mom?"

"Because these CEO clothes have no pockets." She touched Tad's cheek and cooed a soft "Hi, baby boy" before taking the phone from Samantha. Several touches to the screen and she said, "Okay, gorgeous, we need you ASAP here at Jamie's, 403 Beech, and bring Tommy

Mello." She smiled, laughed softly. "No, but I will . . . Yes, now." She ended the call.

Gorgeous? It wasn't so much the word as how Caroline said it. Jamie wasn't sure she had ever heard that tone from her mother. She sounded almost gleeful, intimate in a deeply affectionate way. "What was that about?"

Caroline continued to smile. "A portable generator and this." Reaching into the V of her very beautiful navy silk shirt, she pulled out a ring.

Jamie forgot exhaustion, throw up, and flawed designs. This was her mother. A few weeks of crossed signals couldn't compete against twenty-nine years of adoration. Caroline was also her best friend, and this was exciting! "Oh. My. God. *When?*"

"Maybe four hours ago. No one else knows but you, me, and Dean. And now Samantha and these boys, not that the boys know a real diamond from a ring in a Cracker Jack box, though they probably don't even know that, poor things."

"Can I tell Chip?" Jamie asked. It was the first thing that came to mind, the second being that she wanted him here now to see the cool person that her mother really was.

"Absolutely. But no one else."

"Engaged?" It was *very* exciting. Jamie trusted Dean. He had loved Caroline for a long time, which Jamie hadn't seen then, since there was love and there was LOVE, though looking back, LOVE was a *duh* thing. Caroline deserved this.

"Not engaged," her mother warned. "I'm not brave enough to say that word yet, which is why this came on a chain."

Tad reached for the ring. Jamie opened her mouth to caution him when Caroline stroked his curls and said, "It's okay, baby. It won't break."

Jamie wasn't sure whether the baby just then was Tad or her, but it didn't really matter. She was her mother's child, so *so* grateful to be back. And that sounded like a betrayal.

"I love Chip," she said quickly. "I adore Chip. He's competent, and he just fills me up with hope and happiness and love. But I'm glad you're here."

"Well, isn't *that* one of truths I've come to accept?" Caroline asked. "He and I aren't in competition. We fill totally different needs. Your family with Chip is your future, Jamie. I never want to stand in the way of that. But if I can't be here to help with a problem I caused by giving you a deadline that you might have trouble meeting because (A) you just got married and (B) you have two sick little boys and (C) no power, what good am I?"

Jamie was the enumerator in the family. "You're mocking me."

"No. It's about organizing my thoughts. I'm learning from you."

Jamie felt an oppressive fatigue edge back. "Maybe you shouldn't. I am so in trouble. Is there any way we can postpone the presentation?"

"We can. But do we have to?"

"I'll show you my stuff. It's awful."

"It isn't," Samantha put in, approaching them. "It's not bad."

"Not bad won't get us a deal."

"It's *impressive*," Samantha told Caroline, who glanced at her watch.

"We still have a full day before the meeting."

"I have no computer, two sick kids, and a mind of mush."

"We're here to help," Caroline said so gently that Jamie choked up again. "First, you need sleep." She smoothed a tendril of hair from Jamie's cheek, leaving her hand there.

"Until gorgeous Dean gets us some power, you can do that."

"But Tad—"

"I'll take Tad." Caroline offered her arms.

Jamie was about to say that he was caught between Mamie and Mommy and probably wouldn't go to her when he held out his little arms and went. That easily, he settled in against Caroline, who patted Jamie's cheek and pointed upstairs.

Caroline should have been nervous. She wasn't used to deadlines. A carpenter didn't have rigid ones, or maybe her clients were forgiving, or she was simply always ahead. Same with *Gut It!* Not so business administration, with a progression of appointments that led from one into the other with a domino effect. Yet here she was, digging Popsicles from her son-in-law's freezer, and she wouldn't be anywhere else. If Tad's coming to her like that didn't melt her heart, nothing would. She didn't even care if Roy was cringing. It wasn't about revenge anymore. She felt good doing this.

She actually felt so good that nothing would slow her down. Seeking out Chip had been a win-win move. In helping Jamie, she was helping herself. She needed to be needed. She was needed here. He had said that, as had the look of relief on Jamie's sweet, tired face.

Caroline could do power loss. She could do sick kids. This was where experience paid off.

And Samantha? Well, Samantha was interesting. She wasn't meek or resentful about taking Caroline's help, actually welcomed it, which made Caroline wonder whether the small bulge at her middle was from an affinity for hot fudge sundaes with whipped cream, or something alive. Caroline wasn't about to ask—had made *that* awful mistake more than once in her life. And really, did it matter right here, right now whether Samantha was pregnant? No.

She seemed as clueless as Jamie about what to feed a child who had been throwing up. At Caroline's direction, she searched the freezer until she found a second box of Popsicles and then fixed dry toast, and when Caroline asked if Chip had a little swimming pool, she rummaged around in the garage until she found one.

The pool was a godsend. Water from the outside tap was tepid in the heat, actually perfect for keeping little bodies just cool enough. Once in it, the boys perked up, and while Caroline stayed close, especially to Tad, who was the younger and the less experienced of the two, they were surprisingly adept in the water. Neither was old enough to play with the other for long. Rather, they splashed randomly, or filled and dumped the plastic containers Caroline had found in the kitchen. When she gave them straws, they blew bubbles for a time.

Samantha brought her a lawn chair. "You're dressed too nicely to be on your knees."

Caroline had to laugh. "I've been on my knees all my life."

"Not when you're on TV. I watched several episodes last night. You're good. Both of you."

It was a golden opportunity. Caroline couldn't resist. Deliberately speculative, she asked, "So, when you were watching, did it bother you that I'm old?"

"You're not old."

"Old enough to be your mother."

"My mother is old. You are not."

Caroline didn't know Samantha's mother, but the woman had to be close to her own age. "Why do I want to tell you to be kind?"

Samantha studied the boys for a minute before raising her eyes again. "Because you're right. I'm just . . . dealing with something." With a little breath, she left it. "I look at you on that show, and you're not old. You lead. I expect my leader to be older than I am."

The remark was validating. "Thank you. You put that well. I'm dealing with something right now, too." Taking Samantha's arm, she urged her into the chair. "Watch the boys for a couple of minutes while I make some calls? I need to delay a few meetings."

"You can go to your meetings. I'll help Jamie."

But it wasn't only Jamie. A month ago, Caroline had been a mother and friend. Now she was also a mother-in-law, grandmother, and significant other. The newness of it all had her feeling her way along, but she rather liked the purpose. "I want to be here, too. My meetings will hold a few hours."

She called Dean first, just to hear his voice. Buoyed by that and by the knowledge that he was on his way, she called Theo. He listened while she explained where she was, sympathetic only to a point before asking when she *would* be in. She called Fred, who said he would stay at the bank as late as she needed. She called Dana, who bowed out entirely, which was fine, since Caroline was only including her as a formality. Linda was Team Caro, and it was Linda she called next. Once she had a feel for the Realtor's schedule, she called Brad to reset a time for the three of them to meet.

Having temporarily ceded responsibility for her life to Caroline, Jamie fell into an immediate deep sleep. She was so far out of it that she had no idea what was on her cheek until she brushed it and found lips.

Chip.

She inhaled. Eyes still closed, she wound her arms around his neck and hummed her pleasure. In the next second, the heat registered and she remembered why she was in bed in broad daylight. Her eyes flew open. "Omigod." She listened. "Silence is not good."

Chip smiled. "We're minutes from cool."

"The power company came through?" she asked with cautious hope.

"Dean did. He's out back with two experts hooking up a generator."

Dean. Caroline. *Gorgeous* rushed back. "He gave Mom a ring, Chip. She swears they're not engaged, but I think it's the fifty-something version of that." His hair was sticking up, his skin tanned and moist, which reminded her where he was supposed to be. "Why are you here?"

"School ended at noon. The kids left, so I left."

"What about teachers' meetings this afternoon?"

"They'll live without me. I need to be here. Your mom can't stay all day. Her meetings are important."

Mention of those caused a tightening in her gut. "She and I have to talk. She needs to see what I've done before she goes ahead with all that." Jamie tried to get up, but his torso was angled over her in a way that prevented escape. "Chip," she protested, but he was studying her face, playing with wayward strands of hair.

"You are so pretty."

"I'm a *mess*." But even a little sleep had taken the edge off. Prolonging the escape just a bit longer, she touched his mouth. "How are the boys?"

"Better," he breathed against her fingers. "Your mom has them drinking warm Jell-O. They're asking for cookies."

"And Samantha?"

"Not asking for cookies, but asking the guys a gazillion questions about the generator. It's a whole-house one."

Her hand slid to his neck. "Oh no, Chip. I don't think so. Whole house ones have to be ordered."

"I thought that, too, but Dean insisted that MacAfee

Homes installs enough of them in new construction to have special access."

"But whole-house generators take a full *day* to install."

Chip's blue eyes were smug. "Not when you have three guys who know what they're doing. Dean didn't see the point of wasting time on a Band-Aid when he could do the full fix."

"Are you okay with that?" He looked it, but they were reading in new territory.

"Why wouldn't I be?"

"This is your house. It should be your decision, not Dean's."

He laughed. "Your mom must have been thinking the same thing when she told me it was a wedding gift. Like I mind a generator? Besides, it's not my house, it's ours, and I trust your mom's people." On cue, a low hum spread through the house. His grin widened. "She's an amazing woman, Jamie. I like having her here, and it isn't about child care. It's about family. My sister may be bossy, but her heart's in the right place, and your mom is resourceful and calm. She's one together lady."

With that, for Jamie, reality returned. "She won't be once she sees what I haven't designed."

Caroline didn't know what to expect. She understood that her very professional daughter was shaken. But by the time Jamie had gone through her questions about the land, the marketing decisions she couldn't make, and the designs she would draw if she only had more time, Caroline was seriously worried.

Standing over Jamie's shoulder a short time later, she was silent, eyes on the screen as page after page of designs appeared.

When she had seen enough, she said a soft, "You little stinker."

Jamie raised stricken eyes. "That bad?"

Caroline shot her a punishing look before asking Samantha, who was at Jamie's other shoulder, "Are they bad?"

"They're incredible."

"Incredible," Caroline confirmed. "The details you added to the manor exterior are simple but have a profound effect. The foyer inside is just detailed enough to show how elegant the entries to the condos might be." She gestured for Jamie to go back one screen, then another. "What you've done with the front drive makes a statement, the carriage houses in back are charming, and this house . . ." She had to smile. The single new build Jamie had designed looked suspiciously like Dean's country house might look once the rehab was done. Caroline wouldn't quite admit the potential to Dean, but there it was. "This house is totally inviting."

"It has a younger feel than the manor," Samantha observed. "What demographic are you targeting?"

When Jamie looked to Caroline for the answer, Caroline opened her phone. Seconds later, she connected with Linda, and minutes after that, Linda was headed their way. While they waited, Caroline studied the designs again. Together the three of them had listed a dozen questions by the time the Realtor arrived.

Over the next hour, while Tad napped, Chip watched Buddy, and the house cooled, the four women skimmed over things that they would explore more if the project was theirs, focusing instead on demographics, cost issues, and buyer trends. Beyond that, it was about brainstorming what would work in winning over the Weymouths. By the time Linda left, Jamie knew what she needed to do for tomorrow, which had been Caroline's goal.

Leaving her to work, Caroline found herself talking

ith Samantha in the kitchen. "Would you buy a house
re?"

"If I could afford it."

"Would it bother you if other buyers were empty nest-
s?"

"You mean older?" She popped a Goldfish in her mouth
nd offered the box to Caroline, who shook her head. "No.
love having older people around. They're family when
mily can't be there."

"What if they resent the presence of young children?"

"Are you worried the Weymouths will?"

"Maybe."

"Don't they have kids?"

"Grown ones." Even as she said the words, she had her
hone out and was calling Herschel Oakes. Minutes later,
e had a helpful piece of information. "Between the
rothers? Seven grandchildren."

"Family builds," Samantha remarked. "That has to be
e theme of the pitch."

Caroline smiled, bemused. "It does. Why didn't I think
f it before?"

"You may be too close to the project, or just not a mar-
eter. But you're talking a lot of homes here." She pushed
another Goldfish and talked as she chewed. "Williston
as on the outer edge of commuter towns when I was
rowing up here, but that's probably changed. The home
rices the Realtor mentioned aren't out of sight for Greater
oston suburbia. Quality-of-life issues here compensate
r the commute. Yeah, I'd buy a home here in a minute."
er eyes stopped blinking as they held Caroline's. "I'm
regnant."

And no husband, said that look of defiance. She was
aring Caroline to criticize her. Not that Caroline would.
he liked Samantha. Her gut said that this was a strong

woman who would come to be Jamie's good friend. Caro
line wasn't about to jeopardize that.

"I was wondering," she mused.

Samantha touched the bump. "I'm eighteen weeks. M
parents don't know."

Caroline had an instant reaction to that but bit he
tongue. After a moment's thought, she came at it a diffe
ent way. "Jamie and I have always been this close." Sh
held up two fingers. "We hit bumps this month—"

"She said you weren't talking."

"We weren't. There was a lack of honesty—no, a lack c
forthrightness. It was hurtful and stupid and counterpr
ductive. The longer it lingered, the more it took on a life c
its own. Don't make the same mistake we did, Samantha.

"I already have," she cried in a slightly hysterical way

"Then correct it soon. This conversation we're havin;
you and me? You've mentioned family more than once. It
on your mind."

Munching on a handful of crackers this time, Samanth
considered that. Finally, seeming regretful, she said, "M
family was always close. I could really use the emotion;
support." She nodded. "Family builds. It's a good sale
slogan. I say that as a slightly impoverished version o
your quintessential first-time home buyer."

Caroline was thinking the girl was correct in that, to
She did represent the younger face of the market. If th
slogan appealed to her, it would appeal to three brother
whose children had to be somewhere around Samantha'
age. She was also thinking that someone who was articu
late, direct, and had a certain marketing savvy might im
press the Weymouths. On impulse, she said, "I'd like yo
at that meeting. Can you come?"

If sheer numbers counted, the MacAfee side would hav
won hands down. Theo led the team, looking debonair i

s old-world way. Caroline sat beside him, wearing an-
her of her new outfits, while Dean flanked her, looking
ggedly Dean. Caroline was amazed at how stunningly
mie presented herself, despite being thoroughly sleep-
-prived. Samantha wore a slim-fitting white top over her
arrow skirt, a very New York bump-flaunting look that
as actually a clever marketing choice, Caroline thought,
that it portrayed MacAfee Homes as totally modern.
ranted, Samantha didn't work for MacAfee Homes. Nor
d Chip, who looked sporty and god-awful handsome as
e sat in the background, ostensibly present for moral sup-
ort. Annie Ahl was there. And Linda. And Brad, look-
g awkward as hell.

Conversely, the Weymouth presence was limited to
alph videoconferencing from San Francisco, Grant on
eakerphone from Santa Fe, and, in the flesh, John the
otshot plastic surgeon who'd had plenty of work done on
imself, and Herschel-the-lawyer-with-ties-to-Caroline.

Unfortunately, since the Weymouth brothers owned
e land, they held the cards. Seeming disgruntled from
e get-go, they had pithy remarks about Jamie's de-
gns, Linda's real estate savvy, Samantha's *Family Builds*
nage, and Caroline's offer. They questioned whether
ean's green installations were pure gimmick, and
hether Annie's landscaping plans would preserve their
other's aging dogwoods. Ralph wanted to know why
e Barths, who he claimed were about to affiliate with
otheby's, wouldn't be a safer choice, and, by the way, if
heo was still the one in charge, why wasn't he talking,
nd what role would he play anyway? John declared that
e didn't want Web marketing, which, he said, might
reate a conflict for someone Googling his name; Linda
xplained that any URL would simply include the ad-
ress, and Samantha, having done her homework that
norning, pointed out that nine in ten home buyers used

the Web at some point, with 52 percent citing it as the
first step.

When they seemed to run low on criticism, Ralph aske
Chip why he was there. "If you think your friendship wi
my son will get you brownie points, think again. You l
down your teammates at Harvard and made a mess of you
life. I wouldn't want you involved."

Chip held up a respectful hand. "I'm just the chauffeur

Jamie took exception to that. "He's my husband. He
here to support me."

As much to prevent Jamie from saying something tha
might anger Frank as to make a protest of her own, Caro
line put in a quick "Chip doesn't work for MacAfee Home
but if there was a position, I'd hire him in a heartbeat."

Dean added, "I second that. My subs rave about ho
he is with their kids."

"You're all biased," Ralph scoffed.

"Actually," John told his brother, "I just heard th
same thing from one of my patients. His kids go to Em
ory Elementary."

That touched off a bout of arguments among the bro
thers, starting with the state of the local schools but quickl
moving on to whether the prototype houses should resem
ble the manor, whether an imposing front drive was prac
tical or pretentious, whether their father would roll over i
his grave if tennis courts were built at the expense of a gol
course.

Caroline was still smarting from Ralph's remarks abou
Chip. When the brothers began suggesting terms of a sal
like mandating that freestanding houses be built on two
acre lots and sell for no less than $1.5 million, she bega
to feel that these weren't people she wanted to deal wit
at all. That was when Brad passed her a note.

All posturing. They know they have to sell. Let then

talk. Once they settle and agree to a sale, I negotiate with Oakes.

Caroline was grateful for his words. Actually, she was grateful that he had agreed to come at all. Yes, his job called for it, but he had one foot out the door and could have pleaded a dentist appointment or a migraine or whatever. For all his emotional shortcomings, it had to be hard for him sitting in clear view of his ex-fiancée and her new husband. Much as Caroline wouldn't want Jamie with him, she felt a brief fondness.

Then she heard Ralph Weymouth's strident voice. "Why twenty-four hours? Twenty-four hours is ridiculous. We can't consider competing offers in twenty-four hours. Twenty-four hours won't work."

Caroline knew what to say, but hesitated. Ralph was the toughest of the three. She had watched him during her presentation and could still hear him archly ask what role Theo would be playing. Here was a man's man. Age wasn't the problem; her being female was. She could fight that, push through, be strident right back at him. But she had dealt with enough men in her life to recognize counterproductive before it happened. Meeting with Hersch on Monday had succeeded because of their past. She had no past with Ralph. Her gut said that a reply to him was better coming from someone in pants.

Touching Brad's note, which had been tactically sound, she gestured for him to answer.

He didn't touch his glasses, didn't glance at the papers before him. His eyes remained locked with Ralph's on the video monitor while, with his trademark calm, he said, "This offer stands only that long. We're willing to pay a premium for a preemptive sale—"

"MacAfee Homes isn't the only game in town."

"No, but it's the best one for this job. We've made the

arguments why. If you agree, then the decision isn't hard to make. Absent a preemptive sale, our offer changes."

He was calling Ralph's bluff. Caroline would have done the same, but with less chance of success. Even coming from a male, though, toughness could backfire. She wanted to look at Theo to see if he was uneasy, but knew he wouldn't show it even if he was. She wanted to lean into Dean, but vetoed that idea, too. For a split second, she thought about the simplicity of carpentry, where her greatest decision might be whether to use rosewood or oak. In that split second, she wanted only that.

Then she directed her mind's eye around the table, thinking that she cared about these people and that helping them create something bigger was a worthwhile challenge. Yes, there were risks of giving a twenty-four-hour window. But the risk of letting the fire cool and the competition into the game was greater.

Also, on a personal note, there was *Gut It!* The whole point of rushing to meet with the Weymouths was to have something secured before meeting with Brian and Claire. Before that meeting, though, Caroline and Jamie had to talk.

Chicken Fingers and Spring Rolls, Crispy Beef with Broccoli, Chicken with Pea Pods, Kung Pao Shrimp, white rice, brown rice, and fried rice—Caroline's dining table was covered with takeout containers by the time Jamie and Chip arrived with the boys. Samantha wasn't with them. They had barely left downtown Boston when she announced that she planned to pack and head north.

"When?" Jamie asked in alarm, seeing Samantha as part of the team and therefore deserving of a celebratory dinner. Not that celebrations were in order. Soon after Brad's ultimatum, Herschel Oakes, who had been quiet until then, finally spoke. "We have a lot to discuss," he told the brothers and, shifting his focus to Caroline, stood. "I think we have the information we need. Thank you for coming. If you'll excuse us now . . ."

It was a less than encouraging ending. Seeming to agree, Caroline leaned close in the elevator and said a quiet, "Hersch was being deliberately abrupt so that the brothers see him as in charge. We don't know what they're saying up there now."

No, they didn't. So that was disappointing. And now Samantha. Totally aside from her help at the meeting, Jamie liked having her with them. More important, she sensed that Chip did, too. Two days were not enough.

Samantha's explanation came from the backseat. "I need to get there before I lose my nerve. Or fall asleep." Her hand touched Jamie's shoulder. "You'll give the boys a hug for me? Tell them I'll see them soon?"

"Will you?" Chip asked more sharply than Jamie would have.

Apparently, Samantha agreed with her. "Don't be a prick."

"I'm not," he said, darting glances at her in the rearview. "I'm your brother, and I'm serious. I'd like to see more of you."

"*We* would," Jamie amended, twisting to look back. "There's always room, you know. It's your house."

Her mouth, so like Chip's, tipped into a crooked smile. "I think you just want me here when you meet the folks."

"That, too," Jamie said, only half kidding. She had an ally in Samantha and actually felt bad that they weren't driving north to support her now. Tomorrow's meeting made that impossible.

But life was too short to be distant from family, which was why, after they watched her drive off and then picked up the boys, they went straight to Caroline's—that, and the fact that Jamie was too tired to even think of dinner but was famished.

Tad did amazingly well. Ever prepared, Caroline had applesauce and bananas for anyone whose stomach might still be sensitive, but Tad insisted on sitting on Jamie's lap and finger-feeding himself bits of broccoli and rice. The last ended up less in his mouth and more on her lap and the floor. Champ's tongue swept the floor, and, having changed into shorts, Jamie didn't care about her lap.

Nor, actually, did she care about the fact that Herschel Oakes hadn't called yet. Given the brothers' negativity, she sensed they would wait until the last minute, even if they'd already made a decision, and while that annoyed her, she couldn't sustain anger. She wanted to blame her placidity on the Chardonnay Caroline had opened, but it had more to do with exhaustion from two nights of little sleep. And relief that the presentation was done. And a more immediate and unexpected pleasure.

Looking through the back screen as she carried dirty dishes to Caroline's sink, she thought about the teeny family she'd grown up in and her dreams of it being bigger. That dream was coming true—and on the heels of that realization came one that said the Weymouth project didn't matter all that much in the overall scheme. Effort mattered, and yes, she felt she had done the best she could in a limited time frame. Health mattered. The boys were fully recovered, both of them strong. *Love* mattered. Caroline had Dean, who was at this moment on his hands and knees in the backyard digging up something or other for the two little guys. And Chip, her Chip. He was out there, too, having a ball with the boys in the dirt but also giving Jamie a chance to have her mother alone. If she didn't already love him to bits, his sensitivity to that need would have pushed her there.

She watched Caroline slather on hand lotion before pulling on rubber gloves. With the scent of woods and spring rising from the gloves as they warmed under hot water, Jamie set down the dishes she held.

"About *Gut It!*—"

"About *Gut It!*—"

Jamie hurried to speak first. "I need you to believe me, this change was not my idea."

"I know, baby," Caroline said with a smile. She kept adding soaped dishes to the pile to be rinsed. "I probably knew it all along, but I was feeling vulnerable and I got defensive. Defensiveness is a cloud, sometimes so thick you can't see through it. It's gone now. I feel better about myself."

"Because of Dean?"

"Yes. And because of Theo."

Barely two days ago, Jamie had agreed to lobby on Theo's behalf to convince Caroline to succeed him. She hadn't done it—*such* a conflict of interest—and yet, here was her mother, looking the part, right down to a dusting of blush and mascara, and the neat twist of hair at the nape of her neck. Not even the neon green, soap-covered gloves that went to her elbows detracted from that. Jamie felt positively inelegant beside her.

Taking a dish towel, she began to dry what Caroline rinsed. "Will you take over for him?"

Caroline touched the back of one rubber glove to her chest. Jamie thought she was trying to still a racing heart. But no, she was feeling her ring. It clearly gave her something—*Dean* clearly gave her something. "I fear I may want to," she finally said. "If you think that doesn't terrify me, think again."

"You can do it." Jamie had no doubt whatsoever. From nowhere came memory of the harsh words she'd had for her father before he died. *She's just a carpenter,* he had said of Caroline, to which Jamie had replied, *If she's just a carpenter, then you're just a salesman.* They were both wrong. Seeing Caroline coordinate every detail of today's presentation, Jamie had a new respect for the job. "You've been doing it since Dad died. And now you come home to Dean."

"Actually, I come home to my garage before I'm much good to Dean. I'm a carpenter, baby. That's my first love. I need to make things. I'll always need that. It clears my mind. It *settles* me." She rinsed several more dishes before saying, "Your father died too young. When someone tells me I'm getting old, like Claire did—"

"She was wrong."

"Not entirely. "She rinsed another dish. "I don't believe I'm too old for *Gut It!*, but I am getting older. We all are. I look at what happened to Roy. There's a lesson in that." She handed over the dish, then braced the heels of her gloved hands on the edge of the sink and looked at Jamie. "I have things I want to do besides host. Like this." She hitched her chin at the counter filled with empty takeout containers. "Like working on Dean's house, spending time with your family, going to Canyon Ranch with you. And yes, I want to help Theo. The little I've done has been satisfying. I didn't expect that, but it is. I'd like to give heading MacAfee Homes a shot."

Here it was, Jamie's moment of truth. If Caroline didn't have time to host the show, they were in trouble. Jamie couldn't do it now. "Mom, I . . . I . . . I . . ."

"I know. Not the right time for you."

"But Claire needs to know now."

"Yes." Caroline studied her face. "Your own family has to come first. That's the way it should be. And it's one of the reasons why the changes in my life are good. They'll keep me busy. So. You're busy. I'm busy. Which of us is less busy right now?"

Jamie bit back the quick *You* that was on the tip of her tongue. Both of their lives had gone from simple to complex in the instant when a tree was hit by lightning and fell on a car. If she respected that Caroline was wearing new hats, too, she had to be truthful. "I don't know."

Caroline did. "Me, baby. I don't have kids. I don't have a whole new family to get to know. You'll sort it all out. Things will line up for you. Until then, I'll stay on as host and ease you in as soon as you're ready."

It sounded like a plan, with one possible glitch. "Will Claire agree to that?"

"If we get the Weymouth land, she will."

Epilogue

The rain had let up several hours before, and though the late afternoon sun was more hesitant than Jamie might have liked, she couldn't be greedy. The western sky, framed by the new window in her new kitchen, showed resilient swathes of orange just over the trees, as a dry June breeze pushed gunmetal clouds east.

How to describe what she felt as she stood at her new counter, which was a sandy granite with very practical, kid-friendly veins of burgundy and gray? Grateful for the weather, yes. But now, still, nervous about the food.

This was their first time having everyone in their new home, which actually was the old country house that Caroline had not wanted Dean to buy but then had helped rebuild. By the time it was done, Dean had already purchased another house, this one right next door to Caroline's Victorian. With Caroline insisting that her cats shouldn't have to suffer his dog full-time—and that, BTW, adults needed their own space, too—it was the perfect solution.

It was also the perfect solution for Jamie and Chip. With the prospect of more children in the future and frequent visits from his parents, they needed rooms. The old country house had plenty. And hadn't Jamie drawn the plans that Dean followed in his gut-and-rebuild? Hadn't this exact home design, which so captured her dreams, helped win the Weymouth project?

So Jamie and Chip had bought the country place from Dean, giving his parents' place to Samantha, who was now outside with her eight-month-old daughter Maisie, Caroline and Dean, Chip's parents Donald and Helene, Theo, and the boys, while Jamie frantically whisked a third attempt at dressing.

When Chip appeared at her shoulder, she raised a spoon to his mouth. "Still too sweet?" She was making homemade cole slaw. Well, not entirely homemade. Just the dressing. The cabbage was out of a bag—*no one* seriously cared who cut the leaves—but she had wanted to make the dressing herself. Hamburgers and hot dogs took no brain power. Dressing for cole slaw did. She had a bottle of store-bought, just in case. But this had become her cause, and, with the smell of sizzling burgers drifting in, she was down to the wire.

He licked the spoon, licked his lips, and smiled in a way that would have distracted her if she weren't so focused on the task. "It's *good*."

"I want it great."

"It is great."

"You're just saying that."

"No, it really is. Everything you make is great."

"Is that because I make so little that you're pleased when I make anything at all?"

He rolled his eyes, pulled her close, and kissed a freckle. "It's because even a year later I'm madly in love with you, and because you're a better cook than you give yourself credit for, and because this dressing really is good."

"Yeah?" she asked softly, losing that focus. Even a year later, she was madly in love with him, too.

"Yeah. Mix it in. But first . . ."

He gave her a full-on kiss. Even a year later, that was still special. Every. Time.

"Besides," he said against her lips, "no one eating with us today is as discriminating as you are."

Jamie drew back to disagree. "Your mom is. Look what she brought—three different dinners for the freezer, plus baked beans, pasta salad, and seven-layer bars for today, all homemade."

"She loves cooking. It's her hobby. And she has more time than you do."

"Mommy!" Tad cried, racing in, "Bud-man isn't sharing!"

Buddy was on his heels. "He took Maisie's toy, and he wouldn't give it to her."

"But I didn't have a turn playing!"

"Maisie *wanted* it!"

"Buddy—" Chip began. Jamie stopped him with a touch. Sibling rivalry was still new and not easy for either adult, and while she adored that Chip looked out for Tad, she couldn't let him blame Buddy just because he was older. Tad was three and had to learn to share. Besides, if it was Maisie's toy, Buddy was right.

Bending low, she put an arm around each boy and said as much—and didn't *that* say something? She was the ideological parent, Chip the blunt one. She was the rainy-day activity expert, he the one who taught them all to laugh when they fell. She was the one who still researched problems ad infinitum, while he solved them with a hug.

Tad pouted. "I didn't get *my* turn."

For a minute, Jamie couldn't speak. The child was so like his father in perseverance that she was alternately horrified and touched. She would tell him stories when he was old enough to ask. For now, she simply kept pictures of Jess and Roy on his dresser. He knew to call the faces

Mommy and Daddy. But he seemed perfectly fine calling Jamie and Chip the same.

The reminder was apt. His turn? "With a yard full of other toys? Theodore MacAfee, you are far from deprived. There are a dozen trucks in the sandbox, a water table on the deck, a lawn mower on the grass, and Transformers that Poppy just brought. But what happened to the tee?" She looked questioningly at Buddy. "I thought you guys were batting off it."

"Poppy got tired of shagging the ball," Buddy said, and while Jamie was thinking, *Well, yeah, because the two of you hit more than you miss,* Chip was more blunt.

"And one of you two couldn't do it?"

Buddy looked up at him. "Fido peed on the deck."

"Oh *no,*" Jamie cried, thinking of the sweeping they had done just an hour before to rid her beautiful deck of rain debris.

Fido was the German shepherd pup that Dean had given them as a housewarming gift. Oh, he had checked with them first, causing one of the few arguments between them. Jamie wanted a pair of quiet, clean, self-sufficient cats. Chip argued that a cat wouldn't run with boys who clearly needed to run. When she argued that cat shelters were overflowing, he pointed out that the puppy Dean had chosen *was* born in a dog shelter. It was three against one. So Fido had arrived. They tried to rename him, alternately calling him Oliver, Chester, and Remington over the course of a week, before returning to Fido, which fit the dog, just as Dean had originally said. Now they just had to get him house-trained.

"Oh God, Chip. We're *eating* on that deck."

"Not to worry," Caroline said as she entered the kitchen. "Dean hosed it off." Her eyes were on the boys. "Is anyone here ready for a hot dog?"

"Me!"

"Me! Can I get mine first since I'm older?" Buddy asked.

"Baker." From Chip.

"I think," Caroline said, "that Dean will hand them out at exactly the same time." The two raced out. "Cole slaw done?" she asked Jamie, who shot Chip a *what-do-I-do* look.

He mimed mixing, which she quickly did and handed the bowl to Caroline. Just as quickly, Caroline passed it back to Chip with an affectionate grin.

"Would you take this to the table, like a good boy?"

Chip winked at Jamie in a way that said he got a kick out of her mother, which meant the world to her. Then he, too, was gone, leaving her with Caroline, who had the same huge heart as always, but today a different facade. For one thing, her nails, fingers and toes, were neon blue. For another, her shorts and blouse were white. The irony, of course, was that Jamie, who had lived in a pristine white world before becoming a mom, didn't dare wear it now. But Caroline wore it well. Between those blue nails, her auburn hair, and her green eyes, she was as colorful as ever.

So color wasn't what made her look different.

It wasn't even the diamond ring that hadn't once left her neck.

No. There was a richness to her now, an inner beauty, as though she'd come into her own long after she thought she already had.

That said, she smelled the same. Lily of the valley. Or was Jamie smelling the scent as it rose from the edge of the woods, where yards and yards of the real stuff carpeted the ground, green except for those tiny spikes of little white bells? The smell was ageless. It fit her mother perfectly.

"Are you nervous?" Caroline asked softly.

"With Chip's parents here and Theo—" Distracted, she broke off. "He looks good, Mom. How did his tests go?" Theo had had a minor stroke the winter before, hastening Caroline's ascension. Though he remained president of the company, he had named her CEO from his hospital bed. In the six months since, she had hired good people to help, including a CFO, a new legal head, and Samantha.

"He's fine," Caroline assured her. "Cagey as ever. There are times when I wonder whether he didn't stage that little TIA just to get me on board."

"But you and CEO are a fit. Better than me and kitchen. Yes, I'm nervous." She indicated a Post-it on the wall by the fridge. "I have lists of what all to remember to put out—ketchup, mustard, pickles, olives, and—"

Caroline stoppered Jamie's mouth. "Everything out there is terrific. The table is *full*."

Jamie had a sudden thought. "Lemonade." She started for the fridge, but Caroline caught her arm.

"It's on the table, and if you'd forgotten, someone would have asked, you'd have come back in for it, and all would have been well. You don't have to be perfect, baby. We've talked about that."

"I know."

"But that wasn't what I meant," Caroline said. "Are you *nervous*?"

Jamie didn't follow, until her mother's conspiratorial tone registered. Then her eyes lit. "You mean about watching the tape?" That was the second purpose for the party today. How could she have forgotten? Hel-lo. She'd had a few other things on her mind, like new sneakers for the boys, finishing touches in the guest room for Helene and Donald, and cole slaw dressing.

"It's your debut," Caroline said.

The hosting switch was complete, in part because Theo needed Caroline in the office, and in part because Jamie had taken to it so well. Caroline had hosted the fall project, to which Brian consented once he had a promise of the transition. They had just finished taping the spring project in Maine, with Jamie hosting from start to finish.

"It's also Gina Anderson's directorial debut," Jamie pointed out, pinching back a smile. "Do we miss Claire?" The question was rhetorical. Her absence made things immeasurably more relaxed. And no, the Weymouth property wasn't on the show. It never would be. The brothers were firm about that, and Jamie and Caroline had come to agree. They didn't need *Gut It!* publicity to help sell the development; within months of inking the deal, MacAfee Homes had preliminary contracts on nearly every lot. Without the Weymouth property, the Barths hadn't held much of a lure for Claire Howe, who decided that *Gut It!* didn't hold much of a lure for her anyway, what with Brian intent on keeping the MacAfees and the MacAfees standing as one on who should host. An interim EP had directed the fall project, allowing Jamie and Gina to start fresh in the spring.

"If you're nervous," Caroline said now, "there's no need. Your own personality emerged, and it worked, so if you're worried about what the raw cut will show"—she tipped her head toward the great room, where a huge flat-screen awaited the postcookout showing—"do not be."

'I'm not," Jamie said and realized that she meant it. "I'm really not. Not that *Gut It!* doesn't matter. I mean, I love that we're still doing the show, and the new coffee table book is going to be amazing. But it isn't the only thing in my life."

"That's an understatement," her mother drawled and asked, "I take it you're happy with the latest new architect?" Jamie had actually been through two before finding a woman who could execute a similar architectural vision. Moreover, she had kids of her own, which meant that she was comfortable, in essence, job sharing with Jamie.

"Like her a lot," Jamie declared, more concerned about dinner on the deck. Wanting to make sure everything was where it should be, she linked her arm through Caroline's. They had no sooner left the kitchen, though, when her attention caught on her grandmother's Victorian lace, which now hung on her own dining room wall.

"I feel guilty having this here, Mom."

"Oh, no no no. Do not. This is where it's supposed to be, one generation to the next." They stood together before it. "What do you see?"

"Maybe it's laughing at me and my cole slaw, because I see a bunch of big wide grins."

"Those are happy grins. Satisfied grins. *Fulfilled* grins. I see them, too. What do you think that means?"

Jamie didn't answer. Her throat was suddenly tight. She had her mother back with an even greater appreciation of their relationship, but that was just the beginning. Looking past the dining room, through the great room and out the French doors to a colorfully food-filled deck, where her husband was standing with Caroline's would-be husband, flipping burgers on a huge gas grill, while the boys wandered from adult to adult eating hot dogs and chips, she was overwhelmed.

Then Theo looked their way. His wrinkled face broke into a grin, seconds before an arthritic hand gestured them out.

Neither was about to refuse.

Acknowledgments

Do I seriously have to write about things I don't know? How easy it would be to stick with the tried and true! Unfortunately, it would also be boring. I've always prided myself on making every one of my books different, so I naturally gravitate to the new. Or maybe I simply like new things, and if I do, I feel my readers will, too. Writing about new things is slightly scary at times. Trust me, there was plenty of insomnia where *Blueprints* was concerned.

My medicine for that? Good people, willing to share their expertise with me. I start by thanking Susan Wornick, television personality extraordinaire, who gave me enough information on how the real thing works to make *Gut It!* credible. I also knew nothing about architecture until Jenne Whitelaw and Peter Darlow filled me in enough so that I could picture a real architect's life. My thanks to them. In the field of construction, huge thanks to Bob Gavill and to Ed Foran, for answering my questions. And Ed's crew, which unwittingly made my book real. They were here in my house doing renovation work while I watched and asked questions. And they thought my curiosity was idle. Hah! My apologies for any deception, along with admiration and thanks.

Writing about these fields, I've taken liberties in the name of fiction. All mistakes are mine and mine alone.

My thanks, as always, to my agent, Amy Berkower, and to my editor, Hilary Rubin Teeman, and her talented and dedicated team at St. Martin's Press. Thanks to my assistant, Lucy Davis, whose work exceeds assisting, to Linda Kay, for references and a ready ear, and to Eric MacLeish, for sharing child custody info in answer to every last question I posed. And to my family, truly the footprint on which my own personal blueprints are drawn. Much thanks and love forever.

Finally, my readers continue to be my greatest professional pleasure. With the landscape of the book world constantly changing, they continue to read my books. I never forget that.

Read on for an excerpt from
Barbara Delinsky's new novel

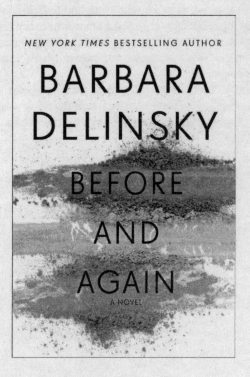

NEW YORK TIMES BESTSELLING AUTHOR

BARBARA
DELINSKY

BEFORE

AND

AGAIN

A NOVEL

Available June 26, 2018, in hardcover,
from St. Martin's Press

Prologue

Mackenzie Cooper had no idea where she was or, more critically, why she hadn't already arrived. Her navigation screen said she was still on the right road, in the right town, but all she could see were woods left and right and a curve of macadam ahead. The turnoff was to have been five minutes past the café in the town center, and they had easily gone ten. During that time, she hadn't seen anything remotely resembling a turnoff, much less the red mailbox that allegedly marked it, although a red anything would have been easy to miss. The fall foliage was a tangle of fiery shades, its leaves crowding the roadside like families at a parade.

A glint in the rearview caught her eye. Braking, she steered to the side until branches brushed the car. She toggled her window down, but before she could get an arm out in a plea for help, the pickup steered around her, sped past, and disappeared over the hill ahead. Assuming the driver knew where he was going, she accelerated and followed, but by the time she hit the crest, the pickup had taken another curve, and by the time she made that one, her car was alone.

She glanced at her phone. It was cradled in a vent holder at the perfect spot for viewing, which had served her well until her map app had frozen. The upper-left corner of the phone showed an ominous No SERVICE where bars should have been, meaning that she couldn't even call or text for help.

"Are we there yet, Mommy?" came a plaintive cry from the five-year-old safely strapped in the back. It wasn't the first such cry, just the first that Mackenzie couldn't honestly answer.

"Almost, sweetie," she said, white-knuckling the wheel through another sharp turn. When the road straightened, she touched the SUV's map screen to zoom in. The larger view showed tendrils where driveways might be— and, *oh*, she just passed one, she realized, but it was a barely there thing, thin and rutted, with no mailbox of any sort.

Turn around, her sane self ordered. But the red mailbox was likely around the next curve, she reasoned, and, if not that, her phone would wake up. Besides, she didn't see a place to turn around. Her SUV was big, the road narrow, and it was snaking wildly through a forest that had no business being this close to the city.

Actually, this place wasn't close to the city. Lily's school was. But being a private school, many students traveled distances each day, which translated into playdates in the boonies. Lily's new best friend had already been to their place twice, easily arranged since the Coopers lived close to school, but this was their first playdate at Mia's. And why would Mackenzie hesitate? Lily wanted to go. She had asked repeatedly, had *begged*. Besides, Mackenzie liked this family. She liked that they didn't live in an oversized Shingle-and-Stone rebuild, that the dad was a carpenter and the mom a struggling writer, that Mia was on scholarship. Edward, too, felt an instant connection—as if the Boyds were people they had both known in earlier, more modest lives.

Mackenzie had made the arrangements with Mia's mom, including drop-off and pick-up times, clothes to bring for playing outside, Lily's love of peanut butter and aversion to chocolate. She hadn't thought to ask about cell reception. Her carrier was the best in their own neighborhood, clearly not so here.

The map screen switched to night mode for several beats, seeming as confused as Mackenzie. She knew it was a glorious fall day. Glimpses of blue could be seen through the high canopy, along with shards of fire where sun lit the leaves, but in every other regard, the day-darkness was unsettling.

"Are we lost?" came Lily's worried voice.

"We are not," Mackenzie said with determination. "Mia's driveway is off this road."

She just didn't know where it was, and, no matter how often she glanced at the phone, it remained dead. Eyes shifting between the road and the SUV's map screen, she zoomed the view out once, then again until she saw an intersection, which was good. At this setting, though, she couldn't judge how far off it was. She was an artist, not a mathematician.

"All I see is trees," Lily said, more curious than complaining. "Maybe Mia lives in a *tree* house."

Mackenzie smiled into the rearview mirror. As dark as the woods were, her daughter's blonde hair sparked with light. "Maybe a *fairy* house. What do you think?"

"With fairy dust around it? And popsicle-stick windows and clay walls? *That's* silly, Mommy."

"Why?"

"Only *our* fairy houses have those. Besides, fairy houses aren't real. Mia's house is made of wood. Her daddy built it, and he's a . . . what did you say he is?"

"A carpenter."

"Uh-huh. Are we *almost* there?"

"I think so. But will you look at these trees, Lily? They're yellow, like your hair. Know why?" she asked as a diversion.

"The green stuff."

"Chlorophyll. It dies off when the nights turn cool. Remember, we talked about that? The colors we see now were always there. We just couldn't see them until the green was gone."

Lily was silent through another twist of the road, then asked, "Are you sure we're not lost?"

"Do I ever get lost?"

"You did when we were driving to the ocean."

"Excuse me, little love. I got us to the ocean, just not the part Daddy wanted us at, but he was sleeping." In the passenger's seat. After a late night of work. "No, we are not lost." But Mackenzie was thinking of turning around and retracing the road to town. If she had a working phone, she could call Mia's mom for directions. Of course, there was still the turning-around problem. The road was undulating with a frequency that made narrowness all the more of a challenge.

"Why's it taking so long?" Lily asked.

"Because I don't want to drive fast on a road I don't know."

"Will you know how to find me to take me home later?"

"Absolutely," Mackenzie said with feeling, though she was thinking it might not be a problem if she didn't get them there in the first place.

"I love you, Mommy."

"I love you, too, baby."

"Mommy?"

"What, hon?"

"I have to go to the bathroom."

"We're almost there, almost there."

According to the map screen, they were nearing the

crossroad. Hoping to get her bearings there, perhaps see a sign or regain her cell signal, at the very least have room for a turnaround, she zoomed in to identify it, to bring the name into view, leaning closer to catch it.

Too late, she remembered that the GPS display of her current position trailed reality by a number of seconds. Too late, she realized that the momentum built climbing another hill would have her barreling down the far side without knowing how close the intersection was.

She never saw the STOP sign hidden by leaves of the same color, never saw the van speeding at her from the right. She felt the terrifying jolt of impact, heard a high-pitched scream from the backseat and would have blindly reached for Lily if the SUV hadn't hurtled into a spin that defied gravity.

She felt another impact, then nothing.

Don't miss more titles from
the #1 *New York Times* bestselling author

BARBARA DELINSKY!